PENGUIN BOOKS

THE ILL-FATED PEREGRINATIONS OF FRAY SERVANDO

Reinaldo Arenas was born in Holguín, Cuba, in 1943. *Singing From the Well*, *Farewell to the Sea*, and *The Palace of the White Skunks* (the first three novels of a five-book sequence) were published by Viking in 1987, 1986, and 1990, and subsequently in Penguin. The fourth novel in this sequence, *The Assault*, is now available from Viking. Arenas is the author of six other novels, including *The Ill-fated Peregrinations of Fray Servando* (formerly entitled *Hallucinations*, which won first prize for the best foreign novel of the year in France), five novellas, collections of short stories, essays, experimental theater pieces, and poetry. He died in New York in 1990.

Andrew Hurley is a professor of English at the University of Puerto Rico in San Juan. He has translated the four Pentagonia novels published in English to date and other writings by Reinaldo Arenas, as well as works by Jorge Luis Borges, Heberto Padilla, Gustavo Sainz, Ernesto Sábato, and Fernando Arrabal.

THE ILL-FATED
PEREGRINATIONS
OF
FRAY SERVANDO

—

REINALDO ARENAS

TRANSLATED BY

ANDREW HURLEY

PENGUIN BOOKS

To Camila Henriquez Ureña
To Virgilio Piñera
for their intellectual honesty

PENGUIN BOOKS
Published by the Penguin Group
Penguin Books USA Inc., 375 Hudson Street,
New York, New York 10014, U.S.A.
Penguin Books Ltd, 27 Wrights Lane, London W8 5TZ, England
Penguin Books Australia Ltd, Ringwood, Victoria, Australia
Penguin Books Canada Ltd, 10 Alcorn Avenue,
Toronto, Ontario, Canada M4V 3B2
Penguin Books (N.Z.) Ltd, 182–190 Wairau Road,
Auckland 10, New Zealand

Penguin Books Ltd, Registered Offices:
Harmondsworth, Middlesex, England

First published in the United States of America by Avon Books 1987
Published in Penguin Books 1994

1 3 5 7 9 10 8 6 4 2

Originally published in Mexico as *El mundo alucinante* in 1966; in France
as *Le Monde Hallucinant* in 1968; in the United States of America
and Great Britain (in a different translation) as *Hallucinations* in 1971.

ISBN 0 14 02.4166 3
(CIP data available)

Printed in the United States of America
Set in Trump Medieval

This is the story of
Fray Servando Teresa de Mier y Noriega—
just as it was, just as it might have been,
just as I wish it had been.
Neither a historical nor a biographical novel
strictly speaking,
but more than those,
this tale aspires to be, quite simply,
a novel.

CONTENTS

HAVANA

I too have been torn by the thorns of that desert, and every day I have left some shred of me there.

Martyrs, Book X

The first thing that shall grace thee shall be the virtue of the eagle, the virtue of the tiger, the Holy War, arrow and shield; and this is what thou shalt eat. But it is what thou though shalt ever need as well, so that thou shall ever walk in fear. In return for thy valor thou shalt go about conquering and destroying for all the days of thy life.

Cristóbal del Castillo:
*General Treatise on the
History of the Mexican People*

PROLOGUE
FRAY SERVANDO,
TIRELESS VICTIM

For many years Fray Servando had been fleeing the Spanish Inquisition all across Europe, constantly beset by the humiliations and hardships that exile and banishment impose, when one afternoon, in a botanical garden in Italy, he came across a thing which brought tears of despair and dejection to his eyes—a Mexican agave, the yucca, or century plant, which is pervasive throughout Mexico. This specimen was jailed in a little cell, behind a protective picket, and it had attached to it a kind of ID card.

The friar had been forced to run for a very long time indeed only to come up against this object that identified and reflected him: a cactus, pulled up and transplanted to a foreign land with its foreign sky. An almost mythic cycle incarnated in the man of the Americas (a timeless victim of all times, a mender of the impossible) may be seen in that brief but incandescent encounter between soul and the landscape, between loneliness and the lost image, between emotion torn by insecurity and absence and the emotion that suddenly erupts, covering, magnetizing, idealizing that thing which when it existed (when we had it) was nothing but that commonplace, now bestowed with the glow of wonder by the impossibility of our returning to it.

Although Fray Servando Teresa de Mier and José María Heredia y Heredia had not yet met each other (and in fact History cannot "certify" that they ever did meet), they must, at similar times, have experienced the same sensation, the same desolation, even though in different settings. Heredia, like an orthodox Romantic, is led by fate to the falls of Niagara, where, more than the grandeur of the landscape, what moves him is the memory of a distant grove of palms. In Fray Servando, man of a thousand dimensions—candid, crafty, sharp-tongued, exalted, an adventurer, a being almost mortally stabbed by the impossible (his country)—the same event occurs in the very heart of one of the most populous cities of Europe, in the midst of a throng of anon-

ymous faces and the clamor of ideas, generally contradictory . . .
The return—that is to say the recovery of the palm grove or the
agave—will be, for both the men, arduous and halting, uncertain,
though finally (fatally) possible.

It is senseless to narrate here, in this more-or-less introduction
to a novel I wrote years ago (and which I hardly remember), the
respective vicissitudes of the Mexican Fray Servando and the
Cuban poet Heredia, nor the reasons for those vicissitudes. I think,
though, of that moment which, like almost all the important moments, has gone pretty much unrecorded by "official" history; I
think of that moment in which the adventurer Servando, now once
again in México, and the poet Heredia, there for the first time,
meet, after the thousand and one infamies they have suffered, and
stand before the vast panorama of the infamies yet to come to
them . . . Both men have seen once more their beloved landscapes.
But really, what have they seen? What can they say to themselves,
to each other? The man who wandered on foot throughout Europe,
having almost unbelievable adventures, the man who suffered
every persecution, the untiring and eternal victim, several times
inches from the holy pyre of the Inquisition, the confirmed tenant
of the most fearsome and terrible prisons of Europe and the Americas (San Juan de Ulúa, La Cabaña, Los Toribios, among others), the
patriot and political rebel, the fighter—he is not exactly the ideal
man to seize and lead the rhythm of the history of his country, or
even of his province, or even of himself. As for Heredia, branded
by his contemporaries as a "fallen angel" for having left Cuba, its
landscape, with a safe-conduct letter signed by General Tacon—he
is also, obviously, not an example to us of stability or of moral
and spiritual satisfaction. The fact that both men lived in the same
place (the Presidential Palace), that history has led the two of them
to converge on the same spot, and from similar situations, and, at
the same time, that history does not take note of that occurrence,
is one of the constant, awful, and well-known ironies to which
history is so given. Therefore, if we limit ourselves, as good historians, to the strict fact, both these figures so important to the history
of our continent would now have to retreat mutely back into the
shadows of it, and disappear—forever?—and with no appeal, down
the halls of opposite wings of its edifice or into the labyrinths
of time.

That is one reason I have always distrusted the "historical,"
those "minutiae," the "precise date" or "fact." Because what, fi-

nally, is History? A file full of more or less chronologically ordered manila folders? Does History record the crucial instant at which Servando came face-to-face with that *Agave americana*, or at which Heredia was suddenly smitten by *not* seeing a palm tree against the sky on that heartbreaking horizon? Impulses, motives, the secret perceptions that urge (make) a man, these often do not appear in history books, *cannot* appear, just as in the operating room the pain of a man savaged by the scalpel will never be talked about.

History sets down the date of a battle, the number of dead, to give some idea of its intensity—sets down, that is, the *evident*, the *visible*. These frightful tomes fix the fleeting, the ephemeral, the fugitive (and there is much of that). The effect, though, not the cause. That is why I have dug more into Time than into History. In that unceasing and always diverse Time, Man is its metaphor, because Man *is*, finally, the metaphor of History, its victim even when he tries to change its course and, as some affirm, actually accomplishes that. Generally, historians see Time's infinity as linear. What proofs have they that time works in that way? With the simplistic reasoning that shows that 1500 came before 1700, or that the Trojan War came before Marie Antoinette's guillotining? As though Time cared about such ciphers, as though Time knew anything about chronologies, progress, as though Time could advance . . . Before the ingenuousness of a man who tries to scale Time, or put it on the scales, file it away, with his progressive or even "progressivist" intentions, Time quite simply bristles, digs in its heels, and will not budge. How, then, can one file away infinity? But Man will not shrug and accept this unyieldingness, and so that endless foliation of codices, dates, calends, and the like. His "progress" . . . What surprises us most when we find in time, or in any given time, an authentic, heart-breaking character, is precisely his (her) atemporality, intemporality, his (her) *now*-ness, his (her) seeming infiniteness. Because infinite, not historical, is Achilles for his anger and his love, independently of whether he actually existed; infinite would be Christ for his impractical philosophy, and that, whether or not History had taken note of it. These metaphors, those images, belong to eternity.

I think the infinite is neither the linear nor the visible, for seeing reality as a parade or a snapshot is to see, really, something very remote from reality. That is why what is called realism seems to me quite the opposite, since trying to subjugate, yoke, that reality, pigeonhole it, file it away, see it from a single viewpoint ("Be realistic!") prevents, logically, our seeing reality complete.

But recently we have not only had (and suffered) Realism but had to suffer Socialist Realism as well, where reality is not merely seen from a single angle but seen from a political angle. What reality can that be, I wonder, which, from that position, that angle, will be seen by the victims of that (partial) reality? . . . The truth is that if we can speak of any socialist-realist work it is that of Alexander Solzhenitsyn. His work at least knowingly reflects a single part of a socialist reality, that which is most obvious and superficial—its concentration camps.

I will never tire of discovering that the tree of six o'clock in the morning is not the tree of noon, nor that tree whose soughing brings us consolation at evening. And that breeze that springs up at night, can it possibly be the same breeze as at morning? And that ocean water the swimmer cuts through at sunset as though it were meringue, are those the choppy hot waters of midday? As time flows, permeates, so obviously and fully, into a tree or a beach or a landscape, can we, the earth's most sensitive creatures, remain insensitive to its signs? I think not—we are cruel and tender, greedy and generous, impassioned and meditative, laconic and rowdy, terrible and sublime, like the ocean . . . Therefore, perhaps, I have attempted, in the little I have done and, within that little done, in the little that I can claim as my own, to reflect not reality or a reality but all realities, or at least a few.

Anyone who is led by fate's strange twists to read my books will find in them not one contradiction but many, not one tone but many, not one line but many circles. I have never thought my novels should be, could be read as though they were the history or story of unfolding or interconnected events, but rather as though they were a wave which expands, flows outward, turns, widens, and folds back in upon itself more wispily and more inflamed, unceasing, in the midst of situations so extreme that from their very unbearableness they sometimes become liberating.

And that is the way I think life is, too. Not dogma, not a code, not a story, but a mystery that must be assailed from several flanks. And assailed not to conquer or destroy it (for that would be horrible), but simply never to surrender to it.

And so it is on that plane, the plane of the inconsolable and indefatigable victim of History, of Time, that our beloved Fray Servando finds his true place. He is the justification and the guardian angel, then, of this formless, desperate, torrential, gallumphing, lying, irreverent, grotesque, desolate, loving poem, this (I suppose I may as well say it) novel.

R.A.
Caracas, 1980

Postscript: I am informed that certain uninformed (and pathetic) informants have informed the information-hungry public that this novel, *El mundo alucinante* (written in 1965 and prizewinner in the UNEAC [Cuban Writers' and Artists' Union] competition for 1966), has been influenced by, for example, *A Hundred Years of Solitude* (1967), and *De donde son los cantantes* (1967). Similar influences have also been found in my *Cantando en el pozo* (*Singing from the Well*), written in 1964, and likewise honorably mentioned in the UNEAC literary competition of 1965. Thus we see another irrefutable proof that time does not exist, at least (especially) for literary critics and reviewers.

Dear Servando,

Since the day I discovered you, as a small entry in a dry and dreadful history of Mexican literature, offhandedly mentioned as "the friar who had wandered on foot all across Europe undergoing unbelievable, implausible adventures," I have been everywhere trying to find you. I've turned libraries upside down, hellish places where the mere whispering of the word *friar* throws the reference staff into consternation. I've written people who turned out to know you at the characteristic distance and by the dehumanized outlines of erudition acquired from history books. I've been to embassies, cultural mission-houses, and museums, none of which, of course, so much as suspected your existence. But in spite of all those setbacks, my stock of information about your life has grown immensely, though the thing that has been most helpful to me in getting to know you, and in coming to love you, has not been the information I've squeezed out of dusty encyclopedias (which are always too exact), or out of those terrible books of essays (which are always too inexact). What has helped me most to "apprehend" you has been my discovery that you and I are the same person. So any reference that I came across before that fateful and almost unbelievable discovery was rendered supererogatory—and I've thrown out almost all of them. Only your memoirs, written in solitude and amidst the scrabbling of voracious rats, amidst the booming of the Royal English Navy's cannons, the jingling bells of the mules passing through the ever harsh and unpleasant, unbearable landscapes of Spain, written in desolation, rage, and sometimes rapture, in justified fury and unjustified optimism, in rebelliousness and skepticism, and between pursuit and flight, the holy pyre and exile, only those memoirs appear in this book, and not as quotations from some mere "other" text, but as the marrow of this one, so that one hardly need underscore the fact that they're yours. And anyway, they aren't yours anymore—they are, like all things grand and grotesque, Time's, brutal and unbearable. Time's, which has just brought you to your two hundredth birthday.

You won't appear in this book of mine (and yours) as a man of immaculate character, or under the characteristic banner of evangelistic purity, or as the irreproachable hero incapable of error or misaction, or who never feels, even just once in a while, like you want to die. Here you will be, dear Servando, what you are—one of the most important (and, sadly, most unknown) figures of the political and literary history of the Americas. A formidable man. Which in itself is enough to make some people think that this novel should be censored.

Yours,
R.A.
Havana
July, 1966

MÉXICO

CHAPTER I

In which is treated my childhood in Monterrey and other things that occurred besides.

We're coming from the stand of palm trees. We're not coming from the stand of palm trees. Me and the two Josefas, we're coming from the stand of palm trees. All by myself I'm coming from the stand of palm trees, and by now it's practically all the way night. Around here it gets to be night before the sun comes up. All over Monterrey that happens—you get out of bed and before you can turn around it's already getting dark. That's why the best thing to do is just not get out of bed.

But anyway. Now I'm coming from the stand of palm trees and it's daytime this time. And the sun's hot enough to crack rocks. And so then, so then once they're all cracked and broken up I pick them up and throw them at my Just Alike Sisters' heads. At my sisters. At my sisters. At my sis.

There I was—resting under one of the palm trees. With those big long sharp thorns sticking out of them. Resting from the race I mean the getaway I played on that big spoiled baby of a teacher of mine. Jackass. I hate him! Because he took the quince-tree switch and switched my back till the switch turned to splinters just because I put three tails on the O and he said you didn't put on even one. He practically breaks my back, and then he expects me not to do the same thing to him when I catch him by surprise. Well ha! King's-ex, I said, and then I made the switch whistle all over the big stuck-up smarty-pants's back. He thinks he's too good for anybody here. He thinks he's this noble Castilian over here looking down his nose at the Indians. He thinks.

So then anyway he spun around like a flash and he tried to catch me. But I took off running over the top of the desks till he grabbed me and made me get down on my knees. But that was just for a second or two because the minute he took his hand off my shoulder I jumped straight up like a bucket shoved head-down in the water.

So then all the boys started to laugh like crazy, but without anybody hearing them but me because there are things I hear that can't be heard. I heard the laughing you couldn't hear because if the teacher heard it he'd lock them up like he did me—in the outhouse. Pee-yoo!

I was locked up in there in the outhouse but I gave this big jump and tried to reach the window that was so high it was practically up in the clouds. But no good. So I jumped again, but no good again. So then I started yelling. And the door flew open. And the teacher, that now he was all covered with all kinds of the strangest feathers, like he was a turkey buzzard with the face of a devil, he came in singing, with the quince-tree switch on fire, and he was ready to shove it down my throat to make me hush ... So that's when I took a big *big* BIG jump because I was crouched down like this, and I jumped so high that my head broke through the tiles on the roof and I flew through the roof and rose into heaven and then I fell on the very top of one of those stabbing thorny palm trees where there was a hawk's nest and I killed the girl hawk because the other hawk, I think the boy, but he was the biggest one anyway, he tried to peck out my eyes. And so I was all tangled up with the boy hawk and I fell down to the ground and it was a miracle I didn't bust and break every bone in my body.

And so I was pulling myself back together from the fall and the way that animal had been trying to peck me to death, when I saw that stupid burro of a devil of a teacher of mine coming running over to where I was. He had set the quince-tree switch on fire and he was waving it around and making all these loud squeaky speeches, which was the first time in my life I ever heard such a thing, and a whole troop of pupils was following him. His retinue, he said, and he was ready to set my innards on fire with that switch.

I took off running through those thorny palm trees, yelling for my mother. But my mother couldn't come right then. She was picking the seeds out of cotton-to-get-the-threads-out-of-it-to-sell-it-to-buy-one-of-those-calabash-things-with-the-money-from-it-so-when-the-season-came-she-could-get-the-honey-water-out-of-the-maguey-plants-with-the-calabash-thing-to-make-pulque-out-of-the-juice-to-sell-it-to-buy-some-little-something-with-the-money-to-give-it-to-the-priest-so-he-would-bless-our-livestock-so-they-wouldn't-die-on-us-like-they'd-been-dying-on-us. And besides, she was dead.

So that's why I figured I was as good as gone—that caravan was going to grab me for sure—so I started yelling at them. And I said things you couldn't imagine. Terrible things. So then the teacher stretched out his hand all covered with hair. And he was just about to grab me when a palm tree (that I guess felt sorry for me when it saw me in that situation) slaps him with one of its fronds that's got those big long ugly thorns on it and it hits the evil old wizard in the back, and when he feels those stickers sticking him in the back he thinks it's a punishment from the devil and so he starts hopping all over the place and huffing and puffing and waving his hands in the air like this and he finally heads off toward the school, followed by all the little brats-of-a-monkey pupils of his, while meanwhile I keep throwing anything I can get my hands on at them.

Well, so, and then—so then I wanted to thank the spiny little palm tree for saving me, so I went over to pet it with my hand like this, running my hand over its trunk. And the thankless creature grabs my hand and shoots all these thorns in it so hard they stick out the other side. So then I *really* got mad. But it hurt so much that even how furious I was went away and all I could think about was dying, so I sat back to die like my mother says everybody is always sitting back to die.

But about then my two sisters got there and when they saw me like that they started pulling me by my other hand to try to pull me loose from the thorns. So I start yelling again and they pull for all they're worth until finally the palm tree turned me loose, so then I picked up, you can imagine how furious I was, I picked up one of the rocks that was lying there close by and I threw it at the two Josefas, at their heads, so they ran off as fast as they could all the way home. But halfway there they turned around again and they started bombarding me with everything they could find, even with the bones of the cows that had starved to death the other year. And since it was two against one all I could do was hightail it away and then take off flying.

And as quick as *that*, and I was home again. And when I got there, there was my mother—with one candle burning on top of her head and one more on every one of the fingers on her hands— and she opens the door with her mouth like a torch holder and she says, "Come in, you demon, and go upstairs to your room. The teacher came and told us what you did. You won't set foot out of this place for the rest of the week."

That was when I looked back and saw all the palm trees twisting and turning around each other and hugging and unhugging one another's trunks, almost like they wanted to pull each other up by the roots, and giving these shrieks so funny and tinny and shrill that my ears could hardly believe their own witness. And their leaves falling off. And all of them twisting and twining with such a strange furious look to them, like they wished I was within reach so they could choke me, waving in a wind that wasn't any wind at all because right then they were the only only thing anywhere that was moving.

"We're coming from the stand of palm trees," I said, and she moved one finger that had a burning candle on it and she put it out in my eye. I started up the stairs, and when I got upstairs I said it again, I said we were coming from the stand of palm trees, and that seemed like it set her off again because she shook her hand like a person does when his hand is wet and she gave me a slap with that hand and all the candles smashed into my head so hard that if I hadn't taken off running I'd have been burned to a crisp.

And now, from up here, I can hear Floirán hopping, and something that sounds like the two Josefas throwing dirt on their heads out there in the yard. But as far as I'm concerned there won't be any games tonight. At all. Not marbles. Not cup and ball. Not anything. Unless maybe . . . But on second thought, no.

CHAPTER I

Which treats of your childhood in Monterrey and certain other things as well that occurred.

So here you finally come. Back from the palm trees, eh? You've been out there the livelong day, dawdling around under the few leaves on the even fewer trees that grow in this miserable part of the country. Thinking. Dodging the sun, scooting in circles around the trees, squatting in the shade of their skinny trunks so you don't get fried to a crisp in that sunshine. So here you come. After you've pulled up every single plant by the roots so you can listen to them cry—the way you cry when somebody picks the chiggers off you.

You didn't go to school and you didn't come home for lunch either.

Listen to the two Josefas yelling and screaming out there, running all over the sand, which is a fine excuse for a front yard. They're out to catch you, I'll tell you for sure, and they've got two good switches in their hands. But where in the world did they get those switches? There aren't any trees left around here.

Now they've got you. This time they've caught you for sure. And here come the palm trees you just pulled up, too, and they're screaming and yelling along with them.

They're going to break those switches over your head this time. You wait—you'll get home and your head'll be in a million pieces.

Your mother'll be waiting for you in the door. And you'll be trying to hold your head together with your bare hands.

And so now your mother shoves you. She hits you over the head with a club two times. And you don't open your mouth, you're such a stubborn little mule and a bucking bronco. You won't let 'em put the halter on *you*, will you?

"Get down to your room," they've told you, and they've put a rope around your neck. So now you're in that room the floor opens up into. And it's not daytime anymore, but it's not night either ... The scorpions are singing, and everything is red-colored.

The scorpions are singing, "Yonder comes the baby Jesus, yonder comes the baby Jesus. Chop him in pieces. Chop him in pieces."

Your mother comes in and cuts off your hands. And she asks you, "Who pulled up that palm tree?" "He did," say the scorpions, the ones that don't sing this time, coming out from under this red-colored rock. So then your father takes out his red-colored knife and he's crying but he cuts off your other hand. The third one. And he plants it in the red-colored sand. (It's getting darker.) Everything is this sort of red color. But it's not exactly day and it's not exactly night either and you can look out the window and see the stretch of sand that's a fine excuse for a front yard go sneaking and sneaking and skulking away, till finally it gets all mixed up with the sky. And over there, way over that way, a hand-plant has started to come up.

Around here there's nothing but rock and stone and sand (and once upon a time *that* was rock and stone too). Monterrey is in the Stone Age. But we're moving into the Sand Age. Pretty soon it'll be the Dust Age.

Everything is *red*. And sand glinting between the rocks.

You can hear the two Josefas laughing and cackling out there, throwing sand in each other's eyes till they're blind, and Floirán throwing rocks at the sky. Of course he never hits it. *You* would, if *you* were out there. But there'll be no games tonight, not for you, and you won't run around all over the sandy yard till the sheets hung out to dry out there are in tatters either, just so you can show those sisters of yours that they're not ghosts. The idea. Sheets being ghosts. The idea.

But just at nightfall, here comes your father riding on a stick horse made out of a quince-tree switch. He's got a whole other reality with him. You can hear his horse, even if he's on foot.

You escape, through the keyhole. You cut off your hands and plant them. Run away. Run. Run. You'll never cut another tree down around here, not with these hands you won't. The only tree in this whole part of the country! Get him! He's running into the rocks! Oh, let 'im go, he'll get in there and the scorpions'll eat him. The *black* scorpions.

The scorpions have gotten together, they've gotten a chorus together for you . . . If scorpions sang once in a while, it wouldn't be so quiet around here in this stinking town. But of course they don't so much as go "shhh." They sneak up on you, they get closer and closer, and if they cry, why, they're quiet about that too. You can feel them, huh?, slipping along first on the tips of your toes. And then they climb up your legs. Your legs are covered with leaves. They tickle your little fanny . . . Here you are out in the middle of this stretch of sand and rocks and stone, and here you're crying. You're running around all over that place, trying to run away, but the scorpions've taken off flying after you, and they catch you and they start pulling off your stalks. They strip off your buds and flowers. They peel off your leaves. And next they're going to work all the way down to your roots.

I think you better think about something else.

CHAPTER I

Which treats of how he spent his childhood in Monterrey and of other things that also occurred.

Sometimes he would leave off hopping and skipping. He would throw rocks, or lie on his back, staring at nothing. And thus the time passed, and thus he lived until he discovered that time did not exist, that it was but that fallacious notion which makes us begin to fear Death—who, moreover, can come at any moment and stop time's passing. There is no cause to be sad, he would tell himself. And he was not sad. There is no cause to be happy, either, he would tell himself. Alone, in the midst of the vast imaginary vegetation he invented (for he had been told tales about the sea, but *that* his imagination could never invent for himself) he would plan slow projects, and in the blistering sun he would then watch them melt and wither (the coming of his resuscitated father); and the glow of the candles had no meaning in the face of the ripping, rending light which he raised up from under the rocks. He imagined himself made of wax then, and he would run to and fro as the End unfolded, dropping off parts of himself like a roast pig too long over the fire. Such an ordinary childhood, among those almost perfectly identical houses. Such a terrible childhood, as all childhoods are, faced with the Coming of Mysterious Body Hair and the Terror of Strange Desires—desires whose shapes stood out red and indistinct against the red of the stretch of sand and rocks and stones. All that remained to him now was his imagination.

And so he did not go to the school nor did he follow the track of the only night heron that had flown past the undulating tiles of the roof. Nor did he pull up the short palm trees with long vicious thorns on their trunks and the underside of their leaves—trees which, besides, had never existed there. Nor did he see his sisters, for they are not yet born. Nor was he witness to that foolishness about his amputated hands ... All of it was imagined. Pure invention, all of it ... The house was filled with voices. And the sandy desert sprouted green and dotted over with trees. And the sky was a constant flutter of birds passing strange ... And he held himself in stillness and quietude for seven years longer, not stirring once from the stretch of sand and rocks and stone ... Nourished on the nectar of his fingernails. Until he was discovered by a bell, which as it was rung with great blows translated him to the origin of all sound. So, seeing in that sound his only possibility of escape, he ducked into his room and waited for his mother to show him his proper course.

Entered his mother pale, with a stone on her head. And he lifted off the stone with great pomp and that night he lay him down and slept on it. And on the next day they saddled the mule. And once and for all, never looking back, he rode away.

CHAPTER II

Which treats of my departure from Monterrey.

On a mule that hardly spoke I left Monterrey one day early in the morning. My mother came to the door and with her arms made over me the sign of a great cross. I was certain the mule laughed, for I looked at his face and I could see all of his teeth. So for that I gave him two licks with the quirt and he kicked up dust and ran through the stretch of sand and rocks, without looking back, until at last we were out of sight.

The first night I traveled alone. But on the second I met with an army of muleteers who as soon as they saw me rushed up to me and attacked me (the savages) and lifted my mule's tail, for as they explained to me it might have been one of theirs, since all their animals had been stolen from them during the first hours of the morning on the day before.

"Thieves come in waves," they said, "and it is but a miracle that has saved thee from being robbed likewise. Look thou at us, who are riding shanks' mares and we must journey to the city of México." If truth be told I wanted nothing more than to turn tail and run. But that horde had respect for no-one and they were gazing at me with some suspicion, for I was the only man not afoot, so I feared that if I did ride away they would set upon me and the matter be yet worse. So therefore I watched until the next night (not even daring to take out the small loaf of brown sugar I had guarded under my saddle). And when they were sleeping I crept away with my mule in tow. But the damnable beast cried, "He's hauling me, he's hauling me!" as though it were a young lady eloped with against her will. And on that, the entire troop awoke with a leap and ran toward me crying, "Ah, so thou wouldst make off with the poor mule." And they soon despoiled me of it. So here I go now, afoot, though I am told I am almost come to where I am going—and indeed those clouds of smoke cannot be other than the Viceroyalty. And so in brief: after much wandering on foot through both hot and frozen lands and across plains so vast that one walks and yet believes oneself to be always in the selfsame spot; after hopping on one foot down trails along the lip of precipices from which the clouds far down below appear to be newly born turkey buzzards; after passing very near a rowdy party of Indians (who had plundered every one of the muleteers); and after sleeping in inns where one is robbed even of one's hair, so, they say, as to make mattresses of it; after all these and other terrible things besides (among which was having my belly near bursting from an *atole* which was served me in the inn, and which the cook had made of sand rather than of corn meal, to save some cost I presume, and on account of which I leave a trail wherever I pass), it appears that at last I am coming to my destination.

CHAPTER II

In which is treated the departure from Monterrey.

The road was not so terribly hard. His way he took in a cart drawn by a singing mule which did not allow him to sleep, for all night it stamped the rocks with its hooves and made a sound like casta-nets. And yet he met this and all the other difficulties inherent in such a long journey, with the high spirits that came from knowing himself saved from that prison of sand, rock, and sun. He was going to the city to "make something of himself." For it almost always happens that the town where one is born grows very small when the hubbub of restless desires begins to be heard . . . and to grow louder . . . and louder still . . . And that is why he slept as soundly as could be imagined in one of the inns along the way. There he ate the delicious *atole*, whipped up out of the milk of a nursing Indian mother and sand from the adjoining rocky waste, but seeing that he carried not the hundredth of a peso about him, he could pay nothing for it. And so it happened that once he was fast asleep, someone—wanting to collect from him the bill—stripped him of all his clothes, though the traveler went on sleeping, utterly unconscious of the event, and the next morning our young man awoke, rose, stretched his arms and legs, and set off naked. And he walked in that state more than twenty leagues without a person crossing his path. Until one day an old woman who had lost her way spied him at a distance and ran off toward the city of México to beseech the Archbishop to build a church in that same spot where she had seen a *vision of God,* Who from afar had waved His blessing over her with a marvelously strange and wonderfully situated and, therefore, divine finger. (The church was duly erected, but the figure that represented the apparition did not suit the old woman and so for that and other niggling protests she was roasted on the untiring bonfire of the Venerable Inquisition.) The young man went on impassively continuing his journey until suddenly, some halfway along the road and in the middle of it, he met with a gang of slaves shuffling along to, he learned, the site of a new cathedral, where it was they who were to build it. It was only these poor souls who at last bestowed a remarkably shabby cape upon the traveler, in which he wrapped himself and plodded on.

CHAPTER II

In which is treated your departure from Monterrey.

You had no great problem either leaving or on the trip itself. The hard part came when you tried to climb up to the city, which is perched at an altitude of about two thousand rods. Who ever heard of founding a city so high! There's never any rain there, because the clouds all sit down there below it.

And just as you come to the city, your hands one mess of red tatters from scaling the rocky sides of the mountains, a hail of bottles rains down on you. There's no end in sight to the avalanche, so in that pelting of empty flasks and bottles you're forced back to the very bottom of the cliff face. "Hast ever witnessed the like?" said a priest emerging from the bottlement. "The rogues think of naught but drink. So their city, which has been filled to the very eaves with bottles of pulque and chicha and alcoholic brews from Spain, is beginning to crumble under its load of glass and shards. Ay, heavenly Father, how will I ever, and after I had reached the top by a miracle, how will I ever climb up again!" And the priest, grabbing the neck of a bottle, brought it to his lips. "And worst of all is that the scoundrels have drunk every drop!" he furiously spat out. And you said, "I think we two if we worked together might build a stairway of these bottles." And so you started in working, and for a month you worked at building that stair unique in all the world. But you finally finished it, a sparkling glassy stairway two thousand rods high that looked as though it scaled the very heavens and that at midday the sun made so blindingly dazzling, with a scintillation of every imaginable color from the polished prisms of the bottle glass, that you fairly had to blink. And then you began the ascent.

And at last Servando and the itinerant priest came to the city of México, quite dizzied and staggering, for they had had to nourish themselves after all on *something* during the long ascent, and since there was no alternative but to avail themselves of the few remaining drops clinging to the sides and bottoms of the flasks and bottles, the blocks for that improvised stairway, that is what they did. So, stumbling and carrying two near empty bottles in each hand, Servando and his companion made their way into the city. At last they had reached the "exalted" City on a Hill.

CHAPTER III

Which speaks of the panorama from the city.

The city, rising from atop a precipice, looked like a tortoise set in a palm tree.

Servando awoke from a maguey-induced stupor as he was trod upon by a caravan of beggars, the nakedness of whose feet being the only thing that saved Servando's face from being squashed. Out of curiosity he followed the crowd of beggars, who in their turn were following a lady following a rope tied about her neck. He dared not ask why, out of caution, but as at the end of the street (which by the way was inordinately narrow) he could make out a cloud of smoke which virtually assailed the very sky, so high it grew, he soon realized that the "doña" was about to be burned at the stake.

The pyres burned night and day at the end of every street, so that heat and soot were perpetual in the city and on summer days made it unbearable.

A mob was crowded about the flames. And as the lady's turn had not yet been called, she took her place in line. Servando was dumbstruck by the beggars' so zealously and anxiously following this lady in particular when there was a long file of victims waiting before the fire. But from overheard snatches of talk he at last made out that this lady was one of the wealthiest women of the city, so that they would follow her to the last moment, hounding her and tugging at her garments and curtsying, hoping that the doña (even at such a critical pass) might sprinkle them with largess—not, be it understood, as a proof of generosity, but as a gesture of her magnificence, for the soon-to-be burnt sacrifice was already well known for her openhandedness.

The pomp of the ceremony might have held some interest for the throngs of the curious, but not so for those who were themselves to pass through that rite of purification. There was, then, a great turmoil of protests in the file of victims, and some even barged ahead in the line and, to the accompaniment of a chorus of hoots and howls and complaints by those who by the elbowers' actions were caused to suffer longer, sneaked into places nearer the flames.

The maintenance of the bonfire was also a great problem, and to solve it some thousand Indians were employed to stoke the fires day and night, obtaining their firewood from any place they could, and even, at moments deemed critical by the authorities, using themselves as fuel. But there were some who did not wait for such resolutions to be taken and instead, tired of the continual search for combustible materials, threw themselves (along with whatever kindling wood they might have about their persons at the time) onto the flames, thereby poking them up for at least a time. When this occurred the flames would take on yellow, blue, and greenish colorations and shoot such fiery scintillations into the sky that one would have thought they were fireworks . . . But now the bonfire somewhat abates in brightness, since its victim is a heavyset priest who has extinguished the flames of several brands. But almost at once the fire recovers its wonted intensity, with unctuous sputters from the priest and a great new load of fine cedar carried to the pyre on the backs of a hundred Indians.

The protests in the line grew more and more shrill and agitated. Some persons seized the flaming lengths of wood and began to burn themselves of their own accord, thereby flouting the orders of the Holy Inquisition and dying an unchristian death, without the final benefaction conferred by a confession. But others waited calmly, and there were many who carried forbidden books, which the Archbishop at that mortal moment allowed them to peruse.

When the lady's turn at last came, she walked forward with great complacency and self-possession, though her bound hands deprived her of some grace, and even made something of a speech (now standing in the very flames), which Servando could not hear but in which she explained why she had refused to have one of her teeth pulled. At last she made a sign to the beggars and said that everything of her person which the flames did not melt or ruin, they might take. The beggars, exultant with happiness, danced around the so-enlightened lady and with pitchforks, metal prods and rods, and even long sticks of wood, anxiously awaited her enashment, assuring one another that gold did not melt. For the lady had stepped into the inferno bedecked quite regally in all her jewelry.

Meanwhile, the protests and complaints of those still waiting in line grew more and more forceful and pronounced, and even somewhat crude. Night fell and many of the spectators returned to their homes. (These spectators were all whites, since the Indians, who did not consider themselves obliged to do so, would not approach those fires even to warm their hands or backsides a bit. From a good distance some might watch the flames flare; some, terrified, would flee.)

Servando, by now weary, walked away (somewhat concerned too that he might contract a fearful grippe from all the smoke he had inhaled thereabouts) toward the Alameda. He did in fact feel a bit ill. He was sixteen years old. But for a few brief seconds, bent double in a fit of coughing on a bench onto which he had subsided, he might have been an elderly uncle. And he was just about to enter precisely the convent that was the seat of those rites. But he had bade farewell to the rigors of authority on leaving the House of his Childhood, and he was not keen to put himself so soon back into authority's hands. And so he sat awhile. The candles in the streetlights along the avenue began to glow. A cart wended by, picking up garbage here and scattering it farther on. A fountain sputtered and spat out a stream of water and then lapsed into its former mute aridity. From time to time the peals of the Angelus were heard, since each church followed its own clock. And above all the roofs of the city rose the steeples (like needles pricking heaven) of its parish churches. At last the young man (the boy) stood up and shook himself, and then he strode off with great strides (as was his custom) till he came to the door of the monastery.

Every little while he would hear a muffled explosion, somewhat like an addled egg thrown into the embers. What could it be but the heads of the bodies burned at the stake as they burst from the fiery heat.

He rapped at the door.

I rapped at the door and went in. The choir of novices, all dressed in white, was already waiting for me. "We have been awaiting thee," they all intoned in unison.

I found myself in the monastery of Santo Domingo, one of the most daunting and terrible places in the world. The vows there are utterly impracticable. Temptation is great and bad example, which abounds, at last drags even the best along in its wake. I hardly know how I escaped falling into its temptations. The choir of novices dragged me to a lateral chapel where a congregation was gathered for a ceremony about to begin. Within moments I shot from it, utterly naked, and making as much haste as I could I slipped up a back stairway to the chapel and took refuge in the arms of Father Terencio. Father Terencio said to me, "Calm thyself, calm thyself," as I attempted to recount to him what I had seen and what at this very moment was taking place on the floor below. And with a multitude of *Calm thyselfs* he helped me sit down on a remarkably hard seat, he ran his hand over my hair, he dried my tears, and he sat on my lap. I, seeing this, jumped up and ran off again, and since I did not know what other thing to do I ran out once more into the street.

And it so chanced that the first thing I saw upon regaining the street was a person covered with scales, as of a fish. I was horrified to think of the dreadful illness he must have been suffering, but I went on walking and a little farther on I saw another, in the same condition as the first, and then another and another. Until at last I asked an old man about these. "But whence comest thou?" he said to me testily. I told him from where I came, at which he began to laugh and he put me the question whether that was on the other side of the world. But finally he explained to me that what I had seen was real enough, for it had occurred that some few years ago a famous engineer had come to the city, hired to drain one of its lakes. This engineer began to dig a tunnel so that the water might be drawn off, but in the meantime he closed off all the city's natural drainage canals and other means, leaving the city flooded, until the artificial drain could be completed. But when it was done, it did not gain the Viceroy's favor, because he liked to see the water flow. It seems that the drainage was all subterranean, and this led the Viceroy to allege that it was the work of witchcraft. The engineer was outraged at the insult to his skill, and so he blocked up the tunnel. And the city was flooded again, until the Viceroy at last relented, and acknowledged the merits of the engineer's work, at which the city was drained again. But then he could not come to an agreement with the engineer on the wages to be paid him. So the city was plugged up again, but this time the engineer was accused of heresy, which is the reason people give for his disappearance into the bowels of his tunnels, where he destroyed all the sluices and valves. And with all this stoppage and unstoppage, the city being flooded twice yearly and then dry, and then flooded again, there was no alternative but for its inhabitants to adapt. Therefore many became fish. And others, whose metamorphosis was slower, found themselves, as one might say, neither fish nor featherless fowl, but somewhere between the two—half fish and half man. The most conservative element of the city had taken refuge on rooftops or on rafts, small boats, and canoes, and so did not lose their original shape, though many died of hunger. And when the lake was at last drained and dry, those who had been fish flopped in dying agony in the mud flats, while those who had remained men returned to their homes. But these—these are the half-fish, living now with the upshot of their indecision. The Viceroy, who had changed into a lovely red snapper, somehow reached the ocean—and some say he is there still, muttering curses and obscenities yet unable to come out onto the shore . . . Thus the old man told me, and this helped me wonderfully, finding him so full of information, to form an idea of just how things in the Viceroyalty stood. I also took the opportunity to interrogate him about the woman I had seen burned the day before. And he informed me that she was a most respectable lady who had been sent to the stake for no reason but pride, since she would not allow one of her teeth to be removed, as every other lady in the Viceroyalty had done, so that in matters of dentition they would not outshine the Vicereine, the Viceroy's wife, who had had the misfortune of losing a tooth directly at the front of her mouth. Rumor and gossip about the rebellious lady spread wholesale and even grew coarser and uglier as the days passed. Most especially when the lady laughed. At last it was said that she had kept her teeth intact as a sign of contempt for the Viceroy, and that by holding the Viceroy in contempt she held the King of Spain, in whose stead the Viceroy acted, in contempt as well, and if the King, then the Pope himself and therefore, *mutatis mutandis*, the Holy Mother Church and therefore, by despising and holding all these entities in contempt and disdain, the lady was, perforce, a witch. And since she was a witch she ought by rights to be burned.

But by now I was not in the least taken aback by these revelations, since I knew very well that the noblest reach of Mexican society was naught but a groveling pack of fawning sycophants and fops and that it was precisely that reason which enabled them to be the "noblest reach of society." But in the lower classes much the same thing also occurs, alas. I had personal experience of this fact when I saw, at my very feet, those most wretched of the city fall, grimacing horribly and spasmodically kicking, raising their legs and letting them drop again, dead on the instant. My God, this was incredible. And so I turned again to the old man who had told me the story of the gap-toothed Vicereine, to inquire of him concerning these dying wretches. But as I was about to put the question I saw him too start up, give a little hop, stick out his tongue, and fall stiff and cold at my feet, before my very eyes. And so I looked all about and all I could see was figures starting up, stiffening, and falling dead in heaps. So of course I ran down the street as fast as my legs would carry me, and all that stopped me was the pyre lighted at the end of the street, awaiting more people to incinerate. A friar was stirring it with an extraordinarily long cross which he was grasping by one of its extremities, as though it were a poker, and as someone in front of him fell into the bonfire and jumped about violently, almost extinguishing it entirely, I could hear him mutter a curse, and say, "Damned riffraff that don't even know where to go to kick off! Eat rotten fish, will you? And there's the upshot of it, by's bones." "Rotten fish!" I said to him. "Why, man, what would you think? Of course it's rotten fish. Dost not see the color they turn before they bust? And dost see how they're garbed, like that? Thinkst thou these miserable folk have the wherewithal to buy themselves a nice fresh fish?" And so it was that I learned how it fell out—our being now in Lent, no one would eat anything that was not fish. But since fish was very scarce (and dear, for owing to the dried-up lake the price of it became terribly inflated, so that only the wealthiest could buy it), therefore most of the fish rotted in the stalls, at which moment the poor, determined to eat naught but fish or die of hunger, could buy it at a very low price, but not before. And with the putrefaction which then lay in their gut, some burst, though still others died of inanition, since even so the means of some of them were not such as to allow them to buy even the fish that had rotted. But this latter death was of course much slower, so that generally people found a proper place to do it in. All this made me see how poverty and superstition always go hand in hand . . . And so, brooding over this great tragedy, which is the misery of poverty, I returned to the monastery of white-clad novices.

And as I came to the high altar, at which a choir of them was crooning softly, I stood there a good space, though without kneeling or praying.

By the time you got there it was already night—you just couldn't get enough of riding roughshod over the town, could you, finding fault with everything. So young and such a grouch! So young, and always yammering about something or other! Even criticizing this holy place, where little angels coo at each other so sweet and quiet. Such an old grump! And so young. You ran off to find Father Terencio, that noble soul, and you got it all off your chest, every single complaint, you absolutely hounded him to death with your filthy accusations. And Father Terencio, that noble soul, not only overlooked your pettiness and petulance but even tried to introduce you into the kingdom of love. But you, you piece of filthy bestial flesh, you rejected him, which was practically like rejecting our Lord Himself. You refused to even let him nestle in between your

legs a little. So you stormed off alone, and that's the way you'll be
for the rest of your whole life long—running away from the very
people you'd most like to be with. Because *I* know—*I* know—you
reject the things you want the most. *I* know that the minute you
caught sight of all those naked novices reaching out their arms to
you, the minute you saw them, something inside you went *pssh*
and crumbled into a million little tiny sparkles of light and your
first impulse was to run up to them, run over to them and strip
off your clothes, get naked and join them. Mingle. But you're so
stubborn. You're such a hardheaded stubborn burro, and a good deal
too smarty-pants for your own good, too, if the truth be known, and
so you trample on your own strongest instincts. You always have
to have your hair shirt on, don't you? So you took off running. But
I'll give you credit—maybe you knew the evil didn't lie in the
moment begging to be enjoyed but in the slavery that would come
of having given in to it, the dependency for life. That lifelong hunt,
that constant unsatisfiedness with what you've got, with what's
right in front of your nose . . . So you ran out of there, running
away from yourself more than just running away. Saying to yourself, "I'm saved, I'm saved, I'm saved." And you *were* saved, too, for
the first time, which of course is the same as being saved forever.

And so you walked all by yourself through the city. And when
you had yourself well in hand, perfectly under control, you came
back (picking your way through the dead) to the monastery. And
behind the pillars of the side aisles you could hear the chant of
those white apparitions, purifying themselves of their orgies in that
sweet tranquility that always follows the letting off of steam . . . And
a youthful visitation of the devil even tried to pet you, caressing
your privates through your white robes—Father Terencio, who very
casually, offhandedly touched you as he gave absolution to all the
young sinners. "Lead us not into temptation, but deliver us from
evil . . . Amen . . . Amen." But you were firm, you clenched your
teeth, and Father Terencio went on down the line with a strange
and ironic wave of his hand. It was his first rebuff in years and
years and years of success. You'd been dismissed.

CHAPTER IV

Which treats of the visit of the Archbishop.

It was all like a dream inside his cell. He clambered up onto the bed frame and pulled himself up to the window cut into the wall high up near the ceiling, far above the level of the eyes of one standing in such a cramped and narrow cell. At this hour it seemed that the city no longer breathed at all, save for the curls of smoke that rose in the gloom of the background, shooting up suddenly sometimes like flickering, sputtering altar lights breaking through a realm of darkness so otherwise dark, so black, and making the earth seem to softly shudder. At first it was to him an awesome and imposing sight, but after a time he became wearied by its constant sameness, so that at last he closed his eyes and imagined it to himself so wonderfully, that little by little he managed to forget those fires, now issuing one had thought from the very center of the earth, as though something far far deep inside were furiously exploding in rage and madness, raving, and shaking off the burden of the heaviness of the world, which now had slid off from on top of it like ants shrugged or flicked off the hide of some irritable beast . . . He fell asleep. He dreamed that he was walking along with a pair of shears in his mouth, and dreamily he tried to fathom the meaning of that dream. But he could not discover it. Even after he had fully awoken . . .

It was then that he hid himself in books and, surrounded on all sides by scrolls and sheaves of parchment, he rummaged nearsightedly through the shelves, searching mightily through everything which had ever been written, and he even imagined what could have been written and yet had not been, or what had in fact been written and then pretended not to have been, so as to be repeated and thereby to bring about the desired effect at last. He had to brush past heavy cobwebs, cut a path through the dusty jungle to the imagined tome from which in fiery flowing letters there would leap out at him that word which had been written nowhere else in the world . . . On the other hand, the books were guarded jealously, and books of interest there were very few. The *Quixote* itself had been kept back in the hold of a ship while customs officers, carrying out the Inquisition's heavy orders, wrangled over whether to let it be admitted ashore, since it "held things of the most mundane and false world." So there they lay, gnawed by book-

worms, riddled by termites, and wetted by cloyingly sweet brandy-
leakings, all those thick heavy volumes, until at last the sailors
were persuaded to smuggle them ashore. That was how one copy
had come into his hands. "One must, somehow, struggle ceaselessly against things that are ill done," Servando would reassure
himself each time he searched through the rows of books without
finding one worthy of his devouring. And at that he would sally
out into the streets and stand and read bills posted about on walls
(many of which suffered from dreadful errors of spelling), until
he wandered back, repeating them over to himself through the
monastery, so continually that Father Terencio at last took an
alarming antipathy to him when he overheard him, during a mass,
whispering to himself over and over, "Tortillas traded for matting."
But Servando did not, even for all those knocks and disappoint-
ments, leave off his forbidden bouts of reading; beneath the bed,
behind the altar, sheltered 'hind the trunks of trees in the patio,
and even in the full force of the sun that ground the paving stones
to powder, he pored over his books and repeated to himself arguments and definitions aloud. And so it was that, before the great
chapel nave, and hunkering somewhat so as not to crack his pate
(so high was perched the oratory), he began to preach sermons in
Latin, aloud, since for his being the best student in his class, he
was also the only novice who might experience fits of ecstasy at
such long and extravagant catalogues of conjugations and cases
(many times those of unfamiliar words and texts extrapolated from
those he knew, on the spot). The other novices would bombard
him with lighted votary candles which hit their mark with uncanny accuracy. And it was during one of those chapel battles that
suddenly there entered (sideways and with great difficulty), through
the central door of the chapel, the Archbishop, in person. Brilliantly lit by a lateral window, his color high from the exertion,
the Archbishop had at that moment the semblance of a whale at
sunset. The Latin master, who saw His Grace enter, tried to calm
the combatants, but with most disappointing results. And so as
Servando kept doggedly spinning out the threads of his now greatly
extended speech while he fended off the flaming candles, one of
the projectiles sailed directly into the prelate's most high and serene forehead and left there a great dent. The Archbishop's eyes
rolled up toward the pulpit whose top scraped the very highest
point of the roof of the nave. He opened his mouth. And from that
mouth there issued a writhing knot of snakes as the Archbishop

fell lengthwise on his back, like a great toad flayed by the preacher's unending tongue-lashing. At that the choir of novices rushed into a circle about the fallen prelate and intoned a solemn Hail Mary, then a *Salve* very very hushed, and then slowly and laboriously helped His Most Excellent self to his feet. Then they knelt before him. The Latin master crossed himself quickly and with the tip of his foot tried to extinguish a votive candle still burning, to all appearances invincibly. Father Terencio, who at that very moment was most discreetly and soberly entering the great nave, stopped as though rendered stone, and then he lowered his head so far that it bumped against the paving blocks of the floor, which momentarily gave the Archbishop another fright, though immediately he interpreted the good father's act as mockery. Servando began then to descend from the pulpit, knocking aside altars, scattering candles, and at last tumbling headlong into a pew, creating no end of nervous fuss among the onlookers and exhibiting something of the same himself, but he recovered himself at once and, holding himself most soberly, he saluted the Archbishop by clapping his hands piously together, fingertips erect. And he began to babble a parody on an epigram by Martial—no doubt thinking he was mumbling a hasty Paternoster—so thick swarmed the readings which by this time the young man had forcibly stuffed into his head.

So you finally succumbed to the poison of literature, and you wound up puttering about, poking through rags and papers, stirring up dust and disturbing the termites and bookworms, all to not the slightest avail. All you got was a jumbled heap of unanswered interrogations, which in fact served only to aggravate your by now habitual uneasiness and mental restlessness. Oh, but you would *know*. And so you *asked*. And you kept on asking, investigating, delving, digging, diving deeper and still deeper, though no man could tell you one jot of what you sought to know (except maybe that you ought to quit all that reading, now, cut out all that stoking, because that way led not only to madness but still worse to sacrilege as well). And that, then, was how you came to speak out so angrily against all those who would criticize you. As it was also how there came to disappear from your cell (I know not by what chaste hands) the instruments of such lamentable unbalance . . . You fell into that well from which there is no escape—Letters— and so you felt more and more alone. You were stricken by the

Blight of Melancholy. But you still kept on declaiming, pro-claiming, speaking out, knocking down unreal doors, and pursuing deep studies of things so rarefied and strange that many there were who were ignorant of their very existence.

Thus, at night, in the midst of your meditations, you might leap from the bed and with great sweeping mute gestures elucubrate, as though spreading not the truth but your very being across the highest rooftops, across nearby balconies and tiled eaves, into the void, down the creaking and precarious rain gutters of the city, down the downspouts and through grates and sewers, the very route by which there had come to you an envoy from His Grace the Archbishop, who, having been apprised of your remarkable learning, had sent to beg that you offer a sermon on the occasion of the transfer of the remains of Hernán Cortés to the cathedral . . . So you began to exclaim that the Archbishop had personally come to visit you, to ask you to give the thanksgiving sermon. And for three weeks you closed yourself up in your room, looking up dates, facts, finding out information so that you might be well armed and prepared at the coming moment, the moment your learning and wisdom should at last be revealed to the world. And yet standing there before the Remains you forgot everything you had planned to say. You looked at the *regidor*, that alderman so hugely fat, resting relaxed, his skin stretched and shining, sitting in the midst of a roiling mob of beggars whose mouths opened it seemed more to clamor for bread than to offer up prayers for the Eminent Dead. And for a great while all you could hear was that single word, the murmur of that potent prayer—"Bread! Bread!"—whose force to sweep men along is greater than all the chants and laments of all the churches in Christendom. You saw the Viceroy smiling upon you, and all the fine Spaniard jackanapes of the pal-ace, the Spanish-born *gachupines*, impertinent monkeys all, the fat lot of them with their smug wealthy wives exhibiting the broken strands of their pearly teeth. And the Vicereine acknowledging with a slight inclination of her head that proof of their esteem for her. From the pulpit the discrepancy of state was yet more patent: On this side the court sycophants, the Spanish purebreds who de-spised the Creoles. Over there the Creoles who hated the courtiers and scorned the Indians. Behind, the beggars and Indians who spat on all the world and looked on all the ceremonial pomp with a slight sneer of irony and disdain.

And so that is the reason, no doubt, that your sermon began

acquiring new—almost magical—colors and hues which many there listening could not begin to understand and therefore found superlatively brilliant. And so it was that you stumbled down at the end, feeling as though you had been run through by hundreds of needles, and you kissed the Viceroy's offered hand and then His Grace's, and you began to hear those bubbling, boiling flutings of the ladies as they fanned themselves and murmured praises of you, blew kisses, fluttered their black eyelashes; and you saw a few who even crossed themselves as you passed before them. Oh, that sermon raised you aloft in triumph. But once you were perched up there you didn't say what you planned to say. You didn't say that.

At that time I suffered much on account of my solitude and so took refuge in letters. Hanging on that promontory mined through and through with the most lustful little caves and caverns, many was the battle I was forced to suffer so as not to succumb. But the hardest and most terrible of all the battles was that one I carried on against myself. At those times I would fling open, with great fury, the books and begin to hop about my cell and I would watch as false and scheming demons would appear in all the four corners of my cell and leap about, onto my hands and before my eyes, screaming, "Fall, fall, fall . . ." But it fell out that one time, finding myself in an extreme of perturbation, the Archbishop came to me himself in person and he requested that I pronounce a sermon on the occasion of the removal of the remains of the Conquistador Cortés, as my fame as a preacher was now well dispersed through the city. And so that very day I prepared the sermon, which for all the haste with which it had been writ came out exceedingly well.

And thus it was that standing before the Remains and before the most illustrious and enlightened persons of the vice-realm, and some of the most mediocre as well, it went out of my head completely what I was going to have said and I spoke instead of many things which nothing had to do with the earthly remains of the Conquistador (which in fact I hoped within my breast would be struck by the bolt of lightning that would have rendered dust what in life never suffered the same most devoutly wished-for misfortune). And as my words flowed from me most fluent and serenely, though by now I gave no thought to what I had been saying, everyone thought my speech most excellent,[1] the speech

[1] Fray Servando Teresa de Mier, *Apologia.*

about which I can now recall not a single word though I believe it turned on a complaint about the scarcity of trees after the Alameda had been despoiled of them. So I was most highly flattered and puffed up by the Viceroy and by the Archbishop also who saluted me with words of admiration though it struck me that his smile had something of an air of disdain in it, for I well knew the hatred he bore against all the Creoles for the simple reason that such we were, but especially if we were erudite or wise in any way.

And, after having taken my leave of all these folk, I was ashamed for having said things which were not those I had had in my mind to say, once I had seen all the poverty and misery arrayed behind the bejeweled garments of fine stuff worn by those royal she-mules. But I put that idea by. Though now it dances through my head. And now I have an inkling how I shall go about the carrying out of my plan, discrediting those Spanish *gachupines* so blue of blood that look at us down their noses for no other reason than that we Creoles have been born in this land which the great idling rogues sack to fill their bulging purses and keep themselves upholstered in satin frippery and colored hose, as though not the sow's ear but the whole hog had been expended on them.

And now the laughter and flirtations of the friars all up and down the corridors. With that, and them, too, I must constantly struggle, to ignore them.

CHAPTER V

Which treats of the meeting with Borunda.

The best preacher in the City of México was I. That was the reason the Archbishop in person begged me, on his knees, that I should be the one to pronounce a sermon on the Virgin of Guadalupe on the twelfth of December. I, who belonged to the Order of Friars Preachers, which was established to save souls, not to exalt the political aims of the state in tedious praise, I, I say, felt no great desire to give such a sermon, at which surely every person would fall into a stupor at the first words. And since nothing at first occurred to me by which I might give some life to that hulking and unwieldy piece of furniture which I conceived that sermon to be, so as to lift the spirits and command the interest of the hearers to the words that I would say, I made many circuits of the patio in the monastery, walking back and forth like some man in extreme agitation of mind, and even pulling all the leaves off the vines in the arbor, still without any fresh ideas coming to my mind for all my perturbation. And it was in that state that I was when (and by now all the trees as well as vines were naked of leaves) there arrived, riding on two brooms, the Dominican friar Mateo, who making a great fuss over me took me in his arms and flew me in great swoops out to the very boundaries of the city, to a cave. "I leave thee here," he said, and he pushed me off the brooms with such strength that I dropped like a stone to the ground. "Enter," I then heard someone say from inside the cave. And since I was not a little befuddled and slow of thought (from the fall I had taken, I mean), I straightaway entered that hole from which thousands upon thousands of bats were issuing terrified, bumping and crashing into one another as they flew off and disappeared.

"*I am Borunda,*" a voice said to me, further frightening the bats. "*Borunda, Borunda, Borunda,*" echoed the bats as they fled screaming and laughing.

"*Come here,*" said the voice of Borunda. And so I walked that way a little ways until he bade me sit down on a most wonderfully comfortable bed, made of the tiny bones of bats. The bed creaked a bit but though I was a good deal frightened I said nothing. A herd of bats came in, singing, and walked farther into the cave to where Borunda was (though I could not see him), but apparently at a gesture from him they walked out again, dying of laughter. "*I AM BORUNDA,*" said Borunda. And with a great leap he was standing in the doorway of the cave, where he pulled back a great curtain made of bats' wings. Borunda's physical aspect was something like a great bellied bowl of a pipe that could move about and talk, but even fatter than that. His flesh hung over his eyes and drooped down and covered his hind parts, which kept him from performing his physical necessities, so he explained to me, which as a matter of course then caused him to be even fatter still.

He began speaking with great panting and puffing, and then little by little his voice rose, till it became so loud, so loud, that thousands more of the bats flew shrieking and crashing into the walls of the cave, many of them dying from the shock or the fright, though several thousand of them managed to penetrate the curtain and find their exit, where there flew so many of them that they clouded the sun.

"I have my ways," said Borunda, hopping twice and falling backward to the floor carpeted softly by the bats' excrement, "I have my ways of discovering," he began, from that floor into which one sank up to the knees, "and I have discovered that thou hast been chosen"—and here he gave me a great heavy slap in the belly—"to give the sermon on the Virgin of Guadalupe." His voice here was but a secret murmur, so that I was obliged to place my ear very near that opening surrounded by two great flapping slabs of meat through which the great toad of a beast spoke. "*Very well,*" he said, and he raised his voice so greatly that I had to draw my head away, which I did with a cry, and gave it shelter in the carpet. "Very well," he shrieked, "I possess the key by which thou canst make this speech the greatest that has ever been given, in all this jurisdiction . . ." And his voice went on rising. The walls began dropping off great blocks of ages-old stone. And bats fell shattered into tiny bits by the potency of those snorting booms. "I possess the key," he repeated, and a hail of stalactites rained down upon us. And then the great whale of a creature stood up, with one heaved puff, and came toward me, shreds of his flesh falling from his body, and raising me up by the neck and throat, he lifted me to his mouth and said to me in the barest whisper, "I think that the image of Our Lady of Guadalupe is from the time of Saint Thomas, whom the Indians call Quetzalcoatl." I expressed some doubt of this assertion, at which Borunda opened his mouth even wider and plunged my whole head inside, so that I could see the tassel of flesh that was his uvula at the back of his cavernous mouth, surrounded by bats that flew from the velvety palate to the tongue, perched on his teeth as they made tiny shrieking noises, and then flew off into the deepest recesses of his throat where they hung from the walls of his throat and palate and fell asleep to the music of the owner's heavy gasps of breath, a panting that was at times so fierce, so heavy, and so strong that it made them sway in its wind like leaves or even at times blew them out through the windows of the nose.

"Well, here is where I die," thought I to myself, "and I am never to preach my sermon," and I recalled Odysseus and his suffering and hardship with the Cyclops, but suddenly Borunda furiously pulled me from his mouth and sat me again on the soft ground. Hopping and leaping, sometimes in great leaps and sometimes in tiny skipping hops, he disappeared, as I watched him, back into the obscurity of the cavernous labyrinth. "Lookest thou here, look'st here," he cried, returning in one great leap, as he began to unroll an endless scroll of cloth on which appeared the figures of animals with women's heads, women with a lion's sexual parts, wild beasts with children's faces, and suns screaming from the expressions reflected in those faces. Then he emptied at my feet a sack filled with rocks and stones of all sizes. "Here is the evidence that will prove the case," he said, in a new voice, a great triumphant cry. "On each and every one of these hieroglyphic stones it is clearly proven and demonstrated," and now his voice was the sob of a tiny lizard, "that the Virgin of Guadalupe already reigned in that better world before the arrival of the Spanish interlopers known by us all as arrogant strutting jackanapes," and after a breath he continued in the same soft throbbing way, "which is logical, I believe, very logical, for did not Jesus say to his apostles, 'Take the word to all the world'? and America, by which of course I mean all the lands of the Americas, even those which we may not know but yet believe in, all the lands of the Americas, of course, are a great part of this world, a very great and excellent, principal part." "*Therefore,*" he triumphantly continued, "therefore the Virgin of Guadalupe did not make her appearance in that filthy cape of the Indian called Juan. Who could imagine such nonsense! Our Lady to appear in that disgusting poncho? No, she came in the coat of Quetzalcoatl, his very own raiment, and when I speak of Quetzalcoatl I am speaking of Saint Thomas, who could never under any circumstances have disobeyed the orders of Christ Himself. This then is my belief, my argument, my thesis, as sure as it is here written before thee. Look at these Yucatecan codices! observe these Zapotecan inscriptions! and these markings of the Zacatecans, the direct descendants of the Toltecs! Here, now look'st thee at this thousand-odd lot of Chichimec stones and tell me that the proof is not irrefutable, the evidence not overwhelming! . . ." Two bats flew out, shrieking, from the mouth of this most curious researcher as he moved his lips, and one of the little creatures clung to Borunda's earlobe and began to sing. At that Borunda with his open palm gave himself such a slap on the ear that the bat was squashed against the side of Borunda's face as though one had squashed an irritating insect, and Borunda himself rendered deaf in that ear, which made him then scream all the louder: "*Here is thy proof!*" And with a great jump the mass of quaking flesh disappeared, leaving a wake of fluttering bats, and then as quickly reappeared, clutching an immense manuscript. And, laying it on the ground, he began to turn the pages, one by one. "Here thou has the *General Codex of American Hieroglyphics*. Here is all the proof thou couldst wish or ever need. Lookest thou at these dots, these figures! How could it be any clearer! But wait—I have still more evidence—wait here and thou shalt see!" And again with a great bound he was lost to my sight in the darkness of the cave, and in a second returned, tumbling over me hundreds of books, each one stranger than the last, in all of which, according to Borunda, one might read in the Yucatec tongue that Saint Thomas had wandered for many years throughout the lands of America and did not go away until he had seen the cathedral of Tepeyac built. I looked at the parade of figures—men with the feet of serpents, women playing the moon as though it had been a tambourine, stags ascending into heaven . . . "Here thou hast material more than enough for thy sermon," he said, and at last the walls of the divers subterranean galleries could stand no more of the booming voice of Borunda, and they began crashing in upon us. The collapse was total. Rocks crashed about our ears, and had it not been for the thick soft mattress of bat excrement, in which we sank or were sunk, we had surely perished. Bats flew squeaking and screaming from the cave, amidst the great clamor of rock. "There thou hast all thou needst, for the most sensational of sermons!" Borunda told me as he emerged, covered with scars and scratches, from amidst the piled-up rocks and boulders, and, helping me then to get free, with great tranquility he sat on one of the ruined rocks and went on talking, as though naught of what had occurred, had occurred. This must be a great wise man, I said to myself as I marveled at his indifference to the complete loss of his work and his very home. "I have tried to make the existence of these manuscripts known, and their contents," he said to me, as though he had read my mind, "but I had no funds to publish them, and the *Gazette* constantly told me to have patience, that others had preference over me. And so, of course, the result of that was that I stood there forever with the manuscript under my arm . . ." "*Not to mention*," he added, and here his voice swelled as though it would crash into the rocks and break them into tiny pieces of dust before it had ever issued from his mouth, "not to mention that Mischief is as ubiquitous as the mass of the Ignorant, and Envy, which always sits in a high place, kicks down all things and all men that have achieved what she could not." That was no cause for despair or disconsolateness, I told him, seeing that he was beating his breast so hard with a rock that the rock was shedding shards and crumbles of dust. "I believe that all you have told me is true," I said, "but yet there may be another sort of people than those to whom you refer, that keep another counsel, and that at the eleventh hour may rescue from oblivion what is worth being rescued. For if not, how could so many valuable and worthy things be conserved?" "And dost thou think thyself such an all-knowing sage and bibliophile, then, to know what has been *lost?*" he put to me pointedly, and took up another rock to lacerate himself. "I shall try to do something," I said, to calm him, for he was taking up yet another sharp stone— but this one he hefted at my head. "What, pray, canst thou do?" "Well," I began somewhat unsurely, "very little time is left me before the sermon, only some ten days. So I hardly think I can embark on a subject so great as the one you have just proposed to me." "Don't say that," said Borunda, and giving a great leap he picked me up by my feet and poised me on his hands. "In ten days there is more than enough time to prepare thy sermon. There is no need for explaining all the evidence, thou canst simply lay out the most important, show the general line of the argument. The rest will be obvious as the background to thy speech, and the peo- ple will understand thee, have no fear. This is the greatest opportu- nity thou shalt ever have to say something new and different, and to interest every one of your hearers and more besides. Come, take this opportunity given thee, for ten days is time more than suffi- cient—was the world not made in six? (Though I tell thee in con- fidence, over that too I have my codex of hieroglyphics that somewhat contradicts that.) No matter—come, thou must begin work at once." And at that, Borunda suddenly, like a gigantic mole, burrowed into the rocks. I beheld a disturbance, like a great earth- quake over all the area, and then after about a quarter of an hour he emerged again with one of the codices under his arm. "Here, tak'st thou this end here," he said, "and walk that way with it, unroll this magnificent scroll, and thou shalt see for thyself, thou'lt have more than enough stuff for thy sermon yet." Thus he spoke, and while I held the one end he had thrown at me, he began to walk away backward, unrolling it. Soon he was backing down the pile of rock rubble, and then backing across the valley, still unroll- ing that endless scroll. At last I watched him fade into the distance between two far hills, naught but a hopping dot giving off harsh puffs and pants that seemed to lay the whole region desolate. And there stood I, fearing that the ten days would pass that still lay between me and my sermon before Borunda should have finished unrolling his hen-scratched and scribbled scroll, so at last I took and set two great rocks on my end and I walked off, as fast as I could, picking my way through that precarious jumble of stones and rocks. The last thing I saw there was Borunda, still backing away from me, fading away into the mists . . . At any rate, there was no cause for me to wait any longer—I had the idea well fixed in my head.

CHAPTER VI

Which tells of The Sermon.

The sacristans on the appointed day rang the bells in every church, calling the folk to mass. The city was one great tolling of bells. And a climbing up and arriving of Indians and Creoles coming from every pueblo and village, by now nigh dead of exhaustion and hunger, and flocking into the great sanctuary of Tepeyac. The women selling bread made of corn and of other cereals had set up their wares very early in the morning, planting the flag of their possession in the most strategic sites. And the most intrepid merchants would surreptitiously pass, under the cover of a burlap bag, small flasks of rum and other drink to rot the gut, at a price in keeping with the importance of the ritual to be celebrated that fine Sunday . . . But the sacristans could pull the ropes no more, so wearied were they, and many of them fell weak, or even dead, from the pulling and ringing. Some there were even who, maddened by the constant clanging, threw themselves from the towers and campaniles of the city, flying for brief moments over the town before they crashed atop the statues . . . The Archbishop made his arrival at the cathedral, casting his benediction to right and left and cursing under his breath (so that only his familiars could hear him) because the Creoles had not made the alley of their bodies wide enough for his ample girth to pass. Behind him marched the Viceroy, smiling the while, and keeping a good distance between himself and His Eminence the Archbishop so as not to tread on the latter's long train, as this once happening on another occasion saw the robust prelate tumbled to the ground. After those two came the Regidor Rodríguez and his completely toothless wife (for to such exaggeration was the lady carried by her devotion to the Vicereine), exerting herself greatly in affectations and reverences before Her Lady the Vicereine in procession beside her, though this latter lady never cast her a glance. Behind them the circle of *oidores* and *cabildos*, members of the governing council of the city, and some petty judges, conversed together in respectful whispers, eyeing the short neck of the Vicereine as though it were the very holy Eucharist itself . . . At last the royal and ecclesiastical procession took its place before the high altar. And sat-down to wait most condescendingly.

But Servando did not arrive. And the sun, falling heavily among the columns along the nave, began to melt many of the costly votives. Then suddenly there fell a sunny rain which filtered through the roof and dripped upon the crowd, and the glistening purples of the Archbishop lost much of their color. As the shower was ending Fray Servando (for at last we may rightly call him by that name) made his entrance, extremely serene and without saluting a soul of those gathered. The Archbishop saw him mounted on a flaming broom, and almost cried out, but immediately caught himself and thought that those were nothing but temptations of the devil, to make him show his fearful weakness for brooms . . . Fray Servando got off his vehicle (for it was as such that he had used it), and the Archbishop, no longer able to contain himself, did at last cry out. The bells stopped their ringing. And a murmur began to spread from the area occupied by the Creoles. Fray Servando looked very grand when standing behind the high altar. He stamped his foot to claim the respect that was owed him. And many a lady fainted at that display of masculine forcefulness. "Señor," spake Fray Servando. And began the sermon in the midst of the stillness of death.

His words were a long combat between the old gods and the new legends. By them were revived the scribbled, incomprehensible codices that Servando had never quite gotten to the reading of. And the Archbishop swallowed the Episcopal ring when the preacher called in doubt the apparition of the Virgin of Guadalupe as the Spaniards told the story, instead translating that visitation to remotest times, even to the arrival of the Messiah, thereby denying all right and reason to the presence of Spaniards in lands that had been Christian since long before their arrival. The Indians were spellbound by his words and the Creoles jumped to their feet, at every moment erupting in enthusiastic applause. Only the jacka-napes Spaniards and divers royal attendants, lackeys, grooms, and the like toadies kept a still and watchful silence, discreetly observ-ing His Most Illustrious person, who in turn shifted about in his seat as though something beneath his ample backside were making him more than a little uncomfortable ... Then the friar's words filled with queer invocations never heard before in a Catholic rit-ual. And then came the Descent of the Divine Plumed Serpents, and the sky, shattering into pieces, opened to admit the New-Recovered-Images. And then the splendors ceased.

And time slowly recovered itself, until finally the victorious Gods took their sacred places in the accustomed niches and altars, in the Kingdom of Futility. The fog cleared away, and the Arch-bishop, moist and irritable, could at last puff to his heart's delight.

Fray Servando brought his discourse to a gentle rest. And at last his voice once more took on the light and human tones and inflec-tions of its beginnings, bringing the assembled populace back down into reality. And so they saw him bend his knee, yet not touch the ground, and intone a soft *amen*. "Amen," then echoed every voice. And then, like a balsam, flowed the religious chants mixed with the various struggling mystical wailings of the Indian voices. It was, on account of all this, most fiendishly difficult to distin-guish the pitch of the Holy Mother Church's chants in the babel of Indian baritones, aristocratic shrieks, and Creole braying ... The Archbishop flung himself out of his pew and stamped away, evis-cerating thereby a pallet of Indian babies the mother had put to sleep on the cool cathedral floor ... The Viceroy came to Fray Servando and warmly squeezed his hands. And all the court ladies gathered about the friar to offer their most heartfelt congratulations on the excellence and upliftingness of his sermon, which none of them had understood. The friar, in such a stately and agreeable manner that he might have been for the moment a noble Spaniard himself, stepped down to the ground and allowed himself to be lionized by the multitude.

CHAPTER VII

In which are treated the several consequences of The Sermon.

Bells peal. Exhausted sacristans collapse and die. On every corner a friar flings at passersby pastoral letters denouncing the Great-Sacrilege-Committed-Against-Our-Lady-the-Virgin-of-Guadalupe-by-a-False-Friar-an-Imposter-Who-Calls-Himself-Fray-Servando-Anathema-Be-His-Name.

It is Sunday, a Sunday in Lent. Indians, Creoles, and the whole gaggle of noble parasites flock to church to hear the marvels of Fray Servando. And from the early hours of the morning an army of the battered, the wounded, the halt, and the lame drag themselves through the streets toward the cathedral. Everyone wants the best seat for himself. But today the "silver-voiced" friar will not be heard, for in every pulpit a sermon of offenses will be read against him. Priests talk of heresies, of offenses against the Word of God and against tradition. They say that Servando has called in doubt the sole, unique, and only true apparition of The Virgin of Guadalupe and that he should therefore be burned in the Holy Pyre. That he should be put to that test to see if that won't rid his body of the Fierce and Terrible Devils that cause him to speak such blasphemies. They say they want to see if that won't free his soul at last, let his sinful soul at last be purified. They say . . .

CHAPTER VII

Which treats of the consequences of The Sermon.

The powerful and the sinful are synonymous in the language of Scriptures, because worldly power fills men with pride and envy, gives them the means whereby to oppress, and affords them impunity. Thus it was that the Archbishop of México, D. Alonso Núñez de Haro, achieved a state of great sinfulness, in the constant and unrefusable persecution with which he begged me to pronounce the Sermon of Guadalupe, which, my being then a friar in the Order of Preachers, I gave in the Cathedral of Tepeyac on the

*twelfth day of December, the year of our Lord seventeen hundred
and ninety-four . . .* [2]

I knew very well that the tradition, or legend, of the Virgin of
Guadalupe in itself held very little interest for Núñez de Haro y
Peralba and that, for that matter, he even doubted it. But he for
his part knew very well too that it was very much in his interests
to maintain the fraud and deception to the people, so as to be able
to reap the benefits of the resulting servitude. To justify himself.
To govern. And, I repeat, to keep the Indians and Creoles servile.
Therefore he immediately sent to have sermons read against my
own, and had me made a prisoner in my own cell as though I had
been a thief or a criminal, and what is more paid no heed whatever
to the eight bulls I sent him with great difficulty, since I was
watched and guarded day and night and allowed to make no request
(at least that they were disposed to grant) whatever. And such was
the extent of his working against me, that at last he enraged all
the people of México against me, a people of itself the sweetest
imaginable but by reason of having little education and even less
of what we might call wits of the sort necessary, easily led by
words, so that I had been pulled limb from limb had I not run for
refuge to my cell in the convent, where I am now, more than
imprisoned, humiliated. For what should I care to be imprisoned
if I deserved it, and thence the humiliation. Though being prisoner
by order of His Most Excellent and Illustrious Grace the Archbishop of México is in fact a mark of some merit, for it signifies
that one is innocent . . . The most terrible thing is that the Provincial has not allowed me even a single book, and what can I do
imprisoned and with no book! . . . Not even my breviary to be able
to peruse it to pass the days and nights, for very little is my sleep.
So that I walk from corner to corner of my narrow cell, thousands
upon thousands of ideas coming into my mind and then scattering
at once for want of transferring them to paper, for that too have
they cruelly denied me. But the worst of all the evils and fears
that bedevil me is that the Provincial will poison me, as he has
done with two novices and a prior, for what reason I can only
guess! Here there is naught but indignation, insult, and contempt,
oppressions of the saddest sort, for those who oppress one are not
even worthy of one's anger . . . And every moment I can hear nothing but that madman Borunda, incessantly whispering to me, giv-

[2] Fray Servando, *Apologia.*

ing me recommendations and advice, proofs (according to him infallible) of the truth of my discourse so as to save myself with them. But I hardly think any of his intricate proofs and evidence will serve me at this pass. And moreover, I am in need of no defense since I have committed no crime or error that would merit it.

CHAPTER VII

On the consequences of The Sermon.

You've been in that cell two long months. A prisoner! And you deserve it, too, for provoking the anger of your superiors. Ay, Servando! What got into your head, to make you offend His Grace!—instead of kissing his feet, like you ought to. But what's happened is nothing in comparison with what's to come—because neither of the two submissions you've made to His Grace has suited him. But out of his boundless pity and mercy, your Archbishop—that holy gentleman—appears to be ready to bestow a part of his magnanimity on you: you'll be burned at the stake, but your hands will be free and you can wear your habits, as a proof of his favor and great kindness. So stop worrying—give thanks that you're safely locked up—or don't you hear that mob of Indians whose Will and Understanding you wanted to enlighten? Listen to them—they're screaming for your head. Even the women selling tortillas have temporarily left their tacos to stand out there in front of the monastery and scream for blood. *Ave María Purísima!* If it weren't for the Archbishop's goodness you'd be drawn and quartered . . .

You can see for yourself how all those people that were so friendly to you before have abandoned you now that you're in this mess. You can see for yourself that you're all alone, that your only hope for salvation lies in the mercy of the episcopate. The Provincial is sick of you, he doesn't want to hear another single complaint from you, and he's even sent more guards to guard you because he's convinced you've got some wild idea of escaping. And he'll sew your mouth shut with a piece of hemp rope that nothing can break if you keep insulting him. And give orders to cut off your head, you just try him, and have your head carried off in a burlap sack. And make your name anathema. And after you're gone lock up your cell with a hasp and lock, because the cell itself is cursed . . . But look here—I think your luck may change. Good news, Fray Servando! Your sentence has been commuted. The Provincial now announces that out of the boundless goodness and mercy of his heart His Eminence the Archbishop of México has extinguished the bonfire laid for you and instead opted for banishment and perpetual imprisonment in the convent of Las Caldas, in Santander, in Mother Spain. Of course with the proviso that any anticlerical remark or attitude on your part will effect an instant reversion to the sentence of death. Which means you'll be tied to the stake. And burned. So don't play with fire, friar, if you don't want to get burned. So that's how it is—you sail for Spain, to be a prisoner the rest of your days and even if your sentence should be reduced, because Spain is nothing but one great prison itself. The soldiers will shove you and push you with their weapons and you'll set out on foot for Veracruz, where you'll board the brigantine *New Enterprise* (a most inappropriate name, but ironies abound) and from there you'll set sail for Spain . . . In the darkness you'll try to look out and see the city and the monastery one last time, but there'll be so much fog that you won't be able to see a thing.

CHAPTER VIII

Which treats of your imprisonment in San Juan de Ulúa.

And so you came to Veracruz, that city named for the one true cross, one day of a rainy morning. And you never saw the ocean, in spite of the fact that you'd sailed it for many a league until reaching the castle wherein you were locked. There you were led to a dark dungeon cell in which there was no manner of telling when it was day or when it was night. You heard the barred door splash in the pool of stagnant water as it creaked closed behind you. And then all that was left to you was to grope through the darkness till you found the water-soaked walls.

At first you merely spoke, but then soon, in a futile waste of energies, you shouted your complaints. And then you started walking, from one side of the cell to the other, back and forth, back and forth, covering it first in two furious steps, the sound of your feet splashing water keeping time. But then the pacing took three steps, and then four, and then six slow steps from one dripping wall to the other, and then, at last, you stood stock-still in the cell. You couldn't see a thing. *I only hear the water dripping in near torrents from the ceiling, as though it were a fountain of spring water. As though the whole cell were but a wellspring just bubbling up at the surface of the ground* ... And so at last you made your tentative way to the bed and began to float atop it over all the surface of the dungeon-cell. You put your hands to the walls and tasted the water. But you couldn't drink it. It was salt.

"Water!" he shouted, for his throat was parched in that lake fit for nothing. "Water!" he screamed, and he stood in the water which puddled the floor and he scrabbled and tried to climb the soppy walls of his cage. "Water!" he shouted, and he struck the bars a great blow with the heels of his two fists and set up a clamor then for a piece of paper and pen, for since he couldn't assuage his thirst, he'd sit himself down to write. Write in the midst of that aquatic hell. Write. Let every mad thought that came into his head be freed. Waste not a one, as now he did when his ideas came and went, disappearing like wraiths of smoke in the prison darkness. So many ideas! ... And yet, he thought, as he roared for water and for light (some new-minted myth he almost seemed), and yet my best ideas are those I never can put to paper, for as soon as I do, or try, they lose the magic of imagined things, and to boot the chink of thought in which they take refuge will not allow them to be seen full face, so that when they at last are taken out and examined, they are wizened, shriveled changelings, not fit for light. And that calmed him some. He even slept a bit, buoyed by his cot, all that early dawn. It was perhaps toward daybreak when a jailer entered with a large bowl, yet with so little food within it that Servando believed they had in mind to starve him. But in time he grew accustomed ... And in that castle, virtually awash in the water, the friar paced from one wet corner of the walls to the other corner dripping and beswamped in sea.

We came at night to Veracruz, so that the only thing a man might see were San Diego's Holy Pyres, to which some hundred Indians were being fed that very night and at whose glorious flames a pack of Spaniards were warming their hands. I saw no more than this, nor wanted to see more, neither. The landscape is always very arid in these places where bishops, archbishops, and viceroys have their seats and hold the reins of power, as though it were Satan himself that ruled. That same day of my arrival, and in the midst of great thunder and much rain which, by the suffocating heat which we had been and were still forced to bear, fell on our bodies and boiled and evaporated on the instant, we started the journey to the castle-fort. And when the soldiers saw that we were completely dry in spite of the torrents which were falling on them and on us all, without a single thought more they shouted that the cause of that mystery was I, who, they said, had entered into a pact with the devil. So at once they pitched me into the blackest and ugliest cell, the cell most mired in the very bottom of the sea, in the midst of which this most execrable and intolerable prison is situated . . . They dragged me to that cell where, they said, they had recently had occasion to torture a woman to such a degree that they pulled out her intestine, and I heard them throw the bolts at the same moment I felt the water boiling at my feet. At that I ran to the bed, which in truth was but a slab of wood with a rag of canvas thrown across it, and there I lay down. And I started to reason a bit more than I had done, over all the chain of calamities that had occurred to me since the moment of my sermon. And yet many times the cold made me drop the thread of my thoughts, so that having nothing wherewith to cover myself I began to pace through the waters of my cell, and as my body was emanating so much heat and fever, the water immediately started in bubbling, so that I managed to warm myself with my own heat. And I thought too about that, for some time . . . At any rate, it fell out that one day (though well might it have occurred at night) I felt something brush my face as I slept. And as the darkness was so thick, in no way could I see what had done this, until by chance I caught it in my hands. I felt, at that, a great pain in my fingers, where some one or some thing was horribly biting me, and I saw (or rather it came to me) that it was a crab. Shouting and calling I leapt down from the wooden plank and began to run about the cell with the crab, which seemed not to want to unbite me, hanging on my fingers. Until at last because of the great row I had made, a jailer appeared. And though it be hard, consider what a simpleton and beast the man was, for instead of freeing me from the creature he set about

beating me for having woken him with my shouts. So with the
blows of the great idiot and the biting of the crab, I believe I must
have fallen half-dead into the water now full boiling. And on the
next day (or rather, when I awoke, for the truth is that for all I
could count, a century might have passed), I saw that the animal
had escaped. And that made me feel truly sad. But immediately I
took heart again, and I began to grope and feel my way all about
the floor and walls, trying to seek out the chink through which
had entered and fled the animal, with the idea of trying whether I
too could not escape through it, for seeing (or rather noting) that I
was so wasted, thought me I could slip through no more space
than had the crab. But I could find nothing. And yet when I awoke
the next day (although only a second of my sleep could as easily
have passed, for all I could measure it), the crab was once more on
my bed, though this time it did not gnaw at my fingers but rather
was snuggled up almost under my chin, as though in search of
warmth. And that made me feel happy. So I set about keeping
watch over this crab for as long as it was there with me and until
it took a mind to leave me (if such can be said of a soulless creature, that it takes a mind), so as to see by where it escaped. I could
well picture myself coming out onto the very sea's bed and from
there floating up to the surface where surely I would find some
way to come out of this dire strait I was in. But first I had to get
me out of that wet hell . . . But it happened that as one of my
jailers entered, carrying the large bowl with the spoonful of food
for my scanty meal, he saw me petting the "soulless beast." And he
set up such a racket, calling me witch and warlock and possessed of
the demon and beast who had sold my soul to the very devil, that
hearing him go on, it even frightened me. And he grabbed up the
animal and stomped it dead. I felt terribly like crying, but for spite
and not to give him that pleasure I hushed and, I believe, I even
might have laughed outright. After that he said he'd not give me
the bowl, though for me I cared little for it, my hunger in fact
having fled me. But later, after I had groped about a long time,
beneath the waters, trying to find the way to escape, my gut began
to writhe and creak. So I stood up. I went over to the remains of
the poor dead shattered beast and I ate them. And then I lay me
down . . . The water had rose a great deal and was almost touching
the ceiling. Upon my straw mattress floating through it I could
hear only the sea, beating and beating against the walls of the
prison. And I asked myself, with all the dangers I was passing

through, what the sea would look like, for though living as if inside or under it, still I had never yet seen it . . . And it happened that one day (or night), through the sounds of the sea I heard someone calling me by all my names. And I was quickly cheered by that, for I had almost forgotten who I was, though I had not forgotten my enemies. "Thou shalt depart tomorrow for Las Caldas in Spain," spake the shadow, which lightened and lightened, as it was carrying a candle. He put the candle on the edge of my cot and turned and left without another word . . . Up to that moment I had been threatened with being sent to be burned, given notice of my banishment and loss of homeland, stripped of my religious titles, merits, and degrees, but nothing that had been done to me, no order given me, had so saddened and cast me down as that toneless voice that had, and even with a touch of indifferent contempt, said to me, "Thou goest to Las Caldas," with no anger or heat, as though I were a chess piece or a rag to be tossed into the rag heap . . . The candle end was still sputtering, but very dimly . . .

I was young and very full of wrong ideas about the world, about other people, and not less about myself. I was young. But the world has always been in the hands of the old, and old men's ideas are strange and different. For that reason, during the months I was there in that prison, I tried to make myself old, so as to understand them. But I could not . . . I paced back and forth through my dungeon cell until the very moment when I heard them coming to take me out. Then I walked faster and recited two or three lines of a poetry composed by myself which, if I may say so, I think were not bad. At last the steps through the puddled waters in the hallway stopped before my door. The candle had long since guttered and died on my cot. So the shadow of my wasted figure blended into the other shadows, and I walked away in darkness.

CHAPTER IX

On the friar's journey.

As the day was falling he was led to the ship *New Enterprise*. He was made to climb down ladders with no rungs and in the very lowermost bowels of the ship he was pitched into a cell worse than that of San Juan de Ulúa, from which rose waves of noxious odors that mingled to produce one great nauseating fetid stench. The friar held his nose (and breath) as long as he could, but at last, nigh suffocating for want of air, he let that pestilence penetrate him so completely that, nigh suffocated now with excess of it, he grew at last accustomed.

And now the ship, through the deep night, sailed into a great bank of seaweed, the fabled fatal sargasso, which tried to seize and hold it, and now it scraped its keel against sandbars risen from the depths, and now, as a crowning trial, it crossed prows with two shiploads of pirates greatly offended when they discovered that the ship carried not the jewels and priceless treasure they had expected but rather nothing in the world but one despicable and insignificant friar (who could as well have been thrown into the sea at the instant of sailing as so unprofitably carried), held prisoner in the hold of the ship, in the depths of the keel, and for no reason but the absurd fact of his having denied the apparition of a virgin which no one had ever claimed to have seen, anyway. The crews of the two pirate ships howled in derisive laughter when they heard the friar's "crimes and abominations," for all the sailors agreed that in those latitudes of constant sun and voluptuous sweat it was indeed a virtual impossibility that any sort of virgin at all should in any wise appear. But with no further trouble, save the death of the captain of the *New Enterprise,* who in his zeal to take their position had himself lowered in a longboat into the sea wherein he disappeared with all his instruments and papers, the ship made its way to the coasts of Europe.

And that night I was dragged away to the fearful and dreadful ship *New Enterprise,* which from being so old and disused was leaking water at all four corners. They pushed me into it, at such a height of darkness that I could not even see the sea in which for so long I had been living, and on which I was now about to be put to live for only God knew how long, if in fact under which I was not to find it my fate to die. Which as a truth came near happening, for hardly had we sailed when the hardships arose which I, from the belly of the ship, had foreseen. A mountain of sargasso weed beset us first, and all the sailors (for I could hear them) had to throw themselves into it with axes and knives to cut that newfangled, impertinent rigging. The ship was almost destroyed, but in fact the seaweed had not come ill, for it served us as food. For a fact, had it not been for this inconvenience we might have all perished of hunger in the middle of the ocean.

At night I could hear and feel the fury of the waves crashing against the walls of the ship and hear too the sailors shouting and calling down terrible curses on the weather, and I felt so bad of spirit that I had a great need to climb up out of that second watery dungeon I was in and see the life above, to feel the palpable dangers accosting it, which for their being palpable were in truth the easier to face than impalpable ones. But I was hard chained to the floor. Therefore I could only listen to the tumult and hope. For something was fated to happen to us ere we reached the shores of Spain, if in fact we were ever to arrive. And so it happened. It fell out that when we were just on the point of touching the coasts of "unclean" Europe, a contrary wind turned the sails about completely and in less than a month we were once more beached on the coasts of México. All the men raged and stormed and wanted to abandon the ship. But the order to disembark did not come, for, as they claimed, I was bound for Spain and there I would be left. And in this surely could be seen the hand of the Archbishop, for he, what he wanted was to see me adrift alone in the midst of the ocean, my flesh ripped and eaten by fish.

And so the ship sailed once more for the land of the Spanish jackanapes, but this time we came across not a single strand of seaweed. And our hunger was fierce, so fierce that I began truly to be nothing but a skeleton draped in dry parchment, and at last there came the moment when I could bear the complaint of my empty belly no longer and I began to eat my chains, just to have some bait to throw to my ravenous gut. And so I ate them all, and in this wise I found myself free. And so, my stomach filled with iron, I slipped as quietly as my inward clanking allowed, up to the deck. There the sailors were having some strange celebration, which at first I could not understand, but which consisted of casting lots to see which of them won it. And the winner, I discovered, would be eaten by the rest. They were so intent upon their lottery that no one saw me skulking along clinging to the rotten ship's railings, and so I made my way forward to the very beak of the ship. There I stood peering into the circumambient darkness, thinking to myself that but a few handsbreadths away there lay the sea, though I could not see it. Just at that moment I saw something I could not make out quite, a great burst of light that shattered the darkness. And then another, and suddenly it came to me that cannonballs were passing by so close to my head that by the time it was through I had lost almost all my hair in that combat, for it was a fleet of pirate ships that had mistaken us for a ship loaded with gold from the colonies.

Straightway the sailors left their dicing and began throwing up the few wooden planks there were, as breastplates to protect us from the cannonade, for the battle had been joined. I ran back and forth and the captain shouted orders no-one heard, until a ball caused him to vanish. The sea by then was lighted by the brilliance of the flames and balls and firing while I, beside myself with delight, peeked over the railing and at last saw it—the sea, red, red, red, from the blood of those who had been blown up in the cannonading and thrown overboard to clear the decks. There was a great clamor and shouting, a great tumult that broke out then when the remaining sailors saw that a shot straight from the pirate ship came and hit the *New Enterprise* amidships and broke her in two. And in three seconds it had sunk. I attempted to hold to some planking ripped loose, but as my belly was full of iron I sank plumb to the bottom of the sea. "Here," I thought, "my end has come," and I gave myself up to dying as I swallowed what must have been a good washtubful of seawater, so much seawater in fact that inflated as a child's ball I began to float upward, and grew so sick withal that I vomited up the chains. After that I can hardly tell what happened, for when I began to regain myself and look about, I found myself laid out on the deck of a grand ship, amid thousands of naked Negroes. By asking about to determine what had happened, at last it became clear that the ships which had attacked the *New Enterprise* had been attacked in turn by a flotilla of slavers. Thus I was here in this packet of slave ships, held as but one slave the more . . . At midday, under a sun that nigh dried up the ocean, some dozen of men came on deck with great buckets and began to slosh water over us, me and all the Negroes. It was bath time. Those sable creatures shouted so when the water was played over them that one had thought it was the Holy Fire itself they'd been thrown into. For my part I was almost happy, because the sun and water together gave me back something of my spirit and because, so I thought, I had been loosed from my captivity by the soldiers, so that I attempted, in a hundred ways, to pass unnoticed in that sea of blackness. I quickly laid aside my clothes and moved toward the center of the slaves, trying always to stay in the way of the most possible sun, thereby to grow as dark as I could. And in truth the life of those Negroes lying about in the boat was most piteous; they were so crowded and huddled one up against another that hardly could they move, and many had to sleep standing upright. The hunger was such that at every moment you might see a Negro fall down dead and be flung into the sea. The others would watch that dead one float on the sea awhile, giving queer cries and screams, but then soon enough they fell silent again, still unable to lie down on the deck. I thought we would go once more to America, by which I mean that part of America which is México, and there I thought I would try to see how I might make things fall out so as not to fall prisoner once again.

But as fate would have it one afternoon in midocean a great shouting was heard, which was like a signal to all that black company of future slaves. They rose up as one and began to call loudly and jump overboard into the water and strike out swimming, so as to come to that place from where the shouting had arisen. The guards killed them without compassion, though the Negroes seemed to mind them not one whit's worth and went on jumping, and though there were some who were saved, the most of them for not knowing how to swim sank and drowned on the spot. In less than one minute the ship stood empty, with the exception of a dead Negro lying here or there killed by the sailors and whom they now set about throwing over the side of the ship.

All was calm. Night came, and the shouts, the cause of all that carnage and uproar, ceased. I looked about me and what I saw was myself naked and exposed to all the elements like a babe in the woods, but I had grown so dark-skinned from the sun that not for a single moment did the men of the crew believe me one of their own kind. And so then I, who well knew the miseries of the species and its weakness for fawning and puffery, pretended great and abject devotion. I bowed to them and with great humility promised eternal fidelity and obedience. And of course as I knew so well their customs (which in fact were no more than my own), I offered myself as a kind of majordomo or jack-of-all-trades, or, to put it straight, servant, and they accepted me with a trace of disdain, so that for any however insignificant failing, as serving them food without bringing water, they might box my ears and say, "Thou savage black beast, thou must learn the ways of humans." They even tried to see if I could learn their language, good Christian

Spanish as they said, which I, with no great cost to my brain, of course, soon enough got. At first, well knowing the little learning possessed by the sailors, most especially if they were Spaniards, I spoke to them in Latin so they might think it was some African dialect. And so the poor benighted creatures did think. So every afternoon, for my own comfort and consolation, I would sit down by the railing and recite pieces from Virgil, though the sad beasts would kick me and shout (in Spanish bad enough), "At it again, thou Negro savage, mouthing thy bestial African talk!" And they would box my ears and threaten to kill me if I opened my mouth to speak any but the "holy Spanish language." And then they would mock and jeer at me while I, in the chastest Latin, would curse their mothers to endless lives in seaside whorehouses kept by Arab brothel keepers. Until at last I made up my mind to shut my mouth, for fear that they might truly do something regrettable to me. So I would beg their pardon with infinite scraping and bowing.

In that way we sailed on, with my never knowing where we might be or whither our course, when one day there appeared a boat loaded with Negresses. The sailors hopped about in delight at seeing those female figures, and began to strip off their clothes and climb about in the rigging and stand on the cabin roof in a state of complete nakedness and provocativeness. Some leapt into the water while others contented themselves with brazenly flaunting their manhoods on our own deck. The other boat pulled up not far off and threw a rope between. The sailors, like so many Mediterranean monkeys, began to crawl across it, and the ship in which I rode soon was utterly devoid of life, except my own. And then there came again that shouting I had heard so many nights before and that had so excited the multitude of Negroes. Thus I soon understood as I had not before that the cry was given up by the Negresses as sailors had their way of them. Or perhaps vice versa. Or both. For the sailors could not be said to rape the sable females, for they had been raped since long before that first shout had ever been heard. Within moments the crew had begun to carry the women over to the boat in which I had remained. The Negresses, who at first resisted, now were agreeable enough and even laughed outright or gave little cries of pleasure. Naked bodies were tangled all about the deck, up against the walls and down through the stairways and passages. And though of women there were plenty, several groups of men could be seen like bees congregating about a single black bloom, a female who always was revealed to be little more than a girl, and the sailors would wait their turns to have pleasure of her body, violating her again and again. The two ships were no more than two great bedsteads given over to lust and lechery, afloat on a steamy sea under a withering sun—fit place for such a battle, which to me seemed almost interminable. But at last the couplings ceased, and then came the moment I had feared, when I saw myself quite literally caught between the devil and the deep sea—for they would have me act as their interpreter to this ocean of female negritude. Things looked blacker for me than the Negresses themselves, for of the babble they spoke to me I understood not one word, so how could I ever translate it for the haughty Spaniards. But at last I worked out a way to communicate to the women what the sailors would have me say. Yet since my features were not those of the women slaves and since many of my translations appeared betrayed by the attitude of the Negresses, the sailors continued to observe me until at last they could not contain their suspicions of me and decided to lock me up in one of the cells in the "brig" as I believe they called it—for their Spanish too was at times incomprehensible to me. And there you may imagine that I never saw the sun. I grew, then, whiter and whiter and they, more and more surprised and angry until at last they saw they had been taken in and swore I was the very devil and even tried to burn me, and in fact only their fear of setting the ship afire finally dissuaded them from laying a pyre. One of the sailors of greatest authority at last suggested that they throw me to the sea. I, whiter than my usual white for the fright I was in, made good defense of myself in my best Christian Spanish, though this had the effect of yet further inflaming their fury. So, hopelessly, I was thrown into the sea. And just before I sank I saw the boat's stern pulling away over the still waters of that latitude, the sailors aboard waving and crying their good-byes amidst great howls of vicious laughter. And then a moment later I saw the ship tremble, or shiver, from some great blow and sink like a stone, just at the horizon. At first I could not give credence to my own eyes, and then I thought it must have been some miracle worked a-purpose to punish their malice (though this thought gave me great mortification, for then I thought that it was a miracle that had brought me to the fell pass I was in), but finally I heard the sound of a great snorting and bellowing over the waters and I saw a giant beast rolling in the waves and shooting a great vaporous column into the air . . . The whale, maddened perhaps by the stifling heat, had crashed into the boat, sinking it at a stroke. I watched it now resting on the surface of the water, as though taking a moment's rest from its easy labor. It was of the whitest color imaginable, and as I swam toward it and climbed up on its hump, cursing at every step, but very softly, it paid me not the slightest heed. Nor when I lay down atop it to rest, where soon I fell asleep. And so it was that I awoke as I was washed ashore by a great wave on the rocky coast of the port of Cádiz . . . It was only then that I first fully saw the animal, now dead and come to rest on the shallow ocean bed. It was a whale of an enormous size, its color now gilded at that hour by the setting sun. I thought it had mistaken its route and that the hot waters of the African seas had stupefied or asphyxiated it. Which, I thought, was why it had come to die on this coast, so as not to go contrary to the habits of its kind as I had heard or read tales of before. Though who knew but that by the time I had mounted atop it, it might not already have been dead.

So you sailed off aboard the *New Enterprise* from the port of Veracruz.

Banished.

And the boat was assailed by scores of storms and tempests great and small.

You watched as the waves swelled and the sails were swept away. And you were calm in the face of that danger which because it was common to all men had nothing to do with you. Nothing to do with you *personally.*

The waters at midocean grew wilder and higher, as though the winds would raise the very deep, and the ship at times, lifted by an incredible wave, would scrape against the clouds.

And you in the keel practically single-handedly holding the mast erect.

And you hearing the crack and roar of the cordage.

And you calmly contemplating the impotence of man before the power of the elements.

Almost happy, perfectly exhausted, standing in a rain that rose from below and fell from above all at once.

But every evening, as the day would fall, calm would come again. *Becalmed.* And the sea would be a meadow smoothed by currents.

And then the bottom-dwellers, as though stirred by the magic air at the surface of the sea, would begin to emerge, to celebrate their rites before your eyes.

It was night, and the winds seemed to hold their breath.

The ship was a sparkling, twinkling point of light leaving a great scar on the motionless waters as it passed.

You saw a school of flying fish swim to the top and out into the air and fly rapidly past, above your head, and then as quickly disappear again into that quiet lake.

The night wore on and the very air was renewed, refreshed, invisibly and continually.

And then the sea newts came, old Triton's sons, and they made love before your eyes.

You watched porpoises come to the surface and sing in chorus around the boat. And you did not stop your ears. The whole wide ocean was one great sparkling phosphorescent glow, like altar lights that flickered and frolicked about the ship.

And you stood in amazement at such glorious sights.

And that fiesta went on and on, the creatures of the sea, the bottom-dwellers rising up strange and weird and floating down out of sight again, and then suddenly, again there was one great sparkling effervescence, in and on and above the waters. And you so wanted to join in that fiesta.

So you threw yourself overboard, and a choir of swordfish surrounded you, singing, and then came the needlefish and other strange-faced fishes.

And a school of dolphins sniffed at you and offered to carry you down to the bottom of the sea. But by then you were a mere fish like any other, so you could not admire those games. So you returned to your ship, amidst a wonderful great rustling in the viscous waters. And so it was from there that you watched, once more, the play of lights from those beings that had become for you once more creatures of deepest mystery. Creatures with a single eye in the center of their forehead. Thousand-legged creatures walking over the water like monstrous spiders. Ferocious creatures that danced upside down, with their fangs in the air, ready to devour anything that passed by above them. Creatures in the heat of rut that swam, sobbing and calling out in voluptuous rapture, finding one another, then bubbling downward to the ocean floor where their union came to its shuddering close.

That was the sublunar battle of life. Then the lights would all submerge. And then all would be a deafening swim of scaly beasts of ashen hue. Strange serpents writhing about the ship in search of crushed or bleeding fish. Aging mermaids that not songs but rather long tired libidinous wails emitted. Rushing sharks awakening to their own implacable hunger. And then, one day toward morning, the great sea-snake with eyes in its tail and smoking tongues of fire devoured them all, all the species one by one, and then circling tighter and tighter about the craft, pulled it down, slowly, from the surface of the sea, and slowly strangling it carried it down and down, to the ocean floor . . . So you had to swim, at last, to the shores of Cádiz—the white city of Cádiz.

You were so skinny, so worn out, so hungry, that it was all you could do to fall in the sand and sleep . . . And every wave that washed ashore caressed your feet. And wet them. And then wet them again.

SPAIN

CHAPTER X

Which tells of your imprisonment in the Chaldean cauldrons of Las Caldas, in Cádiz.

And now—oh good friar—you are to be locked away, here in the darksome cells of Las Caldas, for four long years, in the company of these starving rats with eyes that glow in the dark. What on earth can I do for you that you haven't already done for yourself, or imagined done? You're in this cell now. And you can't hear a thing. You can't see the fields all around, much less see the sea. People here die and never make a sound, here in this place you'd think was made on purpose for being miserable in. And all I can do is leave you here, all by yourself, in this hole where if it were me I wouldn't have the slightest idea what to do, or what to think, and certainly not how to escape. But you—you do. Oh sure, you're already hatching thousands of solutions out of that egghead brain of yours. One step—and not such a big step at that—one step, and you pace the cell. Time and time again. You raise your hands to each side of your throbbing head. And I'll tell you, there are times I'm afraid you're about to start screaming, or to dissolve into wild shrieks of terror. You might as well go mad. But you don't. You've got a plan. Oh sure. And all you think of is that plan of yours. I don't know whether to laugh or cry. You write hundreds upon hundreds of letters—which will never be delivered! But you don't care, oh no, you write. With your goose-quill pen and a stick to scare away the rats—who seem not to care too much for the idea of dying of hunger—you sit in your cell, and you write. Letters to the Spanish royal court. Other letters for His Holiness. Then a good whack at that pack of rats that attack your ankle. And then three more letters, and a whack or two. Write. Write. Write . . . But this is as far as I go with you. I mean I hate to leave you, and so, well, it's hard to go . . . Night is coming on, though, and there's not a candle to be had. Tsk. I don't see any other way—you'll have to write in the crazy gleam of those rats' eyes.

And so, by those lights, you write.

■ ■ ■

"At last! You're here!" cried the rats.

And the cry grew and grew as it echoed all through the con-vent—which was the prison. At last you're here, cried the million voices. (And suddenly the whole world was a scramble of rats em-bracing him and shaking his hand.)

"This will be your cell," said the rats.

This is your cell. But now the voices sounded farther off. As though all this were nothing but a dream. But listen—now the voices thunder again, shattering eardrums and splitting thick stone walls that instantly close up again without giving you a second in which to make your escape.

"You've come at last! At last! You're here!"

At last. And then, through the din of shrieking starving animals, emerged Francisco Antonio de León with a knife between his teeth, applauding. This was a petty, though very high-and-mighty, clerk, a sort of overlord to do the King's bidding, and a henchman of the Archbishop, a man both high and unspeakably low.

"At last thou art in my hands," spoke the terrifying functionary of the King. "Thou art in my hands," repeated León the Fearsome with a great roar like a jungle beast's, and as he slowly stalked closer to the friar, circling him almost hungrily, he swished his great tail about, and at last he slapped Fray Servando in the face with it. The friar raised his hands, not to beg mercy but to shield himself from the horrible stench of the rats and to brush off the hairs the tail had left on his face. León now turned and marched away, followed smartly by the rats, and he carried the friar with him.

They climbed stairs it seemed would never end, but at last they came to the highest, narrowest cell in the tower, worse even than that the rats had ushered him into. And there they cast him. The cell was so high up, that when Servando peered out through a small barred window, itself set so high he could hardly reach it, he could see nothing but empty space. León, surrounded by the rats, fell to his knees and said, "In the name of his most merciful Holiness, the Archbishop Antonio Núñez de Haro y Peralta, and by his mercy thou shalt remain here for only ten years." The friar, his situation suddenly breaking clear upon him, protested. He de-manded justice. And at that the rats broke into gales of hilarity so contagious that even the friar began to laugh out loud. And laugh-ing still, he began to pace his cell, back and forth in one great stride. "I will leave thee here then," said León, but the friar feared being left with the horde of ravening animals. "When thou hast served out thy sentence, then mayest thou protest." And slowly he turned and began to step away, turning again to lock the door behind him. The friar looked up to the ceiling, which on tiptoe he could touch with the palms of his hands. Two or three ants were scurrying about. "If only they would stay with me," said the friar. And at that the rats gathered in formation in one corner of the cell, arrayed from eldest to youngest, and by the looks of them all starving (for they had eaten off their own tails). The ants, though, frightened by all the shrieks and shouts, quickly ran away. "And I too must flee this place as well," sadly said the friar.

What occurred to me in Las Caldas, I am tortured by almost constantly remembering.

I had suffered many calamities since I first fell into the Archbishop's clutches, but what I saw in Las Caldas, and suffered, has no comparison with even the worst of my previous hardships. I had hardly laid my hat on the cot when the rats devoured it before my eyes. I was terrified at the sight of those wild beasts dripping saliva, regarding me with blazing, flashing eyes, ready to devour me at my least misstep or carelessness. Their hunger was grown so fierce that at night the only sound to be heard was the grinding of their teeth in the darkness . . . I had hundreds of letters to write, for I had to denounce the crime being committed against myself and with myself, but the first thing necessary was to save myself from those beasts' ravening fangs. With a stick, then, that I ripped from the ceiling's panels, I sat on a stool (the cell's only furniture) and set about keeping off the rats with one hand, for they gave me never a moment's respite, while with my other I wrote likewise incessantly. I laid out my situation for anyone to see, so clearly did I put it, and I begged not mercy or even clemency, for of that there was no need if justice be done. But justice hardly exists where the government is given into the hands of the powerful. And so I daresay my letters were not even read. So, seeing that by such passive means I would never achieve anything, I began to turn over other ideas. And thus there occurred to me the notion that perhaps if my complaints were heard in person they would be better understood. And since life in Las Caldas could not be born in any wise whatever, I thought only about the means whereby I might save myself. For even the Gospel itself justifies flight when no other alternative exists. And so thus it occasioned that one night during which the rats were more angry and unmanageable than ever and I was on the point of going mad, for no longer could I keep them at bay, it appears that my struggle and shouting attracted the pity of a good friar, who making use of scores of tricks and ruses had soon slipped into my cell. He was an old, sickly friar, all skin and bones, and he spoke like the hoarse blowing of the conch shell. He leaped in one clean leap into the very center of my cell, and the first thing he did was to splatter the innards of one of the fiercest rats of all with one well-directed kick. And then he ate it. "Horrors!" I exclaimed upon seeing the wretched friar devour that rat, skinny as it was and still twitching with the little life it had left, and swallow it down in one gulp. "Think'st thou not that my hunger alone has led me to this," said the friar after he had well swallowed the animal. "I do this to show those creatures who eats whom. Do thou the same and thou shalt surely see that they leave thee in good peace. And thou wilt have put aside thy state of victim for that of aggressor." Saying this, he seized one of the fatter of the creatures and swallowed it whole, without its ever even touching the walls of his throat as I would daresay, so that the animal was still squeaking some as it passed my visitor's gullet. This repast done, he lay down on my lousy cot and rested for some half hour. I could not think what to say to him, though in truth I was astounded to see that the rats had huddled together in the farthest corner of the cell, and some even trembled a bit when they looked at me. That I believe, was what at last emboldened me, and so, so as not to appear weak and girlish in the eyes of that old monk, I very tremblingly approached the pack of cornered creatures and with great delicacy plucked out one of the smallest by the tail. But oh!, soon enough I harvested the fruit of my imprudence. No sooner did the beast feel itself a prisoner, than it began to scream and shriek, and as I had got it only by the tail, it knew how to defend itself well with its teeth and it began to ravage my hand, while I was so frightened and astonished at the creature's ferocity that I did not dare release it. So I began to run around and around the cell with the rat by the tail that was ravaging my hand of the little flesh I still carried on my bones. This uproar had the effect of inflaming the other little beasts, who instantly leapt out to attack me. Had it not been for my blessed friar I had already been in the other world, for he began to kick about right and left so

wildly that one kick took me in the shins so hard that I cried out
in alarm, but at last he had driven back the rats. And peace fell
again. "Thou shouldst flee this place," the friar said to me. "No
other thing ever enters my mind," I replied, and I told him then
all the calamities that had happened and were still happening to
me. "What has happened holds no candle to what is yet to come
for thee." Such a foreboding! And thus spoken, no one could mis-
take its meaning. "For what avails it thee to be a Christian if thou
hast not one jot of cunning or roguishness."

"I have tried," I responded as I glimpsed two rats peeping out
from under the straw mattress, "but *my innocence excludes all
cunning*."[3] "A friar that has no taint of guile is a mythical beast,"
said the friar, laughing heartily, and so lustily that two rats fell dead
on the instant. "That is foolishness,"' he said. "One must have
innocence and honesty, and in quantity, for they are always worthy
and useful, but thou shouldst never show them until thou hast
been cunning, for beforehand innocence is not only not necessary
but in truth, on the contrary, harmful to the cause thou seek'st."

"I do not follow," I said.

"Thou shalt understand in time," said the friar.

"Do you know the legend of the apparition of the Virgin of
Guadalupe?"

"Oh, I know nothing, but neither does it interest me to know.
In the question of apparitions everything one says may well be
true, for there is no way to prove it."

"I can indeed prove it," I said, and now the rats slinked out
with fiery eyes from the darkness and stood in rows before us
two friars.

"Even when thou hast proven it, that does not prove that it is
true. And moreover, an apparition loses none of its truth for having
been proven not to have occurred. The important thing for the poor
is that they be able to believe in something higher than themselves
and their intolerable poverty and misery. And what is important
for those that govern is to keep the poor in thrall to those beliefs.
So everything works out!"

"I do not believe so. You speak that way because you have not
seen what I have seen."

The rats began to snarl and growl. One, which by its looks was

[3] Fray Servando, *Apologia.*

the leader of the gang, scurried over to my visitor and tried to eat his foot. The friar calmly squashed it and threw it over to where the others were now huddled. "I have seen everything," he said.

"And I have seen almost nothing," said Fray Servando, "but even so, with what little I have seen I have satisfied myself that the world is gone much awry."

"I have seen everything," repeated once more the visitor as he stepped to the door. "And so I do not pretend to set things right, and more especially since I have also seen the results of those 'corrections.' I come from a place where the most violent and radical changes have been suddenly imposed. And I come running. Running, dost thou understand? Fleeing! I who fought with my own hands to put those changes into effect."

"That hardly convinces me," friar said to friar.

Now the rats were dancing. In groups of three. But one, who found no partner, was dancing alone. And it did not dance badly. "When what has for so long been sought is finally got," said the visiting friar, "there is no choice then but to die. Oh, thou hast been so disillusioned by those *massacres* in France, but things worse yet might have occurred."

"I do not know . . . the most terrible thing is that one never knows. What if nothing at all had happened . . ."

"By my faith, never! Never! Let things happen! Let there always be something happening!"

"You say that, because nothing overwhelming has yet happened to you, to truly move you and make you lose your faith."

"My faith looks always far above mere results."

"In what do you believe?"

"In myself, which is to believe in almost everyone besides. And that is why I shall never be betrayed."

The other friar stood now at the door. He opened it. And the rats thronged out into the passage. One could hear their little feet splashing in the water. He closed the door after them and began to walk about the cell. The friar watched him and then saw that he had been transformed.

"Thou must leave this place," said the transformed friar. And he walked with great loping strides about the cell, carefully testing the walls with his hands. Then he pushed the cot aside and began to examine the floor. Then he climbed atop the stool and pulled and pushed at the iron bars on the high window up by the ceiling. "Thou must leave this place," he said, clutching the bars as he hung from them, for at that moment a pack of rats had entered, heaven only knew whence, and overturned the stool. The friar fell to the floor, twisting his knees somewhat. But he leapt up again to the bars and began to shake and rattle them until he had freed them from their embedding stone walls. "This is how thou canst free thyself," friar said to friar. And Servando looked out to see the space he would have to fall through to the ground.

"If I fall from this height I shall be smashed to pieces," he said to the friar.

"It holds thy only hope," replied the other.

The two friars made a circuit of the cell until they bumped into one another. The visiting friar let out a shriek, while the imprisoned friar held him tightly by the arms and asked, "What's wrong! What's wrong!" And suddenly he saw that he was clutching a dead rat. But Servando had no time to meditate over this wonder, which moreover did not interest him. Besides, thought the friar, anything might happen to a friar. And that somewhat calmed him. He tossed the dead rat into the corner and instantly the other friar rose out of that corner, standing and crying alarms to every corner of the cell. The friar followed the friar about, but at that moment a stampede of rats came between them and the friar very nearly tripped over them. Outside the cell León's growls could be heard: "I have come for that scoundrel! I have come for that rogue who has tried to kill me!" The friar reflected for a few moments over whether he had in truth tried to kill the other, but at last he was convinced that it could not be. He remembered that he had once let himself be devoured by an anthill so as not to step on even one of those little creatures. "Where is that wild animal?!" cried the wild animal.

And the friar could bear it no longer. He set the stool under the unbarred window, got up atop it, and stuck his head out into the countryside. It was a place which inspired not even pity, but only the desire to flee it and never once look back. Strong winds had blown away the little soil there had been, so that what remained was a dull brown scab emerging from the scalped earth on which not a blade of the hardiest weediest grass ever grew. The friar beheld all this and thought the world had been turned the color of scorched sugar. He looked down into the prison yard too and what he saw there were great rocks, awaiting him below in fits of malicious laughter. But León was coming closer. He was stabbing rats with the toes of his pointed slippers and spreading contagion

through the air with his breath, so noxious that flying insects fell
dead on the instant. And across that lifeless carpet came, inexorably, the Inquisitor. So then Servando, seeing that most terrible and
fearsome machine, gave not a single thought more to the deed. He
leapt through the window . . .

Almost without hope and seeing no manner of being saved, Servando was falling, until suddenly his clothing caught in the bars
of one of the tower windows. And he hung there by a string, his
whole frame unhinged, his head disjointed . . . Two nuns (whose
presence in that place is to this day unexplained), seeing that head
lolling upside down before the window, broke into exclamations
of fear and ran through the passages until they had escaped the
tower, and disappeared off down the rocky path into the desert.
"There he goes!" cried León. "There he goes, dressed like a woman,
and a henchman with him!" And followed by all his friars León
struck out after the two nuns, who by now were tiring greatly.
"Jesus!" cried the nuns. "Jesus!" And León had them shut up in a
cell . . . Our friar, at last having disentangled himself from the bars
though in tatters of clothing and of body likewise, crept into his
cell once more—he climbed up two gratings and pulled himself
into its unbarred window. Once inside, he set the bars back as best
he could and lay down exhausted to sleep. For some time he saw
not a single rat in his cell, and then a quick scurrying zigzag of
lights showed the friar that he had company. And yet still he slept
. . . Now the friar was creeping along the ceiling of his cell, like a
lizard, seeking a way to escape. He would slip from time to time,
and once or twice attempted to cling with his hands to the walls
which, suddenly, seemed almost breathtakingly high as he tried to
scale them. He even fell from the very peak of the high ceiling,
smashing to bits on the cell floor below. The rats scurried in triumph out from their hiding places and began carrying away the
pieces. Each bit of the friar had its own peculiar cry or shout or
groan, so that there were moments when the cell was a chorus
of complaints in harmony—hoarse, strident, sharp, piercing, deep,
rolling, off-key, hallucinatory. But hunger spurred the creatures to
swallow that shrieking flesh, so that their stomachs bulged with
song. And now the rats (screaming inside) ran horrified, as though
pursued by their own interior demons, out into the countryside . . .
As day was breaking the friar awoke. "There is no escape," he said
to the friar. "There is no escape." And the little window-flap in

the cell door opened very quickly and through it entered a bowl which fell upon the friar's legs. The window-flap slammed shut again with the same rapidity, so that he could not even see the hand that had shoved in the plate. The two friars began to eat the little aliment there was in the bowl. It was such a strange food, it threw off odd odors which made the rats stay away all that day . . .

Now the friar again stood before the friar. The moment had come when they must melt into one single friar. They were in darkness, because a good while ago now the wax of the candle butt had sputtered away and turned to the last gutters of a greasy yellow flame. The heat was suffocating. The friar went closer to the friar, and the two felt a shock of fire which almost pierced them both. The friar pulled his hand away. And the friar did also. So that both hands wound up in the same place. The heat is frightful, said the two voices at the same time. But now they were one.

The friar, alone, began once again to pace his cell. He climbed atop the stool and looked out. He saw the countryside shining and winking in a sun so withering that millions of multicolored things (*beings*, he thought, for they called out to him by name) were constantly melting and re-forming, at every moment assuming new, more and more incredible and grotesque shapes. The friar got down from the stool and threw himself again on his cot. And there he lay a good while, meditating on his escape, imagining thousands of possible ways. Until at last he put his feet on the burning cell floor again, and once more peered out the barred window. But he saw nothing. Suddenly, night had begun to fall. The friar raised his open hands up to the level of his face and stood there for a long while. His hands were long and white, and the little light that made its way in through the window cast them even longer on the wall. But black.

"What is this friar doing?" commented some rats that now appeared, hopping about on one foot and shooting sparks from their eyes.

"What does the friar want to do?" said the rats. But this time the friar did not leave off contemplating his hands, which now grew so long that they filled the entire room and the fingers usurped all the light of the ceiling. "To die," said the friar. "To die."

The rats went on hopping about on one foot and singing. They sang with their mouths closed, the way mothers sing as they lull

their babies to sleep when they have no song to sing. The rats
stood all about the friar with lowered eyes, as though in fear, or
hesitancy, or pity.

The friar raised his hands above his head. His fingers had by
now broken through the roof, and they were growing still.

"I don't know," he said at last. "I do not know."

The rats returned to their original positions. They set down their
other three feet and, like simple animals, ran scurrying off into
corners, while the sparkling of their eyes returned to its normal
dull gleam. "At last thou hast answered us!" they cried. And they
returned once more to their language of shrieks and cries and starving groans and growls. And when the friar forgot for a moment to
watch, they attacked him in hordes.

I saw no possible manner to escape my situation save in flight
itself, for the letters I sent, in which I requested that justice be
served, never arrived at their destinations. And to have waited to
serve out my sentence so as, only then, to request that my case
be heard again, as the scurrilous León recommended to me, would
have been shameful.

And so it was that one day when I was awakened by the sun
spitting out lashes of fire, I heard a great hurly-burly nearby my
cell. And then I made out the voice of the perfidious León who,
preceded by a wave of oaths and threats roaring from his throat,
was approaching at the head of a whole squadron of soldiers. More
than ever, I feared for my life. At that moment there raced through
my mind thousands of ideas for flight, but none seemed prudent.
But now the guards were almost at the door . . . That was the
moment when a rat entered, flattening itself so that one would
have thought it was a little plank of wood. And there suddenly
before my eyes was the friar who had abandoned me.

"Go!" the rat-changed-to-friar said to me, in an unbearably familiar manner, "because I have discovered that León will have thee
thrown to the blazes!"

"But how in the name of—" I began.

"No time! The moment has come—out that window! Jump!"

And I was about to leap, when I bethought me of the height.

"I'll be sausage meat," I complained.

So we sat down to consider the alternatives.

"Wait thou then till they open the door and run, before they
can catch thee."

But this idea seemed not wonderful either, for of them (if the sound of their feet were to be trusted) there were hundreds, and I but one man, and unarmed.

"Surely they will catch me even before I can run into the passage, and will have me slivered with their dirks and cudgels."

"Hold one minute," said the rat-friar. And he shot away like a flash. Entering one second later, he showed such a change that I was greatly taken aback—he bore an erection so enormous that one would have thought it was a third leg.

"Jesus!" said I, thinking the saucy creature would have violated me, for from a Spanish friar one must always expect the worst. But great was my relief to hear him say that what was carried there was an umbrella I might use to escape by, and he pulled it from his pants. "Jump, now, thou'lt have no problem with this," he said, and he opened it and placed it in my hands. I, to speak plain, held no great faith in that flight, but now the guards were fumbling at my door. So I took the umbrella and climbed up to the window.

In those few moments the door flew open and the mob of soldiers rushed in, captained by León, who nigh lost his reason on seeing the cell empty. He kicked over the bed and examined the cell inch by inch. And by an exclamation from one of the guards, I deduced that the only thing they found was one wretched rat which, I believe, the savage León squashed with his heavy boots . . . By now I was floating through the air. Below I saw the rocks, which were rubbing and rubbing against one another, to sharpen their points and edges and cut me to shreds if I should even touch them. And at that moment the umbrella turned inside out on me and I began to fall much faster than I would have desired, until a wind came up and lifted me and carried both me and my artifact up into the clouds. I never turned the handle of my ship loose, yet I was fearful that at any moment it might rip apart and let me fall into space and shatter into millions of pieces on the ground. But instead my speed grew greater yet and I continued to rise upward, and now I saw neither the convent nor the abandoned castles which are the only things there are in all of Spain. When at last I began to recover my senses from this flight I looked down and saw that I was nearing the sea. Without another thought I shook the umbrella and threw it some way away from me, though it went on falling with me through the air, so that now I was headed straight for the earth, and I fell into the top of a willow tree. Breaking branches and scattering leaves, I rolled down over the tiled roof of a seaside dwelling. The women of the house, who had seen me fall into the willow tree and then fall atop them themselves, knocking tiles about and causing some damage to the house, dropped to their knees. I, holding the bare skeleton of the umbrella and with a mess of leaves and branches tangled in my hair, must have seemed some strange apparition that they mistook for Divine Providence or God knows what saint descending upon them (since for these things there is never wanting imagination). So, making the most of that confusion, I ran away, the umbrella dragging behind me, up into the mountains nearby, hiding in a thicket of eucalyptus, which is the only plant with the strength to grow in that land of sun and hunger.

CHAPTER XI

The fall and subsequent escape of the friar.

So he flew through the air, and then to earth he tumbled,
Crashing down, head over heels, into a jumble
Of broken limbs and bruised,
Of trees and of his person too,
Into the midst of a convent's praying crew.
But straight up he jumped tho' his pate were cracked
And began to seek anew a track
To take to dodge the Inquisition's rack.
The convent wall at last he leapt clean over
And ran hotfoot across the fields, to cover
His naked body from the sheriff's men
Till he could see his way to México again.

   Poor friar! he stumbled all broken, in that state
Through the open arms of a hospital's inviting gate,
Where "Wait" they told him, so he sat down a good long time to
      wait, and wait, and still some more to wait,
Till he had thought they'd rather him to die than treat
His wounds. He almost swooned.

But finally they put him in a gown
Wide open at the rear, which made him, if the truth be told,
Even more unquiet than before, for the doctors thereabouts were
    bold,
And treat his lacerations not only would they have,
But eke sneak up behind for wicked pure mischief.
So, darting here and there, and keeping full alert
He crept away again, and looked to change his skirt
For pantaloons.
And soon enough in a houseyard he had found
A fisherman's garb strung on a line to dry,
So he replaced the gown,
And with the fishing kit hung right beside,
There came to hand
A purse ready-made to suit him out besides,
And so the new-clad friar was now at last become—
A man.

New-clad, newborn again (almost), and covered thy posterior,
Thou mak'st thy way along a road inferior
For fear of showing thyself upon the wide highway
Where surely León and the rest will lying be in wait.

The friar came upon two shiny *duros* lying in the dirt,
And thinking himself saved, he begged a young goatherd
In exchange for them to lead him where
Safe refuge from persecution he might find.
But the clever lad showed he had an independent mind
By going straight to tattle on the friar
To the authorities.
Flee, Servando! For once again the pyre
Seems set for thee.
Soon as the friar found out the traitorous plot
He cracked the goatherd's head wide open with a chamberpot,
And chased him with cudgels all across Seville
Until of being for once the persecutor he got his fill.
And so once again he resigned himself to flight,
Sleeping as he could by day and creeping down the roads by night.
What sad and wasted life is this,
That promised so much more, but hist!—
Is that a bloodhound howling on the scent?

No, for his nakedness had left no cloth by which to track him.
But still the life is grim—
The farmers' barking curs that snarl at him,
The withering sun that glares at him,
The rough and cloddy earth that halters him,
All nature that conspires to starve him,
And beggars that threaten to carve him
Into steaks for a dinner, or serve him
Boiled instead for soup, for meat on his bones there's none—
The friar is nigh undone.
He walks along sleeping under elms,
Begging for alms,
Praying psalms,
Trying to keep calm,
But wishing, a palm
Of his beloved land to see again.
And see it again perhaps he does,
For well nigh has he lost his mind
In this long flight from dust to dust.
Poor Servando—and as the crowning touch
The highwayman and cutthroat Chalflandín
Will have tribute of him,
And since of money the poor friar's not got a coin
He takes his due out of his skin.

   At last, staggering after many dreadful tribulations
Servando comes in rags to Dos Castillas,
And from there, he thinks, what he must do
Is find the straightest way Madrid to go,
For there, among friends, there's help to seek,
And so through packs of robbers, dens of thieves,
Clever ruses, artful dodges, cheats, tricksters, pricks and peeves,
And all the rest of evil Spain he goes—
Afoot, of course, in spite of swollen toes
And new frights every second.
By thieves he has been robbed and stripped, and worse—
For had he a coin, they've even robbed him of his purse,
So, as they say, he's not a pot in which to piss,
Though not even for that will he leave off his resist-
Ance to the horrors of his times.
To Madrid! For he'll avenge the crimes

'Gainst man and God committed! This
Is his mission.
But he for thirst and famishment can hardly walk,
Nor for long lack of human company can talk,
So soon he feels that all that's left him is to bawl.
But as he sits beside the road and weeps
A drover passes with his mule, and sees
Servando sitting there in misery and tears.
"Here!" he says, "What ails thee then?"
"My life and all," Servando says, "and hunger fit for ten."
"That last at least I can assuage a bit,"
The kind muleteer him tells, and bids him sit
Up on the mule.
"And fool!"
The muleteer goes on, "keep still, d'ye hear?
For Torquemada's near,
And he'd as soon see thee burn
As would that beast León!
So quiet!" And on they went, Servando riding
While the drover walked along beside him.

Soon had the kindly man Servando taken to his house
And called out to his wife that he had brought a guest.
She at that moment was stooping 'oer the dinner pot,
And staightening up she straight back at him shot,
As being not one her words to mince,
"Why husband, how dare thee bring a beggar like this one hence,
Knowing what little to eat ourselves we've got!
To think you'd play the idiot Samaritan,
When all we've got ourselves, is beans and onions!"
"Ungrateful woman," chides the man, "how can you begrudge,
    and whine
Over a mouthful of God's food for a gentleman
That's come upon hard times!"
"A gentleman's pox on the both of you!" she spits—
"You good-for-nothing lout! You smelly pile of—" "Quit!—
Enough! No more!" the drover tries to shout his furious good-
    wife down,
Though for her part, the wife would cry to all the town
Her husband's real and imagined flaws and slights.
Meanwhile, from hunger the friar's head is growing light.

And as the family wrangle mounts
The friar begins to think aloud,
"How sad and angry this world is!
When man and wife instead of kiss
Do fight and bicker all day long.
And truly, if they wish,
I'll buy my dinner of them, tho' with a song,
For that is all the currency I own,
For I'm dreadful hungry, and cannot go on."
"I say, by God, thou shalt have dinner!" swears the goodly man,
"And let her try to stop me, if she can!"
But Servando by now has fainted dead away,
Tho' the termagant wife still gives her tongue full play—
The fearsome, tiresome Amazon of meddlesome, worrisome tem-
    perament, finding that with words she can hardly make them
    flinch, lets fly with another string of oaths, and then, in noth-
    ing loath to tangle physically, she picks up a pickle jug of
    crockery and aiming very gracefully, cocks and hurls, and
    pitches it, and straight it whistles, through the air, at her
    poor husband's oath-parted hair—and he'd have fallen stiff
    and dead from the missile which the witch'd pitched at his
    head, but seeing it coming he'd ducked instead, so the crock-
    ery smashed harmlessly enough on the bed. This wanton de-
    struction made him so wroth with his harridan wife, the
    slothful slut, that with a shard from the jug he severed her
    jugular, and she fell stiff and stark on the hearth. The friar,
    who's awakened, was so shaken by the sight of the wife lying
    lengthwise and the husband upright, with a knife held aloft
    (to slice a loaf of bread), that he fell back, asleep (or fainting),
    without making a peep (or complaint). "Wake up!" said the
    muleteer. "At least there's bread and beer, and beans, and
    onions. It ain't dainty, but here, here's good food!" "Good
    God!" says the friar, "the pyre may've been better." "No, the
    fodder's always better than the fire." "Very well, but then I
    must flee," says Servando.
"Flee? Why on earth, I wonder?"
"Because the sheriff's men are coming yonder."
"And what of that? It's but a trifle, man."
"No, for I tell thee—they've all got rifles on 'em."
"Ha! If they're sheriff's men truly, they've pawned them,

So at best they're bearing broomsticks and the occasional mop
     handle,
And you have nothing to fear."
"Then, my friend, I'll just have one more beer—
And then, after that, I'm off."
"Indeed, that's fair enough—
T' yer health."
And so the two friends talk for many hours, till night,
In company with the wife's stiff (but silent) corpse beside,
The drover recounting the vicissitudes of matrimony
And Servando, his life's long, hard, and bitter litany,
Until toward dawn they both feel greatly better,
The sun is up, the night is past, and lovely is the weather.
Servando—"Is it from here to Valladolid a goodly way?"
His host, the muleteer—"I'll say."
"But even if I have to walk, I must go there."
"I tell thee, friend, thou'rt a fine rider of shank's mare."
"Thou say'st right, for I have my way of varying the route—
For I walk a little ways, and then I change and go afoot!"
"Well put—
But still, I may be in a way to help a friar."
"I thank thee well, but first a Christian burial
For thy wife who's still lying there deceased."
"We'll leave that for another day . . . For now, there's a troop of
     men, the cavalry, with horses ready-leased . . ."
"A robber band!"
". . . who I believe might agree to lend a lad a hand."
"To get away?"
"That is what I was trying to say."
"Hurray!"

And so Servando sets off for Valladolid, his spirits quite new-
     lifted, and as carefree as a kid. Along the road he's led by
     a lad who is not a cavalryman, but instead—of all things
     imaginable—a dealer in old clothes, and all things buyable
     and vendible, and even rags, and he's lent our friar a nag that
     stands not three hands high. And so our very quixotic don,
     he rides his tiny Rocinante, and he drags his heel anon. Poor
     man, he might as well be walking. But anyway—they pick
     their way along high roads and byways, over rocky precipices

and rickety bridges, jumping creeks and fording streams, and streaking past hordes of Chalflandíns teamsters screaming at their steeds (from whom they make a bare escape), until at last they reach the noble town of Valladolid, guarded by that same Chalflandín, the noble robber-king, who this time steals his ignoble mount from him, alas.

"At last—
Valladolid!" the lad delighted to him says.
"Methinks I'll go from here alone. I thank you very much."
"But sir . . . For such . . ."
"Leave me, I say."
"But sir, nay . . .
There is the matter of my pay . . ."
"What say?"
"Yea,
It's twenty *duros* I'm owed for bringing yourself all this way."
"Eh . . . Art thou sure it's *twenty* . . . ?
"Indeed, though there are guides aplenty
Who'd have brought you here for twice that fee."
"But, lad, as you see, my hat's the
Only thing I have of value."
"But it's twenty *duros*, sir, I tell you."
"Begone, I say, for I've nothing to pay you,
Though if you insist on a flogging, then that indeed I believe I can
          deal you."
And the friar, no sooner said than done,
Had walloped the poor boy so, that when he'd done
The lad was dizzy.
"Now go! For I am busy
About settling my affairs."
And so the lad, in tears,
And rubbing his boxed ears,
Retired.
And thus Servando, after many a trial sore
Came knocking at Valladolid's door,
Yet thinking always of getting to Madrid
Where, bedad!
He'd carry out his sacred trust—
Or bust.

(And bust, as we shall see, before it all was done, he almost did.)

CHAPTER XII

Which treats of my arrival and departure from Valladolid.

I entered as pretty as you please through one of the minor gates of Valladolid, and was strolling carelessly through the streets, which all of them are narrow and filled with holes, until I awoke to the fact that the holes in my clothes were greater than those of the streets themselves, and that my body was more exposed than hid by them. It was late in the afternoon and the sun was declining. Of a sudden, I knew not what to do ... Seeing myself in such a sad state, and hearing the ringing of a bell from one of the many churches that bring light to that city, I ducked into it (the church I mean) and with true spiritual zeal I set to praying. And so I remained awhile, so befuddled and sad that at first I did not fully comprehend what was there passing. But my prayers and ejaculations done, I looked about and saw I was alone in the nave although, I said to myself, I was sure that I had seen better than a hundred women enter, who as though by the art of magic all disappeared behind the altar. But I did not wish to rush to find the answer, for a stranger must always be the soul of discretion. And so I sat there, looking about me with apparent unconcern, as again a procession of women marched before me, all most serious and wrapped from neck to toe in black and also long black mantillas draping their hair, and vanished in a trice. And then in a moment more I see the priest, in appearance most grieved and afflicted. I watch him pinch out all the lights and turn, with no further ado, to close the chapel door. I, then, to call some attention to my presence, stood, crossing myself over and over and moving my lips though by now I was not praying nor anything of the sort. At that the father held the latch, then released it altogether and came toward me bustling so, that suddenly I feared he was about to box my ears. "What is the matter!" he said, more cuttingly than courteously, so that I stood taken aback, for not even the highwaymen of Chalflandín had used that language and tone when they addressed me. "Nothing," said I most somberly, at which the priest shouted at me that it was closing time, as though the chapel were a fruit seller's. I begged his pardon as best I could, and so as not to cause a row (of which I'd already felt the first effects), I made him a deep bow and moved to leave, fearing always that that most queer-acting man would cuff me. And I was just coming to the street when I heard the priest's voice calling to me loudly, "Come here, thou!" Truly I desired more to run right away than to return, but according to my design never to call undue attention down on myself (for I knew I was among savages), I turned again and faced the priest, who now began to look to me to be a giant of a man.

"Where hast thou come from!" he said to me, as though I were to be his rack's next victim. The question left me speechless. But nonetheless I lifted my glance, and for the first time beheld the features of that red-faced, fat-cheeked troglodyte, who now looked more the butcher than the ogre. "Whence comest thou!" he shouted again, and now his jowls were sweating great drops of sweat, which threatened to turn the chapel to a duck pond. From without came the chiming and clanging of hundreds of bells, rung with a kind of fury, as though each bell ringer would shatter his instrument. And by now it was full dark . . . I know not why I did it, but I walked slowly, slowly toward the altar and there I knelt and brought my hands to my face as though I were about to weep for very grief, though I did not (nor felt it neither). And suddenly the bells left off ringing, or at least abated their fury. So it was that I confessed to that fierce-looking curate all my wanderings. I told him I knew not whither I was bound and that when I left his church I had nowhere to go, or even knew which way to turn in that city unknown to me, as were each and every one of its inhabitants, who might otherwise have shown me hospitality of their own, or if not, then where to go. And on my sad words I see one of his great ham hands coming toward me, to my shoulder, where it sits. "I too am an American," he says to me, "from the North," by which I figure him for a Yankee. And seizing me, he raises me up by the shoulders with one yank and begins a long discourse on the savagery and bestiality of Spain in the colonies, and on the only way to free ourselves from the great simpletons and bullies. His passion was that little by little, one by one if need be, every Spaniard be killed, and then the Pope. "The Pope! the Pope!" that mad American cried out, in the very center of his cathedral and with such wrath that one would have thought he was leading the attack on the Vatican itself. I stood there in cold terror, for I knew I was in the hands of a madman, as there are many of those who in Spain occupy high ecclesiastical positions. The bells had begun to beat on my eardrums again, but the voice of the Yankee screaming "The Pope! The Pope!" effectively blotted out their sound. "But thou must not worry," he said to me in his strange Spanish, now

somewhat calmed, wiping away the streams of perspiration cours-
ing down his forehead and cheeks. "Here mayst thou stay with
no fear whatever. Only wait a while, for this is the hour when I
hear confession."

And leaving me dumbfounded, he moved off rapidly behind the
altar. I waited for more than two hours, I should think, and many
times I gained as far as the door, wanting terribly to break out and
run, but where to? Where to? In one of my sallies to the door I
suddenly heard a sound of many footsteps from behind the altar,
and as I turned I saw that same procession of ladies, all veiled in
black from head to toe. They were pale, pale as though just issued
from a burial, and in such a rapt, chaste, and mystical attitude that
my peace of mind came back to me in a rush, and I decided to
await the priest who had wrought such a transformation in those
women. At last the parade had passed, not one woman glancing at
me in spite of my saluting each lady as the file went before me
. . . So it was that I came to be lodged in that strange parish chapel,
and as I could find no other place, I made up my mind to remain
two or three weeks there at the most, which was the time I figured
I would require to put in order my defense and find some documents which the wretched thief León had brazenly stolen from
me. Meanwhile, I had to avoid the American father's mad harangues, and try to bear up as best I could, for after all I was a
guest and never lacked for food and bed, neither.

"Here," said that most curious gentleman, when the flock of
women had filed out the door, "and now is the moment for a great
battle," and he grasped the fingers of one hand so fiercely with the
other that I thought he would pull them off altogether, "a great
battle to begin the struggle against the Spanish curs. To make these
streets run with Spanish blood!" "Ah," said I, "yes . . ." and I could
see myself with a forged-steel cutlass hacking Spaniards right and
left. "Not the babe at his mother's breast shall be spared!" shouted
the raving American. And I shuddered.

Those were our nightly chats, after the confession of all the
ladies. From time to time I would try to relate to him once again
the history of my misfortunes, so that he would see that what I
most desired was that all be resolved in the most peaceable way
possible. Justice, which was a sort of byword by me, and the rights
of freedom I always made to take first place. I believed, at that
time, that all could be put to rights by means of treaties,
agreements, and the like. At least so I wished to make myself

believe. But he would not hear that. I think he never listened to what others might say. "Not the suckling babe!" he would shout, and I left off even trying to pacify him. For after all, he was right . . .

And in truth we might even have been able to come to some agreement had it not been for what I had always suspected and which led me at last to flee . . . It fell out that one afternoon, after having walked every infernal street in Valladolid in search of an attorney who was neither a thief nor a trickster, and who'd accept my cause so as to make my arrival at Madrid easier, where I would lay before the King my complaints, and not having found such a man, I entered the church, my feet tatters of flesh from having walked so much over the burning cobbles. And at that precise instant the great file of be-craped women was entering the church and passing out of sight behind the altar, and though I was near fainting from exhaustion, my curiosity got the better of my aching bones, and I made up my mind to solve the riddle that had always so troubled me. As the last mourning-clad lady vanished, I sneaked in behind, and I too disappeared behind the altar. Now the ladies were walking down a narrow passageway that ended in a most tightly spiraled staircase, which made four full circuits before it passed through to the floor above. When they had ascended the stair, they then went, now very rapidly, along a second long hallway and then slipped, very quietly and secretively, through a half-open door, where one would have thought would be the confessional and the confessor. As the last lady entered, I saw the door close. And I had a great desire suddenly to turn back and go to my room, but I did the contrary, and stepping out at the top of the spiraling stairway which was so bothersome to climb, I very stealthily made my way down the passageway and crouched low by the door, my ear to the keyhole. At first I was much relieved, and even taxed myself for ever having doubted that holy man the priest, who was now delivering a long sermon in Latin. But then, tired of listening to that constant murmur, and in a Latin pretty badly botched at that (for the good father put the accents wherever he saw fit), I was about to walk away and return to my readings, when I suddenly heard a kind of sigh from one of the modest ladies there at the service. And then another sigh, but this time deeper. So much deeper, in fact, that it might have been a moan. So I knelt closer and with great caution tried to peer through the narrow

crack one of the hinges had left between the door and frame. So
there I was, squinting laboriously into the room, and what do I see
but the "good" father, utterly naked, quite sweat-covered, with his
member harder than marble and as sharp-pointed as a stick, stepping daintily around through the women, who had knelt in a circle
about him, and he forever reciting his Latin lessons. The priest
walked slowly about that circle while they gazed at him in ecstasy,
their faces reflecting longing and lustfulness, their glance now fully
focused on their priest, forever walking, slowly and rhythmically,
his member of such incredible proportions that I feared it would
reach to where I was kneeling and thrust right through the door.
And so I saw with my own eyes that all this was but the prepara-
tion for what was to come in that room. The ceremony continued
apace. The ladies, now despairing almost, their hands squeezed
together, shuffled on their knees before the friar. And I tell you in
truth that the priest took hold of that part so well developed and
with both hands began passing it from mouth to mouth of the
kneeling ladies (as though, may heaven forgive me the analogy, it
were the host). And they in turn, in attitudes of utter adoration
and idolatry, would kiss, lick, swallow its full proportions, though
the priest had forcibly to take it away from one to pass it to the
next clamoring communicant. The ladies grew mad with waiting
their turns, so the father turned about faster and faster, offering
them all his monumental tool, and leaving their appetites in turn
more and more whetted. So faster still he turned . . . I grew dizzy
. . . I wanted to watch no more, for with what I had seen I needed
nothing more to fully comprehend the significance of that rite. So,
still dazed by what I had seen, and the father's frothing Latin still
sounding in my ears, I scrambled down the be-damned stair which
so further dizzied me that I cracked my head three times on the
treads above, and not till I was in my quarters could I begin to
gather my wits and the few possessions I had and to prepare for
another voyage. It was not the priest's attitude which affrighted
me (though it did indeed make a great impression on me), for such
things I had used to see from my first day in a Catholic congregation. Nor was it the contagion of the flesh (for I had fairly passed
those trials and found myself immune to its lapses), but rather it
was the fear of finding myself involved in such acts, which might
later in some wise be used against me (as the vile administrator
León had on other occasions tried to do) . . .

From Valladolid I departed that same night for Madrid, trying to stay aboard a diabolically uncomfortable Catalonian cart which not only shook my gizzard but nigh rattled my brain loose as well.

CHAPTER XIII

Which treats of what Villa de Madrid really is.

I went, as soon as I arrived in Madrid, to visit Don Juan Cornide and also Filomeno (the present mayor of Havana), who had been very close friends to me since our association in México City and because we shared the principles for which we had been accused of being Jansenists. I had hardly arrived when Cornide gave me the news that the entire convent of Las Caldas had been made prisoner for having allowed my escape, though by my having left part of my hands on the walls, it was showed that no one had helped me in that escaping, so that only seventeen friars were led to the stake. But even that act of retaliation had of course no effect on my persecutors' attitude toward me, for they were on the contrary still calling for my head ... For the moment, I resided with Cornide and Filomeno in their house, with great shamefacedness on my part and great poverty for the three of us, for they were hounded from pillar to post as the saying is, and struggling against hundreds of enemies in high government positions who were determined at all costs to ruin my friends, and to do to me (had they known of my existence) what terrible things go without saying ... Of the eight *duros* I had once had, there were but three *pesetas* left me and those I spent that very night of my arrival on buying my friends and me three of the most abominable glasses of wine in the city, drunk in the vilest-smelling den on a vile-smelling street ... Cornide and Filomeno spent their days working like beasts, running to and fro to solve the myriad of problems which rose like Hydra's heads at every moment; as for me, I set about presenting my case to the court. And so—

With the few documents León had spared me, I would wander lost and friendless through those interminably winding passages which in Madrid pass for streets (passing out *pesetas* whenever I had any about me to give), and never definitely setting straight anything concerning my unjust sentence or my good sermon, which contrariwise was only costing me the more disturbance. And while I would be waiting for a council of drooling old men (considered wise because they could more or less read) to meet and deliberate and meet again to deliberate again, without ever coming to any decision, since to them there never came *pesetas* either, I, tired out now with so much waiting, would wander aimlessly out into the streets, wherever my feet took me. By now there was no place in Madrid unknown to me, though I think I got no use of the knowledge, for one can just as well live there without knowing it, and never thereby miss anything very great. For *speaking of Villa de Madrid, what it is, one implies therewith, disorder, narrowness, crookedness, and tortuosity of streets, without a sidewalk to walk on anywhere, nor for that matter in any part of Spain anywhere, save the West Side or High Street of Cádiz,*[4] thank God, and with so few trees that the fingers of two hands are too many to count them. I say the streets are narrow, and by that I mean that the people have to walk sidewise and never look up to see the sky so that when one person is coming along a *way* (for a street it certainly is not), the person going the other direction must slip into a doorway, jump up and hang on to a window, or throw himself to the ground and wait for the other person to step across him (and as often as not, atop him), so that many times folk are killed in the arguments that result over who is to yield and who be allowed to "step over" (a fine euphemism). The houses lie one on top of another, all with stairways as dark and low as the dwellings themselves, for the domiciles are constructed with such labyrinthine cunning that the light of day never enters. On each tread of the stairs generally there lives a person with all his family, and people must step over, or more usually *on*, them in order to go upstairs. And on the roofs too the people live, for there they construct garrets out of cast-off umbrellas or old tins, which the slightest breeze blows asunder, people and all. And another thing. To walk through Madrid one must always carry a great parasol or wear a helmet on the head, to protect oneself from what is thrown down indiscriminately and without respite from the windows and balconies, for it is so much that unless one go well shielded there is the real risk of life in a stroll. "Gardyloo!" people cry, which is "Watch out for

[4] Fray Servando, *Apologia*.

the water!" but what follows is hardly water (more's the pity, for there is a great want of it to drink in the city), but rather excrements of all sorts, and rot, and slops, so reeking that the air is always thick and cloudy, and the bird who gets it in his head to fly over those parts falls dead from the sky at once. In his days, Charles III had taken note of this and tried to calm and qualify that famous indecency of the Madrileño (as the inhabitants are known). He had installed in some houses a device known as a *secret*, which was a kind of a large drainage pipe the people called Y. But they might have well called it Why? or even What-for? for all the use they made of it; they would sit on it to converse, or perhaps throw out the table scraps and leavings. And since many people opposed the sanitary laws, they had to be arrested, which led Charles III to say that the Madrileño was like a child, that cried when you washed his face. Which was much to the point. It is their way of living that brings them to so many plagues there and causes them to be so ugly and misshapen and never to arrive at their full development. It happened to me that once I was playing with a little girl, no more than two feet tall, and when I asked her age she replied, "Well, sir, I believe I am thirty years of age. Or thirty-one." In general it is said that the children of Madrid are megalocephalic, dwarfened, slovenly, and overly broad-beamed, rosary makers and jail tenders, and all that also is true, for there is no country on the face of the earth any dirtier or more corrupt. So corrupt, in fact, that Nero's Rome, compared to this Spanish court, might well be called the house of God and resting place of all the saints. In Spain even the newborn are corrupt, and babies, just delivered, say not *ma-ma* but some hail of maledictions no Christian might repeat. But the evil comes from above, so that so long as the Queen squanders all her treasure on her *amour fou* (for the French word is used in that depraved court, as the depraved language it is) Godoy, Charles IV will keep step with her and organize still greater orgies, only for the nobility, and to which entrance costs more than a thousand *duros*. (The gossips say that even that money winds up in Godoy's hands.) And meanwhile the common people of the land live in the most desolate misery and poverty and keep body and soul together only with *slaughterhouse blood sausage*, no more than tripe, or *guts*, rotten and stuffed with clotted blood. This poverty is the cause of all the baseness and knavery of the country, for such a hard life teaches the necessity of tricks and wiles to fill the stomach. Therefore there exist in Spain so many kinds of thieves that to classify them one would need a separate dictionary, for each branch has a distinct name, according to what it is given to robbing—so the capesters steal capes, while the skinners strip people of their clothes in the middle of the street and carry them off (the clothes I mean), and this is one of the commonest criminals met with in Madrid, so that there is always a multitude walking about the streets naked as a stork, terrified, and I recall that the first night of my arrival I thought this had been some new fashion imported from Paris (for everyone knows the Madrileños incapable of innovation) ... Vices and moral laxity, like corruption, have no limit, and there is so much prostitution that at every step one is accosted by an Amazon army of ladies making unimaginable suggestions. The last census gave a figure of some forty thousand whores, and that only at the court of Madrid and not counting courtesans, noble ladies, or the Queen. It is the churches where these women most easily and unconcernedly make their offers. There, before the eyes of the priest, who goes on impassively reciting his sermon or conducting the mass! And the truly religious man that protests against these usages risks being stoned to death at his own altar. Which is what nigh happened to me, in fact, who, having found a place in a chapel where I gave masses every week for six *reales*, tried to protest against those acts of disrespect and irreverence the women performed in the midst of the rites. When I communicated my outrage to the canon, he dismissed me. That is, I lost my place, not simply my audience with the man. From this and many other things I deduced that most of the canons in Spain had a great business, conducted quite in the shadows, making allies with the worst moral flaws in man for their own gain, for otherwise, where would they ever amass those treasures that so many of them accumulate? There in Spain the churches are what we in the New World well might call a whorehouse, or even worse, and sooner or later every kind of persecuted thief and robber comes to rest there, for there is no better security than an apse ... Another of the great plagues that strikes at Madrid is sodomy, and when night falls there are streets down which one must not walk, for fear of being taken aback by great surprises. Every night the police capture upwards of a hundred of these wretched creatures, among whom is always to be found a count or other grand person. This vice is punished with burning, but to the pyre go only the most miserable, those who have no-one or nothing to protect them. The nobles of the court never undergo this "enlightenment," in spite of the fact that everyone knows what manner of life they live, and when the fire is at its brightest point, throwing off great sparks and sputtering grandly, they send their pages or valets out to be *fodder* for the flames. Nor is the King either ever touched by that brilliancy which is called *purificatory*. But if in truth there be any one thing that sticks in the memory of one who visits Madrid it is its tribes of beggars and mendicants, who for example leap to open a man's coach-door and help him to alight. But so many of them come with the same intention that the coach overturns and one has to climb out the roof crying and calling for the authorities, who run off themselves in fear. And once one has managed (which is not easy) to escape with his life from that hustle bustle, the caravan of beggars, which fills the streets like flies at a butcher shop, follows one to one's very home. And the man who dares to not throw them a fistful of *pesetas* may find himself veritably quitted of his life instead. This very nearly happened to me once, as you may see when I tell you that seeing the horde of beggars following me and crying out for bread, when I had not a *duro* to give them, I grew terrified, the more so that I knew that poverty is the mother of foul deeds, so that with great circumspection I took the bag where in better times I might have had some brass at least to clink together, and filled it with stones and flung it to my pursuers. As the army leapt after the prize, I made my escape. This would be one of the saddest sights to see in Madrid were it not that such or even worse sadness is always before one's eyes there . . . There is in Villa de Madrid such a number of *thinking* beings as not to be found in any other part of the world. These are people largely from the provinces, dreamers, who come to court in the hopes of making themselves a grand fortune. They lodge in *closets* as we would call them in México, low dark rooms that is, and wait, as the saying is, for manna to fall upon them from heaven. But it never falls, or never has yet, unless it be, all unrecognized, the misery and poverty that crumbles about their ears. These miserable wretches end up becoming *pícaros* or beggars, which is all the same, or land in jail where they are straightway knifed, some say by order of that same Godoy who will have no competition . . . Madrid is surrounded by settlements, *barrios* they are called, which are like villages in which people live as though in the wilderness. Naked men shave in the middle of the street while women sew or shriek like fishwives at one another, for the rows there are incessant and the gambling dens are open night and day. In Puerta del Sol thousands of bodies are counted daily of those stabbed or cudgeled to death. There Juan may dispatch Pedro (or any other) to the other world without the slightest *inclemency* as they say, and no man dares walk through those streets without a pig's bladder filled with water buckled to his belly under his shirt, to thwart the knife and be able to walk on, alive, along the street. The alley called San Ginés is such another forbidden zone, as is many another in the area of the court. Around there the whoring is so brazen that the authorities themselves own the *houses*, so thereby own the whole neighborhood, which then makes everything *official* and no-one pays it the least mind. Along every street one hears nothing but thieves' and molls' *argot*, an underworld *slang* (a word I learned from their very mouths, in fact), accompanied often enough by a pistol shot and the rasping wheeze of a dying man. The most populous, and scofflaw, *barrio* is that of Avapiés, which once had been Lavapiés, which is to say Footbath. A nasty place, indeed. And when there is a *fandango* (which is not a dance but a brawl) of young Turks—stripling Madrileños who call themselves *manolos* in their *argot*—then Avapiés is always the host to it. A gang of Avapiés *manolos* won this distinction in a *fandango* fought with cobblestones on donkey-back. Rumor has it that Charles IV was struck in that particular battle, by a small paving stone, thank heaven. And one day passing by in her coach beside the Manzanares River, where the *manolo* molls were doing their washing, the Queen was shouted down as a whore because the price of bread was up. The Queen had no choice but to flee on foot (for her coach could not move an inch through that mob of swarming wasps), and some thirty of the termagants were arrested, though they later were released again, because the thing had grown altogether too *public*. And so for this and other reasons, now the monarchs will not even go near Avapiés, but leave it to its lawlessness. For *manolo*, one says *curro* in Andalucia. *Manolo* is *Manuel* shortened, while *curro* is *Francisco*, the commonst names of their regions. They are people of no education, or breeding, or upbringing as now one hears it said, insolent, though frolicsome and gay, spirited, impertinent perhaps—Spaniards to the bone, in a word, who with a knife or a couple of paving stones will send a man to the next world if need be, and with twenty insults to boot. They are the bullies, the *thugs* (another of their words), the pimps who're fit to give lessons in't to the world. And their women are as shameless and brazen as they, and among them are to be found all the fruit sellers and secondhand merchants. There the homicides on account of brawls and jealousies are innumerable, and extend to all levels of society: nobles and lackeys, artisans and clerics, and not excluding even the functionaries of justice themselves.[5] Here is one of the best-known verses in all Spain, which is repeated and sung wherever men gather, and which, or so I was told, is attributed to a bishop fully invested, with ring and all. It speaks for itself.

> Oh—
> They kill both left and right,
> They kill both day and night,
> They've killed the Virgin Mary
> And next they'll storm Cal-vary.[6]

CHAPTER XIV

Which recounts the friar's visit to the gardens of the King.

The best thing would have been not to say what I said. But what do I do now? The best thing would have been not to be born. That is what I said.

The best thing would have been to have been a friar in México. Perhaps not even in México City, but rather in my own part of that country. In Monterrey. The best thing perhaps would have been that. That is what I said.

But who can tell whether this is not the best thing. To be here. Waiting. To be thinking about the best way to be. To be at every moment gnawing at myself. While I learn new ruses and fear death. That is what I said.

But I am certain that the best thing is not the best. For the best would have been that I had not been. That I had been noth-

---

[5] José Deleito y Piñuela, *La mala vida en España de Felipe IV.*
[6] Ditto.

ing. And not to be at the mercy of this Madrid heat which stabs a man through and leaves him dead in midstreet. Nor see these frigid colds which with a side wind will freeze a man forever. Nor my life be given over to these constant flights and escapes and that, only to fall again, when I had almost forgot I was persecuted, into the hands of my enemies. Yes, the best thing would have been that I had never been. But then how had I ever known that that was best? How should I ever have known that? That is what I said.

It is that *there is no escape*. It is as though at every moment I am struck anew with the sense of how futile these fleeings are. And yet, I say to myself—Do what thou canst, and *all* thou canst. And so I do. But the worst thing of all is that one can never tell where the limits of possibilities lie. And if all things are possible, then they might as well be impossible, for all that one might do them and they still come to nothing. So that all that would remain would be routine, which swells and bulges more every day, fattening on our lives. But I cannot content myself with routine. That is why I feel more and more asphyxiated as every second passes. And yet I cannot manage to die of suffocation, either.

That is also what I said.

But neither Cornide nor Filomeno answered. We three were sitting, looking out the doorway at people walking quickly down the street, their hands in their pockets for fear of having them picked. Their pockets I mean. From time to time came the cry of someone mercilessly carved to pieces. It was almost night. And I was talking. I was listening to myself. I . . .

"I believe," said Filomeno, and then halted a moment at the cries of a woman whose throat had just been slashed before our eyes by a naked man. When the cries subsided he continued. "I believe," he said, looking down on the woman's body lying in a pool of blood as her tears dried on her face, "that thou shouldst go and pay a visit to a witch. To see whether she cannot solve *some*thing at least for thee." And now the sheriff's men dragged away the killer, who was howling with laughter. One of the officers removed his coat to wrap it about the murderer's body, covering him at least from waist to knee thereby.

"A witch! But aren't there enough of them who come to see us, for us to have to go and visit them? And to boot, what could the witch resolve?"

"More than thou perhaps knowest," Cornide said, standing and stopping his ears, for the clamor in the street was so intolerable that had he not done so, his earpan had been bursted.

"I think he is right," said Filomeno when the shouting had died some. "But when I say 'witch' I mean a real witch, one who would never be burnt because it is she herself who stokes up the fire. They are the most intelligent persons in all Spain. And those as well who carry most influence at court. In a word, the dames that solve the problems."

"But what can such a one, this witch, do for me—when I do not even believe in their existence? And if they do indeed exist, I should prefer not to speak about it."

A great wave of capesters thronged through the street running after the man that had been taken prisoner. Someone snatched away the jacket that had covered his nakedness. The army of capesters ran on laughing, while the sheriff's men came hot behind shouting, "Thieves! Thieves!" and the murderer, naked and as calm as pie, quietly turned the corner and walked away to his house as pretty as you please . . . Silence fell about us again. The hour was late. Down the street came a company of beggars by profession, trying out new thanks-givings to recite to those who might in future aid them. From a distance they looked to be school-boys in a ragged troop muttering their lesson as they came home from school. Then two priests came along speaking heatedly, their arms upraised and waving. And last came seven prostitutes (whose profession could be picked out a league away by the way they were dressed or undressed, and their way of walking) who lost no time in overtaking the clerics and accompanying them. A way behind came an old woman picking up the butt ends of tobacco the prostitutes flung down . . . And now it was growing quite dark, and the terrible heat of the day had calmed a little, and the people, who at noon would have died by only putting a hand out into the street, but who at dusk came out, now grew fewer again as they went home to eat. There was the sound of music, perhaps from the Prado, and if I closed my eyes I might think I was in México City . . . We had not yet lit the lamps, and I asked to leave them that way awhile. So we three sat there in the only door that opened onto the street, in appearance a trio of deformed beasts whose outlines had been cut out of shadow itself. I went on talking:

"I went to see Jovellanos for him to expedite the disposition of my case, so that at last I might feel free of the constant threat of prison, but Jovellanos is no more than another of Godoy's victims,

and even has to kiss Godoy's feet whenever Godoy visits, which
to vex Jovellanos he does many times a day. This repugnant act
was even performed in my presence—I watched Jovellanos bow to
Godoy and then kneel and lower his head to kiss the tips of that
beast's shoe. At that Godoy tapped him three times on the nape
of his neck so that I had thought he would kill him. I ran out of
that place without even speaking to Jovellanos of my difficulty.
Now I have sued for justice to the Council of the Indies, though
well I know they will never find in my favor. There, as everywhere,
filth and indecency has triumphed. And that cursed León has
stolen from me the three keys to the Council—the governor, who
sold himself for a courtesan; the prosecuting attorney, for a boy;
and the secretary, for a threat of being dismissed. At last I sought
an audience with the King. But I was told he had gone off a-hunting
on his land, which he calls gardens. So I went to those lands of
the King, which is like going to all Spain. On these hunts the King
goes on, every imaginable and even impossible-to-imagine thing may
be seen; the only thing not seen is the prey. As soon as I entered
the woods, a band of naked women fell on me like highwaymen,
shouting that my disguise fit me very well, though it had too much
cloth in it. And in a trice I was naked, and I fell then, as I was
pulling on my clothes again, into a gang of women drinking cheap
wine, who for the sport of it poke out one another's eyes and then
go on drinking and dancing; and all this amid howling laughter
and terrible oaths. 'Those are the women for whom there is nothing new to be done,' a boy said to me, surprising me by the courtesy of his words, and more by his smile. 'That is the dance of
suicide. In a while not one of them will be still alive.' And so it
was—I looked toward the group of women and I saw them now all
busied in pulling off one another's arms. The young man went on
explaining to me how the moment came in the lives of those aged
courtesans, or ladies of the nobility, when everything irritated and
vexed them, and when they were jaded and spoiled for new delights
and pleasures, and when, therefore, they made up their minds to
commit suicide. The King, to whose attention this matter had
come, decided to invite them all to a *meet*, so that they might
perform or continue that ceremony at a hunt, as a principal part
of the program. At the moment the women had been conceded a
respite, and were resting. The young man went over to them and
possessed them, one by one; his chore done, he returned to my
side like a man who has kept a painful or onerous obligation. 'Plea-

sure should not lack at any moment,' he calmly explained, 'much less at the moment of death, which for its being ultimate, should be that pleasure most keenly enjoyed. But tell me sir—what is your place in this hunt? For here we all have our offices.' 'None,' I confessed. 'I am but trying to see the King.' 'I can lead you to where His Majesty is, for the women over there are satisfied and for the moment have no more need of me.' And he drew my attention again to the women now sprawled atop one another, emitting terrible snorts and agonizing wheezes as they calmly pulled out one another's hair by the roots. 'So that is thy *office*,' I said, gesturing at the women deformed in paroxysms. But he answered me not. He took me by the hand and led me down an alley of trees, in every one of which there perched an abbot praying, most whistlingly, through his breviary. 'Religion must never be forgot, for then sins would lose their grace, and cease to be sins. Ay, and what would become of us if sin were not? What would become of the world? That is why His Majesty places, in every tree, an abbot, who does not participate in any of the activities of the hunt, but only sits perched in his tree to remind us that we have sinned and to afford us the pleasure of that knowledge.'

"We entered now a grand open field, or esplanade, where there was not a tree left standing, but only people and more people, squatting with their heads on the ground, and no-one spoke or moved. 'These are the drug eaters,' the young man was saying as we went along over the heads of those vice-ridden wretches, who even when we stepped on their heads would not rouse up from their stupor. 'If you wish . . .' the young man said, and took up one of the many devices for burning the drug that were lying about. He sucked at it for a long while and then emitted a great cloud of black smoke and fire from his mouth, and then a cloud of white smoke from his ears. I was greatly affrighted, for I thought he had exploded. But returning the device to the person from whom he had taken it, he walked on over the bowed heads as though they were so many cobblestones. And me after him. And thus it was that we arrived at two great pools of water, one of which was frozen, with large pieces of ice floating at its center, while from the other there issued a smoky steam and the water bubbled, it was so boiling hot. Many people were swimming in them, and would go from one to the other, but only once, for the change was so dreadful that they instantly died and floated up to the top of the water. Some, who at first made use of only one of the two pools (and thereby conserved their lives), would use the corpses like rafts or bathing islands, and they would float on them to distant places. But they almost always at last would change pools, and themselves become converted into rafts. About this the young man offered me no explanation. Nor did I ask, either, for I did not believe it necessary. I could well see that this was the place of the malcontented ... And I had a sudden urge to throw myself into the cold pond, for the heat made me feel as though strangled by flames. And so I did jump in. But once in the water I thought I would freeze to death, and so I tried, as fast as I could, to jump into the boiling pond. And I was just on the point of making the leap when the young man seized me by my surcingle and dragged me to the shore. And as though pulling a donkey against its will, he hauled me away from that place, for I was loudly begging and crying for him to let me swim, 'even for one instant,' in that boiling lake, for my bones were numb with cold ... 'Now I will show you the three lands of Love, sir,' the lad said to me when I had at last subsided and was stretching my muscles again. 'Each of them has its own advantages, but none is perfect.' And so it was that we were walking toward a place covered with flames, and just as we came before them my guide gave a shout and an immense Negro appeared, who without a word picked him up in his arms, as though he were a pebble, and tossed him to the other side of the flames. I saw that and at once began to cry out and attempt to escape, but the Negro had already seized me as well. And with no further ado he pitched me through the air. I passed over, above those tongues of flame licking up and shooting sparks at me, though thank heaven they did not reach me. And the fall was softer than I had thought, since I came to earth (in a manner of speaking) in a very viscous sea which I immediately perceived, with horror, to be composed of semen. Almost fainting, I tried to find the shore, and was swimming for all I was worth. And at that I saw the young man raise his head from that whiteness and shout, 'You are in the first land of Love,' and so with some trouble I kept myself afloat and looked about at the panorama before me. In spite of which every few moments I had to swallow (much against my will) a bit of that liquid so unpleasant to my palate, for I kept bobbing in the sea. And all I saw was men and women—men in full hardy virility and women at the age when they inspire the greatest desire in men, the two tangled together constantly until they fell faint and exhausted and drifted down to the bed of that thick whitish lake.

'If this is all, we can go on,' said I to the lad. So with a long whistle
he interrupted the coition he was performing with one of the
women and settled once more into the arms of the Negro, who
had just appeared in a most voluptuous and lustful attitude. The
Negro picked me up as well. And again we were pitched into the
air. And here we landed on a moist sandy bank with little sun.
'This is the second land of Love. Nor need you be guided by this
order I am showing you, for that is only a narrative convention.'
We had still not had time to explore the place when a band of
women set upon us furiously and tossing handfuls of sand at us
forced our retreat from their country. Once well away and safe
from that fierce Amazon army I could, from a distance, see the
reason for all that, for there were many hundreds of women, and
more women rolling about on the sandy bar, caressing and kissing
one another until they had brought on the paroxysm of pleasure
and could fall in *petite mort*. At that point another battalion would
come on and begin to bury them, with no pretense of ceremony or
pity, in the moist sand, and then return to their stupor-producing
business, until to them had occurred the same as to the buried
ones . . . 'In truth, if this is the second country of Love, I prefer by
far the first,' I said, though the young man to all appearances did
not hear me, for he answered me by saying, 'And now we will visit
the third and last land of Love, and you must know there be only
three, and every person of us is a citizen of one of the lands, or of
all three.' And a quick whistle brought once more, from behind
some tumbled boulders, the great Negro, who, without more ado,
took us up in his arms and flung us away as though we were a
couple of rotten fish. And so we came (after passing through many
clouds and even provoking a rainstorm replete with lightning and
thunder) to fall onto a very soft and cushioned place, where all was
pillows and where music seemed to bubble up from the ground,
but the music seemed base and low, for hardly would one rise to
his feet when he lost the sound of it, for which reason we decided
to crawl along so as not to miss hearing it. And from time to time
there would emerge from the air a gust of what might be perfume,
but it was no perfume but a breeze which seemed permeated by
the odor of a country field just awakened to dawn. 'A most pleasant
place this seems,' said I, and since the heaviness of sleep seemed
coming over me from so much walking and crawling and flying
through the air and swimming, I lay me down on the many cushions and in a moment was asleep. But in a very few moments I

was awakened again by a hand caressing my head, and then moving down to my clothes, unbuttoning them. When I opened my eyes I beheld a man moving his lips as though praying some strange prayer, and as though fearful of not being able to come to the *amen*, or of forgetting it perhaps. Imagining, then, what place I was in, I quickly slipped away underneath the pillows and moved through that place like a fish under water until I hid myself safely at last in a nook inside a pillowcase, out one seam of which I could see what the young man had presented to me as the third country of love. One should, then, imagine something like the land of Sodom, but not much like, for everything hereabouts seemed to obey an order into which there entered not the least iota of anarchy. In contrast to the first land of Love, this place was most clean, thanks to a series of deep canals or channels through which sluggishly flowed the semen down to the sea, which it flooded, to the great consolation of the cloud of white sea gulls flying about. At first sight it all seemed quite neat and nice to me. Although I did not partake of that method in particular, I believe that pleasure knows no sinfulness, and that sex has little to do with morality. There were none there but naked men always caressing and coupling with one another and vice versa. Most of them were congregated in pairs who only talked to and *knew* each other. But even in that there was one thing most strange which at first glance made one wonder somewhat, and then inspired some fear. Though I confess I could not tell quite what it was. Until at last I saw that the pairs continually were dissolving and re-forming with new members. So that one saw that that love was little lasting, and it ended, as all love does, in jadedness and tedium, when one was left with melancholy, a sort of soft sadness. So that a long Indian-file of men zigzagged off into the end of the country, where it disappeared, like a slowly flowing current, in the other current that ran to the sea; and the cloud of white sea gulls seeing them float down, grew very very happy and rushed to attack them, too, not without first making ceremonious curvets in the air in honor of the occasion.

" 'You like not this place either?' then asked the lad, as he delivered himself up to the merciless possession of a great naked man. I waited for the act to finish before I answered him that indeed I really did not, nor did I believe that sort of love had anything to do with felicity, which anyway I considered not to exist, so that it seemed absurd to me to talk of it. 'And moreover,' I said to him, after explaining my theory, 'thou say'st that there exist only these three categories, but then I can place myself in none of them, which shows that what thou hast told me is not true.' 'And yet if thou hast just denied the existence of happiness, it is only natural that thou not be within the fold of any of its categories,' the young man told me, swooning, although then he walked along next to me. 'Nonetheless,' he went on, 'there is one group which is of no consequence, and there it may be that thou'lt encounter thy *thee thyself*. His Majesty has given that group the cognomen *remainders*, for into that group go many persons of the groups we have here visited. Let us go there.' And we began walking that way, a bit more quickly, for a great gang of men was approaching us with their manhoods in the spring of freshness and pointed directly toward our persons . . . So it was that little by little we entered what I came to call the *country of desolation*, and still I believe the name is not far off the mark.

"We passed along a great promenade lined with tall straight poplar trees, which resembled supplicating arms held high. And in a short while I beheld an ancient man rubbing his hands together furiously while he whined his complaint. 'It is of little import,' the young man said to me when I questioned him. 'If you note he has even been banished from his land. For his passion is to strike sparks by rubbing his hands together.' So we continued our walk. I, I must say, was somewhat distracted, looking about a great deal to see what was to be seen, when suddenly I went tumbling helplessly into a chasm to all appearances bottomless; and soon I had fallen to my feet atop a monk's writing desk beside a man writing and then ripping his papers asunder and crushing the pen. And then I saw the man give a great shriek, jump up through the hole I had left, run off to a tree nearby, throw a heavy rope over one of its sturdy branches, and in two seconds he had hanged himself. Aided by my young man I quickly got out by way of my hole, too, and I asked him, pointing toward the hanged man, why he had done such a thing. 'You interrupted him as he was writing his masterpiece, and that has cost him his life.' I could hardly believe it, that I was to blame for his hanging, and I came near fainting from the blow of it. But the lad, who always seemed to divine my thought, replied, 'Do not concern yourself over it, for he'd never have brought his work to an end. Have you forgotten so soon that we are in the *land of the seekers* and therefore of *those who will never find*?' 'But didst thou not say it was a masterpiece?' 'And that is precisely why he'd never have finished it,' the young man answered. So that I, though not entirely convinced by that, strode off again walking. And soon we stopped before a woman trying to give birth through her mouth. And we walked along a bit farther and we came across a man who had pulled out one of his eyes and was trying to put it in his back, so he might see both before and behind. And we walked on and soon stopped by an old woman with a knife whose blade had been sharpened to a fine, fine edge. And she was trying to trim the wrinkles off her face. Then I saw two boys with a very long stick pointed at the sky, and when I asked them what they did that for, what they were after up so high, they told me they were waiting for the moon to come out, so that they might poke it and 'disinflate' it, by which I believe the two mischievous ragamuffins meant deflate it. Still this caused me some mirth, but then made me awfully sad. The boys called after me, saying that as I was taller, perhaps I might help them bust the moon. 'I think not,' I said, and continued my march. And so it was that in a moment I stood before a poet running all about the area, terrified. And when I asked my guide, he told me that this was without doubt a very brave poet, for all his life he had been composing a brilliant poem and now he needed but one word—the last—to finish it, and it was close on to twenty years he'd been hunting it without finding it even by accidentally stumbling on it. And the young man made a motion to the poet to come closer. I was most surprised to see him bow before us in a deep reverence, or courtesy as I believe these Spaniards call it. The young man made him another motion and the poet stood again and showed us the paper, which never left his hands day or night, and bringing it to his eyes, began to read. It was truly a poem like no other I had ever known or heard, and like, I am most certain, no other that will ever be declaimed in the future either. As he read, his words became transformed into an echoing deep magic which more than made me drunk, they transported me, and it was like a wondrous monument in which every stone occupied its precise and necessary place without having even the most miniscule crack or fissure. But suddenly, as the marvelous composition was coming to its close, the poet ended his reading, and left us up in the air, waiting for the end, which lacked but a single word. But the word would not come. So this was as though one had leapt across a great abyss and were landed on the other bank safe and sound and then tripped up on a tiny pebble and slipped and fell

irremediably into the chasm . . . Our great poet folded his papers,
now cracked and yellow, and making another deep obeisance, he
marched off again muttering to himself, 'conquered,' 'torment,' 'so-
journ,' 'extremes,' 'shadows,' 'hands' . . . He was finding and dis-
carding word after word after word, as though he were a man on
a beach, seeking after the perfect but imaginary seashell and only
finding real ones. 'Earth,' 'distance,' 'eternity,' 'leaves,' 'domin-
ions,' 'lang . . .' until the litany could be heard no more. 'He must
find the word someday' I stammered out then. For truly I was
moved by his predicament. I even began to rummage through my
own vocabulary—'sadness,' 'flight,' 'imprisoned,' 'pyre,': . . . But
the young man my guide did not even bother to reply to me. He
laughed and walked on again. And we walked by an old man
weighed down with so many wrinkles no one could even have
counted them, and he had neither hair nor much voice either, nor
the strength to stand, so that he forever squatted, and he was staring as though into nothingness. And since the young man made a
point to walk by at some distance and seemed not even to wish
to glance at him, I took good note of this character, so remote from
the rest of creation. And I asked my guide what that old man might
be seeking, since though he seemed to be waiting, he gave no sign
of waiting for any thing whatsoever. 'You are right,' the lad responded, 'his features do not indicate any stubbornness or persever-
ance, and yet, I will tell you, he is the most obstinate and dogged
of all the people you have seen in this hunt for impossible things.
He is trying to achieve eternity. And for that, what is there for a
person to do but wait? So doubt not the least doubt—that man is
the most misfortunate and unhappy of all you have seen in our
walks, for he perfectly knows that what he has set out to find
transcends the limits of the human.' And so we left that emaciated
old man who looked as though at any moment he might crumble
to dust. But soon we had stopped before another old fellow, with
a long white beard very shaggy, and in one hand he held a mirror
while with the other he bashed himself in the stomach. And the
young man explained to me that this person wanted to see his own
soul, to have a look at it, as he said. And since he felt that his
soul resided in his belly, he beat upon himself incessantly, in the
hope that it would come out through his lips. And we walked on
again, and soon we were at the verge of a great precipice from
which, in a constant stream, hundreds of men and women were
leaping, falling to their deaths far below on the rocks. And yet in

spite of these consequences, that wave of jumping suicides seemed to be growing faster and faster, more and more hurried. 'These are the people who wish to fly,' the lad told me as he held me back from the brink, for at that moment I had grown so dizzied that I had almost plunged headlong over the edge myself . . . And then, since I was somewhat fatigued, I begged him to take me to where I might at least find the King, for that, and no other, was the reason of my visit to these lands. And so the young man, speaking not another word, began to draw me back from that rock-strewn chasm and as we walked away, all along the road we met with and often enough bumped up against an infinity of wretched creatures, all of whom would do some absurd thing contrary to all probability or logic—people trying to make their feet hear, women who attempted to transfer their sex to their forehead, men burying themselves alive, old folk who would have the trees speak, and children trying at all cost to halt the passing of time. We crossed the open space again, for we were returning. And I saw the poet again, who now had exhausted his vocabulary and was trying to combine syllables at random, though as anyone could see these had no meaning. I could hear him as he wandered off into the undergrowth about the alley, murmuring, 'hetergnosto,' 'tonictis,' 'planens' . . . And as we were leaving that clearing I turned and caught sight of the old fellow trying to outlast eternity. He was now more bent and bowed than ever, and the sun, which was now crumbling away in one corner of the world, threw its rays over his smooth, immobile head, so that one had thought that there sat another, though smaller and eternally fixed, orb . . . Of all the things I saw, that empty head scintillating like another sun, now touching the ball of earth, and dying away, is that which has most stayed in my memory and caused me the greatest sadness. For I think it is as though I were seeing myself in that position, struggling futilely against what cannot even be attacked, let alone beaten . . . And as I wished to see no more of these things, I walked on with my eyes fixed on my feet or on the ground, which at that hour of sunset seemed the reflection of a great bonfire set at a distance . . . 'Thou hast showed me naught but desolations,' I chided the lad, 'and for that thou didst not have to make me walk so far. Nor surely are these all of them, neither.' And then I heard myself, that I was shouting, though the young man walked impassively on, nor even looked back. 'And these are not all there are, either!' I shouted at him again, perhaps to tell myself what I was telling the boy. And still

the young man walked steadily on, and only halted when he came
to a stand of pine trees so tall, thin, and ashen-colored that they
must surely have been a thousand years old, if not still older. 'What
more do you need, then?' asked the young man, and for the first
time I saw how tired he was. With a gesture of fatigue he sat down
against the trunk of one of those ancient trees by whose needles
the sun was trying to hold itself up. I did not know what to say
. . . And so it was that I lay back also against a neighboring pine
tree, in which the sun was also struggling to stay aloft, until it
somewhat pitifully was hanging from the lowermost limb. 'I have
not come here that thou shouldst show me what I already know
or have seen and about which or against which I have always spoken . . . No, the only thing I desire is to be taken to see the King,
so I might tell him of my circumstances . . . Nor do I beg for pity,
or mercy, for that would be ridiculous to ask from one who has
never shown it.' And as it was growing darker and darker, my
words grew as heavy as the shadows, and dispersed in echoes
through the grove of pines. The young man leaned over and began
to stare most fixedly. And then he blinked. Raising a hand to his
forehead, he turned away. In that position I divined that he bore
some great sadness, though as well might it have been the effects
of the evening hour . . . 'The King . . . I am the King, and I can do
nothing for you,' he said at last. And he turned so I saw his face,
which suddenly was that of an old, old man, with wrinkled brow
and white hairs which the breeze that sprang up of a sudden began
to blow away. And then with a slight though firmly commanding
motion of his hands, the last traces of his youth took flight. 'But
thou canst indeed help me,' I said, speaking to him familiarly as
though he were still the lad of a few moments ago, so that he
would not note my disappointment and dismay. 'For if not, to
whom do I turn for help?' 'Why do you wish to change that which
most precisely has made you what you are?' he said. 'I do not think
you so simple as to believe that there is any way to liberate you.
The act of seeking that liberation—is that not delivering yourself
up to an imprisonment a hundred times worse? Or have you
learned nothing from our amble among the *seekers*? And more,' he
added, as he stood and made as though to walk away, 'let us suppose that you find your freedom. Will that not be more oppressive
and awesome than the search? Or even than the very prison you
believe yourself caught in?' And he left me, laboriously making his
way through the trees and shadows. I sat there alone, thinking on

future defeats, those which always occur after a victory. And as I was uncertain about the road to take to come back to Madrid, I climbed up into a tree and from there made out La Villa de Madrid in the distance, though not in truth very far off, with its two great columns at the entrance which from where I was perched looked to be marble but which on closer inspection, so evil-minded gossips say, are nothing but bread-dough . . . And that is all," I said. (And as my voice suddenly broke, Cornide and Filomeno were shaken from the lethargy and half-sleep they had fallen into and looked at me wide-eyedly.) "And that is all. So now you tell me I should go and see a witch. You would have me to go and visit a card reader, some great blowsy fortune-teller who will tell me a hundred stupid things and take my money for it. As though I had not spoken to the highest witch at court! And as though the witch had not told me there was no help for my plight!" Cornide and Filomeno stood, both at the same time, and ran to the door of the house, slammed it, and then turned again to me. "We have not the least doubt," they said, "that our little King rides a fine broom. But he did not show thee," and here out in the street one could hear a great shouting and hubbub of drunken men who'd just been stabbed by frustrated cutpurses, "the place where the irreverent, the offended, the insulted live—the folk who most surely will inherit, or steal, the earth. That is why," and now the death rattles faded away, "tomorrow we will take thee to see that witch of whom we spoke."

CHAPTER XV

Which tells of what fell out at the visit to the witch.

And so that's why you're here, standing in front of this great witch's house. But the door is already open, even before you knock! Though it's true, too, that at first you're so stiff you couldn't go in if you tried.

From within may be heard the voice of a woman singing. Or, that is, may be heard a song which sounds as though it came from a woman's throat. From woman's mouth. From woman's lips. (What is that song which I cannot recall though I have heard it times unnumbered?) And the voice of a woman, singing, has called to thee—*Enter!*—in a piercing *fortissimo* that shakes thee to thy boots, thou human friar.

And thus it is that I find myself now passing through a terrible darkness down a terrible hallway, bearing within me, like a wineglass filled with water that not a drop must splash, a terrible fear, for I am alone. (Cornide and Filomeno have told thee they will await thee at the door, for they have not wanted to accompany thee there within.) They have stood a step back from the porch and said to me, "Sayest thou thus and so and then sayest thou to her these things and then last dost thou tell her all the rest." So that is the cause that I am making my poor way through these obscure shadows that groan as I try to brush them aside. But hist! The voice of that woman singing. I hear the voice of that woman singing and I think, "What is that, that I should fear it." Listen! Listen! It's *the same old sweet song.* That song we begged for, to sing us to sleep. Ay! that voice. The voice that hushed us as it rocked . . . The voice that whispered of dewfall loosed by cudgel blows from the clouds and of angels with swords and trumpets.

And out behind the trees . . .

And out behind the trees, the brightness. I am in thy hands, in thy arms, and I am thee thyself. Thou art but a child still, and that is why I sing to thee as I have always done, so thou shalt remain a child. The error lies in having wished not to be so, when thou well knowest that that was always impossible for thee. For one is born to be water, and one is wet, or is born to be man and then one has no childhood. But if one did have a childhood, if one had been a babe once, then one was not born to be man, it means to say. So little it gains thee to try to be one. Thou art but piddling thy time away, trying to be what thou never canst become.

The voice of that woman draws me on.

And now thou hast penetrated the inky shadows. And look, there, in the center of that great apartment, which now seems to rear above you out of blackness, there reclines a woman, naked. More beautiful than all women possible and impossible (which will suffice to describe her), and still singing to thee. *And when, tired and*

*weary, thou enterest the home of thy childhood, I take thee in
my arms and carry thee to thy bed and close thy eyes and tell
thee, Sleep ... sleep ... and as thou wilt not sleep I tell thee,
Rememberest thou those millions of bees the tempest has caught
away from their hive and who perish drowned in the storm, yet
filled with such rain of sweetness in the flowers about ... Re-
callest thou the birds sheltering under the now dripping leaves.
And the flowers lashed by the storm and pulled from their stalks
... And thou sleep'st, because without there falls a rain so hard,
and there is no calm on earth like the sound of rain without while
one is snug a-bed at home within, and the world is made wonderful withal, made to the measure of thy desires* ... "I have been
offended," said the friar, "insulted and aggrieved," and now the
woman closes her lips and the song becomes long, interminable,
and ineffably sweet *hmmmmms* echoing softly. Like a soft hand
nestling over our eyes. "I have been offended," spoke the friar,
"insulted and aggrieved, and all of it for nothing but that I spoke
what I honestly saw and thought. I have been banished from my
country and vilified, only because I struggled to let Truth take its
rightful place above all the cords of meanness and baseness through
which I have had to cut and among which, tangled, I shall surely
perish if you do not help me."

And the song, which was not a song but rather a distant murmur, twined through the friar's words and wrapped all about them.

So she pulled it all out of you—you told her everything, you talked
about all your trials and tribulations, about all the things you'd
written from prison, about how you'd gotten away, about how you
never stopped looking for the Truth, for Justice, for the Right, and
of course you went on and on about what bad shape the Church
was in, and all its clergy, bar none, not even the King himself (and
those "hunts" of his!), and about how everything would've been
better if God had never existed, so He'd never have created the
world, so He'd never be able to be involved to justify such crimes.
You said Madrid was disgusting, and the Virgin of Guadalupe was
more Mexican by a lot than the idiots that were bowing and
scraping to her now, because she'd appeared long before *they* had,
oh yes, and the disgusting, repulsive, foul jackanapes Spaniards
that said they'd brought her over with them to save the Indians
from "barbarity, heathenhood, and moral shipwreck" and the very

Indians who were enraged and dumbfounded at the Spaniards' barbarity, heathenhood, and moral shipwreck. So really, you said, that means that if Christianity got there before the Spaniards, then what were the Spaniards doing there? In Mexico. But since they wouldn't leave, they'd just have to be kicked out. And you were the man to do it. And that you "would see the unjust man held up as high as the cedars of Lebanon." And that you'd walk by and they'd cease to exist. But of course first there were a lot of obstacles that had to be cleared away a little bit—I mean even if they were trifling and nasty, they still weren't all that easy. You said all that.

"I, who am of noble family and well-renowned estate, am persecuted by a dirty rodent, that low clerk and flunky of the King, León, whose name well suits him. And though I am enemy to all violence, I see no other way to my ends, nor for good to come of my ideas, than to do away with him. Once that reptilian creature is dead that harasses me, and indeed, not because he is any way offended by my thoughts or dreams, my plans, my true self, but only so that he may collect the payment he is sent by that other rodent Haro y Peralta, then I will at last be free to work on what constitutes my strength and my greatest yearning—*the independence of my land*. And so long as that crawling clerk is not killed I will have no peace, nor will I ever feel free. For in fact I will not be free. For he dogs my every step. At every instant it is as though I could see him skulking and sneaking closer and closer, to bring me to the cell bars again and to the putrefaction and rot of imprisonment. For he will be content with nothing less than my death. And all I desire is my life. So, therefore, though I rue the conclusion, there is no help but to kill him."

And the friar spat on the floor and ground the spittle with the toe of his boot as though the spittle had been León himself who had been once and for all exterminated. And at that the woman rose and took the friar by the hands and still throbbingly humming said to him, "I believe I can help thee. But tell me this—after thou hast murdered thy killer, who will be next?"

"After that," said the friar, and now the lady was leading him across the apartment, "I should kill Godoy, that lecherous beast."

"And then?"

"The King! The King!" cried the friar, swelling with heroism, and lying.

"And then?" asked the woman, emitting music from every part of her body.

"The Pope!" cried the friar, and his voice echoed so loudly that for a moment it drowned the music. It was a cry of war, like that of his old friend, the friar in the cell at Valladolid.

"Ah, yes? The Pope? The Pope, you say?" said the woman as she passed her hand, humming musical, across the friar's head. And then she said, "Come, for indeed I can help thee, my son." And she said *my son* to him. "Thou art in my very hands' hands, and now it is time for you to sleep . . . Sleep, and recall the millions of ants caught outside their house when the rain came down, and the trees standing stiff and numb in the rain, the shining leaves, bright as though made of tin, and great round drops nestled on them like diamonds, and the leaves that fell, the palm trees' fronds that crashed to the ground, the crackling of lightning, and the little rocks swept along by the rivulets of rainwater till they splash into the great rush of water that carries them away. And you are safe, inside the window. Snug in the heat from the cook stove. Listening to the charcoal snap and sputter. And the ants, at that moment, drown . . ."

"And what of God? Wilt thou not kill God as well?" began the woman again, as they entered a room walled with mirrors, and where the *hummmm* of the music was suddenly muted.

"I do not think it necessary," said the friar.

"But if it were?" replied the woman, filled with sweetness.

"I would not kill Him, for I do not believe He has ever existed."

Silence fell. And the friar saw the figure of the woman multiplying through all the mirrors, parceling itself out into innumerable figures, until it was no more than a whirlwind of women every second gesturing to him, beckoning him to a mysterious ritual. But he controlled himself. And the whirlwind subsided. And he saw her once more changed into a mere single woman, and the mirrors reflecting only her single appearance.

"I believe that I will be able to help thee," she at last said, although now she seemed somewhat worn. "I think, yes, without doubt I shall. And it will not be easy for thee to forget this aid I will lend thee, friar." (And to the friar this word sounded strange, for she had said it with a touch of contempt or mocking she seemed not to be able to hold back.) "I shall aid thee to open well thine eyes, so thou shalt be no more such a village lout, so provincial, so human, so hearty and frank and *gullible*"—the lady paced about the room, and then with an angry gesture she added—"such a puritan . . . so that thou shalt not be so innocent, so patient, so little bright or sly, so little seeing, so *blind*. So without *imagination*. So led by thy nose, so easily persuaded, so easily *enamored*. So that thou shalt learn that what most must be hidden is the truth, reason, right, for rare is the time it is worth its salt. It is a weapon for losers, *friar*, for the conquered and vanquished and stepped upon." (And here the words began to fill with even more anger and hatred.) "Ah yes, I can help thee—help thee see that thou must learn to depend solely on thyself, that thou hast not a friend in the world, but only enemies. *Fool!* For I want thee to know that thou has swallowed the bait, fallen into my trap, been led like a lamb to the slaughter! . . . that thou goest now to a prison where for many a year thou canst contemplate thy folly, *friar*." (And now the word was fully insult.) "Look here well, *friar*, for here thou seest that same *wild beast León* as thou hast called me." And the woman cackled in glee. And then the laughter became a roar of fury. And the roar of fury changed the lovely lady into a paunchy, bejowled, fanged man with arms like tree trunks. The mirrors could not contain the friar's fury, though he said nothing. He only wondered whether Cornide and Filomeno would truly have been capable of so betraying him . . . And León's voice said to him, "Thou hast given thyself over to me, Servando Teresa de Mier Noriega y Guerra," and he laughed cruelly, "thou hast fallen like a bird into bird lime. And how thou hast sung to me! Be not amazed at my cleverness or cunning, but rather at thy own foolish ignorance which has rewarded it."

And here I felt myself utterly lost and cast down. But I bethought myself then, that the best thing I could do for the moment was flee, leave these gloomy meditations over defeat for the time I was safe away. But as soon as I set foot to flight, I crashed into a mirror, which then returned to me my shattered image. And so it was that I groped about through the mirrors, shattering them every one, until at last I found the door. But at the moment I would have escaped, a great barred gate suddenly fell before me, so violently that had I not jumped back I had been smashed. And I heard León's cruel laugh. I turned, and saw him almost upon me, his arms outstretched to clasp me and brandishing some terrible weapon whose name I know not. At that, Cornide and Filomeno (those wretched traitors) peeked in through the bars and, seeing me near strangled by León's powerful arms, took some pity (though tardy) and wanted to make amends for their crime against me, to repair that dirty trick they had played against me much to my harm, and they began to attempt to force the gate, to rescue me. And indeed the gate gave in, at which both Cornide and Filomeno rushed in crying, "Free him! Let him go!" but at a mere tweak of one of León's monstrous arms, both Cornide and Filomeno were changed into tame sheep. Two tame white sheep, so tame that they wagged their tails over to where their progenitor stood and began to lick his boots. And León laughed, a laugh so horrible and fierce that the mirrors jumped from their frames and smashed to splinters on the floor. And the barred gate closed again, falling this time much more softly. And the melody, now neither music nor song, fell silent. "As hot as it is," said León (and now he was once more the marvelous woman), "one cannot survive without removing one's garments. I remain thus unclothed always, I receive my guests in this way, and they in turn always imitate me; the Queen herself, in fact, has followed my lead, and now loses no time before undraping when she visits me. And there is nothing immoral in this, either, but rather only hygiene is in question. So if thou visitest now all the greatest homes and palaces in the country, the seats of the most respectable ladies, thou shalt find them as they came into the world, resting on their chairs and gasping in the heat so that they do not asphyxiate. That is the way of our climate—three months of winter and nine months of hell. What is there else to do? So strip, man. Let us see that indeed thou be'st one. Strip, be at ease. If only to save thy sweat." And so it was that having touched me everywhere, though futilely, the woman swept out of the room. Laughing from every part of her body.

And so it was that very very early in the morning Cornide and Filomeno knock (both at once) at the door of my room. I hear their voices softly but insistently calling me.

They say: "Servando, León is here outside with hundreds of the sheriff's men. Jump! Out the window! Climb up onto the roof and leap over to the next one. And leave now for Pamplona, through the port of Catalonia, for we have persuaded a man to retire the guards, so as to aid also those smuggling clerics whom thou hast befriended. The sheriff's men are all well armed, and León is in a fury. He has already murdered three dozen friars for showing some similitude to the way thou openest thy mouth. Run!"

And that was how it was.

And so in the morning, very early, Cornide and Filomeno call me (the two of them at once), banging loudly at the door and making no end of racket. And I hear them crying, "Up, man, on thy feet, or dost thou think on staying in the bed all day. Arise, arise, for we two are off to work and thy breakfast is cooling on the table."

And that was how it was.

And so at a very early hour the voices of Cornide and Filomeno woke Servando saying to him:

"Up, lazybones, for it is already time to go on thy visit to the witch."

And the friar, half asleep, gave himself two slaps to the face, leapt up out of the bed, and opened the door blinking sluggishly. That was how it was.

CHAPTER XVI

Which tells of my arrival and not-arrival in Pamplona. Which treats of what there occurred to me without its ever occurring to me.

So I depart for Pamplona. Now I depart for Pamplona. I am going toward Pamplona. To Pamplona. So that is how I came to be going to Pamplona with the clerical smugglers, afoot. And I walk straight past the sheriff's men. I am disguised . . . I have changed into a French doctor who died. I am Dr. Maniau. I am no longer I. Dr. Maniau, with two great birthmarks on his eyes (and a scar above his nose). The mother that bore me would never recognize me, for while one brown eye looks up into the clouds the other stares at my boots. Off to Pamplona I go, with Godoy and León hot upon my heels, León snatching up every friar that smiles even a bit, for my appearance, so it has been reported, is very pleasant and agreeable. While I put into practice the latest fashion of the Portuguese: "Glare down thine enemies." And so there is no man that would know me. I leave Agreda by the gate of Fuencarral in a hack that could well be the ferry to hell itself, so stiff and strait and hot is it, and well protected by the smuggling priests and brothers, making a great racket all along the highway so as not to be suspected.

We have ridden out through Fuencarral.

We are on our way to Pamplona. And this hackney coach is rattling over a highway so rocky that it would shake your teeth out. But someone has put the beast León on my track and told him of my new features, so here come Cornide and Filomeno once again to change me, and they so disfigure and refigure me that one would think them possessed by the Black One himself, and my entire visage now is other, so ugly that in comparison the previous face I wore might have been that of an angel. And so we continue our voyage, with not a single *duro* to keep us from dying of hunger on the road, and with insecurity and fear constantly with us. And the coach's wheels at every moment bumping across a man with his throat cut lying in the middle of the King's Highway. A friar dead on my account, a friar that to León somewhat resembled my person (and for less than that would have had his throat slashed by the savage León), a dead man that even I might take for another me . . . And the hackney, creaking and squeaking, rolls and pitches over a sea of dead friars carpeting the whole highway, so that one would be hard put to set his foot on good earth. There are so many of the dead that one cannot see road nor highway, but only friars piled and tossed one atop another. And the coach rolling along over them, its wheels cracking their skulls and mashing out their brains. Onward to Pamplona! For Pamplona! To Pamplona! I have left behind that lecherous and lustful Villa de Madrid where all was naught but filth. I have left behind that unending labyrinth of orgies, foul deeds, and mean tricks. But where am I going to? In Spain, there is nothing but ruins upon past ruins. To Pamplona! And the coach makes the poor skulls of the poor friars explode, pop like sappy firewood, like seeds one steps on when one walks, like crumbling earth, like dropped gourds bursting on the ground, like the heads of friars squashed by the wheels of this damnable, damned, and hellish hackney coach . . . And then night falls, and our hunger grows, and we have still not reached Pamplona. The

darkness rushes upon us and the coach becomes bogged down in
the mess of friars lying piled along the roadway, so that we cannot
go on along the road, and then the mule gives a deep sigh and falls
dead on the spot upon the other corpses. So at last Dr. Maniau
must abandon his hellish car. And so Dr. Maniau steps gingerly
over (though truly it was on top of) the dead friars until he reaches
an open field, and he looks out to find the line of the horizon, but
he cannot make it out. But as one must go on, the smuggling
priests throw Dr. Maniau over their shoulder (that French medic,
that distinguished and eminent man, to be so treated!), and trotting
off they continue their path to Pamplona. Onward to Pamplona!
Our destination—Pamplona! And behold, I am now in Pamplona.
Look at this—Pamplona. Lodged in the house of one of my friends
among the smugglers, sleeping atop a pile of demijohns filled with
wine (the smuggler's great merchandise) that seem at every moment to burst and bathe me in their sticky liquor. Here I am in
Pamplona, then, bathing in wine and drinking it to boot. Listening
to the priests talk about wine, the rises and falls in its price, and
uncorking the casks and demijohns and bottles to reduce the bursting of them.

Pamplona—a walled city girdled by motionless stagnant water
crossed by three drawbridges, the only manner of making one's
way from the medieval world of this village to the other world
that lies all about it . . . It is evening, and I am strolling through
the Plaza del Castillo, the only square or indeed place at all in this
town where one can breathe a bit. And then as night falls I return
again to take shelter in my garret cell. I can hear the creaking of
the three bridges, and I know that we have been left incommunicado, lost in the remote past and stranded. We go backward whole
centuries, until morning returns and the drawbridges lower into
place again. I am coming to the Age of Epic now, since now even
the gate of San Nicolás has closed, so that Pamplona is one long
muttered breath of anachronisms whispered within these dirty age-
encrusted walls . . . Is this not the ideal place to ask oneself why
one must be born? Why must one bear this immutable sentence
whose most dreadful outcome would be absolution? This slow forward dragging of days following days? . . . Is this not the ideal place
in which to doubt? To beg asylum and lose oneself in inventing
impossible solutions? And then to begin to renounce one's faith,
to become a heretic and blasphemer, an apostate of the Word?
Pamplona—the city where flight seems laughable.

I am in Pamplona, and the filthy scummy water lies all around like an oiled mirror slowly slowly licking at the walls. Pamplona— a place of more than quietude, where Dr. Maniau puts himself unanswerable questions: What is a man of the Americas doing cloistered behind these walls? What art thou doing, with that queer foreign name, wearing that expression of a dog just kicked down to kennel? Until what far day will the fact of being American, a man of the wide Americas, carry in itself a stigma not to be washed away except by year after year of flight and exile, the rough and often futile polishing of foreign cultures? Until what far day will we always be seen as creatures of a lustful paradise, walking nude through our vast garden, creatures of sun and water? Until what far day will we forever be considered magical beings led by passion and base instinct?—as though all men were not such, as though all men were not so, as though we were all not led by those same principles of feeling, action, and behavior ... Yes, oh Pamplona, thou art the fit place for meditation, and perhaps the best place of all to die in ... In this backward city which yet holds its retrograde pride intact, as a principle of progress ... Until what distant day are we to remain in perpetual discovery by perpetually unseeing eyes? ...

And in this wise you became soon the old friar of times gone by. You went out very smug and complacent the moment you heard the drawbridges pulled up. And you strolled safe and smug through the streets once more.

And so it happened that as you were strolling along near the wall, oh friar, you were discovered by the evil León (the Indefatigable). And indeed a whole gang of sheriff's men is running after you. You flee down the whole length of the street, but suddenly a new posse leaps out, even closer on your tail. Oh Pamplona, medieval burg ... The sheriff's men are wearing clothes the color of earth (in those places where the earth is earth-colored) and carrying weapons to suit the city. "In the name of God and the King, friar, halt!"

Oh Pamplona, walled city, worn but indestructible ... God and the King ... hark to those voices calling me ...

But the friar, it seems, is spurred on, not stopped, by the shouting of the sheriff's men, and in one hop he is in at a window, has leapt into a house whose family is all fast asleep. From bed to bed the friar leaps, through the howls and screams of terror and the oaths of the roused housefolk, who will go to their graves every one believing this event to have been a supernatural visitation. Oh, Pamplona, within thee all is so retired and withdrawn, so held back, and all is so repeated that the repetitions have become inalterable law. That is the cause why no-one can believe that the flight of the friar, who now is capering over the rooftops, leaping seven water towers, and racing through the alleyway of La Taconera to vault the wall and dive headlong into the fetid waters that will save him, is real. Oh, Pamplona, are not these deeds proof enough and more that Fray Servando is the Devil himself, fallen God knows how or when to the peaceable earth so as to raise Cain once more, as it were, and worse this time, and send man to his prayers?

And León stalks furiously back and forth before the wall, looking over into the murky waters into which the friar has plunged, yet sees not the least sign of the friar. And throughout thy whole length and breadth, oh Pamplona, can be heard nothing except talk, touching that creature out of hell, who before any and all men's eyes could change himself into bird or fish or rushing cataract . . . In which, save it did not rush, were you, oh friar, floating that whole day long in that muddy swamp that circles and cuts off the city, breathing only the air carried on the rocks constantly flung at you by the sheriff's men from the wall, trying to crack your skull. And so it was that, the attackers unable to hit their mark, the friar swam off (keeping under the green slimy surface of the water) to the largest of the drawbridge sites, and there he clung to the chains of the bridge. And you held on to the chains for your life, and rested a moment, but then the drawbridge began to lift, carrying you along hanging to the end of it. The hour of curfew and the closing of the gates had come, and the hinges creaked madly as the great cumbersome bulk began to rise. And so it happened that the friar was flung like a catapult as the ponderous bridge clanged upright against the wall . . . So it was that the whole walled town of Pamplona saw, that evening, the figure of the friar flying through the air, against the glowing sky, like a streak of cometary mud. And the town burst into exclamations of terror, fell to its knees in the streets, and crossed itself in a fit of old-worldly superstition. Mothers snatched up their children and squeezed them to their breasts, wailing and crying. Church bells clanged. And for one moment nothing but prayers and ejaculations—"Save us, oh Lord!" "God forgive us!"—were heard in all the town. Even León was somewhat disconcerted, though but for a very few seconds, when a wad of mud dropping off the friar's clothing fell directly and spotted the hand that was pointing at the apparition . . . And that night there was ruptured for the first time the peaceful, peaceable life of the Pamplonans. Oh, Pamplona, who saw the Devil fly over thy children's heads, who could only salvage from that some wads of wet filth to prove it, and who now art forever spattered by it.

And meanwhile the friar fell most gracelessly into a mud puddle whose softness sucked him even further in. But at least he was outside the walls of the openmouthed city.

CHAPTER XVII

Which treats of the vicissitudes of the journey and the entry into Bayonne.

The dawn was veiled in an angry mist that punctured and pierced, as though the sky were unraveling into fine needlelike cords and cables of steel ice, spinning endlessly out from its very fabric, to follow us, wrap us, tangle us, and trip us up, and to stab us. This is what they call here "autumn."

A while before dawn I managed to give León the slip and make my way out of Villa de Madrid. And thus I came into Agreda and then left by way of Catalonia, which my friends had managed to slip out of without being searched. There I was fortunate to make brief contact with my friends the smuggling clerics who, dropping *pesetas* into every guard's open palm, aided me in my escape, and all their merchandise besides, without any very great difficulty. And then very near Pamplona (a city I have never had the pleasure to visit, though there are many who deny that), my French traders called upon a muleteer who had taken many clerics to France over the Pyrenees. The muleteer came to us with his animal, and I immediately followed along behind as I bade my good friends farewell. In a short while the both of us climbed up onto the mule's back and the mule began climbing up into the Pyrenees ... All I carried with me was the clothes that so ill covered my nakedness, for when I had departed from Aragon on my way to Navarra I was robbed of all I owned. There I was witness to the most ruinous and despotic extravagances of Spain, for the searches of one's person there are extraordinarily severe and thorough, and even worse for confiscating money and all the rest besides, than those at the frontier. Although all my bags and baggage had shrunk by now to one mere small canvas sack of clothing, which the guards spilled out onto the ground, and eight *duros* which they discovered and as quickly pocketed for their own ends, they were not content until they had passed page by page through my breviary, to see whether I had hidden golden therein, and even had made me strip down naked and raise my arms above my head so that one of the guards might peek under every hair of my body, both my head and the rest, to find any riches I might have secreted thereabouts. They lifted my toenails and made me open my mouth so wide that I feared my jaws would be disjointed, and all this to see if under my tongue I held some object of value. And since one of my legs was still somewhat swollen from so much escaping and leaping out windows and running about, the scoundrels thought it might be some trick or ruse to hide some coins there, and so one of the guards (the wretch!) took up a great hat pin and began passing it through my leg in various parts to see what my swelling hid. Could one have imagined such painful humiliation! All this I suffered in silence, in the hope that I might soon escape from their vileness, but at last I could not help but protest when they ordered me to lie facedown upon the ground and one of the soldiers of the regiment took up a hook and attempted to introduce it by the path one may well imagine. But my complaint fell on deaf ears, and they attempted to console me by stating that a great number of smugglers had been captured by this last sort of search, for some would carry there as many as a hundred gold coins or a flask of gunpowder to take to the Revolution. Though of course from me, as it goes without saying, they could get nothing.

And now we are penetrating higher and deeper into the Pyrenees, and what until moments ago was but inoffensive if unpleasant fog and mist is now become a heavy snowfall beating upon us like ingots of ice and piling up about our feet, as though it were on purpose to bury us. But still the ascent continues, and soon the poor mule begins to kick and grow terribly bad tempered. There is an almost constant roar. And I raise my head and see a snow-white mountain listing over us and rumbling and falling about our heads. This driving storm of snow continues until the snow has packed like iron, becoming dense hard ice so that we are no longer walking but now slipping and sliding across it. The muleteer barely opens his mouth, and when he does I cannot understand the babble he speaks, though if one were to ask me, I would say that when he opens his mouth it is not to speak to me at any rate, but rather to the weather, the ice, and in the last instance the mule who slips over it and champs out and tries to bite the icy air . . . And thus we are struggling when night overtakes us, but we continue on, for we fear to stop in case we should be frozen . . . And now we are walking over mirrors in which even the twinkling of the stars is reflected, and where one might track the path of the moon (if there were a moon). The muleteer is ahead of me, dragging the mule by the bridle, as though she were a sled, and from time to time, I confess, I take advantage of the muleteer's never looking back, to get up on the animal and rest a bit while still forging onward. And another sunrise comes. Hunger and cold are taking their toll now, and the step of the muleteer dragging the sleeping or stupefied mule grows ever heavier and duller and more plodding. And I, who no longer have the least desire to go on, lie down on that reflecting hardness and compose myself to die, for the calm of that is most appealing. The muleteer still does not look back but now he halts and digs a small hole in the ice, in which he buries one of the animal's hooves and covers it up again so the beast cannot escape by any means. He comes over to me, raises my eyelids, and then goes back to the hobbled mule. And there I see him take out a knife from the circle of his navel, where no-one ever would suspect that one might hide it, and grasp the mule tightly and with one slash open that thick vein which goes direct to the heart. He then puts his mouth to the wound and begins to drink up the blood of the animal, which is now puffing and panting and trying to escape, though to no avail. "Come here and drink this!" the man calls to me, taking his mouth for a moment from the cut vein out of which is gushing a stream of thick purple blood. And so I crawl over the ice, put my mouth to the fountain, and drink. And on the instant I can feel myself filled with energy, and even for a moment have a desire to run about madly. "Hurry, before it clots!" the man cries. And so I go on drinking that still-hot blood that fills me so with strength, but then which begins to slow to a trickle, and I look, and the animal is a block of dark ice, no more, silhouetted against the ice blue blocks of other snow and ice . . . And so our crossing continued. I had such an excess of good spirits that I thought at any minute I might start braying or give my guide a kick . . . But on the next day my drowsiness returned. I fell exhausted, drained, and once more lay me down to sleep on the ice, which extended for leagues about. And so it was that early in the morning I was awakened by a hand touching my throat, and I opened my eyes and beheld there the muleteer, with his mule-sticker in his hand . . . And the energy I thought to have lost for ever suddenly returned to me, and I let out a cry more like a scream or howl of terror, and began to flee madly across that desolate mountainous landscape. "If ye stay frightened enough ye shan't want to sleep!" the muleteer cackled behind me, in a phrase of justification. But by then my voice was echoing, and resounding, increasing in volume through the chasms and gulleys and against the sheer walls of the mountains, and bouncing about, bringing down the roofs of overhangs and caverns and carving out interior rivers. And that brought on a great avalanche. Entire mountains we saw come unstuck and tumble upon us implacably. The Pyrenees, thought I, will exist no more. I cursed this loud place. And so the muleteer and I began to run, to try to outpace the snowslide, leaving shreds and pieces of our bodies along the way. We spoke not a word to each other, either, for fear of provoking another avalanche. And so we descended, so rapidly that the frozen rocks and earth tumbling down upon us were left at last far behind . . . And so we came finally to a company of men dressed all in black, who were beginning their ascent as we descended. "Those are the friars," the muleteer told me, "who are fleeing the terror of the Revolution. If they remain in France they are almost sure to go to the guillotine." And at that I would surely have shuddered, were it not that I had been shuddering already for many hours. The caravan wended into the distance and at last disappeared, buried under another avalanche that suddenly trembled upon them. We continued our descent . . . And soon we espied another caravan, of men and women both, being buried and unburied by the snow, and that also looked to be fleeing. They passed before us and then they too wended upward, though again a terrible snowslide crushed them to bits. "Those by their look are revolutionaries," the muleteer told me most calmly, "fleeing, I should say, the terror of the Restoration. Nothing in France these days is very durable.' And as the muleteer seemed to note my astonishment and surprise, he spoke these consoling words: "But whatever ye see should not worry ye. Remember that ye be Dr. Maniau and no other, and none of this can touch ye, for ye have been dead now for months . . ."

And so we lumbered on, *and the next day we had come to Hostiz, the both of us frozen through. And the next day after that we crossed the valley of Baztán[7] where the sun*, which falls straight downward, began to melt the snow (which still reached up to our ears, our nostrils, and all our other orifices, however). And so we trudged onward. *By the next day we were in Cinquevilles, from where you can look out at the ocean, at Bayonne and all its surrounding lands, blanching in the fields like a herd of cows. And on the next we passed by Ordaz, the last Spanish village on that frontier, and I grew most eager to find out where the line of France was. "Here,"* said the muleteer, *pointing to a shallow little ravine. I stepped over it, dismounted, and threw myself headlong on the ground.[8] "What are ye doing, man?"* the muleteer asked me. "I have crossed the Rubicon," I replied, "and I am not an emigrant, but a poor Méxican, and all I have is this passport, that was Maniau's, from México to Spain." "But what does that matter," he chided me, "these *gendarmes* cannot read good Castilian, and when they see such a grand person as yerself they will take off their hats to ye as to any great man." And so it was, in fact. *We slept that night in Agnon, the first village in France*, where the muleteer ordered up two new mules (I know not by what sleight of hand). *And on the next morning, to enter Bayonne, which is a walled* plaza, *the muleteer had me get down from my mule and told me to go in amongst the throng of people on the public highway, where for the first time I saw carts pulled by bullocks,[9]* and I even got up on one. But this stratagem was to no avail, for *the guard picked me out by my strange way of dressing, and by the fact that I wore boots and was covered by dust from the road. He carried me off to the mayor's house, where I presented my Mexican passport, and since no-one could read it, they gave me my card or ticket of safe passage. And all this trouble was very necessary in those times of the turbulence, still unrepressed, of the Republic. And I recall it still was a republic, though governed by*

---

[7] Fray Servando, *Apologia*.
[8] Ditto.
[9] Ditto.

consuls, *Bonaparte being the* prime consul. *That day was the Friday of Our Lord's Pains, in the year 1801.*[10]

What to do so as not to die of hunger, my being so upright as not to stoop, which heaven forfend, to begging alms? With my clothes all in tatters and wretchedness seeping out of every pore, I wandered all night through the streets of Bayonne until, standing in a portal, I fell at last asleep. And before cockcrow the next morning (while new and painful sorrows were likewise awakening in me), with the sadness that every exiled man must feel when he has been banished from his homeland, I set off walking again through the city, which I had no knowledge of. And so I came, in a street in the quarter called Spiritus Sancti, to a place where I heard a psalm being chanted in my own tongue . . . I hurried over and, without thinking, rushed into the room from which the chant was issuing.

I was, then, inside a synagogue. And it was Passover, the feast of the unleavened bread and the lamb.

[10] Fray Servando, *Apologia.*

FRANCE

CHAPTER XVIII

Which tells of what things happened to me in Bayonne when I entered a synagogue, and of my life in that city until my flight to save my own neck.

You've never been in Madrid! You've never crossed the Pyrenees! Or been to a single one of those places you mention, or rather criticize. You know perfectly well that the drawbridge catapulted you through the air to Bayonne and that it was pure chance you fell into a synagogue and the Jews got frightened by the thought you might be some evil visitation, since they'd seen you descend like the son of God through the air. And you yourself said, oh you friar you, and these are your exact words, that you "crossed *over* the Alps." You know you did.[11] You tumbled into the synagogue at the very instant the rabbi was preaching on the impossibility of the return of the Messiah who was held in Israel for the sins of all his descendants. And the Jews were sitting there listening in abject, stunned silence to that fierce hot sermon that stripped them of all hope of consolation or salvation, and they didn't like it too much either. And there you came, landing at that very instant, crashing into the rabbi's beard. They had been listening to him with real displeasure, because all he was doing was calling down reproaches on his congregation and telling them what schlemiels they all were, so they immediately hailed you as the new Messiah and attacked the rabbi in a rabid horde and pulled out his beard by the roots. The poor disbearded man ran off screaming into the street, waving his hands and screaming to high heaven. So then all the fanatics in the synagogue crowded around you and lifted you up and put you where the rabbi had been standing before, and they got down on their knees to you and threw off their prayer shawls in an attitude of thanksgiving, and they even kissed your feet. And the ones that couldn't reach your feet to kiss them, kissed the floor instead, and since a lot of the Jews took off their shoes to

[11]Fray Servando, *Apologia.* *"Cruzamos por sobre los Alpes."*

come into the synagogue, everybody that kissed the floor was poisoned on the spot.

And they called themselves "beasts stained by sin." And lo, it was said that these were the hearts that theretofore had scorned the Messiah in Jerusalem. And at last when the chants were sung, and the corpses laid together in a corner of the temple, there fell a silence, in great expectation of the Word. And every man and woman waited, *illuminated*, for thee, that thou shouldst speak to them. And thou spakest to them, saying, "I am not the Messiah, in truth. I am but a simple messenger come from Him, sent to remind thee that the Messiah cannot *come* to thee himself, for He has never *left* thee . . ." And at that, behold, the host of Jews grew hot against the old rabbi, and ran out after him, to kill him if they could. But thy words continued, even until they returned. Thy voice was as cool water, and filled with truth, and though no man understood thee they all wept with delight at thy voice. Thou wast acclaimed and heaped with a thousand words of flattery. They purchased thee new raiment, a robe. And they called thee Hahá, which in their tongue was to say the Wise Man. And they all of them invited thee to be their guest, and to live in their mansions. And in sooth such pulling and hauling was there then about thy person, that a miracle was wanted to save thee from thy admirers. When lo, arising out of the multitude (whose center was thou), there came a most quick-limbed and elegant Jewess, for whom they all, when well they knew who it was, stood aside, as though the waters had parted to let her pass. And she walked erect through the throng of the faithful, coming near and saying, "This man shall be my guest. For am I not the most meet to attend his wants? For I am the wealthiest of all the Jews in Bayonne." And speaking no other word, she led thee away with her . . . And so thou walkedst, full terrified, on the arm of Rachel (whose name in her own country was Finette), out from the temple. Behind thee there marched an army of the faithful, singing praises and hailing thee with blessings. Rachel took thee up in her arms and crossed the city. And in a street she met with that rabbi persecuted by his people, and torn apart by his flock. She kicked him aside with the tip of her shoe and walked erect to her house, a splendid mansion, a noble palace.

This is the hour when it is no longer quite day nor yet is it quite night either. And the shadows, which at midday had shrunk up and squatted beneath buildings or inside the trunks of trees, now have begun to stretch, to lengthen and crawl out of their secret places and flow together until the world is one great spreading shadow ... From your cage, hung from the roof of a great windowed gallery, you watch the sun, midst your own groans and rattles, decline and then sink at the line of the distant horizon. And for one moment all things take on the half-yellow tinge of ripe, turning leaves. The bars of your cage glint and sparkle, but for one moment only. This is the hour at which sounds are transformed to strange echoing throbs, when all things clamor (though softly, discreetly) for mercy or the soothing of melancholy. To your cage come the sounds of voices changed to venerable whispers, and you can look out to the very ends of the city, and even beyond, to the plain beyond spread out to such thinness that it makes one fabric with the sky itself.

The palace rises above all other edifices about, so there can be no secrets for eyes that watch over all from above, without themselves being an object of observation. Those houses, their fronts so brightly painted and bedecked, hardly have any roof at all, and their owners sleep on the floor. That building of several stories, in which innumerable families live, has but one small yard where the women gather to wash and cook. And even the trees themselves seem to lose their upright serenity when viewed from up here above, and seem more like green spiders trying futilely to lift themselves above the dun-colored ground.

But then, those comparisons fade, and the last lights of the day, which were holding back behind some tardy shadow, now shining between the trunks of two date-palms that mark the limit between the city and the plain, bring you memories of other plains, other sandy stretches, other palms. The evocations flutter downward as the shadows fall, like silent birds, their wings extended and held, searching for the one single objective and not finding it, rustling and fluttering incessantly, yet unmoving from their place nor alighting on it either ... And so you sit there transfixed, entering and departing times and places. And when you turn your back to the window and gaze on the ceremonies for your diversion already commencing in the room, night has fully fallen. And the voices take on their usual vulgar tones, their ordinary everyday shrill and shrieking clang.

In the great hall, Rachel, in clothing that sparkled in the light, danced to the sound of a tearful music, while a host of courtiers and their ladies were crowded together in the shadows among the columns, and left nothing undone for the enjoyment and pleasure of the guests. A choir of old Jewish men circulated through the room, with their long white beards, and from time to time one would lift his gaze and offer you a respectful nod, like an echoed salute. Finette came to the end of her dance and at a signal the old Jews began to loose the rope from which hung your cage.

And you descend.

"Oh, Hahá," Finette says to you, opening the bars of your cell, entering, and shutting them again in one swift movement, "will you still not consent to the wedding?" But you do not deign even to respond. Every night the same scene is repeated, the same question, the same silence as reply. And then, as always, Rachel will leave the cage, very saddened and downcast, and will begin to chant a melancholy plaint evoking caravans lost in the desert, dry oases, and solitude. Then the Jewish men will come very gently to your perpetual domicile, make once more the same respectful bows and offer the same propositions. "Don't be so timid," "What if you're a friar, the wedding can be in Holland where they understand such things," "How bad can it be to be Jewish? You'll be a great rabbi. Try it, you'll see," "All Finette's wealth will come to you, my boy." But you refuse to reply to them as well, so they retire crestfallen. Rachel will go on chanting her piteous reproach. And the cage will creak upward for another night.

"Oh woe is me, what fate is mine, to go from one cell to another, and no escape possible. Or if I do manage to escape one cell it is only to fall into another one yet more difficult to force. I hope this prison is my worst. At least until now none has been so hard as this. Ay, because to be hounded by a honey-tongued Jewess to renounce everything and marry her is the most terrible punishment that ever could have been given me. For every day she vexes me with her propositions. And I see no wise to escape me from this cage, even though I have examined its every least articulation. But I must escape, I must, I must!"

Thus raved the friar even as he first awoke, and he would run from one corner of his cage to the other, the cage hung from the highest beams of the many-windowed palace. So he did not see the man down below who approached with his breakfast, and who from the friar's height looked like some minuscule insect crawling through a labyrinth.

"And pray God the rope break! And heaven permit I should plunge to the floor of this stone-paved castle and fall on those Jews' heads and crush them, even though I myself must shatter! . . ."

And suddenly the cage seemed to come loose from its moorings, for a vertiginous plunge began. The friar seized the bars in terror and thought of the irony of these events, seeing that of all the things he had desired in his life and most fervently wished for, the only thing he was to be conceded was that which he had desired in a moment of mere momentary violent outpouring of his feelings! Thus quickly meditated the friar as he fell dizzyingly from his height. And this single moment brought him to the conclusion that in even the most pitiful and painful things there is an admixture of grinning irony and stupidity, which makes every true tragedy not greatly more than a chain of grotesque calamities, infinitely capable of provoking laughter and hilarity . . . With a terrible noise the golden cage (for the cage was entirely made of gold, though it is sad to say so) crashed to the floor and the palace shook with it, and for a moment all that could be heard was a cataclysmic crashing of breaking glass, crystal, tiles, porcelains, and vases, urns, and stained-glass panels. Even heavy slabs of marble were shivered to dust.

Out of the cloud of dust and glassy shards emerged the cook, begging pardon over and over of the friar (for it had been he, the cook, who moved by the friar's lamentations had released the cords by which the cell was suspended, though he had meant only to bring him his breakfast). The remains of the tray were still in his hands. Behind the twisted golden bars the friar was calling out for someone to get him out of there before he suffocated completely. The cook tugged at the gate, and finally he beat it open. Fray Servando staggered out, hopping rather, as the servant brushed off his clothes and again begged over and over to be forgiven.

"Hush, man," the friar said, now walking about, though somewhat unsteadily, "and tell me how to get out of this place."

"Out!" exclaimed the cook. "Do ye think it so easy then?"

"The hardest thing was to escape the cage, and here I am escaped."

"I wouldn't think so. This palace is a great succession of cages, sir, one inside another. Ye have come out of the first, but here we both stand now in the second. From this one to the last . . .!"

"If I walked out of the first I will somehow slip out of the last. And if thou wilt not help me, then I shall do it alone."

"Oh yes, willingly I would help ye," said the cook, and truly his words sounded so heartfelt that of his sincerity there could have been no doubt. "I heard your complaints, sir, and it struck me dumb. That is why the rope slipped from my hand and why ye fell. Those very words ye spoke, I spoke myself ten years ago. And yet look at me here—in those ten years I have still not found the way to escape farther than the first cage, and that by falling in rank, for I came here in the same wise as yourself. The woman's fancy never lights but on the impossible. And when she sees it is out of reach, she takes her revenge. She strips one of his place. That is how most of the servants of the palace, even the lowest of them, came there—by first occupying the very cage that ye were occupying now."

"But why would no-one marry her? Thou—why wouldst thou not have her?"

"For the same reason as yourself . . . or another reason similar enough . . ." said the cook, giving the friar such a speaking look that the friar gave up the inquiry.

"But nonetheless I shall do all I can to flee from here," Servando at last said, and his resolve stiffened the cook as well.

"And I shall aid ye. We shall flee together."

At that moment a group of servants entered the hall, aroused by the racket that had echoed throughout the palace. Servando and the cook, surprised, could do no more than creep beneath one of the piles of glass and rubble that littered the hall. Hidden beneath the glassy hill which at every moment stung and pricked their bodies with its shards, they could still hear Rachel shouting and crying and then her strong voice ordering eternal vigilance of the two thousand cells that comprised the concatenated castle. The friar, upon hearing such a great number, despaired, and would have let out a cry, but for the splinters of glass that had sewed his mouth shut tight . . . "And," ordered Finette, who was exceedingly shrewd, "all that rubble, pass it through a sieve, in case the Hahá should be found there . . . hiding." At those words Servando lost his wits completely. He tried to move within the mountain of debris, but he felt a pain like millions of pins pricking his skin. Within moments the servants had returned with a great sieve and an enormous coal shovel, and so they began to sift through the remains of the disaster . . . And it chanced that when night fell Rachel came into the hall again, and seeing that they had not yet found the friar, sat down and wept, and picking up a handful of that glassy dust, she brought it to her lips. She kissed the dust with such emotion that some of the tiny shards of shattered glass passed into her stomach and her lungs and killed her instantly, though not before she let out a shriek so horrible that all the particles of the remains of the catastrophe were blown about, into a grayish cloud which enveloped the entire room. This was the moment. Servando and the cook seized the opportunity to slip from their hiding place into the mound of dust already sieved, and there they lay them down to hide again.

And so it was that the entire mountain of shivered glass was sifted through the sieve without a trace discovered of the friar, which was one reason the more that among the Jews it came to be believed that this had been a visitation by the devil. And then all the rubble was shoveled into an enormous cart which, toward sunrise, was pulled out of the castle by a thousand Christian servants yoked in tandem to the wagon-tongue. Atop the mound of dust was laid the inert body of Rachel, since the Jews (out of their overweening spirit of frugality) had decided to use that same cart for the funerary celebrations. And beneath the body of Rachel and the mound of splintered glass, the cook and Servando thought they would suffocate before they were free.

Thus it fell out that the cart (pulled by only Christian servants, because it was a Saturday and the Jews could not work) passed through the two thousand cages of the palace, each in its turn opened by another two thousand Christian servants. And at last the vehicle was drawn to the limits of the city, and those men, sweaty and covered with dust, who had drawn it, left it there, just at nightfall, by the banks of the River Dax, where it was overturned, and its weighty load thrown into the current. Thus Rachel's body was buried, while Servando and the cook were disinterred, and this, to the great amazement of the Christians who saw them float away on the foaming waters now colored a million colors by the whirlings of the crushed glassy dust. The sun at setting set the waters ablaze like stained-glass sheets of quicksilver.

"Oh, freedom!" cried the cook, as he floated on his back down the current and recited whole chapters of the *Social Contract*. This piqued the friar's curiosity about the fellow, and he asked about his family and his name.

"Oh," answered him the cook, "I am now the great Samuel Robinson, who at another time was the sage Simón Rodríguez . . ." And then suddenly the current of the flashing Dax dragged him down, so that the friar thought the best thing now to do was make the sign of the cross over the spot where he had disappeared. But then he beheld Samuel bob up a few yards farther on. "We will meet in Paris!" Simón called to the friar, exactly like a man leaping aboard a coach. And then the current made him vanish once again. This time the friar made no sign over him.

All night floated the friar along on the surface of that water, constantly dunked, cast up again, alternately drowned and buoyed, so that it at last became such a monotonous game that the friar fell fast asleep. But in the morning he had lost the little strength that had remained to him the night before, so that he was adrift, and unable to regain the shore, when by good fortune he hit against something metal which halted him in his course. He sank to the very bottom of the river (no doubt a twist of fate), seized some roots tangling there, pulled himself to the bank, and crawled out onto the land.

"My bridge, thou hast ruined it!" a man holding a great sack of gold said to him.

"What bridge?" asked, amazed, Servando, never taking his eyes off this absurd personage.

"The bridge I was building with this gold, to get me across the river so I could go on to Paris."

"But why squander so much money? Is there no other way, then, to cross this river?"

"I truly do not know, or care. I am the Count of Gijón, and I have millions, and if with them I cannot get myself across this river, then why have them at all?" And here he cast another sackful into the flood.

"What a waste! What a terrible waste!" cried the friar, putting his hands to his head and surreptitiously kicking under his soutane the coins that had spilled on the bank.

At that moment a rustic passed by, and the friar took him aside for two seconds. And in not many more seconds the Count and the friar were crossing the river, on the back of the peasant who was also crossing it, but swimming.

"Of what use is my gold to me!" the Count bellowed, "if I have had to beg aid to cross this wretched brook!"

"It has done much good," replied the friar, "for I have just given a ducat of it to this country fellow, to whom it represents an entire fortune."

"One gold ducat!" And the Count's happiness was so great at seeing that his money had been of some use, that he began to embrace the friar and make him hundreds of promises. "I do not know French," he said. "I need someone, then, to teach me all the things there are to see. And to help me spend this gold that keeps constantly arriving to me from the New World. And then there is that money I have invested in sugar, which when I sell it will surely triple my fortune. I am the great Count of Gijón and I have just come from Peru! To Paris, then! . . . I am the Count of Gijón! I am the Count of Gijón!"

And so many times did he repeat those words that when the Count of Gijón at last tired of giving his titles, they had already reached Bordeaux.

CHAPTER XIX

Which tells of my entrance into Paris.

After passing through Bordeaux, where the Count of Gijón spent a great deal of money on wine (which he believed was the finest and most delectable to be had, only later discovering that it was some mishmash from the Canary Islands), we continued our voyage, flinging handfuls of gold about as though it were water, which made me suffer greatly, and I indeed did attempt to restrain the Count somewhat, telling him constantly that he should be less prodigal.

And so we entered into Paris.

The first thing we saw was an excellently uniformed army all carrying weapons as though there were a war. I thought, on seeing all that artillery and the constant parade of colored uniforms, that an invasion must have been mounted against that braying ass Napoleon. But I soon discovered that it was nothing more than the King's supporters who spent a great part of their lives frightening frogs away from under the nobles' windows so that they should not disturb their sleep. Each noble is named to be at the head of one of these armies, and anyone without an army is held in such contempt that no-one will speak to or have any manner of dealing with him. One may well imagine that my most pompous pear-shaped peruke-wearing Peru-milker immediately tried to have one of those armies placed under him, and in fact had it not been for me he would have spent his entire fortune on that one wild-wigged caprice . . . So at last we went on with our travels. Or would have, for of a sudden we were surprised and stopped still in our tracks by a troop of soldiers angrily running across our path, like hunting dogs, after Lord knows what prey or fierce enemy. But when we asked to what was owed this rush of men, whether the Huns had returned to sack Europe, a person standing by informed us that they were only chasing a pigeon that had so little respect for other men's property that it had dared to alight among the Bishop's fields. And so the Bishop's soldiers were leaving every field in their wake trampled, so keenly were they pursuing the little fowl. From the sound of their stamping footsteps as they ran, one would have thought it was cannons fired in a furious cannonade. But then stillness returned once more . . . They had caught the bird . . . We went on our way, the extravagant Count never ceasing talking non-sense and things of no count, flinging gold about like leaves in the autumn, and committing all manner of graceless blunders. Just as we were entering the gates of Paris, we met with a hanged man. The man was dangling from an oak tree, and from the locks of his hair there hung a mangled bird. So this was the owner of the ill-chanced pigeon, the both of them now swaying in the breeze at the entrance to the city, hanged as an example to every bird and bird owner there was. This, and all the other things I saw as we were entering Paris, soon let me understand very clearly indeed that things had returned to their normal state, and that the tumult of the Revolution had passed.

I by now was the Count's *lazarillo*, or guide, and a guide espe-cially to a blind man, and thus I denominated myself not only for that poor Lazarillo de Tormes of Castilian literature, who like me went daily from bad to worse, but also because my Count of Gijón knew no French at all (let alone good Christian Spanish), which in the land of those people is more like being blind than deaf or mute, and he would stand gape-mouthed and stammering before any novel trifle which in the lands of the Americas had already been so little novel as to produce yawns instead of astonishment. The man's simpleness, indeed, knew hardly any bounds at all. But as he had money, all his absurdities were soon pardoned him, and even on occasion praised and marveled at by the greedy French. With him I entered the most luxurious *salons* of the old aristocracy and there met what could be called the *noblest blood of the age*. But soon enough I tired of playing the guide to that brazen Peru-sacker and Paris sycophant—for I, who knew well enough how these Europeans would try to "skin" (for that was what it was) any man come from the Americas, especially if he had any money at all, I, I say, would continually try to counsel with the Count and check his openhandedness, even when he spent money on my own person. But he would grow very heated and wroth, and still would not stop spending money as though it had no end to it. At last, in one of those arguments I decided to leave him to his fate, then, and go my own way—into poverty no doubt, but that at least was a fate to which I had by now to some extent become inured. So I gathered my little belongings, returned to the Count what he had given me, even as gifts, and with a small sack, which I would have almost been able to carry under my soutane without its being noticed, I set out through the streets of what was then being called "the city of wonders." And indeed it was, for the man who sought sin, things of the flesh, or other roguishness, for in nothing does Paris differ from the Court of Madrid save that in Paris the most scandalous things are done in the very streets and light of day. That is why Paris has lost that touch of mystery, that *mystique*, that strangely attractive combination of eroticism and mysticism, which in Spain is still to be found.

Never have I felt so peaceful and independent as when I left that willful and abandoned *arriviste* (who within a very short time was utterly ruined, so much so that he had to beg for alms in the streets), and so I set about living by my own means. But as I was very scrupulous I suffered innumerable tribulations, though I never asked any man's help. And that is how it was one day, when I was near dying of hunger, that I dragged myself over to a bench set along a path and lay down, to die as I thought, but at that moment I heard someone calling my name loudly and quite excitedly, so employing all the force that was left to me, I raised my head and there I saw Samuel Robinson, running toward me.

It was a great stroke of luck that at that moment my old friend Simón Rodríguez should come upon me, for though at times he seemed mad as a hare, he was in fact a quite wonderful person. He immediately tried to raise my spirits by insisting that we set ourselves up in a school to teach Spanish. And so we did. We would give classes in the parks and churches of the city. Samuel found himself some students from among the nobles, and he would teach them in their palaces. It was at that period that we decided to translate the famous *Atala* by the Viscount de Chateaubriand, a translation that was especially difficult for us owing to the great number of botanical names therein which could be found in no encyclopedia or treatise whatever. But we at last finished it, and we sold the first copy of all to the Viscount himself, who happened to walk by our stall. I truly believe that the best time I spent in Paris was that one, owing to my great friendship with Rodríguez; at least, it is that period which now instantly springs to my mind when I think of Paris, and with not a single disagreeable moment to cloud it. For the first time in my life I had what might be called a true friendship. Both Simón and I came from the Americas, we had both been banished, had both survived the most horrendous prisons of Spain. And both he and I had ideas—we never ceased to think about the ways it might be possible to change the world, or at least that part of the world that belonged to the New World, so brutal, bestial, and blissfully though sadly ignorant. Soon I managed to find for myself, after a good deal of most sorry plights, the living of a parish, while Simón established a real school where he set about teaching Spanish in a more orderly fashion. And my friend Robinson's classes were a thing to be heard: they always closed with a fulminating Voltairean speech about Man. People would stand about in the streets to hear him declaim. The greatest part of his students never mastered Spanish, or even one of its primary conjugations, for a fact, but that detail is trivial if one stops to consider that they left his school made real men, hounded and tormented by that vision of the world which Simón had hammered into their skulls . . . To say that this was a time that I will always remember with affection and happiness, is to say too little—it was the only time. As the afternoon waned, after Simón had finished his classes and I had shut up my church, we would go out into the streets and stroll all over Paris. He would walk along parodying Voltaire and Rousseau, saying the most outrageous things about the nobility; I would add to his cargo of knowledge by telling him stories of the clergy and what went on in the court of Spain, which in spite of being true stories left Simón's attacks against the French nobility in the shade, as it were. And thus walking and talking we would come to the Palais Royal where we would take an inventory of the fatuous and useless luxury flung about by the monarchs. Once I remember counting eleven kitchens, fourteen cafés, twelve large theaters and three small ones, not to mention hundreds of *privy closets* with their *bureaux* or money-changing tables and wigged assistants who dispensed lavender-water and orange-water to clean oneself with so that one's backside would always be fragrant. And in mocking all these fripperies we would return, by now in the early hours of the morning, from our strolls, and always with our heads filled with our projects, and feeling, many times, truly weighed down by the seeming hopelessness of our dreams ... But this period of peace and friendship was short, which is perhaps why I remember it with such warm feeling: one morning Samuel received an imperial order that commanded him to leave France immediately. And so he departed, once again to wander and spin out his wonders. While I, who had seen myself in him as I had never seen myself even in myself, had to begin again to adapt myself to my own poor company, which now was intolerable to me. Simón told me he was going to Germany, Austria, Russia. And there he did go, too—*the eternal teacher, the eternal philosopher, eternally ironic and sarcastic and fiercely committed to independence.*[12]

Fleeing myself was perhaps what took me anew to the *salons*, the palaces, the official sites of noble boredom.

I am in the grand *hôtel* of the Viscount de Chateaubriand. Is there anyone of any account not present here tonight? Wherever one turns there is naught to be heard but fatuous and pedantic remarks about literature, so pompous and absurd that they are truly unbearable. No book from the New World is so much as mentioned in these circles, no author, as though the entire hemisphere did not exist ... At last the Viscount appears, in his black, august, and most grandly ceremonial garments, with his measured step and his distracted, apparently unseeing glance. He looks like a being summoned up from some unknown region. A silence falls. Most of the women are reclining on the floor on cushions placed about the room for that purpose. The Viscount's voice seems to issue from the depths of some dark and hollow grotto. It is a mellow,

[12]Germán Arciniegas, *América Mágica.*

melancholy, throbbing voice, slow, and he seems to consider each word, to step carefully across each syllable, each letter, deliberately filling each sound with gravity. It is a voice which does not speak of concrete men or events, but of nostalgias, sadnesses difficult to identify. And every word, every swell of that intonation is accompanied by a matching gesture of gravity and pomp, like a billowing sea, and which appears almost unalterably affected. *Je reste pour enterrer mon siècle*. And he concludes like a prophet filled with light. The conversations begin once more. The Viscount tempers his grandiloquence a bit, and comes to greet his guests. When he offers me his hand, I immediately say to him that I translated one of his books, and remind him that his was the first copy. The Viscount does not recall . . . He smiles with great complaisance and glides away into the throng of people. The conversations swell again. What are these men and women talking about? What are they saying? What is the great topic of the evening? What conceivable importance do these colloquies hold?

In one of the many gatherings of the *salon* I came to know Chateaubriand personally. He was giving a party in his *hôtel*. It would have been ten times better never to have made a friend of him; in that *soirée* as in all the rest, for as long as I was in Paris, in all those gatherings where our friendship was cemented and where I achieved a degree of intimacy with the Viscount, the image he presented to me was of a man excessively sad, reactionary, melancholic. Chateaubriand gave body for the first time to that modern condition known as *le mal de René* . . . There can be no doubt that his gorgeous, deep, and weighted manner of speaking, which was *as though he were unrolling Oriental tapestries*,[13] made most of the genteel and thin-blooded people who heard him tremble and throb. It was most moving, in a sense . . . And so it was that when the gentleman had finished speaking I looked about and realized that those women lounging about on the cushions, or at least those who had listened to the Viscount, were all lying dead and lifeless on the floor. And at a wave of the Viscount's languid hand, respectful bewigged servants hurried in to drag the bodies away into another salon. And the conversation once more resumed.

Now I am in the house of the most peaceable Abbot Henri Grégoire. This is called the "evening of tears" and so far as I could

[13]Artemis de Valle-Arizpe, *Fray Servando.*

discover it has always been celebrated with great success, so that it has become one more of the nobility's *salons* . . . A great silence. The Abbot then at last appears. He sits upon a modest chair, facing his guests. The candles are put out, save one or two left flickering about the room. And out of that penumbral gloom in which the Abbot sits comes his sobbing, at first very soft and low, like a song about to find its key and soar, and then louder and louder, until at last it is a long-held howl, unchanging, neither rising nor falling in pitch, and lasting full half an hour. Two servants wipe away the tears, from time to time, from the Abbot's face. The male guests light their pipes while the women chat in low voices, or comment on his weeping: "Tonight he is in better voice than ever before." "Magnificent." "There is none like him." And some, thrilled, like-wise begin to cry, though very softly, as though they feared they might drown out the Abbot's own sobs. At the end of this half hour the weeping rises in volume, like a sudden deafening chord struck by an orchestra, but only for a few seconds, for then it subsides in brief trickles and drops, becomes more and more sub-dued and nigh inaudible, and then it dies. The *soirée* has come to an end. The tear-wetted handkerchiefs and scarves that the Abbot's servants have used are highly coveted. A polite struggle breaks out over them, but then someone suggests they be auctioned off. The bidding begins, and soon the bids name figures that would require hundreds of gold pieces to pay. The Abbot has disappeared. Taking advantage of the confusion, I too leave the company.

In one of those gatherings I met the Abbaye Grégoire, who by the time I knew him was a most peaceable and tranquil man, that in no way resembled the furious and tempestuous fellow who to the last defended the life of Louis XVI. To these evenings given by the abbot-*conservateur* flocked all the nobility who survived the Revolution, and all the principal personages of France. The loftiest men and the most dazzling women in their highest-heaped hair-pieces . . . The Abbot always brought his *soirées* to an end by tell-ing stories of the distant-seeming past, the guillotining of the King, for example, and then a long session of weeping.

For the society of that time—yearning for the *Ancien Régime*—there was no *salon* more moving and important than the Abbot's, though for myself I could only stand it once.

CHAPTER XX

From the friar's diary.

Have just come home from *salon* of Mme. de Récamier. Nothing of import. *La* Récamier moved constantly among her guests, offering light jests and sallies of wit which provoked no great mirth though everyone laughed greatly at them. Then came Benj'm. Constant (a man of weak frame and bitter character, with whom I have spoken on vrs. occasions and from whom have had v. little satisfaction), and the two went off toward the upstairs chambers. After an hour they reappeared hand in hand and R. smiling like a well-satisfied mare . . . The later the evening grew, the more bored I. On leaving, met a young man from Guanajuato—Lucas Alamán, who woke me from that *lethargie saloniste* when he spoke so feelingly of *his land*, which is mine also, and his great passion, which is likewise mine.

                                                                Paris, Aug. 1

Have made a friend of young Alamán, who invited me to go and visit the famous *salon* of Fanny. There met another haughty young man, v. proud, rebellious, and fiery—named Simón Bolívar (F's lover, as he is of almost all the noble ladies who frequent these *salons*). Told me he'd been a student of Simón Rodríguez, which of course sufficed me to call him a friend as well. Spoke to me of Robinson, and told me that R. was currently in Vienna, though but for a few days. Knew not which way the restless Master would go next . . . Another personage who impressed me v. greatly was Madame de Staël (née Necker). Most attractive and above all stands out from other women (so mannered and haughty) by her small interest in standing out. Asked Alamán to present me to the lady, but at that moment Alexander von Humboldt entered the room. All call him *Baron*. H. was the *pièce de résistance* of the *salon*. He spoke in a most clear and fluent French about everything, and with great discernment and knowledge moreover, though without any show. He knows the New World better than most men born and bred there, and his political ideas are of the most *avant garde*. Many people shivered when he said, "Spanish America is ripe for its freedom, though still it lacks a great man to set it on the move." And young Bolívar, who at every moment had to be pushing Fanny away, for she tired him with her constant *kissy-wissy*, listened most attentively to him, seeming most exalted and inspired. At last, seeing that Fanny would no way let him pay any attention to the Baron's stirring words, he boxed her ears with a slap that sounded all across the room. So then Mme. de Staël laughed, most contagiously in fact. And the Baron talked some more.

Paris, Aug. 16

Young Alamán introduced me to the other *formidable* young man, v. Humboldt. We talked all afternoon here in the chapel and then at dusk we walked out for a run in the Baron's coach. Return to America! It is as though I were there, speaking in the most natural way with the people in the street, my very own street. You can *touch* things. When B.v.H. forgets a detail, I recall it instantly ... We talked about the rivers, which he knows by rote, and even about the most insignificant creeks and *arroyos* ... And of the City of México he has forgotten not one jot, not the name of a single street. He now has found out all the privations and hardships I have suffered. We leave the coach and walk through the streets, and at every moment a new detail springs to our minds. To talk over. To fill us again with that passion. And then we walk some more. It is rather cold, though hardly yet winter. The B.v.Humboldt invites me to his castle ... It is surrounded by thousands of plants brought from every part of the Americas. Crossing the garden we can hear the shrieks, cackles, caws, calls, whistles, and peeps of New World birds I had never hoped to hear again ... And now on one of the castle's many terraces, B.v.H. shows me his essay on New Spain, on which he is now at work. I give him what information I can. I fill him with new ideas and descriptions. I am carried away by my emotions ... In the early morning we take our leave of one another, though with the promise to meet soon again.

Paris, Sept. 30

At last have met Mme. de Staël. Just as I thought, she is a *femme formidable* ... "You come from a place which very soon will begin to exist," said to me when I was introduced. And then we commenced just as we are, with no show of thoughtful reticence or haughtiness of grandeur ... Told her I detested Frenchwomen, who were all bigmouthed and rather terrible, made to the cut of a great frog. She responded that she loved American men, who all were so full of fire, a fire which had gone out long since in Europeans. Told her I could not understand why her house was always filled with such complaining contemptible people.

"What makes man most sociable is his weakness," she answered, quoting Rousseau, that new Bible. "And I am weak," she added in a tone mixing coquetry and confession.

"The truly happy being is solitary," I riposted, still quoting.

"Oh, only the good man remains alone," she added, and there we ended our catechism in Rousseau.

We passed into another hall and there sat down. She then took out a fine cigarette case on which was engraved the figure of Louis XVI, his body on the case and his head on the top, so that they were cut in two when the case was opened.

"It suits him, does it not?" She smiled at me. "It is to remind everyone who sees it that here once a king's head was cut off and that," and here she raised her voice a bit, as though in a fit of passion, "it could happen again at any moment."

"Are you doing something to bring us to that pass, madame?"

"At this moment," she said, as though it were the most natural thing in the world to be talking of, "I am investing all my capital in gunpowder . . . to see whether we cannot blow this empire up, and blow up that pack of Bourbon rogues who are about to ascend to it."

"The unmentionable family," I added, quoting Constant this time.

"That whore," she said, referring to Constant—which led me to believe they had been lovers once.

From the first *salon* there came to us the music from the orchestra, but pretty far off, so it was not terribly hard to bear. Mme. de S. smoked awhile, and then she lay back upon the couch and did not speak. We were in perfect understanding.

"We have missed our great chance. Perhaps our only chance," she finally sighed. "A revolution is not accomplished in ten years, or in a century. It is a long accumulation of eras, of men. And we have now reached the end, and we are besmirching and besmearing it, bedaubing it with our own dirt, changing it, deforming it, and by doing so giving Humanity itself a slap in the face. Such disrespect for Man!" . . . But then she said to me, "And yet, Servando . . . what if we had respected those positions? what if everything had turned out as it ought to have done? would we, do you think, have achieved happiness? . . . I put myself in that position, and I ask myself, 'Could you live without these *soirées*? without these unbearable people? without these walls to have them all in? without a sense of self-importance in the midst of all this pettiness and meanness, this contemptible and despicable social-climbing?' And above all, and this is what worries me most, Servando, would those others, those who hate and want to destroy us, would they be any less mean and petty and contemptible than we are? ..."

She slowly stirred, and lay the ashes of her cigarette to rest in an urn standing by on long silver legs, and then sat back again. She wept for a moment, making hardly a sound. When her tears were spent she took out a v. fine linen napkin which she carried hidden about her in a spot I cannot remember, and patted her cheeks.

"There. Let us walk," she said finally, now once more cheerful and animated. "I have not shown you my apartment."

In Mme. de S.'s apartments. She presented me with a red flag on which is written the words of the "Marseillaise." She showed me her edition of the collected works of Voltaire bound in gold. She reclined on her bed, wrinkling its silks and laces, which crackled painfully, and said to me, "Prove to me that my opinion of the American man is true." And called me a reactionary royalist when I explained to her that my religious vows forbade my performing certain acts which any other man would perform most gladly. She got up. Gave me her hand with v. great courtesy and said, "It is of no import. It was only a gesture of hospitality which I extend to almost all my guests." And with her on my arm we went back to the first floor.

Constant and Mme. de R. were dancing without moving. Fanny and her "fiery" American disappeared behind a post. On the other side of the room, B. von H. and Alamán were v. peacefully talking, the both seated in great armchairs turned toward the dining room. Most of the women were outdoing each other in flirtations and coquetries. Mme. de S. made a polite curtsy before l'Abbaye Grègoire, who took her by the hands and lifted her up and guided her into the crowd.

Paris, Nov. 21

All day in the chapel. A while ago the Spanish Ambassador's private secretary arrived and tried to turn me to atheism with his arguments taken from a dreadfully bad book, just published. After I had reduced his arguments to powder, he begged five gold coins of me and left.

Not a soul in the chapel all day (save that hateful secretary). (Who on second thought probably lacks one.)

Paris, Dec. 4

B.v.H. has departed for the New World. He came to bid me good-bye. We spoke v. little, though at the end I said to him, "If you stay long there, surely we will see each other." "I have no doubt," he replied. And the moment was relieved with laughter . . . When I think of my America, it is of a place too beloved and too fervently desired to be real. Sometimes I ask myself whether it truly exists.

Paris, Jan. 17

Mme. de S. ordered to leave France! We could not even say good-bye. She sent a short message with a warm farewell, though, and promised we should meet again. Seemed filled with serenity. "I am certain that we shall soon see each other once more," she says. And then, "Put off your habits, as you should . . ." There is no need for me to be told that . . .

Paris, Feb. 4

Winter in Paris. Half the city's people have starved, and the other half frozen, to death. The other day I surprised a young woman drinking the communion wine from the chalice, so hard are things for the poor creatures. It nigh broke my heart, so I asked her to eat with me . . . Suicide by jumping from the bridges has become epidemic madness. Cordons of police stand along the bridges to prevent people from leaping the railings into the frozen rivers. But at times the police break ranks and rules and let them leap, where they are splattered on the frozen surface below . . . It is the cold, they say, which has set off this great wave of suicides . . .

Paris, Mar. 11

Have been walking all about the city. Went into a theater but then went on walking. Have seen how one is shunned and reproached for wearing a friar's habits in the street. Most Frenchmen believe it is shocking for a friar to leave his chapel, especially after the time we were hunted, as though we had been *black beasts*, through every forest in France. As soon as I come out into the street, people begin to look at me with anger and resentment. And when I cross one of their bridges, the guards always stand v. alert. I have been told that so many friars have committed suicide that beggars now gather at the mouths of the rivers to strip them of their habits and make themselves clothes, and even costumes for Lenten carnivals, from them.

Paris, Mar. 17

Winter keeps on. What to do. Chapel closed and yet the beggars try to enter by force. If they get in, they will break what little of value there is that is left. But if I leave them outside they will die of the cold . . . I open the chapel and the mob pushes in like a herd of cold wild beasts. They fall to their knees before the altar, though, and begin to pray. Though very distressed, I say a mass for them and make them sing the *Salve*. I have forgotten many words to the mass. If I stay much longer here I will lose my wits.

Paris, June 3

Lost my wits.

Here end the friar's notes. Still, we know that he remained in Paris until Napoleon's second entry, leaving then for Rome in "fleeing the robber of nations," as he himself phrased it. In Rome he asked permission to put off his habits and become a "worldly cleric." And when his petition was at first denied, he had his case sent to the Pope himself, who when he would not hear the case infuriated Servando. Servando therefore prepared an expedition from Sicily to take the Vatican and "cook the Pope's goose" as he himself phrased it. But by the grace of the Holy Spirit and two Sicilians, the expedition was found out, the crew wiped out, the still-friar taken prisoner and locked up in the galleys, and then, once more condemned to be burned.

But the very day of his latest "purification" Fray Servando escaped from his cell, though still today no one knows how he managed such a feat. The Pope, who was to attend the ceremony, was terribly put out, and since the fire had already been well stoked and lit, he saved it from going altogether to waste by having Servando's jailer and all the rest of the galley crew burned at the stake in it, including the confessor and the executioner-to-be . . . The ceremony done (though it lasted until well after dark), His Holiness made the sign of the cross as a mark of absolution of the victims and retired to the west wing of his *holy dwelling*. In the shadows he began to read over his breviary.

CHAPTER XXI

Which treats of the friar's contradictions.

I spent one season in Paris, and had become a bundle of vapors and melancholy (perhaps owing to the weather, for nowhere did it seem to have such influence on me as there), when *l'affaire Napoléon* broke in upon my funk. With a great brazen din he sacked kings, sent nobles and bishops packing, and overturned the state, so that I, who was a witness to all that, grew very inflamed and enthusiastic, and immediately identified my own aims with that new system's, which I believed were precisely what had been wanting. My own merits were in turn soon recognized by Napoleon himself, who placed me in an eminent position in the National Institute and then, even more high and capital, in the Grand National Council, convoked by him to establish Catholicism . . . But I was not long in being disabused of those great hopes for France, and for the little thief himself; for his having crowned himself Emperor, himself and his woman (not much better than his whore), filled me with misgivings, which were immediately proven well founded when it became obvious that France had perhaps changed governance, but in doing so done nothing but change one tyranny for another. And this new government even lacked the grace and charm of the one it had removed. For if before, a prisoner had been carried off to be hanged with iron hoops and chains a-jingle, to the sound of music, and with a certain *je ne sais quoi*, even respect; now, in contrast, he was kicked, shoved, and shouted to the scaffold. I saw, moreover, and with fearfulness, that the very same persons who before the Revolution had held high positions (not to mention their sycophants and lickspittles), now held them again, so that even that most macabre clergy of days past came again to hold parish churches and were even named again to bishoprics. I could see with my own eyes, then, how all the trash of the past rose to the top again, the waters being once more roiled. And therefore I began to fear for my life, just as before, and knowing myself watched, I started inventing a good thousand means of flight, one of which enabled me to cross Paris, make my way across all of France, and come at last to Rome. This was when Napoleon was celebrating the occasion of his first month as Emperor and was parading puffed up and smug through the city to the applause and acclaim of the crowds through which I slipped. So I escaped, and saved my skin . . . And this led me to see that the entire world of political action is a fraud and pretense, the demagoguery of charlatanism. And I felt great compassion for the French. *Poor country!, for certainly I never saw one airier, more fickle, or more given over to trivialities, than France. To sway them to one's will, one has only to speak to them poetically and to mix in, on the one hand witticisms and sharp ripostes, which they adore, and on the other ridicule, which is what they most fear. In France the men are like women, and the women like children.*[14]

[14]Fray Servando, *Apologia.*

ITALY

CHAPTER XXII

Which tells of the friar's negotiations.

And now, oh friar, tell of thy coming into Rome, of the hunger thou hadst suffered on thy travels thence, until at last came thy interview with the Pope, who, with a flourish of his hand, made thee Domestic Prelate and allowed thee at last to hang up thy hated habits. Speak and tell of all thy adventures in that land where the *Città è sanctu ma il populo corruto* . . . Tell how it came about that thy shoes were absconded with even as thou wast riding in a horse-drawn calash. And tell of what a confusion of streets there is, such a crisscrossing that many there are who get helplessly lost in them and never find their houses again, which is the reason that most of Rome's inhabitants walk about with a ball of string, whose one end they tie to the lintel post of their houses and which they unroll as they walk along, enabling them to find their way back home again. Speak, oh friar, of the terrible hunger that assails that Holy City, where the poor cut off parts of their bodies to throw them in the soup pot, and where there is such a rash of thieves and robbers that if one is not one, one is immediately made a saint . . . And of the sad want of saints there is in that city . . . Tell how thou hadst to leave, in a gang of alms beggars, and wrapped in a kind of diaper, because thou hadst been robbed of all thy possessions. And tell how thou cam'st to Florence, and of how excited thou wast to see in one of the city's parks a Mexican agave, ai, a cactus from thy home, caged, it is true, behind a fence, and hung about its neck with a little sign that gave its name. And then tell of the sadness that came over thee then, of how thou wast drowned in it, of how thou bethought'st thee of thy native land, now in the hands of Spanish burros, and how thou decided to set sail for there, now, at this moment, to free it by hook or by crook. And tell then of how thou left Leghorn and crossed to Genoa, at night always, so that thy nakedness would not be seen, until thou hadst woken to the fact that every man of that country was as naked as thyself (for such is the poverty there), and thou couldst see fit to travel by day. And crossing from Genoa, tell how thou cam'st to Barcelona and slipped into Madrid to ask aid of friends and thereby set about preparing for thy expedition of liberation. Speak, oh indefatigable friar, oh Prelate Domestic, speak, Servando, speak.

I will say nothing of my flight to Rome, nor of how I lived there, for I do not want to stir up in my memory such noisome and unpleasant thoughts. Suffice it to say that the Romans are, if not the poorest people that I have ever known, at least the most brazenly grasping. When one takes a coach there, one is charged for the getting up, then the sitting down, the window (if it is hot outdoors and one wishes it open), and then there is levied on one a charge for the air that comes in at that window, if any (for sometimes the heat is so stifling that the coach itself turns to smoke) ... I went to Rome thinking I should come to a holy city, but as soon as I had turned around twice in it, I knew I should see nothing but poverty and squalor in its people, who are plagued by the constant taxes, tariffs, and excises of the Church, which takes advantage of their ignorance to fill its coffers. That is what I saw there, as I had seen everywhere else besides.

SPAIN

CHAPTER XXIII

Which tells of my return to Madrid and of what I did there, until my coming to Los Toribios.

As soon as I set foot in Madrid I went off to see if I could find Tía Barbara (a court lady, but nonetheless noble, who for having aided me in my first escape I called Aunt). This lady kept up very good relations with Godoy, so that she could once again help me if I asked it of her. But she had died. So then, so as not to die myself (of hunger), I set about finding Dottore Traggia (an eminent sage of a most progressive temperament whom the King kept in his court because the good doctor knew the formula for a special drug which no other doctor had knowledge of, and which, so they said, was a panacea for impotency). I looked for him everywhere in the court, but found that he had died. What was there to do then but run off to find my two friends Cornide and Filomeno? And so I set off at once for their house, and coming to it I thought the sky had cracked and was tumbling about my ears, for the house was closed up and boarded. They had, it seems, both died. And so on account of so much dying I started to doubt, and I asked myself if it weren't I who had died, which was what made everything look so funereal to me. So I pinched myself and then pinched myself good again, and I went back to my garret, where I had taken lodging until I could find a better place. It was a place so filthy and every way repugnant that it had gone unrented in Madrid, a city so lacking in housing that even the nobility is forced sometimes to live under the bridges. But just as I had dropped off to sleep, which was no easy matter in that vermin-infested hole, the landlady burst into my apartment, if so it can be called, and woke me up with kicks and blows and a great waving of arms, saying to me in a most vulgar Italian (for the termagant hailed from Italy), that I had to be out on the instant, I could no more stay there unless I paid my rent. And she kicked me right downstairs and out into the street ... I began to wander, then, knowing not where to take myself to make my life easier. But then suddenly there came to me the idea of

going to visit the Count of Gijón's house, who I had been told was
in Madrid. So after walking aimlessly about all of one day, asking
the Peruvian's whereabouts, at last by pure luck I chanced upon
his house. I knocked at the door and as I waited I prayed to heaven
that he had not died.

The Count came to the door in person. I jumped with joy, right
into the house, as I recounted to him all my miseries and tribulations. And he also told me how he had been robbed naked, as he
said, by the thieving French and then how, with the peace of
Amiens, his sugar had lost so much in price that he wound up
eating it, and how poor he was as a result, and how poor also on
account of his not having given ear to my good counsel in the days
when we were together. And so we mutually consoled each other
somewhat. And I stayed on in the house of the Count from Quito.

And it fell out that while this sugar-baron and other great persons and I were talking in the salon of the Count's house one time,
the infernal León chanced to pass by at that very moment, and,
upon hearing me talk, thought he recognized the voice. He stormed
into the house, took up a candle and threw a light on all our faces,
and asked us who we were. But since I had suffered so much hunger for so long, my face was very drawn and unshapely, and since
I no longer wore my soutane, and the house (for being poor and
out of candles) in such shadows, he could not recognize me by
looking, so he marched away at the head of his troop of lickspittles.
But I knew perfectly well that León would not rest till he had
found me, so I immediately began preparations for yet another
flight. And in no more than a few moments Gijón and I were
skulking out of the back door of the house and feigning a calm and
carefree demeanor as we strolled away down the streets of Madrid.

But birds of a feather will find their flock, and since (as Saint
Thomas says) devils have no love for one another, though they
band together to do evil, so León, then, chose Marquina, the mayor
at court, to write out the most damnable order for my apprehen-
sion. This man was known as the hanging magistrate of Madrid,
and so brawling, wrangling, and thick-skulled was he, that in my
first visit to Madrid he'd been no better than a street-corner hood-
lum and cigar smoker at the Puerta del Sol. Surely he had done
Godoy some vile service, that Godoy had appointed him mayor at
court. *Men, the more they are browbeaten by their superiors, to
whom they minister, the more haughty and cruel they act toward
their inferiors. To this bullying dunce was entrusted, then, the*

carrying out of all orders whose administration necessitated despotism and outrageous physical abuse, and he distinguished himself in their performance. And it was the people of Madrid, whom he had so long made to cower, who upon Godoy's fall gave Marquina his just deserts by tearing him to pieces. If all despots enjoyed such success, I say, there would not be so many of them in the world.[15] And so it was that ourselves being already in the streets, the cannibal Marquina sent León a royal decree which only to that particular devil could be sent, for it stated that *For the good maintenance of the life and tranquility of their Royal Highnesses the King and Queen of Spain, Fray Servando Teresa de Mier y Noriega will with all due speed be made prisoner.* Such an order would have made even the most sedentary man to get up and move. And so one may well imagine the hue and cry set loose by León, who immediately filled the streets of Madrid with spies and posted an array of fat constables on the High Street and the street of San Juan de Dios, to stop and interrogate passersby, and more men still about the city, who, mobbing together directly in one's path, made one think that they were standing ready for an attack by a bull or a band of fierce highwaymen, or that Napoleon had invaded. How could the meek Peruvian and I have imagined that those battalions were set out to catch *us*. I myself asked one of the sheriff's men what all the to-do was over, for I could hardly be thought to suppose that it was over myself. "We are searching for the infamous Fray Servando Teresa de Mier," he answered me, which led the Count and me to ask no further impertinent questions, but rather to stroll very slowly and naturally along again, though our hearts were in our mouths. And just as we were about to turn the corner, we saw that army of catchpoles and sheriff's men suddenly begin to give us chase. So we began to run. But from the other direction too, there came at us another squadron of deputies, to close off our retreat. So we were very quickly surrounded. The Count of Gijón let out a cry so ear-splitting that for a moment our pursuers were stunned, and he disappeared through their ranks. But I was still surrounded by that multitude of Pharisees, and trotted off by them to the public jail.

There they flung me into a cell so low-ceiling'd that even sitting down I could touch it with the flat of my hands, and in which the lice and bedbugs were so thick that I could not see the cot when

[15]Fray Servando, *Apologia*.

I first entered, but just a writhing mass of verminous insects covering the whole pallet. There were no windows, but a deafening racket came in from somewhere, I could not tell where, which later I found was made by all the gypsies there who, being professional thieves, were lodged forever in that most respectable inn. The first night I lay not on the cot but on the floor to sleep, thinking I would gull the bedbugs, but they managed, I believe by my smell, to find me, and they came in columns like an army and climbed all over my body and began to prick and bite at it. So there I was, in utter blackness, cracking my skull on the low ceiling, dragging myself about in the cell on my belly and squashing lice and bedbugs every time I moved or touched the walls with my hands. The prison warden himself, when he paid me his morning visits, was wont to kill them with his boots, but the lice one day grew so furious with him for that, that they attacked him and scrambled all up his body, right up to his face, and they put out his eyes. The warden was maddened by this attack, and he flew shrieking from my cell, screaming, the great brute, that it was I that had poked out his eyes. The jailer noted the impossibility of that, for one could see the bedbugs' bites all over the warden's face, but the warden would have it no other way than that I, with my witchcraft, had incited them to commit the crime, for sure it was that they had not done the same to me. So therefore, as my punishment, they had me transferred to an even straiter cell, where I could not even sit me down, but had always to lie lengthwise and had not even room to scratch. In this cell, where a woman had been tortured until she finally died, there were no lice or bedbugs, for the gypsies in nearby cells were so hungry that they ate them all. These gypsies were in cells very much like mine, but some bigger, and all the day long they called out and complained and made a frightful racket. They sang ceaselessly. For example, to say good day to you they would stretch out a song that might begin by saying, "Hail to thee, blithe and pretty gypsy lad . . ." And by the time it ended, they would be singing "So good night to you . . ." for it would be three o'clock on the next morning. Sometimes, I believe in the afternoons, the cell door would be opened and a little tray would be dropped somewhere onto my person, from which would trickle some beef soup I would lap up so as not to starve to death. At those times a great row could be heard among the gypsies, brawling over the food, and it would always end with one of them cut by a razor across the breast, or in an even worse place.

Little by little the gypsies' lice came into my cell, and soon enough I was covered with them, so that once I thought my body might be producing them, or that I was slowly evolving into a lower form of life. My blanket moved of itself, and many times the whole cot. I asked for a pail of water, and in it I would deposit the lice and bedbugs one by one, but in a very short while the bucket was full, and my hair no less infested than before.

Then winter came. My clothes had rotted on my body, so I had no alternative than to cover myself with another blanket. And then indeed I thought I had been covered in a fleece of vermin, for I could feel the *bugs* walking all over my body and strolling even across my lips and into my ears until I thought my eardrums would bust. At last they ate up the whole blanket, so then the cold began to eat at me for fair. Alone, crushed between the walls of that cell not a cell but a living tomb, I could not even tell what time had passed. And for clothes having nothing but a rag I covered my head with so as not to perish of the cold, I brooded on the possibilities of resisting further. And I marveled at thinking how, the worse luckless circumstances grew, and the harder life got, the more determined a man became to overcome it, and how, the meaner and pettier our fellow men were, and the more intolerable our lots, the stronger and more potent the ideas that came and allowed us to combat them. But what most maddened and enraged me were not the lice eating me alive, nor the babble and screaming of the gypsies, nor the cold piercing me, nor the walls every moment growing closer in upon me, nor the nonexistent food, nor the jailers' foul physical treatment of me (for at best I considered them but animals with no souls, so they could not truly insult me), but rather what most maddened and saddened me, I say, was having no good book to read a thousand times if need be, or a pen and paper to write on it, right out to the edge, the flocks of ideas boiling within me. That, and that alone, was anguish to me, though I confess it awoke other anguishes as well, and so I would protest against the lice and rail against the cold, scream at the troop of degenerate gypsies for silence, berate my jailers, throw the tray to the floor . . . and wish sometimes for death. But I never resigned myself to waiting for it there . . . And that was my state, when one day the new prison warden came to me, and said, "Come, thou art to make a declaration." But I answered him, "I have nothing to declare, except that I have done nothing." And he said, "Come at any rate, it will do thee good . . ." So, if for nothing else than to get out of that cell which was a constant torture to me, even if only for a moment of respite, I finally gave in to his entreaties. But once out of it, I found I could not stand. All the strength had left my body, and the lice had sucked out my blood. I could not even remember how to walk. With a beard that now reached my chest, and my body naught but a rickety skeleton, I should think my figure would have inspired pity in the devil himself; and so it must have been, for the warden threw an old coat over me and two guards took me, one at each elbow, and helped me to the judges' seat.

The judges were seated around a very long and very high table. There were about twenty men, or perhaps forty, all white-bearded and black-robed, so that to one unlike myself (who had passed through so many slings and arrows of this sort already) they might have been a most daunting and impressive sight.

"The accused will state his name," said the judges, in a most echoing unison.

"You well know who I am, all of you, and what my name is, unless that petty minister León has given orders that it be changed," responded I.

"Dost thou swear to tell the truth, the whole truth, and nothing but the truth, so help thee God?" the absurd judges continued.

"Do you?" I replied. "Let us go on and waste no more time."

"If thou continuest as thou hast begun, speaking so disrespect-fully, we will send thee to a worse jail yet."

"I do not believe I could be disrespectful to you, for you are worthy of no respect. If you were, you would hardly be acting out this ridiculous pantomime, or be accomplices in the crimes continually committed against my person. And as for sending me to a more terrible prison, you would have to have one built, for there is none such now standing anywhere on earth."

"Art thou a priest?"

"I was forcefully made to be one. To please my family, who believed that that office held the greatest nobility to which a man might aspire. My parents are humble people, provincials if you will, and know nothing of the world . . ."

"Recite thy Paternoster."

"Have a preacher to asses such as yourselves recite it. Not I, who am a Doctor of Theology."

"Servando Teresa de Mier, thou art accused of conspiring against the sacred lives of their Royal Majesties. Thou art also accused of being an inveterate and incorrigible jailbreaker and of the crime that thou art led by an overweening passion to seek the independence of New Spain in the continent of America North and South," and here the voices of the judges cracked and cawed like tin drums, "and of having composed songs sung to thy jailers in which they were painted as burros and jackasses. And of having incited the bedbugs, by black magic and necromancy, to a mortal hatred of our reverend prison warden, leading them thereby to put out his eyes or, failing that, to take his life. Thou art likewise accused of having performed a mass for six *reales* when the price is four. Of having entered church with a muddy foot. Of having composed bawdy satires in which Godoy and Her Royal Majesty enacted the principal roles. Of having insulted the King's mother. Of having complained of too much heat in Madrid. And of having complained of the cold. Of having scratched an ear before an archbishop. Of having been indicted by two viceroys: Branciforte and Revillagigedo. Of having named Queen Maria Luisa as being one of the three royal breeding mares of Europe. Of having no religious sentiment, for thy not having kissed the prebendaries' hems in Las Caldas. Of having renounced the divine disciplines practiced in our convents. Of having criticized the holy relations between the novices and friars of the convents. Of not have put thyself at the mercy of His Royal Highness, Prince León. Of having commented that it was a pity the *Literary Gazette* should be printed on such stiff paper, or else it could have been put to better use by the people of Madrid. Of not having received the title of doctor. Of having complained of mistreatment carried out against thyself by thy jailers of the holy prisons of all Spain . . . Oh, and thou art also accused of having thirty years ago read a sermon which spoke out against the apparition of the Virgin of Guadalupe . . . And as all this concerns the life and serenity of their most Royal Highnesses, therefore thou wilt be held incommunicado, and in solitary confinement, in the cells of the Royal Public Prison. Therefore we hold thee guilty, strip thee of thy priestly habits, and send thee, for the term of thy life, to the prison of Los Toribios, in Seville." So spoke the judges.

At which I said, "Nothing more clearly demonstrates my innocence than this verdict of guilty . . . I will not burden you with my theory of the apparition of the Virgin of Guadalupe, for I know only too well that you will not understand it. Nor will I waste some useless space of time trying with the voice of reason to convince those persons who are paid precisely so that they will punish those who indulge in rationality. Let me then only say that I have never conspired against their Majesties the King and Queen of Spain, not because I have not wanted them dead often enough, which would do the Spanish people such a world of good, but rather because I think it not worth my while to conspire against their lives if you and all the train of opportunists, slaves, and lickspittles were to go on living, for it is you and the other courtly sycophants who sustain the throne. And so since my strength is not so great as all that, I have not conspired, though if I *could* cooperate in a small way someday . . . I entered this jail a young man, and I am let go to another one an old man with death breathing down my neck. Sick and crippled. My crime has been to be an American and not to have shared those false and treacherous religious beliefs believed in not even by those who invented them, but only used, then and now, to bleed the people and subjugate them. I now see no great import in combatting that fraud, but only in combatting those who perpetrate it. That is the difference between the idealistic friar you first imprisoned and this man standing before you now who hungers only," and here my voice rose and I pounded my chest, killing some thousand lice, "only to see the Americas free of all the plagues, taxes, and humiliations imposed on them by Europeans, and who knows that this can only be achieved by total independence."

In short, toward the end of January the rogue León's order came down, to have me carried off to Los Toribios, in Seville . . . Five or six days before my departure, the Inquisitor somehow managed to have me carried down to the infirmary where I could be given the Briefs of Rome. To go down I took off all my clothes and put on instead a suit of clothing made for me and given to me by the Vicar of Madrid. The lice and bedbugs ceased on the instant to trouble me, for they set upon the clothes I had taken off instead. *They shaved me there in the infirmary, and I began to look more human than ursine. But I was still gravely ill. Nonetheless, one day very early in the morning I, along with a sheriff's man, was made to board a calash escorted* by one troop of foot soldiers and another of cavalry. And within a very short while of our setting out, the sun grew so fierce and hot that my ears burst *and I was about to die of the pain, and not being able to wait for the mallow*

*water to cool (for that was the only medication they would allow
me), I plunged my whole head into the pot of boiling water, and
I lost all my skin from that part I stuck into the water, right until
today. Not until after we came finally to Andújar was my cure
complete.* And we wended single file to the prison of Los Toribios,
in Seville, *traveling through snow, so that we were sixteen days
on the road,*[16] and many of the soldiers froze to death.

CHAPTER XXIV

On the prison of Los Toribios and the friar's chaining up.

Escorted by soldiers, the friar rode along inside his coach. The sun
was so fierce it pulverized stones. From time to time could be
heard the wailing of a soldier as he burst. Thus they passed through
Dos Castillas, where they cooked up a soup out of prehistoric
bones. Then they plodded through snowfields that melted at their
footsteps. They crossed Seville and came at last to the prison of
Los Toribios. "He is sentenced to life," said the sheriff's man. And
so the friar was sent to the farthest cell in the prison, and there
they began to chain him up.

From his neck-iron was hung a thick length of chain, and this
was the *main* or *central chain,* which then was passed twice
around his waist, welded to his feet, and then brought up and
clinched to its starting point, his neck. This chain then was passed
through two iron eyebolts, like spurs hung onto his neck-iron, and
these eyebolts in turn were transfixed by a heavy iron bar sunk
into the floor of the cell. Thus the friar was pinned to the ground,
and had always to lie there prone, never able again to rise. Another,
somewhat finer, chain was linked onto the central chain at the
friar's waist, wrapped several times around him there and then
hauled upwards, straight for Servando's head, where it was looped
about his forehead like some iron diadem, then brought down again
to his feet where it clad them in ferrous slippers, so that the friar

---

[16]Fray Servando, *Apologia.*

could not move his head or feet either to one side or the other. Just where this chain made a circlet about his brow, another chain was looped to it, and this chain then was led down, down the entire length of his body and wrapped about his knees like iron garters to hold up his stockings. It made eight turns about each knee and then was passed back upwards toward his neck, wrapped rather unceremoniously around that part of his anatomy, a choker-like necklace indeed, and then guided downwards again and tied in a great bow-knot about the friar's waist. Thus the friar could in no wise move or twist his knees and had also to keep his breathing shallow, for the walls of his stomach had been very tightly cinctured into a mailed fortress of amazing straitness. From this iron corset depended ten chains of the same thickness (which was rib-bony, but exceedingly strong). The first of this gauzy fabric of chains wholly swaddled the friar's nose, passing three times about it, the length of the nose making such a diapering possible; and then that chain made its way over to one of his ears, pierced it like a hoop earring, made ten quick loops about it (though perhaps more, since for a fact the jailers could hardly count their own toes), and then took passage for the other ear, which it filleted only nine times (as later reports have stated) and from there went across and linked itself to the friar's two eyeteeth, wove in and out through all his dentition like an iron picket-fence to his tongue, imprisoned the tongue at seven distinct points and then at last was firmly anchored to his uvula by an intricate sailing-knot—so that this chain prevented the friar from talking or from breathing through his nose—nor, of course, did he any longer smell. The second of the ten ribbonlike chains made straight for his left big toe, twined its iron prison about it, and then made similar cells for all the other toes of that foot. That incarceration complete, the chain was made to form a plastering over the iron wall already built about the foot, so that at last not a glimmer of flesh could be seen, but only the metallic dullness of the interlinked chain, which made it impossible for the friar to wiggle even a single toe of that foot, much less the foot itself, so heavily armored was it. The next chain took its heading on the other foot, and followed the same route, so that both the friar's feet were rendered immobile. The fourth chain was bound about the prisoner's legs in such a way as to weave a fabric between them and to give them the appearance of one single metallic braid, and the veins of his two legs were so compressed that the friar's circulation was considerably impaired.

But from there the chains went directly to the sparse hairs of the prisoner's head, and there they branched out into thousands and thousands of tiny, tiny, chains, so small as to be almost invisible, and whose function was to imprison each and every follicle of the condemned man's head. Thus the prisoner was imprisoned even by his scalp, by a fine-mesh headpiece which gave him such a supernatural air that it frightened even the jailers themselves. Another chain departed along the same route the other four had gone, and it reinforced, by doubling all the knots, ties, welds, cinctures, windings, plaitings, and interweavings of all the others, so that there should be no way in the world that any of the bonds should fail.

Let us glance now at the sixth chain, which had a very special purpose. This chain went directly from the friar's head, bisecting his forehead, and continued downward to twine about his testicles, first one, which it encircled several times, binding it excruciatingly tightly, and then the other. That done, the chain continued upwards through the channel between the friar's two buttocks and was tightly attached to the central chain, so that it was extremely difficult for the prisoner to perform any of his bodily functions, though fortunately these were rendered pretty thoroughly unnecessary by the almost total lack of nourishment meted to the friar. The next, that is, seventh, chain likewise encircled the friar's testicles, but without binding them really, and then made a series of twining circles about the friar's male member, so that when that part of him was fully imprisoned it looked like some mailed, metallic serpent of countless ridges or very pronounced rings. And from the constant friction of these links, the friar's imprisoned member was in a constant state of excitement, which caused him great mortification. Therefore the eighth chain was conducted directly to that locale and, wrapping twice about the stiffened tool, tied it down tightly to one of the chains about his thigh so that at last the friar, obviously, in order to move his organ had to move his thigh, and to move his thigh, to move those chains, and to move the chains had to move the iron rings to which they were attached, and to move the iron rings had to move the iron bars embedded in the prison cell's floor, and to move the iron bars had to move the cell, and to move the cell had to move the entire prison. So to prevent this possibility the next chain went out in a zigzag all across the prisoner's abdomen, and onto this chain were embroidered a network of tiny chains which stretched out across his loins and torso and were stitched into the chains of his neck, shoulders, and thighs so as to make at last one seamless-appearing tunic, impenetrable, and from this in turn the chains went out to knit about his toes and from there to make mail gloves for his fingers. The friar was so besuited, then, that he could not manage a simple movement of his fingers or his toes or any other part of his extremities. And yet this chain too had its appendages, which went out to the friar's eyes and there ramified even further, so that minuscule, infinitesimal chains prisoned the friar's eyelashes, eyebrows, and even, leaving no possibility of signal or escape, the hairs of the nostrils of his nose. The friar could no longer even blink.

But the tenth and last chain remained free. It snaked out from where all the others' paths began, but it hung in the air. Its only function was as orientation to the jailers, so that they might know, more or less, where the various body parts and organs of the prisoner were. His mouth, for example, to give him food to eat ... And yet since his entire face was masked by that metal mesh of chains, it was impossible to make out any single feature, so that finally the prison warden simply ordered the prisoner's soup slopped "somewhere about there," which meant the friar's food was poured approximately where his face was and then the liquid mess trickled through the intricate web of iron chains and chainlets and—sometimes—dripped at last into his mouth. Not *sometimes*. Rarely ... So the friar learned to absorb nourishment through the windows of his nose. At last a jailer (who hated Servando because upon his entrance into the prison the friar had said to him, "I had thought there were only bulls who worked at Toribios, but thou art nothing but a cow") decided the friar's bechaining was altogether too easily broken out of, and he laced new strings of chains through and across the old, so that finally the dungeon was nothing but one great ball of iron wrapped tight onto itself and so huge that it pressed against the walls and almost reached the ceiling. To this great metal mass were bound, on orders of the prison warden, four enormously thick chains welded first to the floor on which the friar was laid and then to the four corners of the ceiling, so that the friar, seen in the shadows of that windowless and doorless keep, looked like some gigantic spider caught upside down in its own web and oozing some dully glowing viscid syrup.

And what of the life of that man locked forever inside that suffocating web? Fray Servando had had much experience in adapting to prisons. This one was hard, then, but hardly impossible. He learned to take in air through the network of chains, and learned to suck into himself the filthy noisome water dashed at him through the metal mesh that hid his face. The soup served (if such a sloshing can be said to be serving) to him of a Monday (always in the afternoon) bedewed his face of a Saturday early in the morning. And by the changes in temperature he experienced through the layers of iron, the heating up or cooling off of his bands, the friar could tell when day came and when retired, when night fell and when withdrew to make way for the dawn. And with the years, penned up in that terrible cage, he would even at last have learned to see—through the iron chains and through the roof—to see the sky, the sun, the vultures slowly circling over the prison's bulk . . . But as he grew thinner and thinner, so thin that his bones were even shrunken, his bechainment grew more tolerable, and he could even now, once in a while, move his diaphragm a bit, and breathe . . .

And in spite of his state—hanging there like a spitted tortoise in its shell—in spite of his jailers' constant watchfulness, and the fleets of ships that came laden with iron chains and bars to be heaped atop a body by now skeletal in the extreme, in spite of the terrible rigors of that confinement, something was lacking. The hellish punishment had overlooked one item. The prison was still imperfect, for something exploded out from that web of thick chains and made it all futile, petty, mean. *Powerless to imprison* . . . For the friar's thought was free. Leaping over chains and walls, it flew, though briefly, yet still unfettered, outside the dungeon, outside the jail, and even when it rested, it never ceased inventing methods of escape, and ways of wreaking vengeance. Thought, escaping as light as mist through the ironwork, ran right under the jailers' noses, fled far away, back in time, to the sandy expanses and rocky peaks and escarpments so white they seemed painted, and it strolled and wandered through cool labyrinthine groves of prickly pear and sage and then made its way into the city of never-ceasing bells. It was sitting on the benches, watching soldiers wrapped in their ponchos march by and hearing hawkers hawking tamales to eat and huaraches for his tired feet . . . Oh, the chains were useless. The friar came and went as he pleased, when and where he pleased, and time passed as easy as could be, for he was free, not careworn and exhausted as in the other days (all his other days, in fact), and now he could do as he pleased. And had it not been for those hateful chains that squeezed his lips shut and penned in his teeth and fettered his tongue—if one could have seen through that armor-plate of chains to his face—one might have seen, like some marvelous little bird, Fray Servando's smile—a smile peaceful, serene, and inspired by some imperturbable and inextinguishable tenderness . . .

But meanwhile the guards were whispering among themselves, fearfully, weaving dark tales about the friar. They saw that massy ball, itself wrapped in constant shadow. They watched its gleams. And the guards quaked in fear. And that fear woke still other fears in them. And so on top of the friar's chains they heaped more chains, and more chains on top of those, to make a grand new web of iron over all. And yet the jailers still feared the friar's boldness and intrepidity, for they told themselves stories of his powers, and they also feared their own part in that cruel and demonic handi-work of enchaining. So they requested a new shipment of chains, which was brought over on two brigantines from England. And that entire cargo of shining new-forged iron links was heaped atop the by-now rusty worsted ball of chain. The walls began to bulge. The prison staggered under its ferrous load. And yet the jailers still feared. They huddled together trembling in the passageway. And then they began to fear their very fears. They huddled in corners and pointed terrified in the direction of the friar's far-off dungeon. At night sometimes a guard would go mad of it, and then reports would be heard in the countryside about, of shouts and screams from the friar's cell, and the rattling of chains, and that the walls (and this part, indeed, was true) would creak . . . So new brigantines came, wallowing through the sea with their loads of chain. And as there were many storms and tempests, and the weight of the cargo very great, not a few came to rest on the bottom of the ocean, so that this became a new charge against the friar—witchcraft, and pacts with the devil to call up the winds—which of course made the fearful jailers' fear even worse. But other ships did make it safe to port. And their chains were hauled by countless numbers of the faithful to the holy prison where the accursed prisoner was held. And those new chains heaped on new chains. And then, at last, there was no one to take the friar's food to him, for every spare pair of hands was enlisted to carry chain. Fray Servando would have to eat chains if he ate at all, for the labor was feverish—day and night the only sound to be heard was the carrying up of chains into his tower and the tossing them atop the now distantly buried body . . . Yet the jailers still feared . . . But at last the moment came. The guards at first heard a creaking, creaking, creaking of the walls, and they cowered in terror and fright. They ran to take shelter in safer spots, and they tremblingly threw their arms about one another, in the lowermost cells of the prison. But still the sound of creaking and cracking followed them. Maddened with terror, they sought still safer refuge. But the very walls were splitting about them. Some strange force or power was at work, and the world was unraveling at the seams. And suddenly there came a creaking more horrendous than any ever heard before, and explosions like the eruption of great mountains buckling, and the walls caved in, the ceilings caved in, the prison itself was caving in. The weight of the friar's chains had at last overfreighted the camel, and the prison building came tumbling down about their ears, for not one link more could it hold up. And as the rock and rubble of the uppermost stories began to fall, it took everything with it that lay in its path. And the friar, still chained, came tumbling down too, through a hail of stone and rock and the shriek of iron shackles twisting and giving way. So it was that all that mass of iron collapsed, floor by floor, turning the prison cells to rubble and crushing them to earth, and by the way squashing, with one blow, all the trembling, frightened jailers. Upon hearing the shrieking of the world about him giving way—iron fetters, rock walls, and bars— the prison warden started to run out across the fields, but a great block of stone catapulted from the buckling walls caught him on the back of the neck and stopped him cold, and then as the friar departed the prison, he crushed that jailer too into powder . . .

The prison, then, was reduced to chaotic and indistinguishable debris, although Fray Servando was still in chains; and since the prison was situated on the slope of a hill, the friar and all his iron trappings began to roll like a great Alpine avalanche, though somewhat more clanking, down the hill, destroying villages and burying whole towns. He rolled all across Seville, running the Guadalquivir out of its banks, pulverizing reeds, toads, and marsh birds, and slopping marsh water everywhere. Then he rolled on toward Madrid, and razed it to the ground. From there he retraced his path, rolling over the Escorial and knocking it into separate stones, leaving not a tree of its gardens standing. He ravaged Dos Castillas, and then rolled down through Cádiz, flooding the whole port. Thus the friar rolled along within the bonds of his chains, which now were beginning to fray and part, so that tatters of his chains were left in his wake. He rolled along until he slammed, still like an avalanche, through the Sierra de León, scattering links. And he rolled along, now somewhat unsteadily (for now only the *mother chain* remained), until he came to the sea. But first he had bumped across some rocky ridges, and the iron eyebolts at last split free. And so the friar fell, free at last, into the waves, which were so choppy and rough and covered with foam that they never ceased, not even for one second, to crash both great and tiny sea crabs against the imperturbable rocks and boulders of the coast. And crush them to powder, too.

CHAPTER XXV

Which tells of my journey to Portugal.

And I fell into the water. And my cassock and cape, being wet through, became so heavy that they made fair to submerge me, so that to save myself I rapidly wriggled out of my vestments and, naked, began to attempt to clutch at and grapple myself to the waves, for there was naught else to hold fast to. And so there was I, calling for a plank to save my life on, when a great roar and bellowing began all over the ocean. The waves grew even more angry, and they began to take on a bright crimson cast. For a while all that could be heard thereabouts was that frightful roar, which sounded as though it came from depths of the inferno to that moment unsuspected even by me . . . And when I managed once more to come out onto the surface of the water and float awhile, in the midst of that dreadful tumult and confusion of sound and furious water, I saw a naval battle the likes of which had never been imagined, at least until then, by men or historians, and within but a very few strokes from where I was swimming in the broth. There were three immeasurably large fleets, or *armadas*, all very well arrayed for the battle. The Royal English Fleet, the Spanish Armada, and the French Flotilla, and these two last began to hurl grapeshot at the first. But then, behold, the English Navy takes aim with its cannon at the source of the cannonade, fires, and the Spanish Armada is decimated, though not before first having run up its colors so as quickly to strike them as a sign of surrender, for thus treacherous and cowardly are the Spaniards at war. And then the combat between the French and English sailors is truly joined, and it seems to go on for many hours, until at last flames begin to consume the French ships and then a deafening series of explosions is heard, and the fleet disappears, to the great pleasure of the sharks lurking about.

All this was like a nightmare to me, and I would even have believed it to have been so, had it not been for the screams and cries of the crews moments before they sank forever into their briny pickling, and had it not been that I had heard Admiral Nelson, in person, give out such a shriek, seconds before he died, that I deduced on the instant that it had to have been the Great Admiral who had been caught by a shot or charge from the conquered fleet, for in the Royal English Navy no sailor would have been allowed to scream such a scream, unless it had been the man who had set that prohibition in force. The English sailors died in silence, and when the sharks aimed the thousand blades of their mouths at the sailors, the most they ever said (the sailors, I mean), was *God save the King* (who of course ran no risk himself of not being saved, being well out of the fighting), and then the wild sharks made sure the sailors themselves were not saved . . . But the most important part of the matter was, for me, not that explosion of the ships of the two fleets, and not the hundreds of keels that had been sent to the bottom, and not the soft cries of *God save the King* from those English sailors whom nothing, not even God, could save. The most important thing of all was, for me, that I grabbed a floating plank or spar or some other indistinguishable piece of wood that had been floating by, I seized on it like grim death, and kicking along as best I could, and paddling with first one hand and then the other, I tried to get myself out of that red-pink sea, wherein the wild creatures of the depths were dying of overingestion, foundering in their own element. So, paddling and floating through a sea of corpses, for often there were so many dead bodies the waves were of human flesh, not water, I made my way shoreward and, as day was breaking on the next morning, I hailed the high coasts of Portugal.

PORTUGAL

CHAPTER XXVI

Which gives some idea of what Portugal is.

There is naught but silence in this city. Silence and starvation. I
have just walked the entire length of the avenue called Aurea and
then down Augusta Street, and I have been much taken by the fact
that no-one speaks. People walk along in silence, and though they
meet up with a friend or acquaintance, no-one says hello, and not
even in Las Delareslas, which is the center of the commercial dis-
trict of the city, did I chance to hear one solitary voice. Such silence. And what a difference between this, Villa Lisboa, or Lisbon,
and noisy Madrid. But this city is no more pleasant or welcoming
than that. In Madrid people veritably feed on shouting and crying,
but here one would think poverty and hunger were so great that
they do not allow even shouting. The hunger is so terrible that a
person who so much as speaks is considered as rich as King Croe-
sus. And thus it happened that just as I was coming into the city
it occurred to me that I ought to ask directions, so I did, of a parish
priest, who rather than answer me pointed with his finger, and
then suddenly I was surrounded, I knew not how, for it made my
head go 'round, by a crowd of beggars—so utterly silent and in rags
that for a second I believed myself hallucinating, which I might
have been, for I had just crossed through all the Bay of Biscayne
on a floating spar rendered toothpick by the explosion that had
sunk its ship . . .

What does one do to survive in a place where one cannot even
beg for alms aloud because speaking is considered a squandering
of riches? What does one do . . . I was walking along lost in that
sort of inward interrogation when suddenly there came to my ears
the blast of trumpets and a roll of drums, and though at first I
thought my ears were playing tricks on me, I was satisfied enough
with them when I saw coming along over the Tajo Bridge a great
army of soldiers that to a stirring drum cadence was entering the
city, like a holy procession turned profane. Suddenly all the "children" of the town woke up. And it was war. And their voices came

back to them—women, in a last profligacy of strength, scream out, and the men, in one last extravagance, run out into the streets and try to turn the invasion back . . . French troops have overrun Portugal. Napoléon, the captain (or corporal) of the thieving horde, the thief himself of power, has promised himself that he shall rule the world, and so there is at least the consolation that you, Lisbon, may feel proud to have been included therein.

And all I could do was survive. I ran (I confess) along on the coattails of my hunger, which was chasing the marauding troops pell-mell, for they possessed the sustenance I lacked. I signed on into the Portuguese Army. And we marched off for Zaragoza. Always fighting, in my role as royal chaplain, against the bellicose French. And devouring without scruple anything which fell into my hands . . . Until I was taken prisoner, for then I completely forgot my obsession with sustenance and took up again my old obsession—escape.

And so I escaped. And I came to England . . . And here I am now, bumping continually against the corners and fronts of buildings, knocking against my fellow pedestrians, for this accursed fog, in which all ghostly misty London is befogged, is a thing I fear I shall never grow used to.

ENGLAND

CHAPTER XXVII

Which relates the new friendships made by the friar and his subsequent escape to America.

Orlando, that strange woman, has taken me to the royal *salons*. And I have met all the noblest persons of the court (all the *rank*, as one might say, to judge by their smell).

That rankest of them all, the female skunk over there with her hair sticking out, is the Queen.

"The Queen," said Orlando, that strange woman, to me. And I bowed to her.

We marched in past a file of dukes and between a rank of counts, all of whom I greeted most personably. And then we mingled into a choir of grand ladies.

"I wonder who that man is that Orlando has brought?" murmured the grand ladies.

"A person from the hot lands," they answered themselves. And broke into laughter.

"Oh, she feels a great stirring for the nations of the sun. Was it not in Egypt, in the middle of the desert, where her change operation was performed?"

"Indeed it was. And from what I can gather, there were nothing but camels about."

"My God!"

Orlando, that strange woman, took my hand, and we passed through hundreds of great rooms.

"I never thought this palace was so grand."

"It occupies a good half of Great Britain. This was all arable land before."

"Where are you taking me?"

"Where might I be taking you, if not to the arms of a woman?"

Orlando, that strange woman, has led me through all the public rooms of the palace. Then through a room made entirely of windows. Then through more *salons*. And now we are standing before the woman.

"Withdraw, Orlando." And Orlando disappears behind the curtains.

"Do you not know who I am?" the lady asks me. She is swathed from head to foot in a black mantle, and only her face may be seen.

There is no doubt that this is a woman of the world. It is evident in the way she sits, and because both her arms and her throat are covered with diamonds that brilliantly sparkle, so that sitting there in her setting of black curtains, sable couch and chairs, dusky carpets, and dressed in her black mantle, one would think her a lighthouse emerging from the gloom.

"No," I reply.

"Lady Hamilton."

"Madam."

"I know that you were a witness to the battle in which my husband died. That is why I have sent for you. I want you to tell me all the details. Tell me how he died. Tell me whether it is true that he cried out. And whether he called my name. And whether he was thrown into the sea. And whether sharks ate him. Ay, tell me what the sharks were like . . . Tell me, tell me everything, and I will pay you an ounce of gold for every word."

Lady Hamilton clapped slowly twice and a most elegantly dressed man instantly appeared, with a book and a quill pen.

"You may begin," the lady said to me.

"Well, madam . . ."

"Two," said the gentleman, making an annotation in his book.

"I hardly know where to begin."

"Six."

"Oh, you are squandering my money, Fray Servando. Come to the point."

"I was there, it is true, but a good way off."

"Eleven."

"Go on! Go on!"

And the friar, in a wealth of detail, began to tell the story. He talked all that evening, through the night, and into a part of the next morning. Lady Hamilton listened spellbound, and, after some two or three hours into the history, she clapped again twice slowly and three very gallant-looking young men entered from behind the drapes. All three were caressed and petted at once by the elegant hands of the lady. And the friar went on talking, faster and faster, in a great rush of fantasy.

"The ships were like great unleashed eagles on the waves, plunging and rising again! . . . And then they began to vomit forth fire, a red fire that rose up to the sky."

"Oh, go on. Go on!"

And the three young men were all undressed at once by the lady's elegant hands.

". . . The three fleets sailed toward each other. And Admiral Nelson came out on deck and raised one arm, which upon the instant was sheared from his body by a shell, and he ordered the battle begun . . ."

"Yes! Go on!"

"The Admiral paced back and forth . . . The Admiral, um . . . The Admiral . . . The Admiral . . ."

"Oh, do not waste my money so!"

"Thirteen thousand two hundred," droned the secretary's voice.

". . . So then, from the Admiral's powerful frame there issued such a howl . . ."

"Closer! Come closer!" panted Lady Hamilton.

"Thirteen thousand two hundred twelve."

". . . A strange cry, like a lion struck by a thousand bolts of lightning. And I say a thousand bolts of lightning, so please note them as three thousand words, since all the lightning bolts were different."

"Sixteen thousand two hundred twenty. Including the thousand lightning bolts," intoned the scrivener.

"All three at once!" pleaded Lady Hamilton.

"Oh! Uf! Whoops!" heaved the three young men.

"Go on! Go on!" breathed Lady Hamilton.

And dawn was breaking . . .

Orlando, that strange woman, and I were conversing on one of the palace's many terraces. Orlando, that strange woman, is the person to whom I most gratefully owe the fact of my not having died of hunger in this distant, foggy country. Orlando, that strange woman, quite literally tumbled across me one day when I'd eaten nothing but fog. And she took me to her palace. She gently conducted me to her bed and laid me down to rest. But then she attempted to bother me, by employing a score of sweet wiles and words of flattery, all of which I put off. This in turn awakened in Orlando, that strange woman, even more interest in me. "I am of royal blood," she said to me. "I come from a line of kings and queens. I was born three hundred years ago."

"You seem remarkably well preserved, then, madam."

"I was born a man . . . of that person I have kept only the name."

"I am glad to know that."

"Just before my twentieth birthday I became a woman."

"Does that often happen in England?"

"My life has been nothing but searching and searching and searching, and never finding."

"That explains your having lived so long."

"And you—who are you? But hush, do not tell me. I know already. My heart broke when I saw you bumping into every wall in your way. It is so hard to accustom oneself to this constant fog— but take heart, for once you have grown used to it you will find it not so great a nuisance, though it is forever an intolerable bore . . ."

"Very well," she said. "It seems you have made your fortune."

"Things did not go ill for me with the lady."

"Then you no longer have need of me."

"You are so straight-spoken."

"When one has lived three hundred years . . ."

"Well, in fact, I believe I do have need of you. With this money I am going to equip and man an expedition to invade México, but I know no-one versed in those matters. There you might be of great service to me."

"And you accuse me of being straight-spoken. What then are you?"

"I have had no time to consider the question. My life has been one long escape from prison. Only to fall again into another."

"Then you should have had much time to consider."

"I almost never considered anything but how to escape."

"I like you, Fray Servando. Tomorrow I will introduce you to every rebel of the age. Every malcontent. Every revolutionary. Really, I like you very much . . . Oh, and do not fail to pay Lady Hamilton another visit. She is a most frustrated woman since her husband died. Nothing has any savor for her unless it comes through her ears, by listening to stories of her husband's death, and in fact she can never achieve pleasure of that other sort either unless it too comes in at her ears, by listening to its hoarse sounds. That may be a proof of her fidelity. We should not criticize what we have no knowledge of, or do not understand. *Au revoir.*"

■ ■ ■

"Father White."

"How do you do. A pleasure to meet you, sir."

"The pleasure is entirely mine, Fray Servando! I know who you are already, and where you come from, and the nature of your 'cause.' I was a Spaniard, but I have even translated my name into English! Before, I was called José Blanco. But I hate the very mention of Spain! And I will go on hating it, so long as it continues to be that vile mudhole of a monarchy it is now! I hate Catholicism and its lascivious rites! Catholicism is a crime against Christ! Our Savior could never have imagined the sacrileges committed in His name! It is horrid and bestial! Degrading! . . . But you will see how we sweep them away! I am so very glad to have met you! You shall be my collaborator in my newspaper! *El Español*, I call it! All the best people from Spain collaborate on it. None of them live there of course! But come! Come, let me present you to a flaming rebel! Angrier even than I, so people say! Ha ha ha! . . . A gentleman one can trust implicitly, Fray Servando . . . May I present Sr. Mina. Señor Mina, Father Mier, the son of kings in far-off America, and deported to Spain and sentenced to be burned at the stake because he said a few silly things about a virgin the Spaniards had invented, like all virgins—Guadalupe her name is—anyway, something of the sort. Father Mier is a strong, angry man, don Javier Mina! He tried to blow up the King, they tell me, but they caught him when he jumped, so he jumped again, and here he is!"

"It is an honor to meet you, don Servando. I have heard of you, when you lighted those gunpowder-filled candles in the Pope's own chapel. We almost lost His Holiness then. Ha ha! So you are one of our own . . . Tell me, then, don Servando, who is it now that you are planning to do away with? Because I cannot imagine that you would be wasting your time . . . And times like these . . . One must always keep one's plots afoot, don't you agree? For example— in México Father Hidalgo started a revolution with four men and now there are forty thousand. I am going there myself. That is my dream. I have more than one thousand men contracted, and all that lacks is giving them the word. For which in addition there lacks a certain sum of money. For want of two or perhaps three thousand gold coins, don Servando, México is at this moment still in chains and the Viceroy still in possession of his pretty head. But do not fear, I will soon find the money . . . I believe the game is worth the candle, do you not agree? . . . But tell me now, are you

in some plot against the Queen? Do you still dream of the guillotine for His Holiness? Confess! Confess! For well I know that you
are a man of many interests."

"I believe my plans and yours coincide, don Javier. In fact I have
written during my stay in London a most inflammatory book,
which I have titled *The History of the Revolution in New Spain*.
I plan to invade México with this book."

"Paper! Paper! What's needed is gold and lead."

"Yes, but for the lead to work, the ground must be prepared.
The great mass of people in my country are poor and ignorant, not
as their natural condition but from the scarce opportunity they
have had to educate themselves. Here we all have read *The Social
Contract*. There the only thing they know is their catechism. We
must open the minds of the Creoles before we open fire on the
Spaniard dogs."

"Then I'll see to the fire!"

"Oh, so will I. Never fear. Did I hear you say that there was a
need for money?"

"Had I money, I'd already be at sea."

"Well, then, I will get it for you, and we will go together to
invade the Americas."

"I did not think you to be a man of great wherewithal."

"But I have words, and they have always served me. Set you the
date and I will bring the gold. And be about getting your men
together . . . In truth you are right: with words alone no war was
ever won."

"I can have all in readiness next week."

"Until then—*adios*."

". . . And at that the great Admiral gave a mighty leap, and the
water sparkled all around," spoke the voice of the friar.

"Oh, go on! Go on! Now!" panted Lady Hamilton.

"And he said, 'To the charge, for we are Englishmen!' And he
repeated the word *Englishmen* two million times. (Please note that
down in the count.)"

"That's highway robbery!" screamed Lady Hamilton.

"Shall I stop?"

"No, go on! Go on!"

And so we departed for México in a nice brigantine, armed to
the teeth. Don Javier gave a shout, and we weighed anchor. The

sails filled. We were carrying two thousand recruits, all good men—
retired infantrymen and mercenaries. Don Javier gave a long impassioned speech as we sailed out of port. And I saw a lady's two
white hands, very very white, and a face on the dock which bade
me godspeed with quiet grace. Success. Success, said her voice, and
then it faded into the fog. It was Orlando, that strange woman.

CHAPTER XXVII

*Which relates the new friendships made by the friar and his subse-
quent escape to America.*

And at last I arrived in England, where I could in a manner breathe
the air of freedom, which had been until that moment withheld
me. England was one great seedbed of revolution, and a staging
ground for expeditions of all stripes, led by every revolutionary
in Europe and even the English themselves. Those two ladies so
tranquilly chatting on that bridge could well have been plotting
the Queen's hanging. And that lad coming along there carrying two
snowballs is indisputably on his way to blow up Parliament.

In order to live in this place, I speedily made contact with a
group of refugees from my own continent, men who at every wak-
ing moment, and some in dreams, were hatching plans for an invasion. From them I discovered that a certain Padre Hidalgo had
begun a revolution in México, that he had done so with fifteen
good men and one woman, and that now he could count more
than fifteen thousand soldiers at his back. And this, for a fact, so
influenced me that I saw my dreams of a liberating invasion take
life once again . . . I also learned, however, that this Padre Hidalgo
had been shot by the Spaniards, but this was a fact little daunting
to me.

I must give credit to two most distinguished persons who saw
after my complete animal and spiritual well-being during my life
in the foggy city of London, and who did so much in that regard
that at last they made themselves perfectly intolerable to me. The
first, as soon as I met her, I could see to be a most eccentric lady,
always dressed in untanned bearskins. The day I took my leave of

her, this woman, like Sappho, threw herself into the sea. She was called Orlando, and she had me know that she was descended from nobility of the furthest rank (which could be confirmed by anyone with a nose for such matters by the odor of the bearskins she wore). She also let it be known that she had been born a male more than three hundred years ago. I listened to all these asseverations with the utmost patience and forbearance, especially since, after all, she was my protectress. I would sit and listen to those farfetched tales of hers, but always I could find to say only that indeed anything was possible—especially given my complete ignorance of English nobility and their customs. She would smile, come to me with great elegance and composure, and assure me once more that of her first origins there remained not a trace (which indeed appeared true enough) and that therefore I should have no fear. I pretended that all this went a bit over my head. (I have always been one to pretend not to understand those insinuations, which have always, it seems, harried me. I have always been the "dunderhead" or the "saint.") Then she would turn her back on me in cold anger, smile, curtsy at the door of the salon and stalk upstairs to her apartments. She would shut herself up and begin to write, furiously, on yellow foolscap, working at a manuscript she called *The Oak*, which held some two thousand of her best poems (a fact she recounted to me on our first meeting). There would be afternoons when I would actually watch her furiously at work on this manuscript, cursing and spitting out words of the most shocking kind, and I began to doubt. I would even wonder, at times, whether she had told me the whole truth.

Through the offices of Orlando, who took me about and introduced me at court, I met my second protectress, a woman who inspired the deepest compassion and, therefore, weariness and tedium. Her name was Emma Lyon, Lady Hamilton. She was presented to me by the Queen herself at one of the Queen's entertainments. She was surrounded and hounded by a hundred of the most elegant dogs at court, idiots to a man, who tirelessly and ceaselessly paid her court. She looked out as through a picket fence of dried-up marquises (old relics who gave no indication that they ever intended to die) so constantly bowing before her feet that at last one lost all respect for them. They bobbed so clumsily that very often their heads would crash together and one or another would fall down dead. When this happened two servants would enter with great gravity and bear the body away into the gardens.

Then the bowing would begin again. And this made me think—were these old gentlemen celebrating a duel comprised of butting heads, to see who at last won fair Hamilton? ... But she was as remote from all this courtliness as a statue of Diana. Since her husband had died she had become a woman decidedly abstracted from the world, though not for that reason any less often in attendance at parties, balls, entertainments, charades, and other gatherings of the like character. People said that this was so as not to displease the Queen. This lady at that moment was making her entrance into the room, arm in arm with one of the witches from *Macbeth* and conversing with her on grounds of the greatest intimacy. I asked therefore whether that play were to be presented that evening in the salon, and on that question a phalanx of irate counts and marquises turned in unison toward the Queen. She was just descending the stair, and she looked toward me questioningly. The nobles bowed, their heads all banged together, and bodies crumpled to the polished floor. The Queen glided, heavily enough, and with a motion somewhat like a slug's, across the corpses. "So much ceremony bewilders me," I muttered. "Why should all these gentlemen, who look still to be reasonably useful men, die?" And at that she had come to where I was standing very stiff and erect, for I did not think to duck my head to her. "And *who*," she said, "are *you*?" "I am Servando Teresa de Mier y Noriega." "And *what*," she asked me, "do you *do*?" blinking constantly like a mouse just waked from its sleep, "I am a friar ..." "It is a new contribution you make to court, then. I do not know whether my dear Emma has had experience of a friar before now, so come with me, Servando Teresa de Mier y Noriega, for here may be her salvation, and yours as well." The Queen said these words with great gaiety and spirit, and she led me off to the much-sought-after lady.

And thus it was ...

The rest of the story is well known enough, I think. As soon as she told me she was the great Admiral Nelson's widow, it escaped from me that I had seen him killed by enemy fire, not two rods from me, and that he had seemed a gentlemen of great courage to me, though perhaps a bit anachronistic. And I added that his cry, just before he exploded, had made my blood freeze in my veins ... "Go on! Go on!" she said, and so I went on, all that night, and on the next morning was taken in a most regal coach to her mansion, where, after we had signed a contract by which she was to pay me one gold coin for each word of my story, I continued the tale in a

luxuriance of detail. Hoarse but with a cart loaded with riches, I
returned the next week to my first protectress's mansion. This lady
was furiously pacing a great terrace outside her private apartments,
and every few minutes she would snatch up her pen and add a new
poem to the already swollen volume titled *The Oak*.

While strolling through those rooms and grand halls I one day
met José María Blanco, who was trying to stab a hat pin some
twelve inches long into the Queen's back, though unsuccessfully,
for it seems the distinguished lady was well whaleboned for the
occasion and the hat pin could not penetrate the corset she had
been laced into. After several of these unsuccessful attempts, he
finally desisted, and he looked my way, to see me observing him.
He came over to me and began telling me no end of nonsense and
not a few things which to my mind were somewhat more judi-
ciously thought out, as for example his unquenchable hatred for
the Catholic Church and for all the kings and queens of the earth,
even if they were atheists. He was so disappointed and disillusioned with his native country that he had changed his name from
Blanco to White and renounced the Catholic Church to become a
Protestant ... This gentleman was the editor and publisher of a
newspaper he called *El Español*, in which every article cast into
doubt the legitimacy of Charles IV of Spain, commented upon his
mother's fidelity to his father and her ongoing chastity, and in-
quired into his father's possible poxiness. White had forbidden the
name of *Spain* to be written with a capital letter. (This, as I later
learned, was attributable to a lack of an upper case in the printer's
font, but White had put the deficiency to good patriotic use.) On
the staff of this newspaper I met one Javier Mina, who seemed
much the saner of the two men, and who told me he had an army
in readiness to embark for the Americas, there to join the Revolution and once landed to leave not a Spaniard's—or any Euro-
pean's—head on his shoulder. I confess I liked the way he talked.
He asked me to join his army of volunteers, to which I readily
agreed. This gladdened him greatly, for he said he had known I
was "one of them" since long before I had formally joined them.
He then confided in me that the only obstacle still standing in
their way was a grievous lack of money, for the English even taxed
the waves the ship was to sail upon. "If it is a question of mere
money, I shall find it for you," I said. And on the next morning I
made my way to the house of Lady Hamilton, where I invented
for her a great lumpy pudding of a tale about the death of Admiral

Nelson, for which she paid me so handsomely that I left with two cartsful of gold . . . "You must have come upon a gold mine," Mina exclaimed in a low and punning manner. But he embraced me most warmly and patriotically. "It is all thanks to my logorrhea," I replied, for I did not wish to go much into details, thinking it wise to keep Milady's secrets, who so generously had rewarded my literary-historical efforts.

And so the fleet sailed from England. I stood quite smug and burning with enthusiasm upon the deck and waved good-bye to the fogs and damps of the corrupt Old World. But I had forgotten the two women who had been my protectresses and who, therefore, had no intention of stopping in their constant aid to me. Thus it was that before we had cleared port, Orlando, at the head of her own flotilla, pulled abreast and begged me the favor of returning to shore with her. I excused myself for my hasty departure, and I rushed to assure her of my prompt return (all this as best I could), but at the same instant I saw another ship hailing us from the other side of the port, and this was Lady Hamilton, who would have made her deceased husband the Admiral proud by her sea legs as she called to me in her husband's name and said she would not let me leave the court, for I was her only consolation. It may well be imagined that I knew not what to do, for when I ran to the starboard side where my indefatigable Orlando still awaited me, my equally constant Lady Hamilton on the port side ordered her men to make up a boarding party to kidnap me away. How was I to escape with my skin from these two harpies of prey? All I could think to do was to throw myself overboard, into the sea. Which I did, for, when all was said and done, it seemed to me better to be a delicacy for the fishes than to have served two capricious women for all my life . . .

I bade farewell to them all, then, from my watery asylum, and rendered myself into the care of the creatures of the deep, who watched me as I sank slowly in my black robes and then turned and swam away terrified from such an apparition, some even crashing into the seabed in their mad confusion. There I was, then, at this crucial juncture of my life, when I heard a great splashing in the water and saw the hair and face of Orlando, who was swimming toward me. And what should be my surprise upon looking closely at her naked body, to see that though her body was not in shape or outline different from that of a woman, in the unmistakable area of the sex there was a great difference indeed. She was swimming toward me laughing and pointing with Her Great Unmistakable Categorical Imperative that swung from left to right and back again as her body slithered through the sea. And it seemed to grow more imperative at every moment. My anguish and chagrin were terrible . . . I saw her smile and stretch out her arms, and I began to swim away as fast as I could. I kicked like a frog along the bottom of the sea, and wriggled like a tadpole, while Orlando seemed to be taking ever more careful aim . . . And when I at last emerged, sticking my head above the waves, I saw the coast of my own continent. The New World . . .

Of all my trials and adventures, this voyage was surely the most like a penal sentence, and one carried out with the greatest fear for my life and virtue.

UNITED STATES

CHAPTER XXVIII

On the friar's vicissitudes and changes of fortune, and the first expedition.

We entered the waters of the United States toward midnight. And we tried to let down our anchor without our being seen by the coastal customs, for we knew well beforehand how intolerable were the taxes and tolls they were capable of levying against us, so as thereby to demonstrate the weightiness of their existence and the necessity to the good maintenance of government; but we could not. They trained on us great lights produced from combustible torches of some sort, and they began to read out a list of our tax indebtedness . . . Javier Mina, I, and the rest of the crew besides, quickly abandoned ship and set off afoot. And thus we plodded, into the dry port of the land of America. The ship we abandoned remained as a payment of a part of the debt, for our foolishly having attempted to anchor it in those waters. We were obliged to pay the remaining part of the boarding taxes by working in the cotton fields of the South . . . And so that we should not change our minds about that while on our way, a squad of Yankee soldiers followed us, armed from their teeth to their toes (where they attached a double-edged razor to their boots, though this tended to cut them in the shins whenever they stumbled). We came, then, to a great plain cut by two long iron bars. And we sat down to wait for the train.

The train moves at great speed and spews out a reddish black smoke all along the track, besmudging the sky thereby. Of thirty boxcars (as they are called), I have counted twenty-nine filled with Negroes, who are so crowded together that they resemble gunnysacks heaped on top of straw matting. It is only the one remaining car that is used for the transportation of white passengers. We are in this last-mentioned wagon, or car, and mile by mile penetrate farther into the red clay lands of the South. And all I can think of is a way to escape from this rumbling, boiling, lurching, horrible vehicle which stops nowhere yet never ceases howling either and which pitches us about so fiercely (as though we were still at sea, for a fact) that it constantly knocks us up against one another and cracks our skulls. One gentleman who was very calmly trying to light his cigar has just died when the cigar, his hand shaken by a sudden jolt of the van on the tracks, went right through his stomach. At the same time two very high-and-mighty ladies, who looked to be a good halfway lulled to sleep, were suddenly hurled out the car window, with no other word than the one or two ejaculated by the passengers who chanced to see them fly out and disappear. Other ladies, sitting forward in the car, are pitched out at one window and blown in again by the strong wind at a window farther back. Sometimes the wind is so strong, in fact, that they land on their own seat again, and once a lady wound up sitting on the lap of an imperturbable gentleman who simply moved to the seat beside him and went on reading his newspaper. This immutability aptly illustrates the experience gained from riding this "line" and coming to know its peculiarities, but I, for whom this journey is the first, and the first time too I have seen such sights, stay as alert as possible at all times, and often and again hold with both hands to the seat back in front of me, trying always to save myself from this meteoric vehicle. We speed along, then, this way for many miles, when I hear a great uproar in the cars for the Negroes. "To yer shovels!" screams the driver, and the stoker screams "We're out of coal!" And one of the twenty-nine boxcars is suddenly uninhabited. "That's the closest thing there is to coal," a lady explains to me, affecting great surprise when she sees the disconcerted expression on my face, and adding, "for all this country produces, you know, is gold, no coal at all. So we just use Negroes, there are so many of them. And like I say, they do look an awful lot like coal . . ." And then the second car is depopulated, so that now we are carrying only twenty-seven boxcars of fuel . . . I look out the window in terror and all I can see is a great streak of black sooty smoke pouring out the smokestack of the engine, inking out the sky entirely . . .

But at last we reach the Southland, as they call it, with one boxcar of this odd fuel still intact. Mina looks horrified. "So this is the land of freedom!" he exclaims, not adding another word, as the soldiers fix a thick chain about his neck. "I don't know, for a fact," I reply. "But it looks as though without a pocketful of money here one is not even allowed the air to breathe." And I watch a chain as thick as Mina's clinched to my neck, too, and then linked

to Mina's, so that we are chained together by that same region of
our anatomy. And without further ado, to the tune of whistling
whips cracking about our ears and other parts, we are marched to
the cotton plantations ... And now we are bent over the fields.
We pick cotton from sunup to sundown, and these "Americans"
(as they call themselves, as though this country were unique on
the two continents!) these Americans, I say, are so bent on produc-
tion that they retard the sun's setting with mirrors and shots fired
into the air. And we are utterly exhausted.

But what are you telling that old story for, oh friar? Eh, friar?
That old calamity? There's nothing original about it; why, people
are still singing that song today. Huh, friar? You don't want to
leave it to the newer generations, then, and just get on with your
travels? Hi, friar! Hee, friar! Tell how you got yourself out of this
bedeviled mess. Tell how you made a hundred and twenty thousand dollars and, at last! set foot again in México. Come on, friar!
Hi, friar! *Viva! Excelsior!* On your feet, friar!

Tell, friar, how on a certain evening, getting on to be late at
night, there arrived at the camp in the cotton field a very old little
old man with bundles bundled up very bulgingly who began to
dance around and yell earsplitting yells. And he awoke thee from
thy slumbers, so that thou didst step out to see what all the shouting was about, and thou didst pat his hunched little humpback to
calm him and didst ask him what his troubles and tribulations
were.

"I have but one trouble," said the old fellow, "but it is bigger
and harder than any other. I have lived ten years with a great giant
of a woman who made me do everything she wished for, and I
detested her, as you may well imagine ... A fierce, hard woman,
who has just died, thank God, and left me, damn her, as a punishment from hell, I know, her entire fortune. So tell me—what am
I to do with all this gold? Tell me! I thought at last I would be
free when the harpy died, and look! The great hulking hag has left
me these sacks of gold and condemned me to be a millionaire. Tell
me—could anyone conceive a more terrible punishment than
this?"

And thou, oh friar, didst make him solemnly the sign of the
cross and offer to lift the great weight from his shoulders.

"Come, sir," thou saidst to the uncle, taking up his burden, "come, and sleep here with me, for tomorrow will you see, freedom will be yours."

"In sooth?" sobbed the fellow.

And thou, oh friar, thou didst lay him in your bed and whisper to him, "Sleep . . . sleep . . ." And the old man said, "I cannot sleep. Who has ever seen a millionaire sleep?"

"Rest easy, I shall keep watch on your fortune," thou saidst, oh friar.

"Oh no. That privilege has not been accorded millionaires. I cannot—I am to stay awake, alone, until my eyeballs dry up to powder. Ay, that damned woman plotted it well. She never once gave me an ounce of gold for myself when she was alive, and now—I am condemned to carry sacks of it to my grave!"

"Sleep!" thou cried'st imperiously.

"I cannot! I must watch over my fortune!"

And so then, oh friar, thou plannedest well-planned new plans. Thou settest in to talk, and thou wouldst not let the old fellow interrupt you once.

"My dear friend, since that fortune there brings you so much grief and vexation, perhaps you should give me a part of it, to use to find the way to free you from it."

"No," said the old man. "Look what our many freedoms have brought us to." And he pointed to a tree nearby where a dozen Negroes were dangling, hanged, like a stalk of bananas from it.

But thou, oh friar, thou never ceased talking for one moment, nor paid any mind to the old man's interruptions.

" 'Freedom, my dear friend, is one of the most precious gifts given to men by the heavens . . .' " And thus thou went on, reciting Don Quixote. " 'To it cannot be equated the treasures held by the earth nor covered by the sea; for freedom, as for honor, life itself can and should be risked; and, on the contrary, captivity is the worst evil that can befall men . . .' And you are captive, captive to that great fortune which does nothing but disturb and unsettle you! Hand me those two sacks of gold and you will see how light and free you feel! . . ."

But as the old man still seemed dubious, and held back, thou, oh friar, who hadst noticed a certain incipient yawn in thy listener as thou wast quoting those words from the ingenious book, thou went on reciting, thanks to thy uncanny memory, in a voice soft and mellifluous, so soothing to sleeplessness . . . To wit: " 'The bachelor, although his name was Samson, was not very big so far

as body size went, but he was a great joker ...'" and dawn was
beginning to show at the horizon, and the old man struggled, but
he was losing the battle with Morpheus ... " 'Sire, a wide, strong
river divided the lands of a certain kingdom,' " and thou camest
at last, by dint of pure intellectual honesty, for by now the put-
upon fellow was about to burst into snoring, to:

> "Hands off, o'erweening ones!
> Let it by none attempted be;
> For this emprise, my lord the King,
> Hath been reserved for me."[17]

And his listener, who now heard nothing, could struggle no
more, and a long scream, like a cry for mercy, escaped his throat.
It was the third morning since his arrival in the quarters of the
camp, a kind of barracks building. And so it was that thou, oh
friar, saidst " 'Vale,' "[18] skipping over one whole paragraph of thy
memorized reading for fear of perpetuating his sleep through all
eternity. And in one hop thou hadst seized the two bags of gold.
Thou squeezed and fingered the money. Thou calculated the sum
of it. Thou wokest Mina (by kicking him in the ribs) and took off
running through the cotton fields. And at every step from thee,
thousands of sparkling rays shot out, oh friar—at every step thou
wast plunging thy hands into the two bags and scattering gold
coins like cottonseed broad-sown in the field. At every step a falling star glimmered and disappeared ... And with the sacks half-
full now, for there had been many streaks of golden light, thou
camest, oh friar, to the shores of the Rio Grande. Little Mina was
right behind. And he began to count the hoard. "This is a hundred
and twenty thousand dollars' worth!" thou wast heard to exclaim,
oh friar. And now, set about preparations for thy great expedition.

So the expedition set out. And thou, oh friar that wast, thou
ledst the way in thy purple robes. Bishop Servando. For they had
named thee Bishop of Baltimore. And so, oh bishop, it was a bishop
that stood on the deck, and seized a weapon, and raised it and
shot, and struck a school of flying fishes dead, for the shot took

---

[17]Miguel de Cervantes, *El ingenioso hidalgo don Quijote de la Mancha (Don
Quixote*, trans. Samuel Putnam, Modern Library, 1949).
[18]Ditto.

them directly in their ever-open eyes. And thou went on, regally walking among the crew, like a violet flame, praying and cursing the winds which grew stronger and wilder every day. And when the ships had sailed into the middle of the Gulf, a great wave, oh bishop, crashed down on thee, and all, all across the bridge, and a cascade of scarlet water trickled from your body. And thus it was that the great batteries of artillery were battered by the waves, and thou hadst begun to fire into the clouds, to tame them. And thus it was that the sailors, after a long wrangle, had thrown the Cuban Infante overboard, to try to save the ship. This fellow had been traveling as a literary man, a war correspondent, and in the midst of the storm he had stood alone, aloof from the turbulence, composing a sonnet to the sea ... And so, oh bishop, thou walkest fadedly all across the deck, and then the mainmast sways and tumbles into the ship. And thou, oh bishop, thou runnest to Mina and orderest the ship put about. "We're going back!" But Mina is shivered by a wave and knocked into the howling, echoing foam. The sailors hurl oaths and blasphemies, not unleavened by an occasional prayer. So that thou, oh bishop, at last seest that it rests with thee to take the wheel of the ship bobbing and dancing and standing on its head in the water, and slowly thou beginnest to discover the secrets of navigation. Taking great care to sink neither thyself nor the boat, thou fling'st thy violet robes into the sea. "The bishop's overboard!" call out ten sailors when they see the robes floating on the water. "But the friar is still with thee!" thou callest out, naked, in reply, and thou attempt'st to take mastery of the situation. Thou clutch'st the wheel again. And the tumultuous circling winds of a waterspout set down their center just at a point on the keel of the warship, oh friar, and the ship is raised up out of the sea and goes sailing through the clouds. And then it drops down again into the boiling spume of ocean. And fish flock to the banquet. Death, riding across the waves, takes out his scythe and dances in great pirouettes. But thou, oh friar, thou swimmest, and swimmest, and swimmest on still more, to where the *tireless reaper* dances, and, seizing his curved tool, thou breakest it in two and pitch'st it in his face. And Death, bawling like a calf, turns tail and runs. So thou, oh friar, plungest once more into the waves and, taking up the tattered, faded purple robes, which thou hast found tangled about a dolphin's tail, thou hast emerged, oh bishop, once more, from the seafoam and waves and constant water, and thou settest thy foot on the land ...

■ ■ ■

Cut out that epic crap, and tell things like they happened! Whoever heard of such verbs! *Pitch'st! Swimmest!* Enough mockarchaisms!

Hardly had we embarked when our ship sank, and the fish thereabouts soon took notice of many of our soldiers. The rest, among them your humble servant, arrived at the shores of New Orleans, supplied with a store of nothing but hunger, and greatly fearing to fall once more prisoner. And so thus it was that Mina, who had arrived there grappled to a fish, decided to depart for Galveston to seek reinforcements. I remained in New Orleans, contracting new men and seeking money in a thousand different fashions, for all the ore I had theretofore amassed lay now at the bottom of the Gulf. Of the sailors, of those who had not succumbed to drowning, many perished by being melted by the sun in that latitude, and the rest fled into the woods where, I was told, they were spitted and roasted by the Indians, though this is doubtful in the extreme, I believe, for as skinny as they then were, after our crossing, I can hardly think they had made a mouthful to such voracious appetites . . . And as Mina did not return, after a while I grew anxious to invade México, and would do it myself, almost. So I set off to find Mina. And there, in Galveston, I found him, without his ever having lifted a finger for independence. I therefore grew very heated with him and read him a list of truths about himself. He promised that from that moment he would, by his word, put the expedition into good order, and organize it all. He would mend his ways. So I set off in another direction to do more of the impossible, if I could.

And after reciting *The Social Contract* twelve times and *The Rights of Man* fifteen, and quoting him the most lovely passages from the Bible, I at last brought 'round an eccentric American to our cause, one Smith by name, a lover of literature and, therefore, a bad poet, and I convinced him to give me a portion of the gain from his harvest, that is the black slaves' harvest—for the frustrated poet trafficked in black bodies with the planters of the South. It was with some misgivings, and resignation, that I accepted that sum, and in return I gave my benefactor a series of lessons in metrics and rhyming. So he, at the last minute, asked me not to leave him or, if 'twere possible, to take him with us on our expedition. But I, foreseeing the difficulties of carrying along a frustrated poet, told him that we could not, that his place was

there, in Galveston, and that I would soon return to tell him new
exploits and adventures in masterful prose for his edification and
delight. And I went off to find Mina, who was still making plans
for how to go about planning what had to be done . . . And soon
we set out from the port of New Orleans, under a quiet sky. But
at the moment of our sailing that smiling sky began to frown, and
it blackened fiercely and began to be shot with bolts of lightning
and to tremble with thunderclaps. It seemed every lightning bolt
went straight for the mainmast of our best ship. The crew, to a
man, mutinied, for they said the expedition was jinxed, and cursed
by God Himself, for a friar was aboard, and this was no fit under-
taking for a priest or curate or other religious person, much less
for a friar. But I, to restore something of order, took out a purple
rag and hung it on myself and, with great pomposity, went out on
deck, pretending to pray and scattering absolutions among the sailors who, continually, were falling or being swept overboard and
carried away by the waves. And in truth my bishop's habits calmed
them some. The storm quieted some too. And on the morning of
the fourth day we came to the port of Soto La Marina. So, after so
long a time, I once more trod my native soil of México, so sad and
desolate there in that port and seaside city, with its low houses
that seemed to beg or suck up sustenance from the very soil, and
battered palm trees which, though open and spread, gave futile
shade from the implacable burning sun.

México

CHAPTER XXIX

The invasion.

I set off, leading the army, marching through the sand. We marched into the village of Soto La Marina, where the women stared at us befuddled and the men (who in these matters are always the more discreet) took refuge in their *patios* or hid out in the hills. I ordered my men to halt in the little town and called all its inhabitants together, to speak to them. And as the first to arrive were the children, I sent them off to gather their parents. Within two hours I had all of Soto La Marina there before me. So I climbed up the trunk of a palm tree and began to speak to them. I told them: *"I took on this charge (the charge of independence) because in this way may be sooner stanched the flow of blood which is spilled in useless torrents all throughout Mexico and across the Americas. For emancipation is inevitable! With Europe its guide and protector, twenty million men who want to be free will cast off their chains, in spite of all the world can do . . ."*[19]

And the women began to clap and shout huzzas. The men kept their eyes on the ground, however, but I, seeing that I was gaining some ground, continued my discourse to them:

"To stand hard against emancipation is to attempt to force nature against its will. The natural order decrees that every colony be freed as it comes to provide for its own necessities and wants. Thus has it come to pass in all the colonies in the world, just as sons, arriving at their manhood, are freed from their sacred dependency on their natural fathers. America has been too long tied to the apron strings of an oppressive nursemaid which has monopolized its trade, and kept it from its proper factories, vineyards, and olive fields . . ."[20]

And the men, at this, lifted their gaze from the ground and looked full in my face.

[19]Fray Servando, letter to Fray Pascual de Santa María.
[20]Ditto.

"*Until now we have not lacked for uprising and insurrection,
but for generals, officers, and arms. These we have here—abun-
dant and excellent ones . . . And uprightness too has been lacking,
for base men drunk with vile passions against the colonizer have
until today stood at the head of the rebels, raving and killing
Europeans for no other cause than that they are so. But we bring
nobler ideas. We bring uprightness that will not bend or sway,
and we promise only to defend ourselves against those who would
destroy us. We raise our voices in a call to civil liberty, fair, just,
and reasonable. We will force no-one to take up arms*, the true
man does not require being compelled to struggle against the op-
pressors of his subject land." (And here I saw the men step forward,
stand stiffer and straighter, become as Mexican as the palm trees
themselves.) "*The man who wages war against us, he will find us
ready—be he Creole or Spaniard; the quiet man who seeks peace,
we will not touch a hair of his head.*"[21]

But by this time no-one was quiet. The people all began to cry
¡Viva México! and ¡Viva la independencia! And so we set out
again, with the village of Soto La Marina behind us, the women
with their children pick-a-back to the rear and the men more in
the van, clamoring for the invasion and cheering us on. But before
we left the village I asked for the curate or priest of the town. And
everyone went off in a different direction to see if they could find
him. They found him at last in the little church, hiding behind
the altar. I went to him, and walked up to him, followed by that
multitude of people, and myself dressed as a bishop, whereat he
fell to his knees and went to kiss my ring. "Is there no mass then
today?" I asked him. "Oh, your Grace," he answered me, fluttering
his eyelashes and making himself charming, "It is that we have
no holy wine to be able to give it." "And what does that matter!"
I cried, "for if it's a matter of wine I've got some here." And unty-
ing and loosening my surcingle I took out a wine-sack brimming
with good strong Castilian brandy, went to the chalice, and filled
it. "Now," I said to the mouselike curate, "now thou canst give
the mass. And give no thought to the quality of the wine, for
Christ was not precisely one of the wealthiest men of his day, and
He never drank wine better than that you have there this minute
. . ." And so the priest celebrated a mass with good hard brandy,
and by the time the chants had ended and he said *Amen*, he was

[21]Fray Servando, letter to Fray Pascualde Santa María.

a bit tipsy and tottering. So helped by an acolyte, he toppled down from the altar. And we left the church, singing out rousing hymns of war, in case anyone still timorously holding back should be inspired and run out to join our cause ... By the time we were into Monterrey we had more than a hundred thousand men armed with sticks, stones, and tools. It was entering that city that we had our first "encounter." So rifle to shoulder or stone in hand, we swept over and wiped out the Spaniard jackanapes that stood in our way. And thus we took their weapons and strengthened our own forces a bit, so that much more safely and sure of ourselves we could march onward liberating towns and villages, swelling our own ranks with the freed townspeople, until there came the time when I looked back and saw that my eyes could not take in the whole of our army at one time. Our men, in spite of the rolling of the plains around there, disappeared over the line of the horizon ... As it grew dark I gave the order to rest, and we lay down on the sandy ground to sleep.

The next day we were leaving the precincts of Monterrey, and had arrived at the New Kingdom of León, continually driving the Royalists back, continually firing our weapons; but then behold, as we were making camp in New León's Land there, the entire army of the City of México, which the Viceroy had sent out against us, began advancing on us. When we had fired all our ammunition at them, and our shot was exhausted, we picked up rocks and stones and began fighting them with those, and sand, so that the sky grew redder and redder with clouds of sand, and taking advantage of the curtain that hid us, we began to retreat, until we reached the fort at Soto La Marina, where we took shelter. There we equipped ourselves with all the weapons and ammunition that was stored there, but I was still afraid we would be discovered, and my fears grew even worse when I noted that the curate had disappeared from the village, for I know well enough the villainy of those wretches.

The first news we had of the arrival of the Royalists was a great crowd of turkey buzzards that began to fly about over our fort. These obscene birds are forever on the track of carrion, and were already long accustomed to the leavings of the sabers of the colonial soldiery, who respect not even the babe in arms, which is why the buzzards follow them so close, trusting in them for their daily bread, so to speak. And these vultures, to tell the truth, were grown so fat from the slaughters of innocents that had taken place, that they could hardly fly anymore, but walked about on the sand with their toes splayed out to keep them up, for all the world like pestiferous black tortoises from some terrible infernal place. And so it was that these disgusting birds had begun taking up positions, so I, soon as I saw them, I sounded the alarm to all the groups. And in all that fortress there was not a hole or chink or bull's-eye in the walls without its rifle barrel peeking out. So the first wave of Royalists served as fodder for those voracious fowls. But then came the second wave, which, cut by our fire, broke up and some of its soldiers began to sound the call for succor, so that in moments there was marching toward us the entire royal army of México . . . Our munitions had run out, so that we had only our own arms (I mean weapons to fight with), not those magazined in the fort, and of course also our own brawny arms. The royal troops were almost upon us, and so I gave the order for close fighting—*To the fingernails!* I cried. And then, having nothing left even to hurl at them, we began to hunt down the turkey buzzards, and we held them by their scrawny feet, whirled them about over our heads, and flung them at our attackers. We kept them at bay that way for all one day. But these projectiles too began to run out, so that at last there arrived the moment when not a single vulture or buzzard was seen in the sky over Soto La Marina. And still the jackanapes Spanish soldiers came on, advancing over the swollen and bursting bodies of the birds.

And so we fell prisoner.

What does it mean to fall prisoner to a Royalist army enraged and starving? It means to fall into hell itself. A part of our soldiery were tied to our victors' donkeys' tails and dragged across the sandy ground while the asses were goaded to make them run the more crazedly. Another part of our men were set astride small burros, that jogged along and rattled their eyeballs and other parts. And another large number, after the donkeys' tails and the burros had all been occupied, were tied together with a great leathern strap, like those used for yoking oxen, and driven by blows, afoot, across that desertlike burning land. And so we crossed all of Pachuca, where the heat was so terrible, and our thirst and the mistreatment caused it to be so unbearable to boot, that there were many captives who begged to be killed. And as though all this were not enough, in each town and village we came to, we were exhibited before the dismayed eyes of their inhabitants, like so many hardened and miserable criminals. We were harried from one offense

to another at the hands of our captors. And when we left the plain
and began to ascend into the rocky crags of Atotonilco, fully half
the prisoners had died and the others were dying. I crossed those
rocks and boulders on the worst-tempered colt in the world, that
at every moment would break into such a bone-jangling trot that
I would see stars in the middle of a blindingly hot noonday. It goes
without saying that the officers of the Royalist army from the first
moment took a terrible hatred of me, and exercised it against my
person, never ceasing to wallop me and hurl insults of every color
at me; or at times they would poke at my skinny vicious mount,
which would buck me off to the ground, with my shackles landing
about my ears. And so it was that from landing so much on the
rocky, boulder-strewn ground an arm and both my legs were broken into bits. And can a civilized man believe that those savage
Spaniard jackanapes (though jackasses might be a fitter name for
what they were), instead of picking me up from that ignoble posture and rendering me some aid, would rather break out in loud
guffaws and mock my state? . . . But what most saddened me was
knowing that all these paid cutthroats and henchmen of León were
in fact good humble decent men, descendants of the poorest and
most ignorant class of Spaniards and who, therefore, could be led
by their noses like tame bears. Often I would try to make them
see the lie they lived in, but their arrogant officers, who already
had a taste of my tongue, finally sewed my mouth shut with hemp
rope, so all I could do was puff and wave my unshackled hands. It
was dreadfully hard work I had, time and again, to clamber up on
my "noble steed" (out of hell was that beast!), only to be thrown
within moments to the rocky ground again. And I cried out to
heaven to let me die once and for all, but I did not pant very loud,
or scream, but prayed all in my mind and even, when my bonds
allowed it, curled my lips in a sneer of indifference and contempt
for all those vile and despicable vermin. Which of course enraged
them even further, for they could see that their tortures and torments had no effect, so they would poke my horse again, and I,
again, would fly headfirst against the flinty ground. Until at last
we came to a halt in one of the mountain villages and I, with a
thousand puffs and grunts and groans and wavings of my hands,
managed to dictate a letter to my friend Agustín Pomposo, in
which I begged him to do whatever was in his power to save me
. . . But my faithful friend could do nothing, so that I was carried
to the prison called La Esquina Chata, in the Dominican convent.

I was given into the hands of the Inquisitors, for them to try me as they might try a fearsome witch. I learned that of the rest of the prisoners, most had perished of hunger and thirst on the way, and that those who did arrive to the cells of the prison died there of terrible mistreatment and ill use ... So I found myself once more before the robed judges. Mired in that black bog. But I would not answer their questions, so that once again I was led off to a cell in the prison. And once again enveloped in iron hoops and rings and chains. I was, then, the first Dominican friar to be held prisoner by his own order in a building of their own, which surely they had never built for such a purpose. But the powerful of the world never forgive any act or word contrary to their own doctrines, and as it is they who have the strength, they have also the privilege of forcing obedience, eliminating anyone who stands in their way or pesters them ... And after three years in that prison I found out that the *Holy Inquisition* had, by and in Spain, been wholly done away with, and that the thousands upon thousands of purifying pyres, which had rendered ash so many persons, were used now only to heat up cooking pots and lend some warmth to poor beggars. I felt, then, somewhat calmer, since at least by law the Inquisition could no longer "purify" me, although on the other hand the government of México still saw me as a dangerous adversary, and was hardly disposed to set me free after having battled so long to capture me. So it was that I was at last transported, though *kicked* better describes my journey, for I will never forget it, to a freezing cell in the jail at Veracruz. Which was almost sinking into the sea.

There they would have left me until the Resurrection, which, given the nearness of my impending death, could not for a fact be far off. But I would not wait for that event to be freed if I could help it, so that I stuck my head between the bars of my cell and tried to make my escape, but all I managed was two great wallops from my jailers, who fished me back when I had a good half my body out the bars. Later I tried to scrabble through the floor of my cell with my fingernails, to reach the boulders of the coast, but I was thrown for my troubles into an even wetter cell. So at last I realized that the only way to leave that jail was through the front door, escorted by a troop of the royal army.

Through the front door, and escorted by a troop of the royal army, I was taken, still prisoner, out of that jail to Spain, for so much did the Viceroy fear me still, that he would not have me in my own land, for fear that I would somehow have his life of him, as I had promised one day (screaming) as he chanced to pass my cell on a visit to those horrendous dungeons.

And so I was taken to sea, bound for senile, withered Spain, where my executioners waited to have done with me. Therefore I feigned horrible sickness on board, as though I were at death's very door. I raved in fits of lunacy and madness all through the bowels of the ship, crying out for a doctor, for I was "consumed by a thousand divers fevers." My furor and outcry was so great that at last the captain gave the order to cast anchor in the port of Havana. And so I crossed the plank to El Morro (the subterranean prison of a massive fortress), clanking my chains and screaming horrible cries.

HAVANA

CHAPTER XXX

Which tells of my escape from Havana.

Summer. Birds, melting in midflight, fall, like boiling lead, on the heads of the few pedestrians willing to risk their lives by going out into the noonday heat. The people are killed on the instant.

Summer. The island, like a long metal fish, sparkles, glints, blindingly glares, and throws off gleams and fiery, fulminous vapors.

Summer. The ocean has started to evaporate. A cloud burning gaseous blue covers the city.

Summer. People, stentoriously screaming, run to the central lagoon, dive deep into its thermal water and, plastering themselves over with bottom mud, try to keep their skin from melting off their bones.

Summer. Women, in the middle of the street, begin to strip off their clothing and run about madly, striking flinty sparks from the cobblestones.

Summer. I, inside El Morro, hop from one side of my cell to the other. I look out the bars of my window and see the boiling harbor. And I start yelling, begging for them to pitch me in the ocean.

Summer. The fever of the heat has made my jailers mean. Their teeth set on edge by my screaming, they enter my cell and soundly beat me. I pray God that He give me a proof of His existence by sending me a prompt death. But I doubt He has heard me. For if God had ever been hereabouts He would have been driven quite mad.

Summer. The walls of my cell slowly change color, from flint to red, and from red to winey scarlet, and from burgundy to brilliant black . . . The floor begins to shine like a mirror, too, and the first molten sparks begin to fall from the ceiling. I can only stay alive by hopping about, but whenever my feet touch the ground, they sizzle. I hop. I hop. I hop.

Summer. At last the heat melts the bars of my cell, and I hop out of this red-hot oven, leaving part of my skin stuck to the sides of the window, where the melted iron still drips.

And in one great leap I leap into the seething waters of the bay and speedily swim across its mouth (which luckily is a narrow one) to the other side, whereon the city of Havana is founded. And I leap the seawall (my flesh dripping off me) and make my way into the labyrinth of streets, where poor creatures run madly from arcades to doorways and then jump, with terror, from marquee to porte cochere to overhang to eave, constantly changing temperature and color. In a fever to find some solace from the ovenlike heat, I cross Calle Del Obispo and come to the park wherein the lagoon lies, which looks to be more of a sea of bobbing heads than of water, and I dive into this lake, drowning the heat a bit by so doing, and at the same time avoiding capture by my pursuers from El Morro, who were gaining on me rapidly . . . But there comes a moment when the waters of this, the city's one and only body of water, become so unbearable from their torridness, that we all begin bobbing up out of them, like a million live frogs in a cooking pot. And so I flop out, onto the shimmering rocks about the lagoon. But I see the soldiers, now almost upon me, and giving off puffs of steam from under their arms, as it looked to me as I watched them, half-melted, ooze toward me in the heat. So I leap once more, over the wall about the garden and the lagoon (now evaporating rapidly), and I take O'Reylly Street, even though it is one of the busiest, jump over the convent of the Dominican sisters, walk quickly through Government House, and as I am crossing the Plaza de San Francisco I clamber up onto, and then over, a cart carrying a band of Negro slaves singing and hooting Lord knows what strange African tune. And so I lose myself, or attempt to, in the pack of black men and housewives shopping for their dinners (and paying no heed to the sun, which has halted as though undecidedly in the middle of the sky like a burning snake coiled into a corner). Then I cross over into the Plaza de Armas, where I am given a great scare to find myself the instant target of a rifle barrel and a cry of "Halt!" though I am much relieved to find it is but a pack of street urchins playing at highwaymen. And I take that route toward the cathedral. I march under the very nose of the Archbishop, who is so startled that he blesses me with the sign of the cross; then I leap into a buggy and call to the driver to get me out of this hellish city as fast as he can. We take the Calle Inquisidor, whose very name is enough to terrify me, so I tell him to whip up his horse and make all speed. We have the foul luck to run over, lying in the very middle of the street like any cur, one of the purebred dogs belonging to the Countesses de Aguasclaras. These ladies, who are sitting half-naked on the portico of their mansion taking some sun (or rather its glare), when they see the mishap, leap up and begin to scream to high heaven, and all the bells of the cathedral start to peal.

So, pursued by the Countesses' private army, by the soldiers from El Morro, by the Governor and the Archbishop themselves, I come, by running across eaves and rooftops, to the seawall, leap upon it, and as I look back I see the enraged ladies tearing the coachman (and even his poor horse) to pieces; so I leap once again into the bubbling bay and hide among the turbid waters of the coast. I then come out a little ways away and seize the first row-boat I come to, and so I depart the port of Havana, paddling with my hands (as there are no oars) through a cross fire from the two batteries—the cannons at the castle (by order of the Governor and the outraged Countesses) and at El Morro (by order of the prison warden and my savage jailers). Tacking widely in great Z's, I at last make the open sea, leaving the Bay of Havana in my wake . . . And paddling through the linked chain of hurricanes constantly forming in these unquiet waters, I come finally to the shores of Florida. As I reach the coast I throw myself, by now more dead than alive, under a sheltering palm tree. I am as naked of clothes as the morning I came into the world, and so hungry that had my exhaustion not overpowered me, I readily would have eaten my own arm off.

United States

CHAPTER XXXI

On new, though old, peregrinations.

And so once again I found myself in that country where for every breath of air one must pay a tax. And again making shift in a thousand ways to keep from dying of hunger, barely keeping myself alive on greens and other vegetables, without much savor either, which the inhabitants bring home from the *greengrocer* and eat (for which, I believe, they are called *gringos*). But I am not going to recount the fat skein of calamities I suffered in this land, in order simply to "get by," for the mere remembering of them (much less the writing them down) gives me fits of shame. I will only name the most honest work I did, to wit: wipe backsides, pick rags, care for aging millionaires and softheaded persons, translate books (the hardest and dirtiest of all work), and collect trash (which I sold in bags as cotton to Northern mills) . . . I lived this sad way for a long while, and then one day I was walking along, with three great sacks quite full of garbage slung over my shoulder, when I heard the news that in México at last *independence had been declared*. And so with the Constitution in hand (for I had thrown down my sacks of garbage), I leaped for joy and landed (as a result of that same exceedingly joyous leap) on my own yearned-for soil. But what foul and rotten luck was mine! for I had not well calculated my jump, and I came down directly on the Castle of San Juan de Ulúa, which was still in the hands of Fernando VII, and so the commander of the castle, General Dávila, took me prisoner and threw me into the deepest dungeon-cell of that entire medieval prison . . . There, with all the time in the world before me, I again read over the so-wished-for Constitution, and I began to emend it, marking it all over in its margins, for there was hardly anything in it but praise for that cunning rogue Iturbe, the fact of which brought on my first twinge (or fit, rather) of disappointment under independence. For could it be, I said, that so much blood had been wasted, and our lives so long endangered and placed at risk, merely so that a new satrap (no better than the old, and without even the

excuse of coming from a foreign land) should come along to crown
himself emperor with all the pomp of ancient Rome? Well then,
said I, this only proves that the war is not yet won, or done. The
struggle for independence is still alive . . . And at that moment, I
began to write my "Letter of Farewell to the Mexicans" written
from the Castle of San Juan de Ulúa. And when General Dávila
intercepted it (or rather wrenched it from my hands, as actually
occurred) and read it over, he ran to my cell and spoke the following words:

"I do not know, for a fact, whose more fell enemy thou mayest
be, the Spanish Royal Monarchy's or the New Iturbean Empire's.
But as I feel that thou mayest do more damage to the Emperor
Iturbe, who is just beginning his reign, than to us, who are in
retreat, I have resolved to free thee."

And I replied:

"You have made a wise decision, for although my hatred of
Fernando and all his royal marionettes and trained monkeys, not
to mention the Mexican burros mixed in among them, is infinite,
the downfall of this false, befeathered and beplumed emperor is
more important, for he crowns himself emperor of his country in
an act which can only bring shame to all true Mexicans."

And so, without further ado, I packed up my manuscripts and
walked, for the first time with legal authority, out of one of the
most frightful Spanish dungeons that had ever been.

CHAPTER XXXII

Which records the friar's colloquy with the new emperor.

"Ah, my dear Bishop of Baltimore . . . I should think you had sel-
dom been attended by an audience so large or distinguished as
that which has come to hear your address on the occasion of your
inauguration into the government of New León. I believe you must
feel most gratified—for after so many and such hard persecutions,
you see your dreams made reality, and you have returned to your
native country with great honor, and with your own and your
country's freedom at last fully achieved."

"Oh, *Señor Agustín* . . ."

"Hmph. 'Your Majesty,' if you please, sir."

"I should think you would understand me when I called you 'Señor Agustín.' We might change that, if it so distresses you, to 'Don Agustín,' or simply 'Sir.' "

"You are very free, *Your Eminence*."

"Let us not play games. There is no need to stand on ceremony with me, *Señor Agustín*, nor to resort to fancy titles. And as for my address, I am happy enough with what I said, because I did not overreach my own possibilities, of which I am most conscious. And above all because I did not deceive myself or try to deceive anyone else, especially my countrymen who heard me."

"But won't you be seated, *Your Eminence?*"

"Fray Servando Teresa de Mier is my name . . . And in truth I'm a bit afraid to sit down, because I might break an egg."

"I beg your pardon?"

"I fear I might soil my clothes with egg yolk, because all the noblemen of the court here are so covered with galloons and feathers that I fear they are metamorphosing into hens."

"Ah, you are so eloquent . . ."

"At least, I have begun to hear them cackle . . . but I suppose I shall risk it. Let me sit. After all, simply being here is much more risky, is it not? I was saying, *sir* . . ."

"Oh."

"I was saying that I am happy enough with my words, because I was honest with both myself and my hearers and because I was not swollen up with pompous phrases, or with promises . . ."

"I believe that any politician who does not make them will find he has a very short career."

"I do not pretend to have any great success, unless it be through reason. To be quite frank with you and not to 'beat about the bush,' *Señor Agustín*, what you have done is nothing but a confidence game, pure hoax and fraud . . ."

"You should show some respect to *Your Majesty*."

"Your Majesty be damned! *Señor Agustín* I call you, and you may like it or not. Your coronation was nothing but a clumsy charade, a vile and dirty pantomime."

"*Fray Servando!*"

"At last you call things by their name! But there is no shame in that for me, or in my name either. Look at my hands, Señor Agustín. There is a reason they are crippled and ugly, there is a reason that there is no doctor that can cure them, there is a reason they can not even bless any longer. Do you honestly believe these hands will accept this show of pomp, this bluster and bluff which you stand as the head of? Do you honestly believe that after forty years of strife and struggle, of fighting always for independence, that I am going to stand for this filthy betrayal of all my ideals?"

"You have said mass again with hard Castilian brandy, it appears, Fray Servando."

"And if I had, you'd not care! What have you against good Spanish brandy? Don't rail against vulgar drinks, Señor Agustín, for where would your 'empire' be without the poison of pulque and chiche to lull the entire country into a stupor and to help you to buy that absurd crown you wear? You and all that rabble of servile dolts that hang about you owe your ridiculous titles to pulque and the cactus that yields it. For surely you do not claim descent from the emperors of Rome? Surely that crown would not have found its way onto your brow without some pecuniary dealings not strictly contemplated in most treatises on kingship? And you ask me whether I am not content, whether I am not most pleased. Well, sir, please be advised that I am not, nor will I be until I see that crown and the head that bears it rolling in the dust."

"You threaten me, Servando?"

"At last, I see, I am no friar, and I am glad of it. For in truth, when one has been made to pass through all manner of torment imaginable, at least there is left to one the tranquility of knowing that there is nothing that can any longer shock or surprise. You inspire no fear in me. I am used to a life of poverty, misery, and constant danger to my life and limb. Indeed, the only thing to which I have never been able to accustom myself is a life of mean-spiritedness and pretense, political trickery. I could, I suppose, resign myself to your 'empire' and pass myself off well enough as just another of those neo-Aztec priests and simpletons that make up its neo-indigenous hierarchy. I might even bring myself to belong to the Royal Order of the Knights of Guadalupe which you in your wisdom have founded and which every man with a grand storehouse or a gold mine may join. But my old habits are enough to keep me. I have been naked, but that has not sufficiently reduced my self-esteem, Señor Agustín, that I would now not speak out against such great absurdities as those which your person incarnates . . . You are my enemy, Señor Agustín, as any man would be who stood in the way of liberty, freedom, and independence. But

you are a still greater enemy of mine because you have no principles, even were they despicable ones, but only self-interest . . . I
hear what your adulators call you—*Tur Vir Dei*—turning your
name about, as though you were a knight of God. I do not believe
that God concerns himself much with that type of knight, first of
all because they are not such. With all those frippery trappings, all
those galloons and feathers and that standard borne above your
head, you remind me of one of those prostitutes in Pistoria, that
only came out during the lusty carnivals held in Italy."

"Enough, Señor Mier! I have heard enough of your insults. I am
about to call the soldiers, to imprison you."

"And that is your democracy! . . . That I am to be prisoner once
more indicates not that I have committed any crime, but solely
that México is not yet free."

And the befeathered guards came in, the courtiers breast-plated
with tinkling medals, and they escorted me away. With great to-
do I was taken to the cells of the convent of the Dominicans, and
there was I locked away . . . But I had never been so at peace as
then, at that moment when I told that preening coxcomb, crowned
emperor by a wonderful sleight of hand, all I had had to say to
him since the first instant I had heard of his coronation and his
system of government . . . And so now, in jail, and by the light of
a waxy sputtering candle, I have begun to write diatribes against
him and to set about preparing for the *true revolution*.

CHAPTER XXXIII

The beginnings.

But revolutions are not won in jails, though true enough it may
be that they are often engendered, or "hatched," there. Such a great
accumulation of hatred, so many blows by the flat of a saber blade,
so many beatings are necessary so that at last that unending and
uphill process of overthrowing governments can be set in motion,
that a prison indeed seems the fittest place for the conception of
revolutions. Thus it was that once again I set about plotting my

escape (ay, always escape!) from that so horribly ventilated prison called Oblivion, whose name I could see was well come by, for, so long as I was there, I constantly lived among the skeletons of those who had preceded me. I slept on those bones, I leaned my elbow on them, and sat, while writing my memoirs, so that at last the skulls lying about came to be most familiar and even at times comforting to me, though I never arrived at a very exact calculation of their number ... I say comforting for it came about that with a sharp-pointed leg bone from one of the old Inquisition's now-defunct prisoners, while a skull looked on smiling, I began to dig in the floor of my cell, with great silence and constancy; and forever trading one worn bone for another newer (for the stone was of an exceeding hardness and would soon splinter them or wear them quite away); at last I saw light. I finished the hole and crept outside, leaving shreds of my habits and my person along the sides of my rocky tunnel. And I hid myself within a barn nearby, the property of two quite holy and extremely pious old ladies, though quite scattered in mind, who ran in to aid me. And what aid those perfectly idiotic old spinsters lent me, my God! No sooner had I explained to them that I was attempting to escape and sorely needed protection, than they had run off (with what I still presume to have been the most elevated of intentions) to the first Royalist barracks they came to. And so I was turned in by my protectresses. And so I lived once more in the presence of my familiar skeletons. And so I set about planning a new escape ...

It was in that deep study that I found myself when, from the Court itself, orders came to my jailers that they should transfer me to the Inquisition's old prison, now renamed The Patio of the Orange Trees, even in spite of the fact that not a weed grew anywhere near the accursed precincts of the jail. So I began to plan a new escape ... But this proved not to be necessary. For one morning as I was attempting to gnaw a way through my ceiling, I heard a great hurly-burly of cries and drums, and I thought I could make out a crowd crying ¡Viva la República!, though I could hardly give my own ears credence. I fell from the ceiling, to which I had been clinging by my fingernails, for they had grown that long. And I pricked up my ears. I heard the shouts much clearer now—it was the Army of Independence which, led by the braying Santa Anna, was coming to free me from my cell, for the false and pretending Iturbe's empire had been overthrown. And so my cell's door was thrown wide open and a multitude of crying, shouting men rushed

in and bore me out on their shoulders. Now there was no doubt—
México had been made free.

The friar, carried along on the crowd's shoulders, immediately
began asking the people questions to find out what type of government had been chosen for the new Republic, and who its president
was, and who its most important leaders. And of course he wanted
very badly to know whether "that beast Iturbe" had been hanged,
and how they could have allowed him to escape, whether some
lackey or caretaker about the chattering magpie of an emperor had
been allowed to spirit him away. The friar begged most urgently
to be informed of all these things, and he kicked at the heads of
those that were bearing him along if they did not give him immedi-
ate and precise answers to his questions. And so, questioning and
kicking, and borne aloft on the shoulders of his admirers, he came
to the vaulted nave of Saint Peter and Saint Paul's, in that city,
where he was about to offer a few words, once more, to all that
enormous mass of people gathered in the city, and flooding the
streets, crowding into balconies, terraces, porches, porticoes, rooftops, and windows, and climbing up into trees where from time to
time one would drop out, the branch he was sitting on suddenly
cracking. A great silence fell. And the friar began his address. "It
is good that Félix Fernández is the new President of the Republic,
though his calling himself Guadalupe Victoria is a thing which
somewhat puzzles me. But to be President, I believe the choice is
good, for so far as I can gather he is the only man among those
who well and truly struggled for our independence that knows how
to read and write," he said. "And indeed my only regret is that the
Republic is to be of the kind known as federal instead of an intelli-
gently centralized republic—that is a thing I never had been led
to suspect."

... And so began, friar, thy new campaign, this one in times
of democracy.

He spoke out, in a voice fevered and filled with sonorities. First
he demanded silence and attention. And then he spoke: "From this
nave I annul and blot out all acts of the empire, the Treaty of
Cordova, the Plan of Iguala, the government by monarchy, but
equally I veto this system, this federal government, rather than a
central republican government, or at the least a federal system
tempered with foresight *and intelligence*." (And here one could

hear a murmur from the crowd. And the new President, Guadalupe Victoria, scratched his ear, though the friar stamped on the hard stone floor once, and then again, and three plaster virgins toppled from their niches and shattered on the heads of the crowd. And silence then returned.) "I have always been in favor of federation," he said, and everyone's eyes near popped from their heads, "but a modest and reasonable, rational federation, a federation true to and in conformity with our scarce enlightenment and the circumstances in which we find ourselves—an imminent war, my friends—which force us to be more than ever united." (And here more murmurs arose here and there, which the friar muted with, now, but a single stamp of his foot and the loss of not a single virgin. Only the Bishop, whose church this was, was heard still to growlingly grumble and mutter. And then the friar lifted his voice so high that the two stained-glass windows of the laterals and chapels quivered, the roses threatened to shatter, and echoes boomed so deafeningly through the long central nave that only a miracle saved the Bishop's hearing.) "I have always stated that in my opinion we should find a mean, a *golden* mean, between the lax and easy confederation of the United States, whose defects many observers have seen and commented upon, and which in that very country has many antagonists, for the country is divided between the Federalists and the Democrats; a mean, I say, between the lax and easy confederation of the United States and the dangerous centralization or concentration of powers of Colombia or Peru, a mean in which, while leaving to the various and separate provinces the very specific faculties for providing for their own necessities and for promoting their own well-being and prosperity, the unity of the whole will not be destroyed—a unity now more than ever before centrally necessary to us, to render us the respect *and fear* of the Holy Alliance." (And here the Bishop looked about for an egress, but he was held back by the words of the friar, whose voice had now become a horrific howl resounding from every wall and booming so sonorously that candles about the altar were shaken loose from their perches.) "Nor should the action of government be weakened and enervated, for now more than ever must it be energetic," and the Bishop was transfixed, "so as to confront simultaneously and promptly the problems of the nation with all its strength and resources. *Medio tutissimus ibis.* That is my vow, my political will and testament."[22]

---

[22]Fray Servando, *Prophecy for the Mexican Federation.*

A great burst of applause erupted within the vaults of the cathedral, nigh shaking it to its foundations. In fact the Bishop watched in terror as all the columns began to quake, and he jumped quickly up and ran. "He that flees now can never be anything but traitor," spoke out a voice which, of course, had to belong to the inspired friar. But there was no time left for reasoning, and so the Bishop flew through the church like a shot, and even at the door paused only to take his bearings before he continued his pell-mell flight to the convent, to the cubicles of the interns. But the crowd, now captained by the indefatigable friar, closed on him. The Bishop ran up a short flight of stairs and began to shinny up a column, but the friar in a second had jumped up and caught the hem of his robes and dragged him down and tossed him to the bellowing mob.

"This is my vow, my political will and testament," repeated the friar, now very somberly, in a voice that barely soughed.

And now the crowd shared among itself tiny portions of meat that once had been the body of the Bishop. *"Si fractus illabatur orbis, impavidum ferient ruinae,"* breathed the friar, and descended the steps of that imposing college.

Now there was no other sound to be heard than the constant pealing of the bells and the clamor of the *folk*, who filled every street. The friar, who had been somewhat fatigued by all this unsettling spectacle, asked to be allowed to retire to the apartment which the President had put at his service in the palace of the governor. "What street should I take, my man, to go to the palace?" he asked a passerby, for the friar was so befuddled by the heat and noise that he had lost his bearings altogether. "Why, Fray Servando Teresa de Mier Street," his guide replied, a man of very mixed parentage, by his features. The friar, vexed at this, thought his leg was being pulled for him, and it was not until he espied his name upon a black plaque at the corner of a thoroughfare, and the same sign repeated at every corner, that the truth broke in upon him. He passed a hand over his now moist forehead and walked on, taking great bouncing strides, to his new residence. A blast on a cornet, which scared him witless for a moment and startled him for many more, greeted his arrival at the palace. And so Fray Servando, the matter coming clear to him at last, marched on, undeterred by the foolish pomp, and he even quite snappily saluted the generals who were so ceremoniously ushering him in. Once inside the palace, which winked everywhere with gold, he climbed an exceedingly long staircase in four great hops, but then he bumped into a legion of twelve most condescending servants who insisted on showing him to his chambers. "Far enough," he said to the squad of footmen and butlers. He raised a peremptory hand and forbade them to enter his rooms. "You may retire," the friar said to the two sentinels who stood before his chamber door to guard his sleeping and his life. "I have been far too well guarded for too long to have to suffer more of it now," he muttered between his teeth as the two guards disappeared down the red-carpeted hall. He then went in and closed the door.

The friar, alone at last within his room, breathed a small sigh of relief.

But look here—from under the bed, from out of the seams in the upholstery, from behind the curtains and out of mirrors and even out of the woodwork there appear friars, ministers, ancient countesses, the most respectable members of the clergy, and even His Honor the President himself who, brushing cobwebs off his coattails, comes toward the friar, saying, "Surprise!, Fray Servando! This is to show our delight at your coming . . ." And with gestures exceedingly refined, his both hands extended to clasp the friar's, the President showed such effusiveness that it was strange more tears did not come to his eyes.

"Long live our globe-trotting friar!" cried their voices, which had been well lubricated for the task by wine. And so the friar spread a large grimace over his face, which was meant to be a smile, and saluted them all with one limp wave. "There is no way out," he said, very slowly and so softly that only he himself could hear. "There is no way out," he said again, and then he bucked up his spirit and smiled as he went forward to meet them.

CHAPTER XXXIV

Of what little happened in a season of calm.

The palace, like a great rectangular bird cage, was a crumbling pile to one side of the Central Plaza of the city. The palace was immense. Its halls and passageways numbered hundreds, as did also its chambers and antechambers, halls, salons, and ballrooms, its high bedchambers and parlors, each with its own room for a privy which could seat an army, its infinite galleries that opened out onto miles-long colonnades. And each colonnade had its own balcony, and each balcony had its railing wrought of fine-spun iron, and each railing curved down into a stair, and each stair led into an arcade, and under each arcade one in those times made one's way into a lovely patio planted with ages-old nopal cactuses rising like mad candelabra, or stiffened phalluses, or upside-down spiders with their feet in the air, high into the hot blue sky.

Millions of useless objects littered the building of unclassifiable style, and so it was extremely difficult to walk, or in any way make one's way, through a maze of pennants, banners, flags, statues, shields, and coats of arms, and all the other objects fashioned from sheer unbridled fantasy that generations of Mexicans had piled into this great shaky jewelbox-coffin-birdcage-folly. And so rusty and decrepit was this truly awesome edifice that from time to time one of the ancient gigantic chandeliers would come unloosened from the ceiling and fall with a thunderous crash of shattering crystal prisms and twisted metal onto the head of some general or other high official, squashing him dead on the instant. A day of mourning would be declared. And the Galleries of Honor would be filled even fuller with the gimcracks accumulated through a long and distinguished life and bequeathed by the deceased—relics now declared sacred, monuments to the country.

Through the palace glide with frightened soft steps the servants, who slip along close by the walls and serve with deliberate grace, holding their breath so the cracked and dusty statues will not topple from their pedestals upon them. And still, the servants killed by falling statuary number thousands.

A few days ago the President, who was walking along most sublimely sipping the blood of an eagle which he had dismembered himself, came very near being killed, as did his wife who was with him, and a number of his closest advisers, when one of the high cupolas with all its cargo of gold leaf crashed down from above and, though but brushing the President's ears, obliterated a number of his most junior followers. For the good fortune of the State, only thirty-seven generals (all supporters of Santa Anna, so people said) and somewhere about a hundred Creoles were killed. These last were, however, all loyal supporters of the President, who at the time were walking close by his side bowing and cringing most amiably.

But it is the servants, of course, with their constant comings and goings about the palace, who most frequently perish. Every day without fail, before the great arcade at the entrance, a line is formed of new servants that are enlisted to replace those recently annihilated. And every day without fail by the rear arcade the most recent victims are removed. Notwithstanding all this, the fervor of the people, their enthusiasm to serve the new President is such that the line at the entrance is always longer than that formed by the lifeless bodies going out the back. The President's support is virtually unanimous. Virtually . . .

Not alone for its style of construction is the palace called the National Bird Cage, for hundreds upon hundreds of poets (lodged to the very roof beams of the garrets) fill its chambers, its grand halls and ballrooms and great salons, crowd its passages and corridors, stroll through the galleries, gardens, and patios, and compose—always they compose. They are to a man composing works that will be universally proclaimed *works of genius*. In the afternoon, and sometimes even of an early morning before dawn, the jubilee of those creatures, who have just discovered a rhyme *par excellence*, the unparalleled word, can sometimes grow to deafening proportions. They dance hand in hand in a ring, they almost seem to be trying to beat their wings and fly away, so transporting is their ecstasy. They call down the Muses with exotic dance, they posture and declaim. They pass into deliriums of recitations. The President has instituted a Poets' Reserve within the National Bird Cage, and in it there may find a perch any poet that composes a sonnet (or ode) in his honor. (And the task could not be easier, since to the eternal glory of the Spanish language *Victoria* rhymes perfectly with *gloria*.) President Guadalupe Victoria has spoken: "He who is on my side shall rise." And so every day a great procession of bards and Delphic vessels wends into the palace and is lodged under its flaking roof. From the farthest islands, from the jungle, from savage tribes, from desolate Siberia and even from the courts of France and Spain, every day sees the arrival of some peregrine troubadour. The doors of the palace are, by presidential decree, thrown wide. A roll of sheets of manuscript, on which are already inscribed the occasional verses for the occasions of this regime, carried under the poet's arm, makes a way for him into the Preserve of Poets.

Nevertheless, from time to time in the chirruping peace of the Poets' Preserve a note of discord may be heard, a different song is sung. And then there will come a shriek, and one of the President's canaries (or several) dies at the hands of a vulturous horde of contending songsters. The offender has misrhymed, linking the name of the President in a less glorious fashion than is the wont thereabouts. The President himself is, so they say, never apprised of the bloody events that sometimes transpire within his realm. It is his adorers, swept away by indignation, who take justice to themselves. The President (praises to his name) declares that he is a sworn enemy to all violence. And in fact when these sanguinary events occur, the President (long may he live, and reign) will be found strolling through the immemorial cactuses. In spite of all, though, at times the President (may his glories forever shine) asks his singing choir to what might be owed the change of timbre in their songs. Why is there a missing voice? But they immediately reply with fulsome praises, resounding calls of glory, applause that may sometimes last for weeks. The President (sainted may he be) then smugly retires to his regal quarters and, to the sound of the praises ever rising, he falls smilingly to sleep. Indubitably, the President (may he live forever) is a protector of poets. A lover of poetry.

But there are times too when the delirium of his followers and admirers, the applause, and the constant cries of "Long live our Great Liberator!" "Long live the empire killer!", combined with the recitals of long odes and honeyed sonnets, overpass the usual limits. And at those times, His Honor the President, who finds his sleep disturbed, rises a bit irritated out of bed, goes in his underclothes to the Presidential Box in the mezzanine overlooking the greatest hall of all the palace, and, with consummate grace and serenity, brings a single finger to his lips. The songbirds suddenly cease their songs. And then the President turns and passes down the halls once more to his bedchamber, and he enters and crawls into bed.

And now, with his eyes closed, he thinks once more of the exalted multitude, the multitude which applauds until its hands sting, the multitude which he can silence with a single index finger laid across his lips. "But all of them were not there," he thinks, and his eyes almost flutter open. "The two most important ones were not there," and his eyes drop closed. "I must not forget them." And then he sleeps. The silence now is absolute.

The silence, the great calm, filled the hallways, chambers and apartments, and fell like a mantle over the motionless statues.

But when it came to Fray Servando's room, it stopped. The friar spoke: "At last," he said, "those trained parrots have shut up." He stood up, still amazed that the fluttering and cooing of the poets had ceased, and he tried to find out at what hour of the day this marvel had occurred. He looked out through the great windows with their drawn curtains, and he saw other windows that opened on still other windows, and so on and on and on. He raised his eyes, but he could only just make out the dizzingly high roof, and nothing of the sky. He stood beside his enormous bed and then made a circuit of his spacious room. By the time he had come to the door of it, he was panting with the exertion. "It's worth your life to see the sun in this monstrosity," he said. "This is worse than crossing the Pyrenees." He went out into the Great Hall of the Generals, where a few poets, hiding behind the pillars, were tuning up a low-throated trill, and he hushed them with a brusque gesture with one hand. With the same motion he attempted to halt a gang of servants, ministers, and nobility who were reverently approaching him. But his gesture proved futile, for the procession continued to advance on him. They had something most important to remind him of. "This is the last straw," said Fray Servando. And so in one great jump he crossed the Consular Chamber (more than a hundred yards long) and tried to hide in the old Gallery of the Viceroys. But his persecutors were following hot on his heels. "Today," they were saying, "is the day . . ." And some of them burst out in prayers of thanksgiving. One lady, who seemed to want desperately to detain the friar, threw her thick breviary made of gold at him. The book clanged into the great pilgrim's head, at which Fray Servando, enraged, and understanding nothing of the gibberish issuing from so many mouths at once, stopped dead still in the very center of the salon swimming in centuries-old artefacts, and he yelled, as loud as he could yell. His shout shook loose a statue of a viceroy, which fell onto a Chinese-Indian maid left over from the old royal staff, and killed her. The crash of the falling statue set off a chain of destruction—every statue in the hall toppled, like a row of dominoes. The hall itself was threatened with annihilation, and the friar took advantage of the cataclysm to slip away, since at any rate the statue shards by now had made a wall between him and his persecutors. He crossed the nigh infinite Gallery of Immortal Martyrs, went briefly through the Hall of Perpetual Heroes, and now breathing hard and with dragging step, he passed through the Court of Children Who Gave Their Blood Too for Their Land. He looked all about to find an object he might hold on to. But everything was so monumental that it gave off an air of unreality, and was so huge that for one to grab on to one of those gigantic children a stepladder two stories tall would have been necessary. And so finally he staggered weakly into the Hall of Buffoons, crossed the passageway filled with emergency privies that ran alongside the Hall of Justice, and came into the great salon, always seeking a ray of sunlight to follow to its source, out to the balconies and out of doors. There in the grandest hall of all the palace he stumbled, almost fainting, on the steps of a dais upholstered in a drape of crimson velvet on which were embroidered the columns of *Plus ultra* in golden thread. To keep from falling he clutched at the velvet covering, and he caught his breath there and wiped his face and breast dry on the cloth. "If the President will not give me a new apartment this very day," he said, "tomorrow the Revolution begins again." And then he pulled himself together and, like a man mortally wounded, he dragged himself, his feet hurting so dreadfully that moans escaped his dry and cracking lips, across the Court of Accords, the Pavilion of Arms, and entered the galleries in which several oils of "honest nudity" were hung. He studied them awhile. But suddenly, furious, he recoiled. Before him, in a frame all royal black and gold, had arisen the figure of "His Highness the Emperor Carlos V, fully armed with lance and socket, crimson plume, and scarlet sash." Servando tried to spit upon it, but his throat and lips unfortunately were too parched. And so he went on, and at last, clamoring for a priest to make his last confession, he saw, at the end of a long, long passageway, the light from out of doors. Staggering and stumbling, so weary had his journey been, he ran out into the corridor, crossed the twelve wrought-iron balconies of delicate tracery, and for an instant he glimpsed the great standard on which were hung the national shield and coat of arms. But these objects he saw from the rear, for they faced outward, into the Great Plaza, so that all the friar could truly see was a mass of iron rusted by the rains. Still gasping for breath, yet breathing somewhat easier, he groped his way along the railing to one end of the enormous balcony, and lapsed onto a bench. The heat was suffocating. He tried to give himself the consolation of resting his eyes on a spot of greenery, so he turned them to a patio that lay along that side, and he was relieving them by the sight of the branching cactuses, when the voice of one of the poets, who wished to read him his "Apology to the President of the Republic," rose up to him from the garden. Immediately Fray Servando stood and leaned over the balcony, and for a moment he was dumbfounded. The man (far along in years), armed with compasses, triangles, rulers, and a good hundred other articles which Servando did not know the names or uses of, was reciting a kind of litany of the names of all the kinds of columns and pillars of the palace, and the tiniest details of them, the number and position of the pilasters and architraves, the quantity of friezes, bas reliefs and high reliefs and cornices and volutes, the composition of the plaster and stucco for the walls, every kind of tree that lived in the garden and the exact number of leaves on every one, and finally even the different families of ants which lived in their boles and branches. And then he paused, as though to catch his breath, but then began again, this time somewhat more parsimoniously, to note, alphabetically, every word which had been used in a great vellum folder on whose cover could be seen the title *An Inventory of Paving-Tiles* (in golden letters two inches high). The friar, from his balcony, read to himself the title of that work in progress. He even spoke it several times aloud. And then, enraged, he threw himself onto a spiny cactus (a prickly pear, in fact), slid down its trunk, stood before the would-be apologist, and cuffed him. But the poet stood wrapped in his own imaginings, and then continued his composing. Now he was counting the spines of the cactuses in the garden, the kinds of stones and pebbles that gleamed there, and indicating the notes shrieked by a kestrel which had been attracted by the shine of his bald spot and was hovering overhead with keening cries. Fray Servando slapped the man again. But the writer was as though in a state of grace, a mystical trance. "Ten thousand thorns of one inch long," he was chanting. "Eight Corinthian canopies," now he crooned. "One thousand five hundred bronze door knockers," he brayed. And on and on he went, numbering, naming, noting, murmuring, lost in another world. Finally Fray Servando saw that it was futile to try to unseat the poet from his hobbyhorse, and so he left him (although the kestrel was now threatening to pull out his eyes), and climbed up again, this time by way of a stairway, to his own balcony. "I will be the poet of hammock and fan," he thought to himself as he subsided into exactly such a device swung from the balustrade. Now he was calmer. "At least," he thought, "my friend Heredia never goes so far." And he looked out, to see if he could see that poet, but Heredia still had not made his appearance there. "Ah, well," thought Servando, "perhaps he is lost in one of the hallways, or a scaffold has fallen on him, and he will never come . . . And maybe that is for the best," he thought, grown somewhat indifferent now and fanning himself with his hand. "Because at times he can be as unbearable as the rest." And then he recalled the night before, and the rehearsal for that dreadful tragedy called *Sulla* (translation by José María Heredia y Heredia), where he had seen the poet in one of the boxes, seated next to the President (who had unlaced his boots) and with head inclined, making gesture after gesture of sycophancy to his "protector," bowing his head mock-humbly to the audience as the curtain fell, and actually almost blushing as the ladies (who had not understood a word of it all) broke into loud, sustained, and perfectly customary applause. He saw all that old-hat show of lapdog insincerity, and he pitied it, although of course it had disgusted him as well. And that Roman tragedy, and that whole sea of gold braid and jewels and décolletage, he thought, were there gathered in honor of the Virgin of Guadalupe, in commemoration of her anniversary which was at hand. But then his choler, as it had risen, fell. But the cooing and unction of the poets came to him again, and although it was not terribly loud (for the President was still sleeping) Fray Servando found it unbearable. So he tried to distract himself some way, to take his mind and ears off that contemptible sound, and he looked about for a sight that might serve to entertain him for a while. His eyes ran over the palace grounds, sought along the circle of the horizon, looked for some spot of brightness. The tower of the cathedral loomed before him, though, the clock with its terrifyingly engraved numbers, the indefatigable hands moving ahead inexorably with little jerks. And so, in irritation, he looked out toward the Avenue of the New Houses of Cortés, but the houses were old and decrepit by now, hunks falling off their plaster-and-adobe walls, and the spectacle of them lowered his spirits even more. He turned his eyes to the Gate of Flowers (*where not a tree grows,* he thought), gazed a moment at the Plaza of Midday where he saw the prison house the President had just erected there on the site of the old Botanical Gardens, and then, almost in pain, he turned to the Central Plaza, hoping perhaps there to find a sight he could look on without horror or disgust to him. There stood, still untoppled, the statue of the old King Carlos IV. He shook his head, and his vision was rattled by the façade of the cathedral chapel. Its style, the dripping, peaked, mazy convolutions of its baroque excesses, the slavishness of it to long-dead Churriguera's manic designs, horrified the friar, and for a long while he could not bring himself to open his offended eyes. "What need is there of so much flamboyant frippery?" he thought, at once resentfully raising his eyelids and fearful of laying them on still another horrendous sight. And so with half-closed eyes (as a precaution), he passed his gaze lightly over the fronts of the buildings that lay about the palace—the Mint, the two houses of the Treasury, the Plaza of the University, all of a style more crude and brusque than simple rustic or even calm Roman or Norman. And yet it was not horrifying, what he saw, so that, taking courage again, he looked over to the Central Plaza. "I think I should look at people and animals instead," he thought. And so he watched a woman with a parasol slowly making her way across the square, and then a man on horseback and a coach. And then, through the now-deserted plaza, there trudged the tragic figure of a water bearer, his two great clay jugs strapped to his head, as though they would pull his head off backwards. Fray Servando watched the boy (for though stooped, the water bearer had not yet reached his majority) as he crossed the burning pavement, and he wanted to close his eyes again, but he watched transfixed. The boy patiently walked slowly on, his bare feet sizzling on the white-hot bricks. As he came to one of the age-pocked national monuments he lost his balance, stumbled, and the two water-casks were thrown into such a pendulum-swing by the misstep that his head was torn from his neck. The body, spurting blood, fell to the ground kicking like a hen. "My God, what horrors!" cried the friar. "There is a conspiracy to keep me off this balcony forever more." And he looked at the water bearer again, whose lifeless body now was still. Water from the clay jugs that had been smashed to sharp-edged pieces flowed all under him. When Fray Servando had recovered himself a bit (for now the heat was suffocating), he looked again for a cool place to rest his eyes on. He looked out toward the Merchants' Gate, which was thronged with scribes, tortilla vendors, and prostitutes, and suddenly the figure of Father José de Lezamis, balancing atop a boulder, caught his eye. The father was preaching, in that voice of his so like a whining child's.[23] "Thank heaven," thought Fray Servando, "something at last I can rest my eyes on." And he smiled as he looked down on the padre. But then he realized that no one was paying the preacher any mind. The letter writers and scriveners scribbled on, writing their lecherous or insulting documents, the tortilla sellers were calling out their wares as loud as their lungs allowed, and the prostitutes carried out their ages-old offices with utter unconcern for the father's saving words. And so Fray Servando looked again toward the priest who with great emotiveness continued to speak his homily. And so as though that were the straw that broke the camel's back, Fray Servando banged his fist against the wrought-iron rail, gave up all thought of the palace and its surroundings, and sought to find some consolation in the landscape, in that *wide valley* of México, out on the horizon. "The valley . . ." whispered Servando, and he attempted to find that place, known better from books than from his own experiences. But the mountains suddenly rose all about him. Before him there was naught but a suffocating ring of peaks, a circle of mountains which, in parallel concatenations, rose almost to the clouds. And so, he thought, once more, *once more*, I am in a prison. And he looked for a way out. Enraged and terrified, he ran about the balcony, looking all about, to find a way to flee. He looked toward the east, and his eyes ran up against the range of the Sierra Nevada and its two fearsome volcanoes Iztachuatl and Popocatépetl, threatening to fry him to a sizzle; he swiveled his head about, to the southwest, and his nose bumped into the Sierra de Las Cruces, sweeping up like a curtain of dark iron. He ran to the front of the balcony, and

[23]"The gate that concerns us here was the site of the preaching of Father José de Lezamis, an apostolic gentlemen who came to New Spain as the confessor of His Eminence Francisco de Aguiar y Seixas, Bishop of Michoacán, when that distinguished personage, on the persuasion and advice of Lezamis, accepted the Archbishopric of México City. Transferred to this city, Father Lezamis was named a priest to the Cathedral in September of the year 1818 . . . The pastoral zeal of this ecclesiastic not being satisfied with preaching in his church, to which not all those went who the priest would have desired, he resolved to put up a dike against the torrent of corruption which in those days flooded public customs, taking the word of God to where many might hear it, and for this he chose the Merchants' Gate, and every Sunday he would go there to preach, standing precariously atop a great rock or on a bench." José María Marroquí, *La Ciudad de México*, 1900.

as he looked out toward the north his hands could almost touch
the peak of Tlalpán. He hopped about like some frantic marionette
and looked toward the south—the spurs and promontories of Tlalóc
almost crashed into his forehead. And so he turned about and
turned about, like some poor cornered creature, seeking a way to
escape, but wherever he turned, he found naught but high walls
and escarpments, blind alleys, fortifications rising almost straight
upward which could offer him not the least glimmer of hope, or
snowy mountain peaks glinting and sparkling in the sun like
knives and showing, but very rarely, a tree trunk (covered with
spines and thorns). And so by the time at last his gaze met the
Cicoque Peak with a brief shock, and he saw that that lovely
mountain was but another wall, his eyes were filled with tears. "It
is a spell, a hex, an evil eye," he said. "They want to destroy me,
they want to see me die bricked into a high-walled moat. They've
built a prison I can never get me out of." But he was planning his
escape, he could already feel the horror, what a new, and even
more terrible, banishment, would feel like, when he lowered his
view and by pure chance caught a glimpse of a small outcropping,
only about fifty yards high, and covered with trees. Was it, were
those trees, a miracle? And suddenly he realized that this was
Mount Tepeyac, in whose basilica was kept the image of the Virgin
of Guadalupe. His eyes rested on that modest sanctuary, and
seemed to take some rest from it, as well, for it seemed to be
floating in a transparent mist of coolness. Looking at that place,
nearer by far to the palace than those other mountains, he began
to laugh out loud, for he felt that there had come to him a revelation. There he was, laughing and looking at that little peak, when
the first chants began to sound. And he saw, with surprise and
dismay, that from the sanctuary there was issuing a procession of
people. The image of the Virgin preceded the parade, carried on the
shoulders of the faithful. The solemn procession had begun. For
this day was the twelfth of December, 1825. *Again this year the
procession files out from the Sanctuary of Tepeyac, enters the village of Santa Veracruz, crosses the bridge of Mariscala, turns down
the street of Santa Isabel and takes the Alameda Walk, and as it
comes to the bridge of San Francisco, it marches solemnly toward
the Cathedral. The throng of people is overwhelming, and the tumult of the bells is deafening.* And as the procession has gone all
this way, Fray Servando, standing alone in the Deserted Palace (for
almost everyone, including the President himself, has joined the

throng), has never ceased speaking. "What infamy is this!" he cries. "How is it possible that I have not been invited—me!" And here he strikes his breast with his clenched fist, pulls out a handful of hair, and undoes his surcingle and uses it in a fit of self-flagellation. "I—who am the person most closely associated with that idol. I— who am the true liberator. What outrage is this," and he goes on lashing himself, "and where can we be heading, if that mob of scoundrels, robbers, tricksters, confidence men, and provincial hoodlums has seized this chance to lead our way? . . . How dare they ignore me in such wise. To them I am now good for nothing but to ridicule. They all want to see me dead. But I will bring that parade up short. Those scheming ragpickers will see . . ." And with that he was about to leap over the railing of his balcony and run to where the procession was. He had it in his head to jump up and topple the image of the Virgin itself. But he suddenly heard a voice behind him, and felt a hand, which had seized his shoulder, holding him back. *"Prodigious flood,"* the voice intoned, *"be calm, and hush thy mighty, terrifying roar. Soften the mist that swirls about thee, and let me gaze on thy face serene once more."*[24] Fray Servando stopped. He turned toward the poet still calmly reciting one of his interminable poems of nature, and his eyes almost popped out in fury. "By God," he said through clenched teeth, "is parodying your own frothy confections all you know how to do? Look at that. Look at that parade. And me here—me—and my deserts go unrecognized by that rabble. I am forgot. Am I no longer a prophet to those people?" The poet turned toward the procession, and he softly answered the friar. "A prophet in his own land . . . Listen to me, Servando. All things must perish. It is a universal law. Even this world, so lovely and so shining, in which we live . . ."[25] But he could not go on. Fray Servando sprang and fell upon his throat, trying as best he might to choke him, and then muzzling and tying him with his thick dirty girdle. And then he picked him up over his head and carried him over to throw him into the wild mob of naked Indians dancing along the way, when suddenly he felt a small stab of compassion. Poor wretch, he thought. He is a fugitive, like me, and he has a right to his life like all of us, especially since he's no idea what it is. And so he set him down on a sun-blasted balcony. The poet, his hands tied tight, wriggled

[24]José María Heredia y Heredia, *Niágara* (1825 version).
[25]Heredia, "En el Teocalli de Cholua" (1820). ("In The Temple of Cholua").

like a snake though he could do nothing to get on his feet. "Preaching in this country," said the friar, "is like making crucifixes out of water." And he leaned on the railing again and watched the procession go on. *Behind the image of the Virgin comes the Royal Tribunal, the Audiencia, and then the other courts-at-law, the holders of all the many offices there are, the Consular corps, the religious communities, the lay brotherhoods and sisterhoods and the arch-fraternities with their banners and flags blazoned with crosses, and bearing also high processional candlesticks; and then farther back, the folk. Before them, the President (in the old place of the Viceroy), the Archbishop, the Canon Superior, the Dean, the old Cabildo or Town Council, the nobility of the city and a train of their invited guests. And at the very head, presiding over all the train, there is a dance of Indians, as it is their custom, since the days of their heathen-hood, to perform. And over all, the bells, pealing loud.* The friar followed the parade yet a while longer. Then he attempted to scream, but his voice unaccountably failed him. He stepped back from the railing of the balcony and like some automaton of the century before, he began to loose the poet's bonds. When he had done, he helped him to his feet again. They looked at each other in silence. Poor thing, thought the poet, he is old and set in his ways. He lives in the past. He sets up a row about everything. But soon he will be dead. One has to forgive him his tantrums and harangues . . . Poor devil, thought the friar as he set his dusty clothes to rights, he comes from a savage island, and he wants to befriend these savages of another kind. He does not know. His beginning lies in exile. I should have more pity. "I find it strange," he then said aloud, "that you are not in the procession. Has the President forgotten your presence here, too, then?" That voice, thought the poet, that keen, cutting, bitter voice has always been the thing about him I liked least. "No," he finally replied. "It is simply that I did not go. I hate to mix with the rabble." "Then," said the friar, raising his voice so as to be heard above the pealing of the bells, "the best thing for you would be to leave this palace and preserve your body undefiled." He has insulted me yet again, thought the poet, and he said, "I am with *you*, Fray Servando, and so I am with the best of all the nation." The friar was frankly disarmed by this, and he knew not what to answer. He stepped to the railing once again and contemplated the throng. *The dance. The Indians almost naked swaying in rhythm to the tune of a native song—which they call* areyto *in their tongue—and which they themselves parody in a most melancholy voice. First they move slowly, as though in a funeral march. Then they take hands all about and look up at the sky. And then they hop about on one foot, kick up their feet behind and kick themselves in the back, cry out most horribly, pull out their eyes with their fingernails, stab themselves in the heart with a nigh-invisible dagger they hide among their fingers. But the survivors continue to dance, growing more and more frenzied and spirited, until at last they are ejaculating prayers in their native tongue, slitting their own throats and leaping mortally from cliffs and walls, attempting always to reach the divine image, its share of grace. At last a muted discharge from the heroic National Guard, standing on the rooftops of the ministerial edifices about the square, ends the orgiastic frenzy. The procession solemnly marches on. At no moment have the bells been silent.* And now the poet and the friar, stunned almost faint by the discharge of arms and cannons and the constant clanging of the bells, withdraw from the balcony and go to stand at opposite ends of a long, long colonnade where each man breaks out into furious diatribe. Both speak at once. Both whine, harangue, denounce, complain. They tell of their long peregrinations, their pains and torments and inner anguishes, the sadness that comes of banishment and exile, and then at last they stand on spindly, wobbly rocking chairs and go on speaking, waving their hands about in gesticulation, stamping their feet until they have kicked the seat bottoms out, losing their balance from time to time and tumbling to the echoing floor. "For of all the misfortunate miseries, which are manifold," Heredia says, gesticulating and looking up toward the palace's lightning rods, "none are so terrible as the poet's, for not only must he suffer calamities with greater force of sensibility, but he also is bound to try to understand and give them name." And on he spoke, shouting, making his *apologia*. Then the friar, in the midst of his speech of protest, looked at the poet and thought (though he never ceased to speak): He is a crybaby. Suffering is a distraction, an amusement for him. He is always talking of death, but he is careful when he goes down the steps into the garden. At the same time he was going on aloud: "What mockery is this," he said, "not to have invited me. There is some plot afoot. They wish to annihilate me, wipe me out, for they know I am the most extraordinary political genius of all time." Listen to that, then thought the poet, Listen to that. In all his memoirs, and all so badly written, at that, in all of them the only thing he does is talk of Fray Servando. Himself, always himself. Look at him like a peacock strutting. He is nothing but a great show-off, an exhibitionist. But the poet had still gone on reciting the story of his life, telling the innumerable calamities which had hounded and were still hounding him, and the poet went on declaiming ... That romantic spirit that he has always had blows everything out of proportion, the friar thought, Such exaggeration, as the friar was declaiming his *Prophecy for the Mexican Federation*. He tells me he has been hunted across mountains and peaks like a wild beast. He talks to *me* of such things! To *me* he describes persecutions! Though he was still going on with his *Prophecy*, stamping, kicking about, hurling threats into the air, a froth of saliva collecting at the corners of his lips and sputtering at each spat-out word, and knocking apart the chair, which had now lost its back and two of the stretcher rungs. He's a crotchety old curmudgeon, thought then the poet as he began to declaim his *Hymn to the Ocean*. He complains and kicks and protests over everything, he would have everything pulled down and re-begun again, and put to rights, its *errata corrected*. He says dreadful things about President Victoria, who somehow swallows all this old man's senile cranks and nonsense, though I am not sure that if I were in his place I would. The poet's voice in counterpoint to his thought was now soothingly whispering, "Burning mirror of the sky sublime."[26] He is a madman. After he has fought so long for independence, he now declares he will have nothing but a centralized constitution. This man would correct the Old Testament ... and his meditations over the friar ended just as his declamation of the poem did, so that instantly, so as not to lose his impetus, he continued on by breaking into *The Death of the Bull* ... Could there ever be a more contradictory being, thought Servando, though his voice was repeating one of his earliest successes, a discourse on the Republic: "I give thanks to heaven for having restored me to the warmth of my native land, after twenty-seven years of the most vicious and atrocious persecution and terrible labors; I give thanks to the New Kingdom of León, where I was born, for having elevated me to the high seat of this Chamber of Deputies."[27] He tells me he loves simplicity, the friar's thoughts were going on,

[26]Heredia, "Himno al Océano" (1836 version).
[27]Speech given by Servando T. de Mier as Deputy to the First Sovereign Constituent Congress, to formulate protests against the law (1822).

and yet he spends his life composing songs to waterfalls (which he calls "cataracts") and volcanoes and bulls and the ocean . . . Listen to that speech, thought the poet, as he began reciting "The Pleasures of Melancholy," just listen to that speech. How dull and uncomposed. What a dreadful poet he is—not even at the most terrible and awesome moments, when he was about to be burned at the stake, for example, could he construct a line of poetry worth anything more than the paper he used to write it on. And he thinks he has the right to criticize me. Me—who am . . . "And who are we," interrupted the voice of the friar into Heredia's poem and thoughts, "who are we, huddled in this palace, but useless *things*, relics in some museum, rehabilitated prostitutes. What we have done will serve for nothing, for we dance to the music of the latest little cornet. For nothing. And if you attempt to correct the errors, you are a traitor, and if you seek to civilize the bestialities, you are a cynical revisionist, and if you struggle for true liberty and freedom, you are about to meet your doom . . ." The poet fell silent, listening to those words. The friar went on speaking, arguing, making his voice echo through the halls of the deserted palace where from time to time might be heard the rumble of a falling column or a statue that shattered on the parquet floors. "And is that true liberty?" rose the friar's voice to heights unheard before. "To serve that brutal mob that reduces all great things to schemes and grand absurd abstractions, that rabble which has confused bad manners and vulgarity with sweet democracy? Riffraff that thinks democracy means going about half-naked, showing one's gifts to an adulating throng that is actually capable of kissing those gifts? Is that *the end* we have sought? This unrelenting hypocrisy, this constant repeating that we are in paradise and that all things are perfect? For are we indeed in paradise? And does indeed," raising his voice to such terrible volume that the lightning rods on the peaks of the roof were blasted from their moorings and crashed down into the statue of Carlos IV, shattering it at last to bits, "does indeed such a paradise exist? And if it does not, why should we go on trying to invent it here? Why deceive ourselves? Have we seen the land that was promised us? Have we found the consolation and rest from weariness? Is there nothing more to be desired?[28] Well, no.

[28]Fray Servando here mocks the words of Fray Diego Durant, in his *Historia de las Indias de Nueva España y* (sic) *Islas de TerraFirma:* "Ya emos hallado el lugar que nos ha sido prometido; ya emos visto el consuelo y descanso dese cansado pueblo mexicano; ya no hay más que desear."

No. No. We have not found it yet . . ." And he tried to go on, but
the chair let out one last groan, and Fray Servando, sputttering and
cursing, tumbled to the floor. Instantly Heredia stepped down from
his improvised pedestal to help the friar to his feet. "Leave me
be," said Fray Servando, turning in anger against Heredia the moment the poet touched him. "I can get up by myself. I thank you."
And he began the task of getting onto his feet again. He's a proud
old man that's set in his ways, a touchy one, thought the poet as
he watched Servando creakily stagger erect. He's a curmudgeon,
and he has hallucinations. He's always seeing visions, always
thinking they're going to spear him from behind or shoot him in
the back. I've watched him walk down the halls looking over his
shoulder to be sure no one catches him unawares . . . I cannot trust
too much in that coxcomb, the friar was thinking as he struggled
up. He may not be what he seems. Whatever it is that he seems.
For he seems too many things. He publishes a newspaper called *El
Conservador* and at the same time declares himself on the side of
Santa Anna's revolution. He goes about constantly complaining
about the heat of this brutal climate and then writes a *Hymn to
the Sun*. No, I do not think the man bears too much trusting . . .
He was making his way to another chair, to finish his discourse
on, when there erupted (now with unprecedented vigor) a new roar
from the people in the Plaza. Both of them, the friar and the poet
too, ran to the edge of the balcony and leaned out over the crowd:
*The commonfolk, filled with religious zeal, also want to touch the
divine robes of the figure. See it, touch it, and die. The common
folk howl. They pray and clamor for pity, they raise psalms and
prayers never heard before. The crippled flounder as though they
would stand and walk; whores for a moment leave off their trade;
beggars put out their hands but cry for nothing but love; those
with pustules and sores scrape off their bloody scabs and cry for
purification. Some of the faithful walk on their knees toward the
canopied Virgin, others crawl on their bellies and give moans as
though in dying agony; a number of old women lick the ground
where the holy image has passed. A child somehow slips past
the religious cordon about the figure, pushes his way through the
crowd—which has raised its hands to heaven, broken into hysterical tears, and begun to faint in weariness and ecstasy—and runs
through the brother- and sisterhoods until he comes at last to the
great image displayed above his head. Sure that thereby he will
achieve eternal blessing and salvation, the child reaches up to*

*seize one of the garlands draped about the Virgin's robes. And as
he is raising his hands, as his hands reach out, one of the holy
sisters, horrified at the boy's sacrilege (for he would touch the
sacred dais), takes out a pistol from the carved pages of her breviary and shoots him in the head. The boy falls, flailing his arms
and legs. The people in the crowd about the spot cross themselves
holily, and the procession continues on. Moments before it enters
the cathedral, a* Salve, *exceptionally clear, runs like a shiver
through the Plaza. And, above all, the bells . . .* Calm was established once again. Fray Servando and Heredia stood openmouthed
and mute and stared at the long retinue behind the Virgin, now
moving away in the harsh light of midday. I must speak, thought
the poet. Something must be said before we both go mad. Something, anything. We must break this deceiving spell. He looked at
Fray Servando and saw that he was distant, remote, faded, almost
intemporal, floating in the midst of a booming, echoing fog. At
times he raised his hand in what might have been a sign of benediction, though the poet could not tell, to bless a person visible only
to the friar. Poor old man, then thought the poet, looking at that
blurred image almost dissolving in the implacable glare of that
noon, he may have his thousand faults, but he was man enough,
and more, to suffer his banishment, he got through it all the best
he could, he never bowed his knee to any man, or any power—he
did the impossible, he achieved what he set out to do. Above and
beyond any defect, he thought, he is a hero. Or better yet, *a man.*
A true man. And the poet was melted by a great pity for that faded
figure. He almost thought he would take him in his arms, weeping
and begging pardon of him. But when he spoke he said, "Did you
not see, Servando, how excellent the last rehearsal of *Sulla* was?
The President himself has praised it." Little by little Servando was
emerging from the mirages he had imagined about himself. He
contemplated Heredia standing there before him in an asphyxiating
suit of winter clothes, and he saw in the poet's face an almost
unheard-of sadness, a sadness which looked almost unbearable, and
which bore no relation to the words he had just spoken. And the
friar thought, he betrays himself, he is a bundle of contradictions,
he is a crybaby and a melancholic. But there are times when he
does things which leave me perplexed. He has wept for his op-
pressed country as well as for himself. And I grant, I suppose, that
he has written one or two verses that are not bad. All right—real
poems. Excellent poems. That is more than enough to win my

respect and to keep my friendship. And Servando even thought that that was the moment to manifest his admiration and respect. But when he spoke he said, "Dear Heredia, you know very well that I cannot waste my time on pantomimes which are not even original. And besides, one can see at once that you translated that play of Jouy's when you were on a journey—it is mined with potholes. It is a botched job of bad plagiarism," he ended, and he turned his head toward the procession. *The Virgin's toilette was a dazzling jewel-show of a thousand precious gems and pendants, rings and bracelets, massive pearls of more than three carats in mountings of gold filigree, and her dress was likewise made of richest gemwork. This splendid raiment completely covered the image, which advanced on a silver litter atop an altar of diamonds on which was figured a peak adorned with herbs and flowers, all made of precious stones. And on the peak itself, sprouting from the very rocks and precipices, a rainbow carved from rubies, surrounding the image sprinkled with innumerable tiny pearls like drops of dew* ... Staggered by the brilliance of so much jeweled splendor, the friar caught at the railing of the balcony. And he watched that grand procession—the worshipful generals, the clergy as always beside the President, the dance of the starving Indians, the miserable raving folk that drowned its rages in prayers and supplications. He clutched the baluster, and listening now to the constant pealing of the bells (for suddenly it had grown unbearable), he thought the infamy of it all would kill him, that if he stood in that spot and looked at that spectacle for one second more, he would burst, that the mockery of it would destroy him. And so (as the bells began truly to madden him) he raised a hand into the air. And as he watched, the great palace began to crumble before his very eyes; it shuddered and collapsed to the sound of short sharp explosions, pops, it began to vanish, as though folding in and burying itself beneath his feet. The bells sounded far off now, almost like a song, and muted. And then he saw the poet, disappearing with the palace, and he had a moment's pity for that contrary creature. He beckoned him to his side with one crooked finger. And the two, standing together, watched the procession, composed of tiny ants, disappear with the palace's last column, with the city's last houses. And suddenly they found themselves on another balcony, standing amidst the chant of millions upon millions of birds the likes of which the two men had never known before, and surrounded by trees which at every moment were exploding in

more flowers. They raised their eyes and saw about them a mighty
city, with its two huge lakes, and all its people in canoes. They
walked down the great stairway that opened before them and
strolled out into the gardens filled with birds of every kind, from
every region, and with unknown animals, with hundreds of servants feeding with gentle fingers even the tiniest lizard. The friar
and the poet walked on through that park as though they were in
a daze. They silently looked at each other. And they nodded in a
kind of joy. Farther on they stopped. Birds were fluttering about
them everywhere. Fray Servando lifted his arms and they were
covered at once with falcons and hawks, gray geese, and thrushes
that had filled the woods with trilling. He laughed in glee, and on
the edge of his teeth there perched goshawks and hummingbirds
that instantly began to sing, keeping tune with his delighted laughter. And then, overcome with the emotion of it, the friar began to
softly cry. At once a flock of chaffinches perched on his ears, drank
up his tears, and flew away, breaking into unexpected song. Fray
Servando looked at the poet and he saw him to be a magnificent
tree filled with doves, teal, parrots, owls, and dormice. (At that
very moment Heredia composed his *Ode to Athena and Palmyra*.)
Finally the two men looked at each other joyfully and began to
walk along under the trees, in a whirl of light and shade. They
came to the lake, where wild ducks and cranes greeted them with
a great honking and quacking that cleft the air. They took off their
clothes. They swam a while. They made themselves new clothing
out of some brilliant sparkling leaves they found. And they lay
down underneath one of the great twining vines inhabited by singing monkeys that now began to chant a song superior to every
other musical sound the two men had ever heard. And there they
fell asleep. They were so happy that they could forget the time
marked off by the seasons, and they promised not to waken. But
suddenly a great noise was heard, and then another, and another.
Then there was a roar of cannon that clouded the sky, the stampede of a cavalry, and immediately the tramp of armored men, *an
army of dust, sweat, and iron*. The conquistadores had arrived.
Fray Servando and the poet had only to open their eyes to see the
terrified flight of birds before a troop of men erupting into the vast
garden, pulling down the eyries of falcons and eagles, treading on
defenseless quail and whippoorwill, and plucking quetzal, the royal
firebird, bare. One of the soldiers confused Fray Servando with a
dying heron, and he raised his weapon and shot, with such accu-

racy that had the friar not ducked away he would have surely perished. Meanwhile, Heredia, hiding in a clump of leaves and feathers, could not breathe for horror. The shrieking of the birds spread through all the region. The friar, once more at the verge of madness, raised his hand again, and on the instant the park was changed. It was the time of the great peace. The true season of calm. In every hermitage sacred incense burned, for now the gods did not want human hearts, but a sacrifice of sweet sap. An *areyto* floated through the air and filled the city with its notes. Fray Servando and Heredia descended the great stairway of the palace and entered the House of Mist where the King, Montezuma the Sorrowful, was at the celebration of the Renewal of the Fire. This rite was necessary if his people were to obtain fifty-two years more of life. The great festival unfolded perfectly. The fire was passed from hand to hand as the King gave his blessing to it. The torch came to the Peak of Citlaltepétl. Prayers burst forth like shooting stars, and the city was lit with a necklace of sputtering, flashing brands. And then the celebration went on. The poet and the friar turned and looked delightedly at one another. They were about to leave the great world-renewing rite, to stroll through the rest of the grounds, when a restless song rang out behind them. Both men turned and looked disconcertedly as four hundred naked youths came forward to the dais of the King and sat down all about it. And immediately they began to pass about calabash-gourd cups filled with arousing drink. The reed flutes, pipes, and tambours began to play, and then the youths began to dance. Fray Servando, enraged, desolate, lifted his soutane and with it covered the poet, who did not want to leave that spectacle, and then dragged him off to the outskirts of the city, out where the music (which was now taking on great frenzy and arousal) was somewhat less horribly compelling. The friar was terribly fatigued, but he lifted his hand once more, and the two friends found themselves in the President's Palace, on the balcony again. They stepped to the railing once more and looked out on the procession which now was engaged in a spectacle in the very center of the Central Plaza. *The Indians, the nobility, the image of the Virgin advancing like a glowing barge over a sea of uncovered heads, over the people and over the religious communities. And each community, each fraternity and sorority, each guild bears an angel with one symbol of the Passion. Eighteen is the number of the angels, all richly ornamented, and now passing as though in review before the palace.*

They bear: the first, the lantern the soldiers bore; the second, the thirty pieces of silver; the third, the purple toga of the soldiers' mockery; the fourth, the dice; the fifth, palm leaves; the sixth, the lance or spear; the seventh, the sponge; the eighth, the robe; the ninth, the pillar; the tenth, the crown of thorns they put on His head; the eleventh, the chains; the twelfth, the ladder; the thirteenth, the three nails they nailed Him up with; the fourteenth, the false scepter with which they mocked His royalty; the fifteenth, the scourge; the sixteenth, the hammer; the seventeenth, INRI, the scroll of the superscription that Pilate had put above his head; and the last, the cross. The first fraternity had passed, and now was passing the second religious community, and again the angel with the lantern was in procession beneath the friar's feet. "No!" cried the outraged Fray Servando then, and again he lifted his hand. The bells ceased. And now the friar and the poet were walking through a great rocky waste dotted with cactuses that reared up menacingly. Far off they could make out a settlement thrown up beside the lake. They walked all that night through that wasteland, eating prickly pears, which brought on terrible attacks of indigestion and a bellyache, and on the next morning they set out for the mountains, to go and visit a peak known as Tepeyac, where a religious ceremony was to be held. At last, drugged by the sun and by the juice of the spiny plants, they came to the range of hills. They saw, standing out against the sky along the ridge of one of the peaks, a great file of natives picking its way through the mountains, marching toward the little sanctuary where the idol Tonantzin was worshiped, the spirit the Indians called Our Mother. The poet and the friar stood in wonder at the religiosity of that civilization. And then the first scream was heard. The elect of the faithful were entering the temple, where they lay down on a slab of stone. At once the priest, making the grimace appropriate to that mortal pass, wielded the obsidian knife and pulled out the still-beating heart. The friar and the poet looked once again at that great procession filing slowly into the temple, where the priest awaited with dagger aloft. "Jesus," both said, as with one breath, as soon as they could speak again, for now the blood was flowing down the hillside and into a deep *arroyo* where Indian children were playing and the vulture was fluttering at his feast. The friar was so sickened and faint that he could only move two fingers of his hand. And the landscape was transformed, but only partially, for still a procession of men continued its way before his eyes. Terribly shaken, the friar and the poet carefully picked their way down the mountain. Hiding among the branches of a tree, they studied this new parade from a point closer to its flank. These were people very like the others, yet dressed like the friar and the poet. They seemed impatient, as though vexed that they had to wait in the line. Fray Servando, who had already begun to tremble, looked then toward the beginning of the file. And there he saw, as he had feared, the fire, blazing on the horizon with flames that almost reached up to the clouds. He tried to make that scene disappear. So hasty and horrified was he, though, that he raised both hands this time, and he was flung violently into a future he did not recognize. But still, there were the flames. Flames, licking upward, filled the whole room in which the friar had come to rest. Flames, and within them, a person telling the story of the friar's life. Puzzled, confused, and curious, the friar listened to find out what was to be his own end, but the fire was raging about his sandals, the tongues of it were flicking up to singe his robe. He dropped his hands. And he was once more standing in the Presidential Palace. The poet, who had no interest in knowing the future, neither anyone else's nor his own, was waiting for him there, in the colonnade, before the Plaza, looking impassively down on the procession there. The friar was still panting, and his robe hung in tatters about him. He felt a scream welling up inexorably in him. But he beat it down again. He walked over to the poet and standing beside him, his hands resting on the railing, he contemplated the scene below. *The procession marches out of the Plaza and away, into the cathedral. The other churches had been asked to ring their bells even louder at this moment of entry into the sacred nave, when the cathedral bells began to peal. And so it was: at a signal agreed upon in advance, the mother church rings her bells, and all the churches of the city rush to follow. And now, within the nave, each Deputy to Congress and each ecclesiastical leader, each man in turn with his hands clasped between those of the Archbishop, swears faith eternal to México's principal patroness, the Holy Virgin Santa María de Guadalupe. After the solemn vows of faith, the Archbishop turns to the altar to offer up thanks, and he begins to recite the Te Deum. At that moment the ringing of the bells is crushing.* The friar, as from a distance he beheld that ceremony, felt a dreadful chill. And he thought that now had come his moment of death, for the heaviness of that mockery of faith, of all the vileness he had witnessed, surely at last would sink him. And suddenly, hearing the renewed tumult, which drove him ever nearer madness, he had one revelation more—that he had been tricked and deceived his whole life long. But since he could not clearly explain to himself what that deceit, that fraud, had consisted of, he walked to the center of the great balcony, climbed upon a rocking chair that he had declined to climb on earlier, but which like the other creaked in protest, and he stretched out his arms. Before he lowered them again, he glanced at the poet in awe at the great procession, and he thought he had best not take him with him this time, for this was a journey from which he well might never return. And he dropped his hands. Then he himself seemed to drop somehow . . . He was now in the midst of the Great Starry Night. The night of questionings. The night which drove Van Gogh to madness. The night that had made Emmanuel Kant doubt. David's first night. This was the night which had unhinged or enlightened all men in all civilizations. Under the twinkling (sputtering) light of the constellations, the friar walked all along the outdoor colonnade, back and forth. What was the answer? Where were the signs, where the solution? He lifted his gaze again and stood stock-still, contemplating the whirling procession of the stars. For hours he stood rigid and motionless there, watching that glowing and inexorable procession, that imperturbable harmony. And then came the great revelation. He thought: The object of every civilization (of every revolution, of every struggle whatsoever, of every purpose) is to attain the perfection of those constellations, their inalterable harmony. "But," he said aloud, "we will never arrive at that perfection, because there is always in men some disequilibrium, some unbalance." At that moment Heredia, who overheard a word or two, ran to his side and held the chair, which was rocking crazily under him. But the tottering friar took no notice of the poet looking up at him bewilderedly, for over his head revolved all the planets, and the friar himself, bathed in that splendor, was asking himself question after question after unanswerable question. Again he thought, now to himself, that if all the universe were governed by the harmony of the stars, if everything, save man, were subject to that Law, then indeed that imbalance in man did exist. And now, utterly sure of that asseveration, he tried to go on. He stood even stiffer on the chair seat, he made several dizzying passes with his hands. And immediately, the bells fell silent and ceased to peal and the procession vanished. Silence was absolute. Where the city had lain, now there were only cane fields. And later, immense forests. And then later, at last, came the waters to cover the whole extent of the plain which the friar from his height stood over. And still he stood firm. He saw the waters transformed into a ball of fire, and the ball of fire change slowly into white, white, white snow blowing and whirling all about. And then he made up his mind to go to other distant lands, to live in a time where memory did not exist, but only a vacant present. The beginning. The revelation. "God," he at last spoke aloud. "I will go to God." And he crouched a bit and raised his arms. But the chill, the dreadful shivering chill (and now much worse than before) came over him once more. The friar had a moment's doubt. He was afraid, seized with fear. Afraid that at the end of that vast country he was to travel, no-one would be awaiting him. Afraid to float forever in a vast emptiness and nothing, whirling through a vacant time, through an inalterable solitude that contained not even the solace of belief, the consolation of a simple faith. Afraid to be left utterly stripped of illusions . . . he stepped back. He lowered his arms. And he plumped down on the seat. The pealing of the bells came redoubled to his ears again. *Bells, bells that alter time; bells that drive birds to a frenzy; bells whose pealing shatters stained-glass windows; bells the echo through the two arched naves; bells that so enrage volcanoes that they burst and spew in fury; bells that unleash lust in the dancers dancing to their peals; bells, bells, bells—drowning the noise of the orgy spreading wild across the city; bells, bells, bells, crying Let everyone pray that this most holy Virgin protect our lives; bells, bells, bells, And let this devotion to the Virgin of Guadalupe spread to all classes of society; bells, and twelve women are violated by one cunning youth who slips quickly through the crowd; bells, And let there not be one balcony or door that is not richly and luxuriantly adorned; bells, bells, bells, muting the noise of the bandidos who kick down the doors of houses and enter them to rob; bells, And let banners be raised, whether richly or humbly confected, and let on balconies be shown the image of the beautiful patron saint, Our Lady; bells, bells, bells, and the tumult grows ever fiercer and more turbulent, and the shrieks and cries of lust more overwhelming; bells, and a woman runs naked through the shrieks toward a group of men who instantly seize her and possess her; bells, bells, and the president's henchmen carve up alive anyone who looks askance at the government's "heroic policies"; bells, bells, bells, and the Presi-*

dent and his lovely wife flee down a tortuous alleyway, miracu-
lously saving themselves from the shots fired about them; bells,
And let the image of Our Lady be praised with banners and flags,
with flowers and veils, with standards and any other adornment
which imagination, good taste, and faith may suggest; bells,
and the lights of the city are raised high, and above the houses
of the city there looms up the cathedral, its towers decked with
torches and lamps, chandeliers in its naves ablaze, the noble
pile become a golden icon; bells, and lava buries the city; bells,
and the friar, hysterical, scales one of the palace's tall towers
and threatens to jump to his death, while Heredia supplicates
and holds him by his surcingle; bells, bells, bells, and they begin
to grow softer, to grow quiet, to hush, because the ceremony
now has ended.

For a moment the silence is deafening. But then begins the solemn prayer. Fray Servando and Heredia descend from the tower
and in silence return to their balcony. As they come out onto it,
night falls. From the chapel rise the notes of a mass sung in Latin.
At last the image and its attendants return to the Sanctuary of
Tepeyac, marching to a *Salve* very, very slow. It passes in silence
through the plaza and crosses the devastated city. The friar and
the poet stand and watch the cortege as it fades into the shadows
of the hill of Tepeyac. Then they turn and look at one another,
standing very still. In the air still resounds the last vibrating hum
of the mass's solemn chant. "Today is the premiere of my play,"
Heredia says, and he thinks, Poor man, he's so old he doesn't even
understand that this entire procession has been for him, in his
honor. Where in the world did he get his habits singed that way?
"I have told you I will not come," Fray Servando answers him. "I
will not waste the little time I have left to me on costume parties."
I will go, thought the friar. He is so young, after all, and so alone,
and this is not his land.

Then he walked over to a rocking chair and spoke again.

"Let us sit here and wait for the President," he said, raising his
voice somewhat. "I want him to move me—tonight!—to a room I
can see the plaza from."

"He will do that, undoubtedly," Heredia answered, and sat
down.

And both the men began to doze there, facing out over the city,
rocking in their rocking chairs. Anyone that saw them would have
said the both of them were fast asleep. But still from time to time

one might have heard Servando's voice as he muttered in his sleep, and Heredia's too, as he rehearsed a parody of the lines of a poem which he is yet to write.

CHAPTER XXXV

In which the friar gazes at his hands.

Every morning the old friar rises before dawn. He opens the windows of his bedroom and looks out over the park, where birds are trying to outdo one another to see which can scream the loudest. Every morning he then turns and walks over to the bookshelf, takes up a book at random, glances a moment through its pages, and grumblingly returns it to its place.

Every morning the President, Guadalupe Victoria, enters his apartment, always with an inquiry after his health—"And how are our ills getting on today, my dear don Servando?" "How would you have them get on?" the testy friar invariably replies. "I go like the Republic, from bad to worse."[29] Testy, because for our dear friar the battles are still not over. Testy, because he can never forget that he could not manage to induce men to adopt a centralized republic, but has had to accept (though always under protest), resign himself to, this federalist system which so slows and bogs down the wheels, as he never tires of explaining. And because he will never be able to accept the fact that the "swift emperor," that man who so hated him, and whom he so hated, was allowed to escape. Servando had begged the death penalty for him, to nip in the bud, extirpate at the root, weed out once and for all, that evil of empire, to ensure the peace, and to show the next ambitious soul, some other would-be emperor, that any new attempt at empire would be suicide ... (And although Iturbe did later find the end the friar had wished for him, on the scaffold of Padilla, Servando will never forget that when he had pleaded for Iturbe's execution, the government would not see fit to grant his request.)

[29]Artemio de Valle-Arizpe, *Fray Servando*.